BINDER

THE PRICE OF TALENT: BOOK TWO

SPICY DYSTOPIAN SCI FI ROMANCE

AK NEVERMORE

DEDICATION

Thanks again, Mom

CONTENTS

FREE PREQUEL

What you don't know can kill you...

BEFORE KARA MET FLYNN, she was property of the Source.

The genetic research facility owned by a powerful international conglomerate dominates the Northern Hemisphere. Valued solely for her DNA and her talent to bind matter together, when she receives her summons to breed, she panics.

Rescued from the brink of death, she's offered the chance to escape and find her own destiny.

But the journey through the desolation of the Outside is fraught with peril, and the golden halos marking her as a Talent also paint her as a target. Kept ignorant of everything beyond the facility's walls, Kara grapples to survive in the hostile wasteland. Humanity purists and roving gangs are only a fraction of her problems, because the Source, and Riegel, her contracted mate, aren't just going to let her walk away…

Download it at: aknevermore.com/breeder

A HEADS UP ON CONTENT

This book explores themes which some readers may find uncomfortable or offensive. This one's got elements regarding pregnancy and parenthood that might catch you in the feels. In addition to that, if violence, smut, various kinks, salty language, references to alcoholism, drug use, abuse, and generally unsavory behavior are triggers for you, please put this novel down and back away slowly.

Still here? Awesome. Just remember, it's a fantasy, people. Don't try this stuff at home.

TERMS

*Talent [**tal**-uhnt] noun*

1. *An individual denoted by halos surrounding their irises with the ability to manipulate reality, i.e. Breakers, molecular destruction; Binders, molecular cohesion; Shifters, translocation; Fixers, transfixation; Finders, spatial orientation.*

   – Excerpt from A Treatise on Talents, *Third Edition*

"First say to yourself what you would be; and then do what you have to do."

– Epictetus

Three days prior to the attack on the train

Otto rolled his head over his shoulders, admiring the dark-haired little minx picking up her clothes as she left his room. The directive he'd just implanted into her psyche would last until she reached the arena. He chuckled, imagining the look on her face as she broached the arched steel doors and realized she wasn't wearing a stitch, her thighs inexplicably sticky.

It was a pity they weren't more so, but despite it being well past midnight, Titus had summoned him. The man rarely felt the need for sleep and didn't much care that other people did.

Otto rose, dressed, and washed; his cherubic cheeks still pink with exertion. That one had been an energetic lover once she'd realized how much she wanted to please him. He smiled at his reflection and pushed back from the sink. It was time to go see his Patron.

His low whistle bounced down the Source's stark-white dormitory halls. Though less prestigious than the tower's posh accommodations,

Otto preferred their anonymity. As one of the few Binders outside Albanach's stables, he was already enough of an outlier.

The Patrons' monopolization of lines was stupid, though not unexpected, given the flawed logic behind maintaining the purity of each line of Talent. In practice, it only exacerbated the declination of what should've been ascendent.

It was also intentional, and the sole reason Otto had taken up residence at the facility.

He passed the Lucite and chrome seating of the dorm's lobby, more suited to a medical pod than a social space, giggles filling the air. A few Talents reclined around a table in the corner, sucking down tubes of amnio-paste. They smelled of the club district, sweat and glimmer still glistening over their skin. One of them saw him looking and pinched a rouged nipple through the gossamer of her dress, lips pursing to blow him a wet kiss. The others laughed.

Otto smiled blithely back. She'd be the next one on her knees.

He pushed through the rotating glass doors, into the rotunda. Suspended lace-work bridges of iron webbed above the chill granite space. The air was crisp, perfumed with the medicinal redolence of chlorine. Painfully clean lines of exacting topiaries surrounded the fountain at the rotunda's center, modified carp swimming in its too-blue depths. Otto felt a momentary pang for the sultry winsomeness of the sea—

His longing was immediately ousted by the Source's entertainment value.

In front of the jag leading to the arena, a small crowd of leering Breakers had gathered. Ostensibly shielding the minx from eyes other than their own, they leered as she shoved her limbs into tangled garments.

Otto smirked. The bitch should've just danced with him when he'd asked. Granted, he wasn't the most attractive of men, but manners mattered, and it wasn't as if he were repulsive… though perhaps at the lower end of average. He wasn't complaining. Beauty came to bad ends in other environs.

He approached the transport platform. The Fetch at the dull grey slab was wholly engrossed with the show. Otto cleared his throat. The man's eyes flicked to him and away.

A surge of temper shot through him. His moist fingers plucked at the man's sleeve, sending out talent. "You'll shift me to Titus's offices, then be unable to think of anything but bedding that large Breaker at the end."

The man's demeanor instantly changed and colors ran as he pulled talent, shifting them to the other side of the facility.

Otto was alone in front of the mahogany double doors, the Fetch gone before he could draw a breath. Perhaps not the wisest use of his talent, but certainly satisfying to imagine the man being pounded to a pulp when he propositioned the behemoth. Breakers had little tolerance for such advances, though Glory knew they weren't opposed to the practice behind closed doors.

Otto walked into the reception area, smiling at Titus's secretary, Marina. She didn't return it, waving him through. He entered his Patron's dimly lit chambers just in time to see the man throw back a handful of pills. Interesting. Titus's headaches must be getting worse, though his last refresher had only been a few weeks prior. Something must've gone against his directive, triggering them.

"Ah, Otto. I have a job for you. I need you to flip through BrNC37's memories. There's a particular incident I want the details on. It happened right as he was entering the Creche and involved that Jester girl."

Otto's ears perked up. Kara Jester had been of particular interest to him throughout the years. It was unfortunate she had so much Breaker blood. Something about that line made them resistant to coercion, not that he hadn't tried.

He inclined his head. "I'd be happy to. If I may inquire, how have your migraines been?"

"Worse than usual. That's the other reason I summoned you. Here, do whatever it is you do."

Otto bowed again, hiding a smirk as he walked around the large cherry and chrome desk. Titus put his drink down and leaned back in his chair, going limp at Otto's touch. He flipped through the man's mind, reviewing what'd happened since the last time he'd invaded

Titus's psyche to coerce him. The binds were holding well, and he'd been staying the course he'd been set to…

Otto's brow creased as he got to the past few days. Things had changed dramatically. He made several adjustments to Titus's directives, reinforcing the desire to obtain the girl at any cost. Given the vector readings at the lake, Kara was far too important to let go. Otto stepped away and crossed to the other side of the desk.

By the time he resumed his position at its front, Titus was sipping bourbon again.

"Very good. I feel much better. Now, I have another job for you…"

Otto inclined his head. Eager to leave as soon as possible, he barely heard the man parrot back the directives he'd just implanted. Mother needed to know that the Unmaker had been found.

CHAPTER ONE

duality [d(y)o͞oˈalədē] noun

1. *Talents of balancing natures; Breaker / Binder, Fixer / Fetch, Finder / Shade. With rare exception, each innately finds the other repellent. The phenomena is believed responsible for the unpredictable outcomes regarding offspring.*
2. *The offspring of a duality.*

– Excerpt from Glynfyls: A History

"…Those presenting as dual Talents are strictly prohibited from holding public office. Any individual in violation shall be subject to the permanent nullification of their talents and censure of their House for a period of ten years…"

– Lord Kanov, Chief Judicator,
Glynfyls Supreme Court

FLYNN SAT, head hanging, hand running up the back of his neck. He'd fucked up.

Eyes stinging, he collapsed into the plush wing-backed chair, fingers trembling over cracked lips. The wicked contusion staining his flank jolted fire alongside his spine. He grimaced, accepting it as penance. He'd promised he wasn't gonna do that again...be that animal.

Christ, it'd felt good.

It always did. Until he came back to himself and saw the aftermath caught in the half-moons of his nails, the creases at his wrists. The memory of what he'd done leaving him shaking with that goddamn gnawing in his guts for a drink, trying to forget how much he'd liked it.

They'd deserved it.

He chewed his lip. What right did he have to make that determination? Shit, he'd earned worse...but Kara hadn't. Neither had his kid.

If he still had a kid.

His gaze slid across the expansive room to the curtained fourposter bed. Her form lost in shadow, an extension of self, taking up every bit of talent he was pushing her, searing his insides raw. He didn't care, the burn was nothing. He'd crawl through hell to save them. His eyes dropped to his hands, knuckles ragged and swollen.

He had. Jumped right into the fire, and it'd only made things worse. Goddamn his temper.

They'd all know what he'd done.

What he was.

"... I swear to God, I wish I was a fucking twist, then I wouldn't have to pretend..."

Flynn scrubbed a hand over his face. For once in his life, he hadn't, and he'd pissed away House Scot's political power in the process. If he confessed and registered, Cal might be able to salvage some of it. Maybe enough to protect her.

There was a soft knock at the door, and the massive oak slab was pushed inward on well-oiled hinges. French wheeled in a sterling coffee service. The flickering light from the marble hearth bounced off its polished curves onto the glossy pastries at its side.

Christ, he'd just wanted a cup.

"The constable major will be in his office within the hour, per your request, sir," the man intoned, working the cafetière. He'd gotten old. Flynn took in the familiar livery and stiff mustache waxed into precise loops, bone white instead of the salt-and-pepper grey he remembered. "I've brought suitable garments. Will you require assistance?"

Flynn's eyes went to the freshly brushed jacket and trousers hanging from the bar of the cart. French handed him the cup and saucer with a flourish, then stood, awaiting his pleasure.

The enameled china chattered in Flynn's hands, and he fought the urge to wing the fucking thing into the fireplace. "You're gonna have to find a different jacket. The last one I borrowed from Lot didn't work out so well."

The seams would split when they cuffed him. The press would love that. He took a sip of coffee. Christ, it was a far cry from freeze-dried.

French began making him up a plate of pastries. "That shouldn't be an issue, Lady Breakspear sent over several options, along with this." He took an envelope from his breast pocket and held it out to him.

Flynn's stomach lurched. Shit. There was only one thing the First Breaker could want to speak to him about. He stared at it for a long moment before taking it from the man.

It was unaddressed and heavier than it should've been, thick cream parchment with a raised wax seal the color of dark cherries. She'd used her signet to stamp a stylized 'B' into the blob. French held out a slim blade before he could ask.

Flynn's hands went through the motions, opening it by rote, though it'd been years. No exotic perfume rose up with the gold-lined flap, and the page within was free of ill-conceived prose. Two words stared back at him.

Breaker Business.

What the ever-loving fuck?

They weren't outing him… Anger devoured his bewilderment. It had to be blackmail. He flung the missive into the flames. Not up here ten goddamn hours, and he was already hip-deep in political fucking intrigue. They'd expect something in return for keeping this quiet...if they could. There'd been more than just Breakers kissing the ground out there. Flynn bit into one of the pastries French had set beside him. Still...it gave him time.

"What're they saying in the city?"

"The aid-workers are reporting any number of improbabilities, everything from aliens to the second coming of Christ, but those whom survived the Sons' attack have been markedly silent. One wonders how long that will last."

"Until their wallets become noticeably thicker. How many nobles were on the train?"

"Just your party. The hour was a bit too raw for your brethren," French said, topping off his coffee. "I've taken the liberty of scheduling Ernesto to attend to your needs before Assembly begins."

Flynn glanced at the butler, reading all he needed to in his eyes. Bastard had known exactly what he was planning. Had he known what was in that note? Christ, he wouldn't put it past him. Man was worse than Cal with that shit.

And now it was time to play the part.

Flynn ran a hand through his hair. French was right. Those fucking assholes wouldn't take him seriously without a three hundred unit cut. Borrowed clothes were bad enough.

He reached for the navy trousers. The faint odor of cedar clung to them, like they'd been in storage—Jesus, she'd sent Richard's clothes. What would possess Phyllis to break out her dead husband's wardrobe for him?

They were loose but the right length. French held out a starched white shirt, eyeing the bruise discoloring Flynn's back. The butler knew better than to comment, his lack of expression conveying enough. Flynn ignored him, hissing as he shrugged it on.

"Ernesto will be awaiting you in the east drawing room. Shall I stay with the lady?"

Flynn bit at his lip, not wanting to leave Kara. Shit, he didn't have a choice.

Hands were at the rug beneath him, just waiting to pull it out. He wasn't gonna squander however much time he'd been granted to keep her…them…safe.

"Yeah, I don't want her to be alone." His voice cracked.

"Of course, sir. I shall send word should the lady wake prior to your return."

Flynn crossed the plush carpet to the bed, the fragrance of lavender rising up to meet him as he pressed his lips to Kara's brow. She looked so small and wan beneath the thick fur coverlet. Pulling it closer to her chin, he pushed her more talent, the steady draw chafing his channel. He didn't care. She…maybe they…needed it more than him.

Dear God, please let it be they…

He dashed a hand across his eyes, and the butler gave him a solemn nod. Flynn left the room, shoving everything down so he could play the fucking part.

TITUS FLIPPED OFF HIS OXFORDS, mouth curdling at having to enter the smokey room in his stocking feet. Salist lounged against a white sheepskin bolster beside a raised platform. He waved invitingly at the one across from him, the long mouth-piece of a hookah between his lips, despite the early hour.

"Your aversion to furniture with legs is tiresome," Titus grumbled, crabbing down onto the floor opposite him.

Salist smiled, tendrils of cerulean smoke wreathing his face. His amusement, watching Titus try to arrange himself on the floor with some modicum of dignity, was tiresome as well.

"I've enjoyed your hospitality often of late, it was time I returned the favor." Salist clapped and servants entered, laying out an array of odd foods meant to be sopped up and eaten with a spongy-looking pancake.

Titus eyed it all warily, planning on sticking to his typical breakfast of bourbon.

The dark man laughed, flashing the platinum fillings in his back teeth. "Come now, you must try the injera and misir wat, I insist." He tore off a piece of the unappetizing mass and swept it through some ruddy slop, smacking it up with relish.

Titus sniffed. "Spice doesn't agree with me."

"Very little does. I would think you more affable, your proxy set in motion. Quite the coup smuggling Riegel north like that. Orin may suspect, but the rest of the board is clueless. Rache is such a greedy thing, I don't believe the possibility she's being played ever crossed her mind."

"Orin's been compensated for his silence along with those nanobots of his. I hate to admit it, but they're worth every unit. May I?"

At Salist's nod, Titus threw up a holo, layers of smoke striating through it. A moving landscape resolved, jarring with the first person perspective, the hum of tires in the background. Beside the visual there were a series of graphs, tracking Riegel's metrics. He'd crossed the border early this morning, leaving the no man's land of the Outside for that of the Northern Territories. Two thousand plus miles of unutilized resources. Once Glynfyls was on its knees that would be Titus's to plunder as well.

"Quite comprehensive, isn't it?"

Titus smiled around his bourbon. The man had no idea. Salist's eyes narrowed, and Titus pinched off a bit of that pancake. It smelled sour. His lips pruned around the scant mouthful, and Salist laughed again.

"An acquired taste, perhaps. Here, this will be more to yours." He motioned to a bowl of what looked suspiciously like diced tartar.

Titus called for a fork, amused at Salist's amusement. The smoke in the air was having a sportive effect upon him, and was the reason he rarely dined with the man in his chambers, but the meat was good. He'd eaten most of it when Salist spoke again.

"Do you think Riegel will be able to harvest the Jester girl before the boost kills him?"

Titus sat back against the bolster, chewing. "He's not meant to. She'll be under lock and key until the Introduction, but another has that well in hand. What I'm betting on, is Riegel wreaking havoc in the city. If he can't manage that by abducting Talents, imploding in their midst should do the trick. Has the amended deal been offered?"

"Petra will deliver the new terms when he reaches Glynfyls."

Good. Titus grinned into his bourbon, pleased at the neatness of his plan. Riegel to throw the city into chaos, and his troops to sweep up the mess. He'd have every Talent in Glynfyls back in his labs before month's end, and the damned board on its knees begging for his cast-offs.

"One of my concubines saw the Commandant and Nora Jester out dining last night. That makes twice this week, doesn't it?"

"It does, and they've tickets for Kasham's opening of that staged bordello of hers."

Salist laughed. "It's a burlesque theater, and you know you're expected as well."

"More like live porn."

"What of it? I've never known you to turn your nose up at a viewing."

"I've never tried to pass it off as art." The cheek of the woman was abhorrent.

"You and your art. Regardless, it'll be entertaining."

Titus doubted that very much.

"So who is he? The Shade. Don't play coy. You've that look on your face." The dark man licked one of his long, lean fingers from base to tip.

Titus smugly pulled up Scot's infamous reel, still enjoying its irony. His people had finally been able to stitch together a timeline for the reprobate. He flicked another holo of the boy's extensive rap sheet beside the first. Salist, thoroughly engrossed in it, stroked his thumb across his parted lips.

"Laughlin Scot. After that little gem was recorded, he fled south. The first year he spent Outside racking up a litany of misdemeanors. Public intoxication, assault, soliciting prostitutes…there's a gap, then I have him serving two years in Kensbot for an assault conviction."

The headshots taken at his admittance and release were drastically different.

"My. Didn't make friends there, did he?"

"A couple of my Peacekeepers took an exception to him. Brix does enjoy carving up the pretty ones. Apparently Scot came very close to dying."

"Shame, he's a bit rough, but could've passed for one of yours. I didn't realize a Shade's physiology mirrored a Breaker's so closely."

"It doesn't, which is intriguing, given the importance the Original Houses place on line purity. I'd give a great deal to get him into my lab."

"I'm sure you would," Salist chuckled, still nibbling at the spread before them.

Titus swept the images away. "My people are chasing some rumors of his involvement with one of the gangs Outside, but as of now, there's a total of five years I can't account for. I'm assuming whatever he was doing, it was unsavory. The operatives in Glynfyls have been forwarded the information. I have it on good authority House Scot is going to try to install the boy as First. His father's dismal performance is one of the reasons I've been able to move so quickly of late."

Salist dusted off his hands and sat back, sucking at his teeth. "And if he gains it?"

"It will never get that far. Should Laughlin Scot feel the need to make a name for himself, my operatives have the means to ruin it."

KARA'S EYES SNAPPED OPEN, mouth dry with panic.

Flynn had left her, and he felt very far away.

She lay there in the grey half-light, heart pounding, wanting to cry, watching freezing rain slap against windows twice as long as she was tall, the splatter and slide of it sloughing away the residual terror from her nightmare.

Ugh. Stop it.

He'd said they were safe, at Meddleton in the North. She took several deep breaths, her anxiety fading enough to feel Flynn's concerned reassurance flowing through their bond. She struggled to pull herself up against the mounds of pillows behind her, head spinning as she looked around.

The room was huge, its navy silk-covered walls framed with dark woodwork, windows swathed behind tapestry fabric of swirling blues and greens. Heavy curtains of it were tied back with braided cords at the sculpted corner-posts of the massive fourposter bed she was in. Kara watched firelight play across the canopy above, her fingers idling through the ruff of the thick fur coverlet... something niggling at the back of her mind, a half-remembered dream...

Who was Flynn up here?

"My House has a lot of influence..."

That felt like a serious understatement, but if the jerk had told her there was a crystal chandelier hanging in his bedroom, she would've thought he was full of—

Someone cleared their throat, and she tugged the coverlet to her chin. A man in black livery had approached. He must've been in one of the chairs by the fire, there was no way she'd have overlooked him otherwise. The tips of his snow-white mustache were fixed into loops.

Kara gave a weak laugh, overcome with the worst urge to tweak them.

Unperturbed, he executed an exacting bow. "My lady. Welcome to Meddleton. Lord Scot requested I sit with you whilst he attends to business. I'm Cornelius French, major domo of this estate. If there's anything I may do to serve, you have but to ask."

"Is he—"

Kara's vision swam, her sense of Flynn abruptly strengthening. She shut her eyes, willing herself not to throw up. When she cracked them again, the butler was at the bedside with a cut-crystal glass of water. Her mind flashed back to the train crash. Had she dreamt Miriam and Shelby were okay?

"If I may assist you?"

She nodded gratefully. He helped her up and held the glass to her lips, the crisp liquid washing the sting of bile from her throat. The door on the far side of the room opened and Flynn came in. She drew in a sharp breath, choking on her mouthful.

Who was this man?

He hurried over, dressed to the nines in a claret wool jacket and double-breasted waistcoat, his unruly locks gone. Cut close to the sides of his head, the top had been left long and worked into sculpted waves off his brow, his stubble trimmed precisely above an intricately tied cravat.

He took her weight from French, patting her back. "Hey, easy, you all right?

She stared at the Flynn-that-wasn't and he colored, settling her back against the pillows. Kara motioned weakly at him. "Lord Laughlin Scot?"

"Uh…yeah." He glanced at French with dark-rimmed eyes, and the man bowed, then left them. Flynn sat at the edge of the bed, taking her hand in his and kissing her knuckles. His own were all torn up. "How do you feel?"

"Like shit."

He barked out a laugh. "You must, using that kind of language."

"Where'd you go?" She traced the split between his first two fingers.

His expression clouded, and he looked down, flipping her hand over in his. "Into the city for a meeting about yesterday." His tumult of emotions made her head spin. She closed her eyes, nauseous. Flynn's lips pressed against her forehead. "We'll talk about it when I come back."

Kara's anxiety jumped. "You're leaving again? Why?"

He traced the contour of her cheek with his thumb, grim. "I lost my temper after I found you out there. Bad things happened. If I don't go do damage control, worse things are gonna. I'll be back as soon as I can. You need to rest, Binder's orders." He kissed her forehead again and stood.

"Wait, I need—will you help me into the bathroom first?"

"Depends, number one or number two?"

She smiled. "One, you jerk." He scooped her up with a pained grunt. "You're hurt?"

"Not as bad as I should be."

She lolled against his shoulder, too tired to decode his doublespeak. That debilitation of her talent was back, dragging at her. Not that it'd really gone away since the garage, but it'd been manageable. This wasn't. She sneezed, his aftershave teasing her nose. An inexplicable hatred for it came over her, wanting that combination of machinery, sweat, and wood-smoke back.

Flynn pushed open a door, his footsteps echoing off grey slate walls. Her stomach clenched at the overpowering odor of disinfectant. A vague memory bubbled up of puking in the shower and a slick of blood running down the drain…

Bad things had happened.

He sat her down, and she leaned against him, dizzy—

Her eyes startled open at him cleaning her up and gently lifting her into his arms again.

"The Binder's gonna be back to check on you. Let French do the talking."

Kara managed a little nod. The talent he was pushing her increased, along with the accompanying burn she felt on his channel. "Stop, it's hurting you…"

He tucked her back into bed, his hand lingering on her abdomen. The fear she felt from him… Understanding stole over her. Glory. He was afraid the pregnancy had been terminated.

He looked away, blinking. "Get some sleep."

A stab of guilty ambivalence went through her. If she'd lost it…the possibility of having her talent back warred with the knowledge of what it would do to him, but why was offspring so important? His lips pressed against her brow. She forced a smile, empty at the prospect of breeding.

"… I thought women lived for that shit…"

Not this one.

CHAPTER TWO

First [fərst] noun

1. *The individual elected from amongst the heads of a line to speak for the collective, traditionally spearheading relations between factions. Each line elects their representative based upon criteria deemed pertinent to their bent, the amount of talent a candidate is able to pull often trumping all else.*

– Excerpt from Glynfyls: A History

"Relations between the lines are heavily dependent upon a First's political acumen. However, history has set a strong precedent; in particular, regarding dualities. Of the three, the most contentious has even been between Shades and Finders. Inherent to the nature of their talents, Finders delight in ferreting out secrets in equal measure to a Shade's obsessive need to conceal things..."

– Lord Talos, Preceptor of History,
Academy of Glynfyls

FLYNN STALKED down the long hallway, his heel strikes loud in the shocked silence of the crowd lingering before session. They stared at him like he was an apparition.

Christ. He sure as hell felt like Jacob Marley back from seven years in purgatory, wrapped in the goddamned chains of his sins.

The gawkers drew aside until he passed, their frenetic whispers swirling in his wake. Someone took off running toward the transportation gate, probably to cash in on his appearance. Fucking Glynfyls. Teeth popping, Flynn approached the double doors leading into chambers.

The heralds standing at attention eyed him as he passed. He snorted at this year's livery; puffy gold jackets and black tights. The tunic and trews he'd had to wear way back when suddenly didn't seem so bad. Shaking his head, he entered the six-sectioned amphitheater and descended the marble steps, the low murmur preceding his arrival dropping out.

Lot was sitting in the First Shade's box at the center of it all. Flynn grabbed one of the tall-backed chairs and put it behind his.

His father stood, pinch-faced. "Didn't expect you."

Flynn offered his hand, trying not to bristle at Lot's bullshit. "My priorities have changed."

His father's mouth soured, but he shook his hand. A murmur started in the room like a switch had been flipped. Flynn sat, swallowing his irritation. Yeah, priorities. He needed to suck it the fuck up and play the game if he wanted to protect Kara.

Shit, if he didn't want to be nullified.

He looked around at the other Houses. Some nodded when his eyes met theirs. Most refused to acknowledge him.

Julia definitely fell into that category.

It took him a moment to recognize his ex. Any doubts that she was different evaporated, the kindness gone from her face. Angular and cold, she was nothing like the girl he remembered. He felt sick. Christ, that was on him.

The speaker banged his gavel, reading out the agenda.

Not one fucking thing about the attack on the train. How was that possible? Flynn sat seething as they droned on about replacing the planters on the building's front steps.

He glanced over at the Breaker section, biting the inside of his cheek. Phyllis wouldn't meet his eye. What game was she playing? A page handed him a packet of papers, cringing back as Flynn snatched it from him.

Goddamn it. What was he doing? Flynn just stopped himself from riffling a hand through his hair. Two hours left of this time-suck before he could leave. He flipped through the packet and stopped. There'd been an addendum.

House Crandall was calling for a formal inquest into the attack.

Flynn broke out in a sweat. It'd give him a chance to speak, but Christ, the last thing he needed were a bunch of fucking Intelligencers trying to figure out what'd gone down out there. Once Glynfyls' secret police got involved… The rug beneath him was slipping. It wouldn't be long now. He looked around the room again, trying not to glare at Crandall.

He was the only other First Flynn recognized. He couldn't place who'd ascended for the Fetches or the Binders. Cal hadn't been joking when he said things had changed, it was usually a lifetime appointment. Too bad the order of business wasn't any different. Flynn swallowed a rude noise as Lady Firth took a dig at the statue in Lady Harrington's roof garden. Christ, even the petty grievances were the same.

"Now ladies, we've, ah, agreed to disagree on this matter." The two women huffed, glowering at each other. Speaker Riggs cheerfully ignored them, dottily scanning his paperwork through half-moon glasses precariously balanced at the end of his bulbous nose.

"Very good, ah, Lord Crandall…I believe there's a matter you wished to address?"

Bartholomew Crandall stood. His sharp gaze skated over the Assembly members to meet Flynn's. Shit. He fucking knew something.

"Yes. I found it remiss there wasn't anything on the agenda regarding yesterday's tragedy and thought to open an inquest, but seeing Laughlin here, perhaps we can save ourselves the trouble and hear what transpired straight from the source."

His lips twitched that stupid, greasy little mustache of his upwards, and Flynn wanted to hit him. Not a chance that word choice was a coincidental. Fucking Finders.

"Hmm, well, yes, that does seem, ah, fortuitous." Riggs smiled kindly at Flynn, oblivious to the subtext. "I'm pleasantly surprised to see you there. The press certainly painted a dismal picture, I hope the rest of it's as unfounded. Ah, if you'd be so kind as to tell us what happened yesterday?"

Flynn stood, schooling his expression. He moved to the rail at the front of their box, jamming his hands into his pockets to keep them out of his hair. "I can, and appreciate the opportunity to do so." He smiled genially across the floor at Crandall, positive the asshole was trying to pull talent on him. Good fucking luck, Flynn'd cloaked himself from talent before he'd left Meddleton.

"Yesterday morning, the train transporting my entire House was attacked as it crested the plateau. The Sons deployed explosives and a nullifier. Our car was thrown to the side, and those ahead of us were completely blown apart. It's my understanding a squad of Breakers disabled the unit and prevented their craft from taking off. I owe your line a debt, Lady Breakspear."

Phyllis inclined her head, still not looking at him. Goddamn her—

"And where were you, Lord Scot?"

There was a glimmer in Crandall's eye and a questing at the edges of Flynn's cloak. Arrogant prick was trying to find the truth of Flynn's words. The only thing he was gonna find was a tack on his chair after the Assembly broke for lunch.

"After evacuating everyone, I was trapped in the passenger car when it slid down the embankment. What I want to know, is how this was allowed to happen. Word had been sent up prior to our departure that the Sons were building a presence in Hamlin, and nothing was done to address it. That's absolutely unaccep—"

"Yet, you were on the plateau when aid-workers arrived. What portion of the events did you witness?"

The part where I found my fucking wife bleeding out on the ground, you smug motherfucker. Flynn bit back the words, fighting to keep his temper. "The aftermath, Lord Crandall. The wounded and dying. My intended among them."

A murmur began and flashes came from above. The observation gallery had filled with press.

Flynn rocked back on his heels, a muscle in his jaw jumping. Fuck it, they'd come for a show, he might as well give them one. "Instead of grilling me, the Assembly should be begging Stonefist to come back. If he hadn't been hamstrung by your petty edicts, the military could've—"

A harsh laugh from the Fixer's section cut through the Assembly's shock and stopped him cold. Familiar and not; Flynn's nape prickled with dread.

"Not back a day, and already full of insight. Tell me, did you find it at the bottom of a bottle, or beneath some whore's skirts?"

Flynn flushed, and Julia raised a dark brow in challenge. Christ, she was coming out of the gate swinging, and everyone in the room was salivating for it.

He ignored the jibe. "To assign the security of the railway to the Constabulary is ludicrous. The edict entrusting over a thousand miles of track to a department already strained policing the city—"

"So you'd prefer it to be done by force that's ineffective at keeping the border secure?"

Goddamn it, she wasn't gonna give him a pass. "This border thing ticked up, what, three years ago? In all that time, nothing has gotten by Stonefist, save for the Sons your policies have allowed into the Northern Territories. So, yeah, I think those odds are pretty good."

"Will you be betting on them later in hopes of clearing your debt at the Pony?"

Clearing his debt…?

Julia flashed him a pitying moue. "Aw. I'm sure someone will be around to remind you, they're used to dealing with deadbeat drunks trying to squirm out of their responsibilities."

Snickers and gasps sounded around the room. Flynn grit his teeth, Christ, he'd deserved that, but now wasn't the goddamned time for it. What the fuck'd happened to her? He'd been an asshole, but Jesus fucking Christ, it didn't justify this level of vindictiveness eight fucking years later, especially not on the goddamned Assembly floor, and the rest of them were just letting her have at it.

Fuck this. Especially with Crandall on the prowl.

"Look, I don't dispute the fact that you've got a valid gripe against me, but as acting First, I'd think you could put it aside for the good of Glynfyls. Feel free to berate me after session." She started to say something, and he raised his voice, talking over her to address the rest of the room.

"I came here today because of a serious security breach that affects every single citizen of the Northern Territories. This goes beyond Stonefist. Not once has the Constabulary ridden the line in an official capacity, nor do they have the manpower to do it. In speaking with Constable Major Grimes earlier, he informed me that it was an unfunded mandate, and apologized profusely over his inability to comply. I find the oversight appalling, and, given your moratorium on shifting, totally unacceptable. It's criminally negligent that the main means in or out of Glynfyls was left vulnerable to attack."

Gasps and murmurs shot around the room, and Julia colored. "What right do you have to speak with the Constable Major?"

"Really?" Flynn laughed. "He's an elected official, not the emperor of Xian. I set a meeting. Can you blame me after what my House just went through?"

"That's absurd—"

"Are you doubting my sincerity, or my commitment to keeping my family safe? I'm sure Lord Crandall will be happy to verify the truth of my words."

Crandall smoothed two fingers around his smirking lips to trace his goatee, clearly amused at the jibe. Fucking Finders. "Lord Scot's presence at the Constable Major's offices this morning had been noted. It was assumed he went to give a statement."

Goddamn it, that motherfucker was already keeping tabs on him.

"I did, and apparently that's not the only unfunded mandate or onerous code directly affecting the security of Glynfyls and its port. Your inquest should be focused on how best to protect our remaining means of transporting goods that doesn't take three weeks to go around the Greberian Peninsula."

Riggs cleared his throat. "I think we've gone a bit farther afield than—"

"I want to know about the murders," a woman's voice shrilled. "No one's saying anything about that."

Flynn's stomach dropped, his attention on a slight woman in the Finder's section. The room had gained a heavy expectancy at her words. A few years older than him, she looked vaguely familiar. "Murders?"

"Yes, Lord Scot," she said tartly, flicking a dark curl from her brow. "Thirty some-odd men were savagely dispatched. I'm more concerned about the possibility of someone capable of that being loose within our fair city."

"I'd hardly call the routing of an enemy force murder, Linda." Lady Breakspear sighed. "What do you think would've happened if the military had intervened?"

"I think a code of conduct would've been followed and men would've been left alive for questioning!" she shot back, her pale cheeks flushed.

"Questioning. What questions do you need to ask?" A large man grumbled from the Fetch section of the room. Flynn struggled to place him… Lord Peale. "They're Sons, and we're Talents. Our existence is an anathema to them. They kill us because their 'Holy Mother' has decreed that'll somehow reverse the Surge. There's no reasoning with that kind of crazy. Whomever took care of that trash did us a favor."

There was a murmur of agreement throughout the chamber, and she sprang to her feet, incensed. "They're human beings that deserved a fair trial!"

Flynn stepped back from the rail at her vehemence. Was she one of the turncoats or just delusional?

Lord Peale leaned forward, glowering. "They deployed explosives and a nullifier, that's a clear indication of intent as far as I'm concerned! Not to mention all the Talents they hunt down and slaughter. Do they get a fair trial as well?"

A man in the next box put a hand on his arm. "There's no need to make this personal—"

"Not make it personal?" Peale shook it off and rose to his feet, shouting. "By God, Eric, they hung my son by his ankles and skinned him alive! All these flaming idealists have no clue what they'd visit upon us had they the chance. Scot's right! They never should've been allowed to get a toe across the border, never mind a staging ground. I won't be silenced on this any longer!" He directed the last at Julia, and her lips twitched in amusement.

What the fuck?

Lord Peale's words sucked the air from the room. Everyone looked away, having their own horror stories from a friend of a friend, someone they knew, a loved one. The Sons' stain of hatred festered beneath the subconscious of every Talent. Why the hell had the threat within their borders gone unchallenged? The room was full of guilty faces, wondering the same thing.

All but one.

Julia smirked, the air rife with the stink of their fear and cowardice.

Flynn bristled. There was no way in hell he'd be a party to it, and they needed to wake the fuck up to what was on their doorstep. "The Messiah's calling in the chapters. The Sons believe judgement day's at hand. This won't be the last attack and the Sons aren't alone. The Source is coming."

Flynn met Crandall's eyes and the smaller man returned his stare. Acid in the back of his throat, Flynn's next words burnt as he spoke them. "The border should be closed now, and we need to prepare for war."

Fucking Cal. He hadn't seen the man since the crash, and he wasn't sure what he was gonna say when he did, but it sure as hell wasn't gonna be admitting the old man had been right.

<hr>

THE DOOR to Cal's study banged open, doorknob cracking into the chair rail. He kept writing. There was only one asshole that made an entrance like that.

"Fine, I'm here. Now you wanna tell me what the hell you're trying to rope me into?"

Cal glanced up, the haze from his cigar breaking and swirling around Rogan helping himself to the good scotch on the sideboard. He grabbed the bottle and crossed the room, plopping down unceremoniously into the chair across from him, browned up like a nut. The Breaker topped off Cal's glass, then lazed back, clunking his booted-feet up on the desk. White sand fell from the treads, leaving little piles on the numbers from the fall harvest and bouncing across Cal's actuary reports.

"You mind?"

"Not a bit." Rogan grinned, taking an appreciative sip and motioning for a cigar. "Well?"

Cal shrugged. "The usual."

"Then how can I possibly say no? Oh wait. No."

Asshole. "You can't. I need you."

Rogan rolled his eyes and caught the trimmed cigar Cal tossed over. His halos flared, lighting it. "You gonna buy me dinner before you fuck me? Not for nothing, but I'd prefer some tight young thing to you."

"Think you've more than met your quota for a while, don't you?" Cal bristled.

Rogan grinned at him with zero remorse. God, he was an arrogant son of a bitch… Cal snorted. Water under the bridge like all the rest of it. He should've known better than to dangle Kara in front of him, but what choice did he have? Less than now, and this couldn't be helped either. He settled back into his chair's permanent divot.

"I need you to pick up where you left off training her."

"That it?"

"Yeah."

Rogan rolled his eyes. "You're full of shit. What's the catch?"

"No catch."

"Jesus, you're a lying asshole."

Cal sipped his scotch and pursed his lips. He'd have to give him just enough to hook him. The rest could wait. "She's bred." God willing.

Rogan shot back his drink and poured another. "When'd that happen?"

"Sometime last week."

"Funny, you failed to mention that when you called me up here. Anyone I know?"

"No, don't imagine you do."

Rogan scowled at him, and Cal grinned back around his cigar. The Breaker sighed, dropping his feet from the desk. He looked around the room, eyes lingering on the random things shoved into the jumbled bookcases lining the walls. A baseball glove. Thumb-bell from a Schwinn long since turned to rust and blown away… The detritus of a childhood they'd shared hundreds of years ago, before the Surge shot everything to hell.

"I can't stop it, Rogan."

The Breaker sighed, tapping off his ash. "No one asked you to."

"That's bullshit."

"Lifetimes too late, my friend, and it isn't gonna make any of them less dead."

"No, suspect you're right on that count, but it'll let me rest a hell of a lot easier when I join them."

Grunting, Rogan topped off their glasses, both of them remembering other conversations in other lives, all of them with similar stakes, steadily increasing over the millennia. They wouldn't get a fourth chance to stop the enemy.

Shit, they shouldn't have gotten a third.

MOTHER STOOD on the garden terrace of the tallest tower in the temple complex, staring blindly out over the azure waters of Halja. A warm breeze played across her bare scalp, the strands of gemstone shards encircling her limbs heating pleasantly in the morning sun. Their brilliance was painful to look upon in the light, though she could no longer see them with any physical sense. Aetherically, her energy was dazzling. Sight had been a small price to pay for the multitude of vistas open to her now. She smiled, listening to the tonkle of bamboo chimes, the breeze playing through the verdancy of her garden, all the sounds and smells of humanity a distant thing.

Well, not all of them.

Otto groveled amid the sharp stones of the garden path, his hair tonic jarring with the heady botanicals around them. A discordant note within the symphony of hibiscus and rose. But then, what was man but an off note?

They all thought themselves so very clever, but only one had ever been a worthy opponent. She could almost admire Cal's coup hiding the Unmaker in plain sight. That irked, but wasn't anything she couldn't turn to her advantage. Nor was Otto's ill-conceived abduction attempt on the plateau. The universe, yearning as it was for correction, continued to aid in her endeavors.

If Cal hadn't done so already, Otto using the Sons to attack the train would trigger her old enemy to summon Rogan, and the Breaker would come running.

Her faith would be rewarded, all the players back on the board, along with an opportunity to curb Otto's willful nature. Mother tapped her lips with a jewel-encrusted finger, throwing rainbows of energy across her son's stodgy form. He fidgeted beneath her regard. So very contrite.

And so very feigned. Unable to coerce Otto's compliance thanks to his father's contribution of Breaker genetics, she was forced to fall back on good old-fashioned manipulation and guilt. They were by no means the lesser of her skills.

Mother placed a hand on her son's thinning brown hair, sighing with all the benevolent disappointment she could muster. "I forgive you for acting out of turn." His shoulders sagged a fraction, then pulled away sharply from tendrils of her talent moving inside his skull.

But not before she'd gotten a read on him.

Oh yes, he was positively seething. It was difficult not to cackle. "I feel your vexation and share it, but we must carry on."

She moved to one of the stone benches scattered amongst the elephant's ears and palms. Otto rushed to take her elbow, though she didn't need his help. Her milky white eyes saw far more than his own.

"Plans are to proceed. Glynfyls must be in as much confusion as possible. Your botched attack has put the city into a state of alert, but I want them positively frantic by the time Titus sends up his troops.

Return to the Source and keep him on target. Our timetable has just moved up considerably."

"He's been fractious with the changes to his directives. His migraines are getting worse."

"Then I suggest you refresh him on a more consistent basis."

Otto frowned, raising his head to look out over the parapet. "What of Kara?"

Mother ran her dry fingers under his chin, pulling it toward her. "She's where I need her to be, and beyond you. A Breaker won't submit to your will, never mind a bonded one." She laughed as he ripped his face from her grasp, but she'd already seen his dirty little secret. He'd already tried to bed the girl and failed miserably.

"And Scot?" Otto gritted out, his cheeks flushed like bright apples.

Mother tapped a tapered nail against her teeth. Laughlin Scot's pedigree had the potential to become problematic, but she needed Cal's attention focused on the boy while other plans were afoot. "He's serving a purpose. Our objectives stay the same. Return to Titus and carry out my instructions."

Otto gave a begrudging nod and bent to peck her cheek. He pulled a dull white stone from his pocket, rubbing it with his thumb as he looked out over the green blue sea, then gated away.

Mother tilted her face to the sun, smiling as the band bound across her brow warmed. Four shards were entwined within the golden circlet, each as big as the ball of her thumb. One of silvered quartz, one of topaz, and two of a deep amethyst. An empty setting lay over each temple, wanting a ruby and an emerald. She ran her fingertips across them. It wouldn't be long now.

CHAPTER THREE

Breaker Business [brākər biz-nəs] noun

1. *A sensitive matter unique to the Breaker line not discussed with
   outsiders.*

– Excerpt from The Way of Honor

*"Gates were installed throughout Glynfyls and the oldest of the remote
estates by the original founders. The secret of their creation has been
lost to time, but their functionality persists. One only has to envision
their destination and step through one of the many pale stone arches to
make it a reality, completely eliminating the need for a Fetch."*

*– Lord Talos, Preceptor of History,
Academy of Glynfyls*

"LAUGHLIN, A WORD."

Damn, he'd almost made it. Flynn looked longingly at the gate only
a few strides away, fighting the urge to dive through to Meddleton. He
turned, trying to keep the dread from his face.

Phyllis Breakspear hadn't changed a bit. A tall, handsomely built woman, her grey-streaked auburn hair swept up off her brow and was held back by a black mourning ribbon.

Fitting, since she was about to bury him.

"Lady Breakspear." He bowed over her extended hand.

"Oh please, you needn't be so formal." Phyllis kissed his cheek. She'd been his mother's best friend, and he'd always liked her—at least until she'd sent that fucking note. She reached out like she was gonna brush something from his sleeve, then dropped her hand away.

"You'll have to forgive me. The last time I saw that jacket—" Her lips tightened, and he felt like an ass. No wonder she hadn't met his eye during session. "I always liked it with the pewter waistcoat, but the bronze looks nice; you've warmer coloring than Richard had."

"I appreciate you lending them to me. I'll have them returned as soon as I've something suitable." He frowned at the crowd. It wasn't gonna be fucking breeches.

"Oh, don't bother," she laughed, dabbing her eye. "I'd saved them for Billy, but his shoulders aren't nearly so broad, and I don't believe they'll ever be. I'd heard through the grapevine the sad fate of the jacket Lot lent you, and had hoped they would suit."

Flynn shoved his hands into his pockets, wondering what else she'd heard. Fucking Miriam. He wasn't gonna be able to scratch his ass without it becoming front page—He jerked away at Phyllis's palm cupping his cheek. Christ, what was it with older women treating him like a poor orphan?

"Walk with me, won't you?" She smiled at his reluctance. "It won't take long, I promise."

Flynn sighed, offering her his arm, and they started toward the promenade.

The Assembly Hall was a huge domed structure with two large wings surrounded by a complex of architecturally dissimilar—but no less ostentatious—outbuildings. Shifted in from God knows where, they ranged in size from intimate pavilions to a coliseum for tens of thousands situated on the hill's edge. Wide glass tubes connected them all, allowing for traffic between structures regardless of the snow. The entire thing reminded Flynn of a set up Leo'd had for his ferrets when they were kids.

The promenade was the most elaborate of the glass-encased walks, housing dozens of restaurants and shops between the coliseum and the administrative portion of the campus. It hugged the western slope of the bluff rising through the center of Glynfyls. High enough to clear the squalor of the lower city, it boasted a stunning view of the mountains in the west and the bay to the north. On the rare days when the wind was strong enough to thin the heavy fug of coal smoke and less desirable vapors blanketing the city, the plateau to the south and east could be seen as well. More often, the clag choked through the streets of precariously listing buildings, thick enough to chew.

Flynn turned away from the view, the memory of it coating his tongue with that distinct foulness that was Glynfyls. God, he hated this fucking city.

The lunchtime crowd milled around them. Men tipped their hats and bowed to Phyllis as she met their eye, and the women simpered behind their fans at Flynn. He sighed at the complicated gowns and coiffures, unable to imagine Kara dolled up in any of it. A memory of her running through the frost-silenced woods, dark hair streaming out behind her, filled his mind's eye. Her smile as he caught her, pressing her back against one of the sentinel pines—

Flash bulbs went off.

Flynn blinked, a crowd of reporters had gathered at a respectful distance. The promenade drew a sharp line between the world of the nobility and the commons. Here, and on the hill above, there were strict rules of conduct. On the lower rungs of the city, none existed.

Phyllis and he ignored them as they strolled past the shops, Phyllis pausing often to idly finger a scarf or sample a sweet. A gentle hum of conversation, the clack of ladies' boots, and sweep of full skirts against the flagstones murmured in the background. Wide brass-bladed fans above lazily circulated a warm breeze, rich with the scents of tapas and the spicy notes of the perfumery at the far end.

Flynn's stomach rumbled. Damn, he wished he had an io-bar.

"Did you want to get something to eat?"

"Ah, no. Thank you. I need to get back to Meddleton."

Phyllis's brow furrowed. "I'm sure you do. How is she?"

"Recovering."

They'd stopped in front of one of the florists' booths. His eyes lingered on the proliferation of hue and scent. Did Kara like flowers? Shit, he didn't even know what her favorite color was. He pulled a long-stemmed rose from one of the polished wooden buckets. The blossom was fixed to retain the dewy blush it'd had on the morning it'd been plucked from somewhere in the Deep South.

"I'm told she's an excellent shot."

A smile ghosted across his lips. "She's skilled at a great many things." He put the rose back and caught the eye of the woman making up posies. She set her work aside and bobbed a curtsy.

Flynn motioned to her wares. "Have it all sent to Meddleton, along with whatever you have in the back."

She stammered for a moment before bobbing again and hurrying to do his bidding. Phyllis watched him with a bemused expression. He colored, jamming his hands into his pockets.

"Was she the one who set your nose?" He nodded, and her eyes became calculating. "Binder and Breaker…"

Flynn couldn't stop the smile from spreading over his face. Kara was gonna stir things up, all right. He couldn't think of anyone else in Glynfyls that was a duality. The nobility was gonna shit themselves.

Phyllis's brow knit and she smiled with him. "Don't you just look like the cat who's been at the cream." She considered him a few seconds longer. "What you said in session, you've changed. Grown up while you've been gone. What have you been doing all this time?"

Flynn shrugged. "Stealing cars."

Phyllis laughed and gave his shoulder a little push. He chewed his lip. That probably shouldn't be his stock answer.

"Seriously, Laughlin. You've been gone for so long…"

He sighed, not imagining people's heads tilting toward them or their steps slowing. Whatever he said would be on everyone's lips before it left his own. "Figuring things out, I guess."

The florist came over and presented him with a receipt. He signed it without looking and handed it back. Two men began gathering it all up.

"Well, I'm glad you came to your senses and returned to us, although I would've preferred you'd done so in a less spectacular manner. It's made quite an impression on my line." Phyllis didn't exactly frown at him, but she wasn't happy.

He kicked at the granite flagstones. "I did what I had to do."

"And now that you're up here?"

"What d'you want from me, Phyllis?"

She worked her jaw like she was rolling something around and enjoying it immensely. "You used to be more fun."

"I used to drink."

"Can't say anyone will miss that, though your sense of humor's a steep price for sobriety."

"There's not a damn thing funny about what I just saw during Assembly."

"No, there wasn't." The amusement left her eyes. "It will be even less entertaining when some tragedy befalls House Peale over the next few days."

Flynn snorted, then saw the look on her face. "You're serious."

"I am. Make no mistake, Laughlin, Julia Cree is dangerous. She can't buy or bully the Breakers, so she's alienated Stonefist and gutted the army's funding. The rest of the lines she's cowed or corrupted, and she doesn't tolerate defiance. Right now, Lot and I are the only things standing between her and complete control of the Assembly. To get it, she just needs one of us to fall." Phyllis laughed at his expression. "He and I have come to an understanding. We've been voting as a block, hamstringing her where we can, but the rest of the Houses—"

"Think he's an asshole."

Her eyes sparkled with amusement again. "Lot's delivery has always been problematic, regardless of the message. You know as well as I that he was never meant to be anything more than a place-holder. Believe me when I tell you, it's something he's keenly aware of."

Flynn's mouth curdled. Great, one more thing the man could hold against him. "And your note?" he asked, done with the guilt trip.

Phyllis shrugged, inspecting her ring. The gold-filigreed setting held a ruby the size of a pigeon's egg. "Breaker Business is Breaker

Business. You're not a Breaker, so it's none of yours. What happened out on that plateau falls under my purview, and I will deal with it."

"Does Crandall know that?"

"Lord Crandall knows a great many things, including when not to try me." The steel in her voice took Flynn aback. "You need to take up your mother's mantle. Deirdre meant for you to be First Shade, and all of us are desperate for someone to wrest power from that creature. I can't do it alone, and Lot can't muster enough support to be effective. Crandall will keep his peace and remain neutral for as long as it benefits him to do so. I suggest you step up quickly and make it worth his while, because she's just made it very clear you're her next target."

Flynn gave a low laugh. Fucking Glynfyls. The maneuvering and machinations made him ill.

Phyllis's expression hardened. "She won't stop with you, Laughlin. Grab a paper on the way out. The press has been very busy eviscerating your mystery woman. Speaking of which, the Ladies and I—"

Phyllis's hand rose to flutter at her throat.

Motherfucker. Flynn gritted his teeth, pushing past her. His temper had jumped enough to tint the promenade crimson. He couldn't deal with this shit right now.

"We're not finished—"

"Like hell we aren't."

Flashbulbs peppered him as he passed. The murmur of the crowd a hushed frenzy, crashing in around him. They pulled back from his path, their eyes sucking at him as he stalked to the gate.

He stepped through it and into Meddleton's foyer, some three hundred miles away.

OTTO TURNED FROM THE CROOKED, grime-encrusted window, not bothering to keep the distaste from his face. Below the city's sixth rung, it looked like a flock of birds had spent the past several hundred years shitting over every available surface. Higher up the hill, the Assembly paid for clinkers to shift the hardened fly ash away, but no one cared down here. For all he knew, it might be where it ended up.

The room was free of ash, but that was entirely due to the window being nailed shut. Dirt was another matter. It caked the floor beneath the tenement's hanging furniture. The thirty-five degree tilt to the room made anything with legs an impossibility.

Anything inanimate, at least. Barton perched in one of the woven, rope chairs, reviewing today's rag sheets atop the hanging plank that served as a table. Titus's favorite procurer of Talents was, well, to put it mildly, odd.

The articles were laid out in front of Barton in two precise rows, folded with exacting edges to show anything mentioning the Scots. There were a fair number. More than Otto would've expected, considering they'd just arrived at Meddleton, albeit dramatically. His mouth pruned. They shouldn't have arrived at all.

He climbed into the other chair, his left leg bending and the toes of his right boot scraping the floor. "What happened? I thought you'd extract her from the farm, that's why I held the Sons back in Hamlin."

Barton's eyes snapped to him, his tongue darting out to moisten his lips. "Titus wants her bred, and I couldn't. Wards set, same as Meddleton. Keyed."

"So? You're a Fetch. You got into the tubes easily enough."

"Different." Barton's right eye twitched, his hand drifting upwards. He began to absently gnaw on a finger. "Old woman's a Radiant. Tied in…ties, keys, keyed different." He pulled his abused digit from his mouth as if catching himself at it. A bead of blood welled up, and he whisked a cloth from his pocket, wrapping the wound.

Otto watched him warily. Having been inside Barton's bizarrely structured mind, he put very little past the procurer. Though Otto didn't think he was in danger personally, it was best not to agitate him. He carefully slid a newspaper away from the rest, allowing the man to collect himself.

The publication was one of the more sensational rags Glynfyls had to offer, and had his favorite still; a shot of Scot's face from that infamous reel. The article hashed out all of his past exploits in great detail. Otto had to admit, it did make for juicy reading, and sex sold papers. All of the newsstands he'd stopped at had been cleaned out.

The stories running in all of them were largely the same. Lord Laughlin Scot had returned to Glynfyls with a mysterious woman after a stint in the great unknown. They gleefully speculated as to if he would take up his old habits, and brutally assassinated the conjectured character of his companion. His suspected whereabouts ranged all over the globe, but none came close to the truth.

Otto studied the man's photo. Titus didn't think Scot would be an issue, but there was something—

"Dangerous."

He looked up to find Barton watching him intently. The procurer pulled a folder from beneath the papers and handed it to him. Stills from the plateau.

Otto gave a low whistle. "Where did you get these?"

The man blinked at him, first one eye, then the other, on a rolling delay. Otto supposed it didn't matter, other than the fact that someone was working very hard to bury the entire incident. No one was saying anything publicly, and that in itself was troubling in a city which thrived on dirty deeds and innuendo. He was convinced Mother had nothing to do with the cover up, though she'd make it play into her hand. She needed Scot for some mysterious role in her grand scheme.

Otto couldn't help but question the wisdom of that. His gut told him the man was going to be an issue, and these stills did little to change his mind. He flipped to the next one. Thirty-seven Sons slaughtered over the course of an hour. Eviscerated in most cases, their innards splayed across the frozen tundra.

"One man's work. Precise," Barton mused. His halos glimmered a sickly shade of prune. "No trail. Tastes like a Shade and not. More. Other." He licked his lips and pulled a still from the stack, admiring the spatter of viscera captured by the hoarfrost.

"You're sure?"

Barton gave a slow nod. "Artistry. Economy of movement. One, other." He sighed wistfully, then slid out the bottom one, his tongue flicking across his lips again. "This was just fun."

The still on the table between them was of the train's engine compartment. The remains showed none of the aforementioned artistry, and Otto's normally iron-clad stomach lurched. Suffice to say, they'd suffered. Excessively so.

He pushed it back to the procurer. Barton took it up eagerly, ogling it like other men would a porno. Leaving him to it, Otto flipped open the file Titus had forwarded, carefully looking through Scot's arrest warrants. He had a hot temper to be sure, most of the altercations over petty grievances or women. All of them involved alcohol. Weaknesses to exploit, but nothing to suggest Scot was capable of such cultured cruelty.

Kara's file was considerably thicker. Everything from her birth pedigree to her Creche entrance scores. Years of holo. Otto was sure Barton had watched most, if not all, of it. The notes on her physicals were intriguing, her Breaker genes listed as recessive.

That was patently false.

Otto sourly adjusted himself at the memory, knowing full well the woman moved like a Breaker. He'd tried to corner and coerce her at one of the few fêtes she'd attended. The attempt hadn't gone well, and begged the question: where were the training logs, sparring partners, or equipment requisitions? Otto personally understood the drive all Breakers had to perform physically, half-blooded or not. She would've required some kind of outlet, but there was nothing.

"Not logical," Barton said, rousing Otto from his musings. The procurer pulled his finger from his mouth, pressing the spot he'd chewed raw.

Nasty habit, that. "The potential variable is troubling, isn't it?" Otto reached for the last paper. It sat a little apart from the others. Unlike the rest of them, there was actual information on the page instead of supposition. Laughlin James Scot was to Introduce his intended to his line and wed, Thursday at Meddleton. It went on to include a statement from the Scots that the woman in question was not a native of Glynfyls, but that no further information would be forthcoming until after the ceremony.

"I'm assuming you've seen this?" Otto asked, motioning to the article.

The procurer grunted, jerking his head at the black and gold servant's livery hanging from a peg on the wall. He was good at what he did, of that there was no question. Kara would be sequestered at the estate and out of reach until the Introduction, but afterward, her first stop would be the Assembly.

"What role has Titus given to you?" Barton asked, gnawing on his fingers again.

Otto wriggled out of the chair and stood awkwardly on the canted floor. "Facilitating." He ran his thumb over the stone in his pocket, gating back to the Source, and to more even footing.

———

KARA CHEWED her thumb as French escorted the Binder from the room, the two of them speaking in hushed tones. If that had been any indication of what a northern Binder could do, it was no wonder they hadn't had any idea what her talent was capable of. Just assuaging her exhaustion had spent the man, and she could already feel it creeping back. The nausea had never left.

The door closed behind them and the room suddenly became that much bigger.

Kara curled into a little ball. Alone.

What was wrong with her? The Binder had told French she just needed sleep, but that wasn't—Ugh. Nora would've known. Abject misery crashed down over her. She flinched at the soft knock at the door sounding above the pop of the fire.

Kara dashed a hand over her eyes. *Oh Glory, what now?*

A trail of liveried servants entered, laden with more flowers than she'd ever seen. Arrangement after arrangement kept coming through the door, large urns being shifted in…

They covered every surface; the industrial desk with mechanical bits scattered across it, the occasional table between the plush winged chairs, the top of the stone-veined mantle. A massive spray of roses hid the intricacies of the inlaid gaming table in the far corner.

Then that weird jump of sensation—Flynn was abruptly closer. Her eyes went from the joyful riot of color to the rectangle of hallway. He was back from the city, but he wasn't happy…not that he had been since they'd crossed the border.

Still, when he appeared, it was with a wide smile and a bouquet of daisies in his hand. He bowed with a flourish, presenting them to her. Kara laughed, stupidly bringing them to her nose. They wouldn't smell unless the fix was removed. His brow creased, and he wiped the moisture from her cheek. She batted him away and gestured at a massive urn of lilies that'd just been shifted in.

"Daisies are the best you can muster after all of that?"

He grinned, pulling off his jacket and cravat. "You like them?"

"They're wonderful, but why so many?"

"I didn't know your favorite, so I got all of it." He climbed into bed beside her, Kara's stomach lurching as his weight settled. She closed her eyes and curled up against him.

"Sorry." He sighed, undoing the buttons at his throat, and putting an arm around her. Her nausea settled at his touch, and his emotions mellowed at hers. The talent he was pushing her jumped another notch. It did more for her than the Binder had.

"Between this and the Introduction, there's not going to be a bloom left in the North."

"Christ, French rope you into that already? You were supposed to be sleeping."

"I kept having nightmares…" She forced a smile at his frown. "He kept me company until the Binder came. I had no idea what a big deal the Introduction is supposed to be." Or what a big deal Flynn was supposed to be…

He played with her fingers, his lips against her hair. "People up here get off on that shit. I'm sure Cal's gonna go all out and use it to set up my bid for First. So, what's your favorite?"

Something about that first part made him really uncomfortable, but the look on his face… Had he asked her something? "Hmm? Oh, flower? I always liked the orchids in the botanical dome, especially the orange ones. Alb—Cal used to take us on picnics there."

"Orange… that your favorite color?"

"Just for flowers, otherwise I'm very fond of green." She felt him smile.

"I still can't believe Cal's a Patron. We thought he was out surveying apiaries."

"Apiaries?"

"Yeah." Flynn laughed. "Where d'you think all this comes from? It's honey money."

"I've never really thought about it...money, that is. We just scanned our barcode." She turned her wrist over, and he ran his thumb across the bold tattoo.

"You gonna keep it?"

Kara started at the possibility of having the last vestige of her old life removed. "I hadn't thought..." Tears pricked at her eyes.

"Hey, hey," he murmured, gathering her up against his chest. "What's wrong?"

She sniffled, shaking her head, and playing with the edges of his waistcoat. "I don't know. Ugh! Sorry. I hate crying, it's so stupid." It wasn't that she missed the Source, not exactly. Certainly not the Creche, with its petty feuds and power struggles, the constant testing and sampling... Riegel and Ielle were just at the top of a long list of people she never wanted to see again. Still, there were some she'd miss...

To her horror, a sob escaped. Flynn's arms tightened around her, his lips pressing against the crown of her head.

"I'm sorry." She wiped her eyes. "I just... I miss Nora." A mashup of feelings came from him and a heaviness filled her chest. Another sob snuck past her lips, and she felt very small against him in that big bed. "I'm sorry, but I do."

"Shh...hey I get it. She's your mom." His voice cracked, and Kara lost it, weeping into his neck and wishing she could bind it all up and shove it away with everything else she didn't want to deal with. The thought of using talent made her feel worse. Flynn smoothed her hair, a rumble coming from his stomach. She laughed, wiping her nose on her sleeve.

He grabbed his cravat from the floor. "Here, use this damn thing. I'm starving, and you gotta be hungry. Let's get something sent up, anything you want. What d'you like to eat?"

Kara took the square of aubergine silk. He wanted her to blow her nose in this? She looked around the room at all the flowers. The servants had disappeared. They'd set the last of the arrangements on the floor, making random floral islands. An abrupt longing for the coop filled her, bleeding into guilt. There was no going back, not to any of it, and it was her fault.

She wiped her face and sniffled. Ugh, she was a pathetic mess… and he was right, she was hungry. If he said anything, he probably meant anything—she laughed, and he raised his eyebrows expectantly.

"You'll think I'm dumb, but I woke up with the worst craving for a baked potato with this awful cheese sauce they used to serve in the Creche…" She sniffled again, feeling another tear escape and hating herself for it.

Flynn wiped it away. "That for the potato or your mom?"

"The potato." She smacked him, and he grinned.

"Well, that I can do something about." He hit a bronze plate on the wall. A soft chime sounded, followed by French's disembodied voice.

"Sir?"

"I need a couple of baked potatoes sent up with awful cheese sauce."

"I will instruct the kitchen to make it as distasteful as possible. Will that be all?"

He glanced at Kara, and she nodded with a sheepish smile. "Put a crapload of chili and broccoli on one of them, and a steak next to it."

"Very good, sir." The chime sounded again.

Flynn kissed her brow. "See, all better."

"You really live like this?"

He looked around the opulent room and sighed. "Not for a long time, but it's how I grew up." His hand drifted to her abdomen, and she felt him burying his anxiety. "I asked Bernice to come… The Binder couldn't—he couldn't sense anything."

Her brow wrinkled. "I'm not surprised. He wasn't very talented."

"Yeah." Flynn's smile was completely unconvincing. "You're probably right."

A stab of annoyance went through her. Why was he was so invested in offspring? She started undoing the buttons on his shirt, not wanting to think about it. His chest was an excellent distraction. "I can't believe I felt bad for you when we met."

"Did you?"

"Of course. I thought you were a sub, living in a shack that smelled like dog pee."

"That was my jeans. I didn't exactly have a regular laundry service."

"Honestly, I liked the way you smelled better then, even with the pee. That aftershave is gross."

"Really?" He pulled up his collar and sniffed at it.

"Really. It's like overripe fruit…musky pomegranate."

"What?" Flynn laughed. "Is that even a thing?" Shrugging at her look, he closed his eyes, settling back against the pillows. "Fine, pick whatever you like."

"I just like you." She slid her hand across his chest. He gave a sigh of contentment, kissing her forehead. She listened to the slow beat of his heart. A kind of hum accompanied it, more a feeling than a sound, lulling them both. The nausea that'd been tormenting her subsided, and she was surprised to find she felt almost human with it gone.

"Was the bad thing like what happened at the 'Pinion?"

A burst of his anxiety. "Is it important?"

She trailed her fingers across the rise of his pec. "I killed two guards and the pilot before that pack attacked me. I see that red mutie every time I close my eyes."

"I put it down, I can't stand those fucking things."

"Because they can sense you cloaked?"

"No, dogs and I don't get along, mechanized or otherwise. Cal had one when I was a kid. It hated me…most animals do."

"Cats like you."

"Cats are weird."

"Can I get one?"

He laughed. "A cat? Yeah. There's probably some in the kitchen. I'll ask French. If not, we can get one from the farm. Which did you want?"

"I can pick?" She propped herself up on an elbow, wondering at his delight.

"Yeah, Kara, from here on out, whatever you want is yours."

… *"I want to be happy"*…

Had she spoken those words only yesterday? It seemed a lifetime ago and surrounded by all this, how could you not be… Except Flynn hadn't been…and wasn't now.

He moved her thumb from her lips. "Hey, I know this sucks. Gimme a week or two to get shit settled. Rest up, we get through this Introduction, and then we can figure out what our normal is, okay?"

"Is shellacking your hair down part of that?"

Flynn scowled. "It won't lie flat otherwise."

"Good." She mussed it. Laughing, he rolled her onto her back, messy strands across his eyes. Her heart leaped, heat building in her core. He was such a beautiful man—

"Stop tempting me, woman," he rumbled, his lips brushing hers. "I need you better." Kara trailed a finger down his abs to tug his belt free.

"The Binder just said I needed sleep."

"That's not sleeping, and you said his talent was for shit."

"It was, but feeling you, our echo—I don't know how, but remember back at the farm? It helps."

His eyes closed with a ragged breath, her hand slipping inside his pants to trace the crown of his hardening length. That weird resonance between them deepened. Flynn groaned, his cock bucking against her hand. "Christ. You Binders and your fucking logic… You feel so fucking good, Kara, but I don't want to hurt you."

"You won't." She raised an eyebrow, stroking him. "And I bet I'll feel better after…"

Flynn captured her wrists and pinned them above her head. "I told you to stop tempting me," he murmured, nipping at her lips.

"Are you tempted?" she asked between long slow kisses.

His fingers threaded with hers. "Mmm. Every time I look at you."

"Yeah? She raised her chin, his mouth hot on her throat. "To do what?"

"Nasty, filthy things…but not tonight." He nosed into the hollow beneath her ear, chuckling at her pout of dismay. "Brat. That wasn't a no. Do you trust me?"

Her brows drew together. "Of course."

"Then close your eyes and stay right like that."

She looked at him for a moment longer, then did as he asked. His weight shifted from the bed and his footsteps crossed the room. A cabinet opened and there was rustling before he returned.

"Ah—Keep them closed," he chuckled again, a silken weight pressing against her lids. "Lift your head…good girl. You might trust me, but I'm not sure I trust you."

She huffed, letting him tie the blindfold, anticipation building low in her belly. He pressed her back against the pillows, his fingers at the ties of her nightgown, slowly dragging the neckline down over her skin, stopping just short of her aching breasts. The caress of the thin cotton left prickling need in its wake. She went to free her arm—

"Did I say you could move?" he murmured, raising her hands back above her head. "Naughty girl. We're gonna have to do something about that." Silk trailed across her breast bone, along her throat, elbow to fingertip, then encircled her wrists, cinching them together tight. She gasped as he tugged her arms upward and fastened them to the headboard.

Kara wet her lips at the sound of his pants hitting the floor, squeezing her thighs together. The blindfold amplifying her desire, the dark spice of him tinging the air, enflaming her need. He smelled so good… "Afraid I'm going to run away?" she asked breathlessly.

"You're not going anywhere, Kara," he rumbled. The mattress shifted beneath her. "You're mine, and so goddamned beautiful all tied up for me." His fingers teased the nightgown's neckline lower, and she whimpered, her shoulder blades pulling together. "Shhh…let me play."

Flynn's mouth captured her peaked nipple through the cotton, its gentle rasp an exquisitely excruciating barrier keeping her from the soft wetness of his mouth. She moaned as he sucked at her, tongue flicking the turgid point of flesh. His fingers trailed up her thigh—so slow, oh Glory, so painfully slow—drawing up the hem of the nightgown, her over sensitized skin on fire with its passage.

Kara squirmed, wanting—needing—more… "Please, Flynn…"

"Ask for what you want." His touch brushed up her inner thigh to ghost across her panties. She groaned, hips rising to chase his fingers.

"Touch me, m-my… oh…"

His breath feathered over the apex of her legs, chilling the damp fabric clinging to her dewy folds. "Say it. I won't until you do." He nosed over the seam, the sound of his deep inhale triggering a rush of heat to her core, soaking her panties clean through. Flynn's finger hooked the sodden cotton, drawing it to the side. "Goddamn, you get so fucking wet for me. Tell me I can have a taste, baby. Tell me to lap up all this cream."

Kara whimpered, the restraints digging into her wrists as she writhed. "Yes, please, yes…"

He slid the ruined scrap of fabric from her hips, down over her legs with torturous care. She bit her lip, fighting the urge to rip free and kick the stupid things away.

"So fucking beautiful. All laid out for me." His voice was honeyed gravel, rough with need and sweetened with sin. Their link burned with his hunger for her, and her desire to be devoured.

Kara shivered, her breasts painful points, the ache between her legs sweet agony. Teasing hands traveled the length of her body, her skin pricking and pebbling beneath his feather-light touch. He returned to her core, inhaling again with a low moan. "Ask for it."

"Please…" She wet her lips. "Please eat m-my, my pussy, please…"

"Mmm. Good girl." His mouth fastened on her with a rumble of satisfaction. Tongue delving deep, hands bracing her backside, lifting to shoulder her thighs farther apart, and feasting. Kara cried out, writhing against her bonds, riding the storm of his desire into her own.

"You're so fucking sweet," he murmured, fingers at her clit, exposing all of her to the soft ministrations of his tongue.

Her knees pressed inward, trying to jerk away. "N-no. That's too —" A finger breached her opening, and then another, scissoring and curling. Behind the blindfold her eyelids fluttered. Oh, Glory—

"Shhh…that's a good girl. Relax…"

"I want you, Flynn," she moaned. "Please, I want you in me when I come…"

The rhythm of his fingers faltered, then he pulled his hand away, beard tickling her skin as he skated up her body. His lips found hers, the musky tang of her passion on his tongue when he kissed her, deep and languorous.

The blunt tip of him swept across her entrance, easing her wide in agonizingly unhurried increments. She raised up to meet him, and his hand caged her hip, pinning her to the bed. "We do this slow, or not at all," he breathed raggedly, his forehead against hers. So much tangled emotion behind that block he threw up over their bond…

"Then I want to see you…touch you…"

A pause.

He tugged the blindfold off, leaving her blinking at the inrush of light, and him above her, the glow of the fire backlighting him like some kind of God. "Goddamn, you're fucking beautiful." He dashed a hand over his face, then reached up to release her wrists.

"What's wrong?"

Flynn shook his head, and kissed her breathless.

She wrapped her arms around his neck, feeling all the things he couldn't say. "I love you too, and I'm not going anywhere."

He buried his face against her neck and sank into her, her walls fluttering around him, urging him deeper. The bond connecting them rife with shared pain and pleasure, fear and longing, and the intensity of rightness between them.

Her, feeling him, feeling her.

He groaned against her mouth, bottoming out within, breath coming fast. His eyes opened, halos washing the snowy linens with verdigris fire, the gold of hers painting the canopy. Talent gathered in the room. His brow furrowed, tendrils of it plucking at them, expectant… wanting…

They moved together as one in a sultry undulation of flesh. Talent grew with each slow thrust, the burn of their halos brighter. Everything else falling away. Her nausea and exhaustion, his fear. A soft pulsation of passion and power cocooning them in their own world. Building. Cresting. Breaking over them in waves of staccato bliss carried in a melody buoyed by oneness.

Flynn brushed a lock of hair from her sweat-stippled brow. "I won't lose you, Kara."

"I'm right here, aren't I?"

He nodded, kissing her softly. "Yeah. And I'm gonna make sure it stays that way."

MARCOS SAT beneath the simulated blue of the dome encapsulating several acres of manufactured wilderness, tugging at his collar. The damned heat in this place… it brought back too many memories of Diytan. The glade Nora had chosen for their picnic was idyllic otherwise, but his mouth curdled thinking about that sole smear on his military record. He supposed a volcanic eruption wasn't something you could be held personally responsible for, but the annihilation of so many of his men and losing their objective was a bitter pill to swallow.

Nora laughed, reaching over to undo the top button of his jacket. Her fingers on him made him sweat more. "If it's too warm, you can take this off. Picnics are supposed to be casual." Her own arms were bare, and she'd kicked off her sandals to bury her toes in the grass.

Marcos wet his lips with a sip of fizz. "I wasn't bred to be casual, Nora."

"No. You weren't, were you?" She hugged her knees, smiling up into the botanical dome's greenery like it was some private joke. Ficus trees surrounded them, feathered automatons flitting through their branches, their songs on staggered five-minute loops. A brook trickled through the long columns of roots, the subtle hint of an algae bloom in the purified air. The geneticists must be playing with protist resilience again.

"Is the Deep South anything like this?"

His lips twitched at her thoughts mirroring his own. "I suppose it's a close approximation. The amount of insects down there always surprises me, and it's noisier than you would think. Primates hooting and yelling over the birds…" Explosions and the screams of his men—

"What does it smell like?"

Dead bodies.

He started from the memory. "Smell like? It smells like everything's in bloom and rotting at the same time."

"Then this is more of a sanitized approximation than close. Like everything else here."

Marcos helped himself to the chicken salad, resisting the urge to glance at the surveillance drone hovering in his peripheral. "Can I make you a plate?"

"Please." She smiled. The checkered blanket spread beneath them had been set with a simple meal Nora had brought in a wicker basket. She had a fondness for the quaint dining practice. Though he knew Albanach was responsible for introducing her to it, Marcos had to admit to its charm. He prepared her a plate and gave her his pickle—she liked them far more than he did—and opened the flash-vac of dehydrated potato thins to share.

"Will you have to go back?"

"To the Deep South?" He ran a mental tally of the operations the Source was currently embroiled in. Land grabs, border disputes, that regime change that'd been dragging on… "I doubt it, Pax's been boots on the ground for the past few years." Marcos frowned. Since Diytan, to be exact. "He's competent, though I can't completely discount the possibility." Especially if the boy kept sulking around like he had been since Kara bested him.

"He's your eldest son from the litter before Riegel, isn't he? What was her name? Gerta?"

Marcos stiffened. "Greta. Pax is one of her offspring, yes."

"And yours."

Marcos shrugged, picking the grape halves out of his salad. The concept that the byproducts of his mandatory copulations should be more than that rankled of late. "One of many, what of it?"

She looked at him with those blue eyes, and he couldn't hold her gaze. "It's just…lately I've been thinking of family—of Kara. Have you heard anything?"

Family. The word made his mouth pucker. "Nothing specific."

There'd been reports of an attack by the Sons, but she didn't need that weighing on her. He pushed salad around his plate. If Pax went missing, would he care? Only so far as lamenting the loss of a good soldier. Save for him and Riegel, the others hadn't distinguished themselves enough for him to pick out of a line-up… His mind flashed back to the crowds of Diytanese refugees, desperate for any word of their families. Marcos frowned again. His lack of emotion for his own offspring bothered him. His scowl deepened, recognizing it as a symptom of what was really wrong.

And the Source was responsible for that.

Nora twisted her ring, ignoring the plate at her side. The light filtering through the leaves struck the planes of her face, more angular than they'd been a week ago.

"You're not eating."

"My appetite of late hasn't been especially hale."

"Then you won't mind me divesting you of that pickle—"

She gave a cry of mock outrage and snatched it away. "Careful Commandant, if you start taking liberties like those, I'll have to rethink my good opinion of you."

"Wouldn't want to do that, especially with how much I've laid out on theater tickets."

She laughed, crunching on the briny spear. "Opening night of Kasham's burlesque review isn't my idea of theater."

Marcos lazed back onto an elbow. "Just trying to broaden your cultural horizons."

"And here I'd thought you take any excuse to spend time with me." She smiled coyly.

"There's that, too."

A series of notes sounded, and her face paled. "Were they scheduled to release a kaleidoscope today?"

Marcos swore. "No." He swept up the checkered blanket, scattering their picnic as the air above filled with a symphony of color. Wings of vibrant blue, oranges and pinks fluttered across the dome's strata, soaring on the artificial breeze.

He tented the blanket over them, Nora pressing against his side. His breath stuttered at her nearness—

And then the patter of corpses began.

Butterflies rained from the sky, the simulated bird song drowned out by the hum of sani-matons appearing to vaporize them once it was clear the geneticists' latest attempts to breed a plaz-resistant pollinator had failed yet again. That, the algae… what were they trying to cook up now? Nora nuzzled under his chin, and his nostrils flared at her scent, a whisper of talent building between them, muting Laurellai's ire searing through his bond.

"Have you ever seen them as they're supposed to be?" Nora whispered, flinching from the pattering of winged bodies from above.

"I've seen how a great many things are supposed to be, especially recently."

She pushed away to search his eyes, that little triangle between her brows, and then a smile on her lips. His hand raised to her chin, thumb brushing across them, her pupils expanding in the muted, red-checked light.

"Won't you kiss me?"

The whisper of talent prickled his skin, and Marcos's bloodlust surged, wanting nothing else—

That was a lie. He wanted more.

He took his hand away. "I won't share you." His voice cracked. "Not with Laurellai, and not with him."

The hum of the sani-matons stopped. Marcos dropped the blanket, the organics of their picnic gone, along with any trace of the kaleidoscope. Nora's smile remained. She set about picking up the scattered dishes, looking ridiculously smug. He held the wicker basket for her and raised an eyebrow. She laughed.

"Did I miss something?"

"Miss something? Why, I've no idea what you mean." Her eyes glinted with mischief. "You must be imagining things."

His lips curved up in a smile to match hers. "You're right Nora. I believe I have been."

CHAPTER FOUR

Introduction [in-truh-duhk-shu n] noun

1. *A wedding ceremony between Talents of differing bents in which the bride is held in seclusion before the formal presentation to the groom's line.*

— Excerpt from Glynfyls: A History

"The bride's seclusion before her Introduction provides an opportunity for reflection upon the enormity of abandoning her birth-line for another. A small taste of what will equate to exile, it also allows her to become acquainted with the oftentimes jarring expectations of the House she's entering into..."

— Lady Chatterly, Precepta of Social Graces,
Academy of Glynfyls

FLYNN STEPPED out of the lift, wishing he was back in bed. Not counting the scant hour he'd just grabbed, it'd been at least two days since he'd actually slept. He rubbed at his chest, the burn on his channel almost gone.

That was weird, considering he hadn't let up on how much he was pushing Kara, but she'd been right. Being with her skin-to-skin had made them both feel better. Not that he looked it. He snorted at his reflection in the hall mirror, trying to smooth down the inevitable cowlicks.

Goddamn. There he was, older and thinner, but the Scot heir was back.

Christ, this was really happening.

Fuck my life.

Hair a lost cause, he continued into the foyer, stifling a yawn. French wouldn't have woken him up if it wasn't important, and there wasn't much point in delaying the inevitable. Still didn't make walking into the east drawing room any easier.

It was one of the smaller chambers Meddleton boasted for entertaining, though the dark cherry panels and plum silk moiré lining the walls weren't any less decadent. Two of his oldest friends stood by the pink granite hearth, speaking in hushed tones. At least, they'd been his friends up until a few years before he'd left. He wasn't sure what to expect from them now. By the way they broke off with whatever they'd been talking about and openly appraised him, the feeling was mutual.

The awkwardness of the moment wasn't helped by the absurdity of their outfits. He'd seen a smattering of men in breeches and hose on the promenade, but had hoped to hell they were on their way out. So much for that if Charles was sporting them. Christ, the man was in fucking heels—Flynn suppressed a groan. He didn't care what the latest craze was. There wasn't a goddamned chance he was wearing that shit.

"So it's true." The taller of the two men came forward, his head full of tight curls so black they shone blue in the firelight. He extended his swarthy hand to shake Flynn's.

He gave Jacques a warm smile, clasping it firmly. "It's good to see you, and I guess that depends on what you're referring to." Flynn motioned for them to take a seat.

"That you're really back." Jacques sat on the edge of the gold damask settee, turning the rim of his bowler in his hands. Charles took the chair nearest the hearth. "This is at least the third time they've reported your return, and the pictures plastered over Glynfyls were so sensational… Well, you know how it is. Now that I see you in the flesh, I have to wonder what really happened out there; you were positively covered in blood."

Shit. Flynn scratched at his jaw, taking the other armchair. "A lot of people got hurt. Miriam had a pretty severe head injury, and Kara was mauled by the pack they were running."

Jacques paled. "My God. Is she all right?"

"Yeah, but it was close." Flynn leaned forward to make himself a coffee from the service on the table between them, ill at how close. "So, you've ascended?"

Jacques' blue eyes clouded. "Yes, I've been the head of my House for almost four years now."

"Sorry to hear about Kristof and Silas. Your brothers were good men."

Jacques nodded faintly, twisting at his cuff. "The past several years have been difficult on multiple fronts. I can't tell you how glad I am you're here. I'll ask you plainly, have you bonded her?"

A broad smile spread across Flynn's face before he could help himself. He looked down into his cup, then at them. "It's good to see you both, but I'd planned on being at Assembly tomorrow. What's so urgent you and Charles had to come out?"

They shared a look, and Charles rolled his eyes with an affected sigh. He appraised Flynn critically, arching a sculpted brow. His dove grey breeches and coat were exquisitely tailored, but it didn't make them any less ridiculous, especially with those shoes.

"I'm inclined to like this woman very much if she's the impetus behind you coming to your senses and having your nose properly set. Why you ever felt the need to walk around disfigured, I'll never understand. Now, if she can only convince you to wear something other than fifteen-year-old hand-me-downs—"

"My wardrobe's a top priority, I can assure you." Flynn's sarcasm was lost on Charles, but Jacques smoothed his drooping mustache, hiding a smile.

"I should hope so, lord knows you've never been able to dress yourself." The spry man sniffed, flicking a lock of auburn hair from his brow while eyeing Flynn's disparagingly.

He reached up and mussed it more just because. It earned him one hell of a look.

"To be blunt," Charles enunciated, "the circumstances under which you left were unsavory. We're here to assess the situation for the line. The others felt Jacques had the best chance of surviving your temper. I tagged along for moral support, and to provide legal witness, should things prove unchanged."

Flynn tamped down his irritation. Charles was infamous for his sharp tongue, and he wasn't saying anything that wasn't true. Once upon a time, that brazen honesty had been why Flynn had liked him. It was a rare quality up here…and it made him fun to mess with.

"I'm here to ascend and take First." He bit back a grimace as the words left his mouth. Fucking Cal. "I'm not the man I was. I'm sober and gave up brawling, so I can assure you, you're both quite safe."

Charles blinked rapidly, and Flynn broke into a broad grin at seeing the slight man speechless. Not that he could blame him. Those last few years, beating the crap out of people and getting shit-faced had been the only reasons he got out of bed…unless his third reason to keep breathing kept him in it. He glanced up at the ceiling, trying to keep the stupid smile off his face.

"You do seem, ah…different. Apart from being sober."

Jacques' smile matched Flynn's. "He's in love, Charles, just look at him." The smaller man rolled his eyes again. "I didn't think I'd see the day."

Flynn colored, not comfortable with the word, but unable to deny the truth of it.

Ever practical, Charles waved the sentiment away. "We're here to give fair warning. Both Jacques and I fully back you for First, but politics are dangerous at the moment. People are being pressured. Talent alone won't be enough to secure your claim."

"The entire line's been approached by Julia's people and told in no uncertain terms that if we nominate you, we'll suffer consequences," Jacques said sourly.

"Not to mention Morris, Leeds, Gent, and Glass all have less than glowing opinions of you," Charles added.

"No, they hate my guts." Flynn put his coffee cup down, not trusting himself with it. "Since when do other lines try to manipulate nominations?"

Jacques and Charles shared another look.

"You've been gone a long time, Flynn. Anything that threatens Julia's power is fair game." Jacques' mouth contorted. "Including your intended."

Flynn growled at the implied threat, and the dusky man flinched back, holding his hands up in apology. *Shit.* Flynn ran a hand through his hair, giving Jacques an apologetic smile. "Sorry, I'm on edge after yesterday."

Jacques searched his gaze before nodding. "I apologize for being crude, but I'm speaking from experience. Julia saw Bea after her Introduction. I have strong suspicions about exactly what that visit entailed."

"Miriam mentioned something about that..." Flynn ran a hand over his jaw. Cal was gonna have fucking kittens, but it'd serve the man right. "You know, Kara'd be happy to look at Bea when she's recovered, she trained as a medic."

Their eyebrows rose in unison. Christ, they should, considering what he'd just spilled.

"It's true? She is from the Source?" Charles asked, just shy of slavering.

"Yeah, she's a Binder."

The hope that bloomed over Jacques' face was pitiable. Binders up here... He knew what Flynn was offering him. The man turned away, overcome. "I—I'll speak with Bea," he stammered, his voice raw. "We won't keep you."

Flynn nodded, standing with them. Tightlipped, Charles put a hand on Jacques' shoulder. The man was a mess. Flynn followed them to the door, watching them disappear through the gate. He leaned against the jamb, eyes sweeping the foyer.

Everything was the same, right down to the massive urns of fresh flowers his mom used to have set around the lavish space. He wondered if French had done that or if they were the spillover from what he'd bought. Either way, it was too easy to imagine her coming down the sweeping staircase. No wonder Lot was staying at the flat.

Footsteps echoed through the hall, and Flynn sighed. Another meeting he was dreading. This one wouldn't go as smoothly. He snorted. If you could consider being blackmailed into taking First after your entire line had been threatened by a jilted ex who wanted you dead smooth. Christ, he wished he was at the coop.

"My turn. Get your ass in here," Cal snapped, striding past him in a cloud of smoke. Sighing, Flynn trailed the old man across the foyer to his office. It was a hell of a lot cleaner than the one at the farm, but the positioning of the furniture and the jumbled bookcases were the same. They just cost a couple million units more.

"I didn't say you could sit."

Flynn straightened up and jammed his hands into his pockets, grimacing as his back twinged.

"What's the matter with you?"

"I got hit with a platter when the car went over."

Cal poured himself a glass of scotch. "I would've thought your aversion to Binders ended when you bonded one."

"I let them do my shoulder." Flynn grumbled. "How is everyone?"

"Shaken. Those sons of bitches had Shelby locked in a goddamned storage bin with three other women. Miriam's recovering, but Jon's a mess. He's back to sleeping on the couch in his lab. Lot's car was behind ours, so he never saw any of it. Cliff and Leo are back at work. What about Kara?"

"She's better. When I left, she was sleeping."

"The baby?"

Flynn felt ill. "I don't know, Bernice is coming tomorrow."

His grandfather took a slow sip of his scotch. "You sure the Sons were up here for Kara?"

"Yeah, one of them said as much."

Cal's eyebrow rose. "Friend of yours?"

"No, but they're pretty difficult to avoid down south. You were the one who taught me staying on someone's radar's the best way to keep off it. I knew the one who ran his mouth, and recognized a handful of others. How the hell did they get this far north?"

"Think you know the answer to that question," Cal said, sitting back in his chair.

Flynn's fists clenched in his pockets, his temper spiking. "Whatever bullshit power struggle's going on with the Assembly's no fucking excuse. Christ, how can we not muster a response when one of our critical assets is hit? There should've been a system in place to get auxiliary troops there regardless of who's goddamned purview—"

Cal narrowed his eyes, taking a long drag of his cigarette.

Damn it. Flynn looked away, running a hand over his beard. How the fuck Cal always got him to spill shit… He needed to keep his mouth shut.

"I'm assuming the Constable Major chewed your ear about what a joke they've made of his department. Would've been nice to have had a heads up on that tête-à-tête. Since when do you start taking meetings, never mind before noon?"

"I dunno, Cal, right around the time my wife was mauled by a pack of dogs. When the fuck did we stop exterminating every last Son that put a toe over our border?"

"Five, six years ago, some feel good bullshit. Think the gist of it was 'if they only got to know us they'd love us, we aren't so different', blah, blah… You've got to admire the idealism, but it doesn't hold up real well against the Sons' ideology. Seem to remember there was a clause in there to reinstate punitive measures should certain criteria be met. I'm reasonably confident yesterday fits the bill."

"Reasonably confident." Flynn laughed. Un-fucking-believable.

"I don't take squat for granted anymore. Not with how quick everything your mother built has gone to shit. You notice who's sitting in chambers on your jaunt this morning? Strong voices have been eliminated. Firsts met with accidents or scandals. We've been left with scared old men and young fools to lead us, while trade falls off at a steady clip, and we become even more isolated." He took another slow drag. "We're ripe for invasion."

"And what d'you expect me to do about that?"

"Seems to me you've already stated your intentions. Suggest you hop to it. In the meantime, why don't you tell me how you're suddenly qualified to give orders to a squad of Breakers?"

Flynn's stomach dropped. "They didn't have to listen."

"Didn't they?"

"Kara would've died. I didn't have a choice."

His grandfather rocked the edge of his empty glass on the blotter. "And after you found her. You have a choice about that?"

Flynn ran a hand across his mouth, watching Cal pour himself another three fingers of scotch. "No."

"Bullshit. What'd they have on you?"

Fuck, he wanted a drink. "Gimme a cigarette."

Cal tossed his pouch over. Flynn's hands trembled, rolling one. Shit, what the hell was he gonna say? He pushed back in his chair, wincing, and lit his sad attempt, the harsh smoke cutting into his lungs. He frowned, picking a bit off his lip. He'd smoked worse, but not by much.

Cal sipped his scotch, waiting.

"I did odd jobs for the Sons. One of their captains has a gripe against me. Big enough that I went south for a few years. I ran into them again bringing Kara up. It was his guys on the plateau."

"Odd jobs." His grandfather's mouth tightened. "Being muscle and running contraband, I'd wager." Flynn scratched under his chin, not denying the allegations. "How the hell'd you get into that line of work?"

"Knew a guy." He hoped to hell Cal would leave it alone.

"Before or after Kensbot?"

Flynn coughed, sitting up straighter. *Shit.*

"I gotta say, you made it pretty easy to keep tabs on you with all the arrests early on, then the two years you served in prison. It's the rest of it that's always made me curious. Where'd you disappear to? You did one hell of a job going dark."

"I don't wanna talk about it."

Cal slammed down his glass. "And I don't give a shit. You're under the microscope, boy. Everything you've done is gonna be spread out in the public eye, and I'd prefer to stay ahead of it. Now start spillin'."

Flynn pinched off another drag. Everything would get him hanged.

Christ, he deserved to, but if Cal couldn't sniff him out, there wasn't a chance in hell anyone else could. He'd give him the bare fucking minimum.

"A guy inside hooked me up with a merc outfit. I ran with them for a few years. Did some work for the Fuil. You called."

Cal tossed him another cigarette. "Watching you roll the last one was painful. That was one hell of a CliffsNotes version, the goddamned Fuil, Flynn?"

He shrugged, trying to downplay it. "Wasn't really a conscious decision."

"Then it had to do with a woman."

Flynn lit the cigarette off the smoldering nub between his lips, avoiding his eyes.

"They gonna come looking for you?"

He shrugged, Tracy wouldn't.

His grandfather was back to staring at him across the blotter's expanse. He didn't look pleased.

Flynn blew out a fitful stream of smoke. What was he, fucking ten? "Look, I got myself into some shit. Prison dried me out. I've been sober since, better at keeping my temper." Christ, that was a goddamned joke lately. "Women took longer, but this past year, I was done, with all of it until you called and shot that to shit."

He took a long drag, looking up through the layers of haze at the bronze panels lining the ceiling. There were a hundred and thirty-six of the damned things. Used to be a leak at the corner of the chimney. Someone must've fixed it, all the patina was gone. That had to have been a shit job.

Cal kept staring at him. Waiting for him to let something else slip. Fuck him.

It was several more minutes before his grandfather ground out the butt of his cigarette in his big crystal ashtray. "Fair enough. You're not the first Scot to have trouble with the law, but piece of advice, come clean to Kara. Take your lumps and have done before she hears it from someone else, or picks up a goddamned newspaper." Cal pushed the pile on his desk at him.

The front page had a still from that fucking reel. Flynn exhaled, stubbing out the butt on his grinning face. Wasn't a chance in hell he was telling Kara shit.

RIEGEL STEWED in the dingy apartment, waiting for Petra to come back from meeting with her people. He flipped through the newspapers again and snorted. Newspapers. Glynfyls' lack of technology was appalling and from what little he'd seen of the city, the entire dirty enclave deserved to be razed. He wouldn't even be able to get a decent meal if whatever the squat woman had brought back was standard fare. Some kind of a curry… Riegel ran his tongue around his mouth, appreciating the fact that he was able to chew the indistinguishable meat. His stomach burbled menacingly. At least, he assumed it was meat.

His gastrointestinal upset could be attributed to more than the food. His eyes kept drifting back to the front page of the *Tribune*, his mouth twisting in disdain.

Laughlin Scot.

He'd bury the bearded ape. If it hadn't been for Scot, he'd be mounting Kara right now. For that, there would be no bringing him back from where Riegel planned on sending him.

He scanned one of the articles gleefully dissecting the man's character, splaying his perceived perversions across the page in excruciating detail. None of it was particularly shocking in Riegel's estimation, but he'd been cautioned that Glynfyls was considerably more conservative than the Source. If this was any indication, puritanical was a more accurate descriptor.

The door opened and Petra slipped in with a bag. She threw it at him. "You need to change, else you'll draw too much attention." Riegel opened it and sneered at the coarse workman's garb. She shrugged. "Then take your chances. Since all that yesterday, constabulary's been pulling in odd people for questioning. If your size and silks don't qualify you, those eyes of yours will."

He grunted. One of the unfortunate side effects of the boost he'd been fitted with after being plucked from Ielle's tender mercies. Every time he pulled talent, his halos bled a little bit more across the whites of his eyes. The pleasure of feeling all of that power coursing through him was worth it. Petra had brought him to a Shade when they'd first arrived with the intention of cloaking them, but for whatever reason, it hadn't worked. Riegel thought it rather quaint how uncomfortable that had made them. He stared at Petra now, and she turned away, muttering about "flashing colors."

He pawed through the cheap garments and flicked the shirt onto the table. She could've at least gotten something to compliment his coloring. Orange made him look sallow.

"I've hired a whore to take you around. Plenty of hillies in the district looking for House guards after yesterday. That'll give you access to the upper rungs. Should make buying yourself more time easy. Bring them to the place we shifted in. Someone'll be watching."

Riegel frowned at the new terms she'd foisted onto him. He'd agreed to retrieve Kara, not collect samples.

"More Talents you deliver—"

"Yes, yes, the more time I have before you detonate something in my head. I know."

She nodded, but clearly didn't trust him. Well, life would be particularly miserable for her if she was as stupid as she was ugly. She scuttled into the bath, closing the door firmly behind her.

The lock clicked.

As if she needed to worry. He pulled out a deck of cards. It was somehow more satisfying to feel them in his hands than selecting them on a plaz screen. He shuffled them awkwardly. Petra had mentioned there were several gambling dens in the district. If nothing else, he was looking forward to Glynfyls satisfying his baser impulses.

***

KARA LEANED against the window sash, looking out over expansive snow-covered fields bisected by tumbles of stone and neat weathered grey fencing. Just past a gentle rise, a large stone structure was set against a backdrop of forest. Thick with ancient pines and bare limbs gnarling from trunks bleached and blackened with age, the sky crowned them in a startling hue of azure she'd never seen before.

Not a cloud, not a line of smoke, not a sound. They could've been the only living things amidst the untouched, frozen vastness.

She felt so small here. Behind her, Flynn stirred beneath the coverlet, a large furry lump belonging to this place in a way she couldn't articulate. He was more here. So much so, she wondered how she hadn't seen it from the beginning. The air vibrated with his potential, expectant. Waiting. For what she didn't know, but the heft of it was stifling.

Her gaze fell on the sprays of roses covering the gaming table. Blushes of pinks and peaches amongst ivories and creams. She pulled one to her nose, hitting the node to release the fix on them. A wave of scent washed over her. They would rapidly decay as they faded, but go out in a burst of glory. Their lush fragrance pushed back at the pregnant atmosphere.

Flynn's arms wrapped around her waist. "You're up early."

She turned, pulling him down for a kiss. "This is late, but I almost feel like myself."

"I'm glad. I feel better, too…you were right about our echo—you released the fix."

She swallowed a surge of anxious nausea. "Was that wrong?"

"No." He pulled out one of the chairs to sit, his smile sad. "Fleeting things, enjoyed so briefly. A fix. Changeling of vanity for soul."

He colored at her startled look, mussing his hair.

"Lord Scot's a poet?"

"No. Not me." He turned away, his jaw with that set to it that meant he wasn't going to elaborate. "If you're feeling better, I need a favor."

"I'll trade you." She pursed her lips, tracing the sharp line of his sideburn. "I liked your beard longer. It's not as soft now."

"Then I'll grow it out. An old friend of mine and his wife are having trouble conceiving. You think you can take a look?"

Another wave of nausea came over her at the thought of using talent, but he'd just asked her to look… "Sure, I should be fine in the next day or two," she hoped, forcing a smile.

"Thanks…" He swept a thumb over her abdomen. "You feel up to seeing Bernice? They brought you some clothes…"

No. "Of course."

He stood with a sigh that was both terrified and relieved. Taking her hand, he led her to the long row of built-in closets on the other side of the room and opened one.

Her wardrobe from the Source hung there.

Kara flushed hot and then cold, that creeping nausea rising into her throat and choking her. She fled to the bathroom, trembling fingers pressed against her mouth.

Everything she'd ever eaten retched through her lips. Repeatedly.

When it was over, she rested her cheek against the wall's cool slate.

Flynn peeked in, looking baffled. "Uh…you okay?"

She laughed, stomach sore, and her throat burning. She stood and grabbed an insipid pink toothbrush from the sink. The paste made her gag. Choking back the sick, she brushed with a vengeance.

He edged into the room, running a hand up the back of his neck. "Ah, we can see Bernice later…"

She spat the vile foam into the sink.

"No. We're doing it now." He wanted to know if she was bred, fine. Maybe then he'd shut up about it. Grabbing a brush, she ripped it through her hair, contemplating just cutting it all off. She pushed past him and went back to the closet.

Her eyes fell on that stupid top with the scratchy mesh panels. She tore it out, and everything else that even mildly annoyed her, throwing them into a pile on the floor. The majority of the closet's contents were at her feet when she was through. She scooped up as much as she could hold, marched it over to the hearth, and threw it in. Bits of synthetics smoked and curled then erupted into flames, filling the room with thick, black smoke.

"Uh…"

She whipped around to glare at Flynn. He held out what she hadn't been able to carry like some kind of peace offering.

Her mouth crumpled, and she burst into tears, hating herself for it. She collapsed into one of the chairs, pulling her knees up and hiding her face as she wept. What was wrong with her? Feeling his bewilderment didn't help—Ugh! What was he going to think of her?

The air in the room cleared, and he knelt in front of the chair, peeking at her through the valley between her knees, halos glowing. Behind him, smoke roiled behind one of his cloaks.

Kara laughed, limply wiping her face. "I'm sorry, I don't know what's wrong, I'm all over the place… This isn't like me…" She shook her head. Was this everything she'd been burying? There was no other excuse, besides her stomach being a mess…

Her wretched guts growled, and she laughed again. The last thing she wanted to do right now was eat, but she was abruptly starving.

"What can I do for you, Kara?" The concern in Flynn's voice made her brow wrinkle.

There was a soft knock at the door, and he frowned, ignoring it.

She shook her head. There wasn't anything for him to do. As soon as she could use her talent, she'd bundle all of it up, all of this… whatever it was, and that would be that. Until then, she'd just have to deal with it.

The knock came again, louder, and he swore.

"Let me—I'll be right back." His halos flared, setting his cloak over the roaring mass of flaming textiles in the hearth. Riffling his hair, he stood and went to answer the door.

Kara stared at the flames, ignoring the low murmur of voices. She felt a momentary pang as a skirt was outlined in flame. The lint on it hadn't been that bad. Ugh. She needed to be rational, but all of this was so much. Flynn, Meddleton…

Who was she out here?

Stupid question. She was his predestined, genetically engineered mate, designed specifically to produce his heir. Anything beyond her womb didn't matter.

There. That was rational.

And awful.

A tear eked out from beneath her lashes, and she dashed it away. The door closed, and Flynn came back over, taking her hands as he knelt.

"That was French. I asked him to send up some breakfast."

"What did he want?"

He looked away. "Ah, Bernice is here, but I told him it wasn't a great—"

"Get her."

"I don't—"

"You're not going to be satisfied until you know. Just get it over with and put one of us out of our misery." She pulled from his grasp, turning away and wrapping her arms around her knees, exhausted by all of it.

He ran a hand over his jaw, his hurt and confusion coloring their bond. She wished she could block him out the way he blocked her. After another moment, he stood and left the room.

Tears pricked at her eyes again. She was so stupid. He'd only done exactly what she'd told him to… Miserable, she watched the conflagration of her clothes die back to an ominous shell of glowing black carbon, her eyelids heavy.

Furtive voices woke her.

"That's not fucking possible."

"I don't know what to tell you. Energy's never wrong." Bernice sounded exasperated.

"It has to be, I haven't known her for ten days, how the hell can she be three weeks pregnant?"

"Who knows what the Source is breeding? They've tinkered with every other part of our genome, why not gestational speed?" She sighed. "Poor thing, the stress on her body… I'm not surprised by what you're describing, her hormones have got to be a mess, and she's part Breaker to boot."

"What the hell does that have to do with anything? Are you telling me this is normal?"

"Nothing about this is normal. The Ladies and I'll be here Sunday for tea… I have to tell Phyllis about this, Laughlin. Be gentle with Kara until then. Pregnancy is terrifying enough without the rest of it."

The door opened and closed. A loaded silence.

"How much of that you hear?"

Kara didn't bother to sit up. "Enough."

He flopped down into the other chair, his face grim.

"I didn't lose it."

"No, but something else is going on. How the kid's that far along…"

Good. The sooner it was done with, the better.

"Maybe Cal knows something." Flynn forced a smile. "There's another potato if you're hungry… I didn't know what else to get you. Shit, Kara, what d'you like?"

She glared at him over her knees. *Not being pregnant.* "Potato's fine, thank you."

His face tensed, and he turned away. "You can call down for whatever you want, just hit the panel. I've gotta go to Assembly, but I'll be back for lunch."

He stood. At some point, he'd gotten dressed in a smart navy waistcoat with an overlay of variegated paisley. His cravat was a brilliant teal. He took a maroon jacket from the back of the chair and shrugged it on. The figure he cut made her stomach hurt. He was so handsome and kind, and he loved her, she knew he did…

So why wasn't she happy?

He gave her a peck on the cheek. "I'll see you in a couple hours."

Kara nodded faintly, and he left the room.

Then she dropped her face to her knees and wept.

CHAPTER FIVE

*fade [**feyd**] verb*

1. *The rapid progression of condition once a fix is released, bringing an object to its natural state, had the fix never been imposed.*

– Excerpt from A Treatise on Talents, *Third Edition*

"While possible to completely rebuild a subject's psyche via coercion, any previous societal value is lost with the erasure of identity. It is far more effective to remove traits and experiences deemed subversive and embed desirable behaviors in their stead. Pain triggered by preset parameters has proven effective in curbing entrenched tendencies endemic to the subject's persona..."

– L. Merkel, Head Geneticist,
The Source

JULIA SAT at her desk gazing through the far window's clouded squares of leaded glass. With the leaves off the trees, she could just make out a faint haze on the eastern horizon from Meddleton's chimneys. She and Laughlin had counted them once. There had been forty-two.

The memory was remote, like something she'd seen on a stage, and the feelings it elicited were disjointed and visceral. He'd always been a selfish cad, never bothering to be discreet with his philandering, or to temper his drunken rages. Fool that she was, she'd turned a blind eye to all of it.

Until that last night.

Her pen ticked against the blotter, its spatter contributing to the Rorschach already staining the violet pad. So much of her life had become occluded in a sticky fog, but that… All her deficiencies called out in vulgar, exacting detail, punctuated by his grunts and Charlotte's cries, the leering crowd held spellbound as he ravished her maid over the doilied arm of her grandmother's Eastlake settee—

That was excruciatingly clear.

The pen stilled in Julia's white-knuckled fist. Mouth twisting, her mind shied from the aftermath. From someone… Pain lanced behind her eyes, a man's silhouette fleeting, the void filled by her son.

Henry was all she had. The rest of her House… Her father's absence should bother her far more than it did. They'd been close once, hadn't they? Pain stabbed through her temple, and she cursed herself for being a pathetic little fool. As if it mattered.

Laughlin was the issue. After building her entire push for the incursion around the possibility he'd been harvested, here he was, and spouting patriotism of all things—

No, it'd been Flynn. Handsome as the devil and that grin—

She cried out, gripping her head and reaching for an amber vial at the corner of her desk, pouring a jot into her teacup. Calm descended as she sipped, the headache receding. She turned the cup on its saucer so the chip in its rim faced away. A hairline crack clipped the wing of the bluebird on its side. It would spiral…

Julia had purpose.

She parsed through the thick file Titus had forwarded her. The thuggery outlined within wasn't surprising. Laughlin would probably alienate everyone in Glynfyls by the end of the week. It was too bad there wasn't a whiskey convention in town to speed the process, but it wasn't his only vice she could exploit. Tucking her lank hair behind an ear, she wiggled the top drawer of her desk open and removed a ledger.

A name halfway down the first page jumped out at her.

Sylvie. She was adept at putting men in compromising positions. Julia jotted a quick note and rang for a maid to take it. This early, the courtesan would probably still be abed. Julia busied herself with accounts, waiting for the woman to answer her summons.

Roughly an hour later, a fragile beauty glided into the room swathed in lace with her rose-gold hair piled high atop her head. She perched at the edge of the stiff-backed chair in front of Julia's desk. Sylvie's skin was the color of almond milk, her bosom strained against the keyhole of her bodice. This season's fashion suited her. Julia sniffed, smoothing the flaccid lace of her own.

"You wanted to see me?"

"Yes, I've a new mark for you. Laughlin Scot."

The girl's crystalline green eyes twinkled. "Oh, I've heard about him," she purred, nipping up the newspaper from the corner of the desk. "Do you really think he bought out an entire florist—"

Julia thrust her pen into the blotter. "To needle his father, I'm sure. He's too self-absorbed for grand gestures." She flipped the ruined implement away. It fell on his file, bleeding out across the pages. Why couldn't he have just died in a hole somewhere?

"The papers have him absolutely smitten. They say he's already bonded her." The whore's rosebud lips pursed, leafing through the society section. It was rife with speculation about his upcoming nuptials. The money the Scots were said to have spent was obscene. "And she's rumored to be so ill… It's really terribly romantic."

Julia bit her tongue. All of it show for his bid for First, she was certain. "Is that going to be an issue?"

"No," the whore trilled. "If he's even half as delicious as they say, I'll take the job gladly."

Julia frowned at her eagerness. It was indecent, but that's what she paid her for. "You'll take it regardless," she said, handing over a bank note.

Sylvie smiled, tucking it between her breasts.

FLYNN STALKED down the hall to chambers in a militant mood. After spending half the night trying to catch up on Glynfyls' politics, then all that shit with Kara—

His steps lightened, and he laughed.

People turned to stare with disapproving frowns.

"Drunk already." A woman sniffed as he neared. Her companions made sad tsking noises. He pantomimed tipping a hat to them, not giving a shit what they thought.

Kara was having his kid.

He passed the heralds with a wide grin. Damn, they looked straight outta *Macbeth*. They smiled back, one of them giving a little salute. Flynn laughed, taking the steps two at a time to their box. Murmurs followed in his wake.

He sat, glancing up at the observation gallery. Shit, it was packed. A stunning strawberry-blonde met his eye. She smiled invitingly, and his grin faltered. A whore. Had she come on her own or did someone pay her to? As if the fucking perfumed notes rolling in from his past mistakes weren't bad enough—

"They're all here to get a glimpse of you. Most of the city's been hell bent in thinking you'd been harvested." Lot glared at him like that was his fault.

The gavel fell, and the chamber went silent. The speaker read out the agenda. Taxes, an outlying bridge needed to be repaired. Someone was taking grievance with a zoning matter, and the border.

Flynn tuned it all out, his thoughts back at Meddleton. Pregnant women were supposed to be emotional, weren't they? He tried to dredge up what little he knew about the subject.

Lot kept swearing under his breath at the whore in the balcony. She leaned toward them, threatening to fall out of her dress. It barely registered. Pages came in and out of the room, delivering notes and taking them away as the business of the day progressed.

A vote came up on a proposed tax authored by Julia's father. It was narrowly vetoed and would've put a serious dent in their honey profits. Flynn glanced over at her box. Her smile wasn't friendly. What had he missed? They were on the zoning grievance, and Lot was getting agitated.

"…an independent committee! This should have no bearing on my standing within the Assembly!"

"You were acting chair, Lot. Protocol dictates that you be held in abeyance for the remaining council season or until this matter is sorted out." Papers shuffled and there were mutterings of agreement. A quick vote was held. The abeyance passed. Flynn's eyes widened. House Scot had just been rendered a non-entity. What the fuck—

"Wait." Lot stood before the speaker could lower his gavel. "I'll accept the ruling and go without comment, but there's a matter that can't wait until next season." Murmurs filled the hall.

"If he's going to go quietly, give it to him, Riggs!" There was laughter, and the speaker snorted good-naturedly.

"Go ahead, Lot. I think we all know what's coming."

Every eye landed on Flynn. Sweat broke out across his brow, and he resisted the urge to wipe it away. It was happening too quickly; he wasn't ready—

"This is preposterous, the measure's already been passed—"

"Adlothian will be held in abeyance, Mistress Cree, but the Assembly has never denied a member from passing leadership of an individual House," Lord Riggs interrupted dryly, turning to Lot. "Ah, I believe you had something to say?"

Lot glared at her, tearing off his cuff and slamming it back onto his opposite wrist. "My natural born son, Laughlin James Scot, has challenged and ascended. He is head of House Scot."

"Enter it into the log as uncontested. His parentage is well established. Welcome to our ranks, Laughlin. It's about time you stepped up." Riggs dropped his gavel and the bang went through Flynn like a bullet.

What the fuck had just happened?

They adjourned for lunch. Lot motioned for Flynn to stay, about half their line descending into the amphitheater to meet them.

"Julia's just bent us over a barrel. Mind your fucking manners." Lot shoved him forward and smiled at the forming crowd. Flynn did a double-take. He could count the number of times the man had tried to be pleasant on two fingers. "You all remember Deirdre's son, Laughlin."

There were nods, and Flynn shook hands.

"So you're back from Krakataw, Malai, Sieson, or wherever else the papers have had you for the past eight years. You wanna clear that up?" Lord Leeds asked, doing his damnedest to crush Flynn's hand in his.

He returned the pressure and the man grunted. "Nowhere nearly that interesting. I spent a lot of time Outside. Figuring things out, I guess."

Leeds's eyes narrowed in speculation. Yup, Horace still hated him.

"I hope one of them was sobriety," someone muttered from the back.

Flynn shoved his hands in his pockets, lifting his chin. "That you, Ned? Yeah, actually. I haven't had a drink in almost five years. I'm finding it easier to keep my temper as a result, so you're safe."

A few of them chuckled, and a man his age came forward to shake his hand. Flynn grinned at him. Ned was a good guy. He regretted punching him, on top of a shitload of other stuff.

"Can you say the same about my sister?"

Flynn colored, remembering what the fight had been about. "Yours and everyone else's, I've come back with my intended."

Ned clasped his shoulder. "That's good to hear. You were a real ass at the end."

"Yeah, Sorry about that." Several others approached, and it was more of the same. Damn, he'd been a fuck up.

"You ready?" Lot asked when there were no more hands to shake. Flynn nodded, starving and eager to get back to Kara.

A lanky form fell into step with them as they made their way out of chambers. His father lengthened his stride, putting distance between himself and the younger man. Flynn wished he could do the same. Goddamn it, Klaus was the last person he needed to renew his acquaintance with. Why was he even here?

"Lord Scot, now is it?"

Flynn's mouth hardened as he stopped to face him. Other than wearing his hair a little longer, Klaus hadn't changed a bit. The blond man was tall enough to look him in the eye and a belt notch shy of gaunt. He struck an affected pose in his satin breeches and brocade jacket, his shirt open at the throat and gin on his breath.

"How are you, Klaus?"

He ran his eyes over Flynn with a half-smile on his pouty lips. "As well as I can be, all things considered. Daddy finally kicked it a few years back, forcing me into this nonsense, but look at you, suddenly head and bonded to boot, if rumors are true. And so pretty! I wouldn't have recognized you without the whore in the balcony to point you out. Not with your clothes on, at least. To date, I've still never seen a cock quite as large as yours, and I have seen more than my fair share… I suppose it's too much to hope your time away has cured you of your prejudices regarding male companionship?"

And that was Klaus. Right out of the fucking box.

"It is."

"Honestly, Flynn, an asshole's an asshole, or a mouth for that matter, what difference does it make if it's mine or some woman's?" He shook his head, ignoring the look on Flynn's face and smiling up at the whore in the balcony, waggling his fingers at her. She gave a coy wave back.

"If you insist on depriving me, I can attest to Sylvie's skills. Woman can do marvelous things with her tongue, and I know her and Melanie get on. She's been eagerly expecting to resume her role as your favorite. Shall I tell her you'll be by the Pony later?" Asshole said it like he knew what the answer would be.

Flynn desperately wanted to hit the man.

Intensely aware of the audience that had gathered around them, he plastered a smile across his face. "The only place I'll be later is Meddleton." He turned to walk away.

"Spoiled now, are you? It must be true that she's from the Source. Those women are supposed to be the finest whores money can buy. You know where I'll be when you feel like sharing, and you can settle up your tab."

Flynn stopped dead, trying to blink that crimson haze away. Since the plateau, it was always right there, waiting. People around them edged back, and conversations dropped off. His fists clenched in his pockets. Fucking Klaus. He couldn't afford to lose his temper, even if the man deserved to be beaten.

"Gerrard knows where to send the bill. I'd advise you to keep a civil tongue regarding my intended. Her character and virtue are beyond reproach. If you, or anyone else, insinuates otherwise, I'll give them cause to regret it." The last came out as a growl, and he fought his temper back down, slapping another fucking smile onto his face. "Feel free to keep the whore, and send Melanie my regrets. I've no use for her, or any other."

He turned from Klaus's incredulity to the shocked expressions of the crowd, his smile becoming genuine as he strode to the gate, a flurry of resumed conversation at his heels.

KARA WAS BRUSHING her teeth for the umpteenth time when Flynn peeked around the bathroom door like she was something that needed to be defused. Laughing at his expression, she finished up and buried her face against his chest, feeling awful about it.

He wrapped her up in his arms. "You good?"

"No, but I'm better than I was. I'm sorry, Flynn. I'm having a hard time adjusting to everything, I don't mean to take it out on you."

"It's okay. I thought of something that might help." He tried to swallow a smile, then gave up, grinning at her suspicion. Her traitorous stomach rumbled.

"Hungry?"

"Only when I'm not throwing up."

"Dining room's on the way." Taking her hand, he led her to the door with a glance at where the urn of roses had been. "They fade already?"

"No, smells have been making me really sick. French had them shifted somewhere. I should've kept the fix on them. I couldn't stand it after you left."

"Makes sense, I guess. Roses, eggs, aftershave…"

"Toothpaste, coffee and, ironically, whatever they use to clean up barf."

"Sounds rough."

"It has been."

"Coffee, huh?"

"Sorry."

Flynn shrugged and ran a hand over his beard with a funny smile.

The corridor they stepped into was wide, paneled waist-high in dark wood. Creamy white plaster domed high above it to an arched ceiling. At its apex, ethereal light fixtures of bronze and whisper-thin glass dripped back down toward the floor. Tall windows recessed with plush cushioned seats faced the oaken door behind them. Kara went over and looked out. A formal garden and opposing grey stone wing at least four stories tall lined its far side.

"How many people live here?"

"Ah, I'm not sure. I mean, there's us, Cal, Miriam, and the triplets, but then there's a lot of people that keep it running, too. I'm not sure how many of those there are anymore. French would."

He laced his fingers through hers and led her down the hall, into another wing. Their footsteps fell silent on thick carpets. Works of art and bookcases heavy with tomes and antiquities lined the halls, pillars arching at their intersections. The paneled walls gave way to ones that'd been papered in rich colors, shot through with metallics. Kara stopped to run her hand across it, and he smiled.

"My mom put that up. She told Cal she was tired of everything being so formal around here. You should've heard the fit he pitched."

"I like it. Why didn't she do the ones by your room?"

"My room's in Cal's wing. That one down there was hers and Lot's. It okay if we check on Miriam before we go down? It won't take long."

"Sure, I've been wondering how she is, that laceration was pretty serious."

He bent to kiss her. "Thank you."

"For what?"

"Not biting my head off."

"There's still time."

Smiling, he tugged on her hand. A few turns later, he stopped at a door and knocked. A muffled voice called for them to enter. She felt his stomach drop as they stepped into the room.

The parlor was jarring after everything they'd just passed through. The woodwork had been painted a flat ivory with gold accents, and everything was done in pinks and purples. Miriam was settled on an over-stuffed, tufted couch in a formal gown of deep mahogany taffeta. A man in ebony robes and a tight cap over his sparse grey hair sat beside her. His eyes narrowed at Flynn with unveiled distaste.

"Oh, there's my Laughlin!" Miriam held her arms out. Flynn ignored the man and went to hug his aunt. "You've got good timing, Father Benson and I were just talking about you."

Flynn gave a very proper bow. "Father."

The man's gaze dismissed him and fell on Kara. His eyes were the kind of toffee brown that should've been warm.

They weren't.

She blushed, making an awkward curtsey, her toes curling in the carpet's thick mauve pile.

He sniffed, turning back to Flynn. A burst of his irritation flared through their bond. "Laughlin. I was disappointed to hear you didn't wait to Introduce the girl before you bonded her, though not surprised. If nothing else, I suspect it's brought you back to us. The Lord does work in mysterious ways. Far be it from me to question his wisdom in this matter, but I won't condone your sin by holding the ceremony at St. Michael's."

An overwhelming loathing for the man came from Flynn, but he laughed, returning to Kara's side. Father Benson frowned at them. "Honestly, it makes very little difference to me where it's held. Lot was the one who insisted on it. As far as I'm concerned, Kara's already my wife, and there's no need for any of it."

She tried not to laugh, hearing the "You sanctimonious asshole" edited from the end. She wasn't the only one. Miriam wrung her hands, watching Father Benson's lips prune. He stood, flicking his gaze over Kara again. Flynn put his arm around her, a soft growl escaping him.

The man's mouth puckered into a liver-spotted sphincter. "The Source is a Godless place, as are those that dwell there. I'll expect you at mass. You'll need to be shriven, and she'll require instruction."

Kara was positive whatever that was, wasn't happening.

Father Benson met Flynn's eyes like he knew it, too. "In the meantime, I'll continue to pray. Miriam." He nodded to her curtly, leaving the room. She fell back against the cushions, her hand fluttering at her breast.

"You're feeling better?"

She gave Flynn a long-suffering look. "I was before all of that. You need to mind your manners, Laughlin James!"

He snorted. "That man has never liked me, and the feeling's mutual. After the way he just treated Kara, he's lucky he was able to walk outta here. There's not a chance I'm setting foot in that church."

Miriam puffed out her cheeks but didn't say any more about it. "Yes, I'm feeling better, thank you for asking. The two of you all right? Kara, you look pale."

She smiled, trying not to stare at the scar slicing across Miriam's forehead. It was a better job than the one above Flynn's collar bone, but only just. That was the best Binders here could do? "Yes, I'm fine, just tired."

Miriam's eyes unfocused, and Kara bit back her annoyance at the woman reading her energy. Flynn glanced down, his apologetic smile tempering her mood.

"Bernie was right…" Miriam shook her head. "Not that I'd expect her to be wrong, you understand, but you're so much farther along than you've any right to be… If I hadn't heard it from her first, I would've thought the accident messed with my ability. You remember when Sue got kicked by that horse? It played havoc with her talent for a good six months—"

"How's Jon?" Flynn asked, cutting her off.

"Shelby's staying with him. He's in a bad way. That man's nerves… It's horrible timing with all that needs to be done. Kara, the planners are coming tomorrow to suss out the details for the reception, and Luann will be here tonight. You're running out of time to have your Introduction trousseau made up. God forbid you end up with something off the rack."

Kara had no idea what that meant, but the way Miriam said it, it sounded scandalous. Kara bit back a smile, tempted.

It was erased by the sense of dread from Flynn. "I'm not wearing tights, Miriam."

"What?" Kara laughed before she could help herself. He shot her a dirty look.

"And I'm not responsible for the fashion up here, Laughlin." Miriam sighed, waving him away. "You can take it up with Luann."

He swore under his breath as they left the room.

"Tights? Do I want to know who Luann is?"

He bit back the first thing he went to say. Whoever she was, Flynn hated her. "She's a couturier, seamstress…whatever. Woman's always finding a reason to measure my fucking inseam."

Kara stopped short, her frown evaporating before it'd formed. They'd come to a sinuous three-tiered staircase descending into a grand foyer.

There were no words.

They stood on the center balcony, steps at either end bowing out to hug oblong walls, then meeting at the next landing and bowing out again to end their sweeping descent on a floor of gleaming stone. The wide balustrades were made of wrought iron and alabaster, carved into fanciful creatures hiding within a forest of stone. Kara traced her finger over a pixie peeking through the foliage, her eyes rising to the fresco surrounding an elaborate medallion in the center of the domed ceiling. Its chandelier cast the warm amber light of electric bulbs over oil paintings adorning emerald silk-lined walls.

How was this place real?

"Impressive, huh?"

She nodded, backing up against him to take it all in.

Flynn wrapped his arms around her. "Before, I never knew if someone liked me for me, or for all this."

"What do you even do with all…" She turned to him with a laugh. "It's excessive."

"It's yours." He dipped his head, brushing his lips against hers. That hum between them swelled, clouding her thoughts. He pinched the bridge of his nose like he felt it, too.

"What's changed, Flynn?"

He took her hand again. "Shit, that's a loaded question. All of it.

This place. Glynfyls. The North. We were supposed to be safe up here. You were supposed to be safe, but it's all wrong, and Cal fucking knew it. Someone's gotta—I dunno. I don't have it figured out yet."

"I mean your talent…our bond. Last night. It's all different."

"I dunno why." He shrugged, slowly leading her down the wide marble steps. "But when I pull, it's like there's more, but it's… I dunno how to explain it."

"And that man?"

Flynn stopped by one of the massive stone urns decorating the first landing. Ivy laced through magenta peonies as big as her head and spilled over the railings, greenery trailing to the floor below. "That's a whole other can of worms I don't have the time, or the patience, to deal with." His voice was pained. "I got bigger problems. Come on, I gotta be back in chambers soon."

"Tell me. I want to understand." They came down the final curve of the stairs to the foyer's floor. Their watery reflections trailed beneath them as they crossed the expanse of intersecting geometric slabs. She could feel his reluctance, but after a moment, he began.

"I saw Julia…my ex. It's like she's been scraped out and filled up by someone else. Since I've been back, she's brought up two measures directly against our House. The last forced Lot to abdicate. Our line's leaderless right now."

"What does that mean?" Her eyes roved the room, trying to take in everything. One of the men in the portraits on the far wall bore a striking resemblance to Flynn and Lot. There was something else familiar about him, but she couldn't place it.

Flynn gave her a little smile, looping her arm through his.

"Our ruling body, the Assembly, is set up for plebiscites. Referendum voting. There's one hundred and forty-four Original Houses, all ranked by line, beneath a First. Everyone gets a vote. That's fine for administrative stuff, but when there's a big decision, like war, it goes to Quorum. Firsts take input from their lines and vote accordingly."

"What if there's a tie?"

Flynn shrugged. "Two hundred years ago, when we had an Overlord, he'd have the final say. Now there's a lot of arguing and bribes until someone capitulates. With Lot benched, the Shades'll be locked out of the vote. We have to elect a new First before Julia pushes the incursion that far."

"What happened to the Overlord?"

"Last one fucked up. Didn't use the power he'd been given, and basically let the Source waltz in and harvest half our population. Glynfyls almost fell. The Talents that were left cast him out and changed our entire system of government. Anything associated with the man was expunged, including his name."

"So you don't even know who he was?" She laughed. "You'd think you'd want to."

"No…up here, having your House die is pretty much the worst thing that can happen."

"They killed his entire House?" That was awful.

Flynn shrugged again. "I assume so. The North isn't particularly forgiving."

An arched hall led beneath the main staircase. It shot back through the estate and opened into an immense ballroom. Two walls were made of blue-tinted panes and the third boasted a fireplace almost the entire length of it. At least three dozen citrus trees were shoved in one corner.

"Shit, those are new," he mumbled, then grinned at her. "I never bought anybody flowers before. Guess I overdid it."

Kara laughed. "You think?"

They went down an oak-paneled corridor into a dining room with intricate brass-bound doors leading to a snow-drifted portico outside. Servants dodged them, removing draperies and rolled-up carpets.

Cal sat in the center of the hubbub at the end of a table that could probably accommodate fifty. At least that many little plates were spread over its linen-shrouded expanse. Flynn pulled out one of the tall seats for her.

"What's all this?"

"Catering samples for the Introduction. Don't know why the hell they've gotta test 'em out on me." Cal scowled, motioned to the servants dusting and polishing. "All of them are busy evicting spiders. So what's the word?"

Flynn loaded up a plate, relating what he'd told Kara. The two of them exchanged angry glances. She picked at a roll, stomach burbling.

Lot walked in and thumped a stack of papers onto the table. "They're bringing up the border. Mark slipped me a copy of the amended proposal. I'll let you guess who suggested ceding a hundred miles of territory to the Source as an alternative to an incursion."

Flynn sat back, shocked. "That'll annex our holdings. Why would —Christ. I was an asshole, but I've been gone for years… Why would she want to ruin us?"

Kara tore off little pieces of bread in annoyance. No one would look at her. What weren't they saying?

"For the life of me, I can't imagine why Julia's gone down this path, but as to undermining us? House Scot's economic outlook's heavily tied to Glynfyls'. If we fall, no one else'll be able to stand. She just cut the legs out from under us politically, makes sense to hit us financially next. Lot, you need to go back and act as council. There's too many undercurrents Flynn doesn't know about."

He looked sick. "So that's it. She's working with the Source."

"That's my read on the situation. I'll have my lawyer, Merchant, work up something. Won't be able to hit her with it until we've got hard evidence, but I don't think it's a bad idea to have a charge of collusion against her in the hopper." Cal lit his cigarette and turned to Kara. "Rogan'll be here tomorrow. He said he'll meet you in the gym, regular time."

Rogan! Her pulse leapt, a huge smile spreading across her face. The inverse crossed Flynn's. Crap. "Um, there's a gym?"

"Yeah," he growled, shooting Cal a dirty look. "That's what I was gonna show you. Who's Rogan?"

Her cheeks warmed, and those blue motes in Flynn's eyes flared. She laughed at the barrage of jealousy screaming through their bond. "My trainer from the Source. You'll like him."

Cal coughed. "I doubt that very much," he muttered.

Flynn looked like he did too. "Should she be training right now?"

Kara glared at him, no way was he taking this away from her. Flynn completely ignored her, his jaw set.

"Yeah," Cal said, unperturbed. "Breakers need a consistent physical outlet. Only gets worse when they're breeding. Trust me, Rogan being up here's gonna be preferable to her going off the deep end. None of it will hurt the baby. Push comes to shove, her physiology's built to give birth on the battle field."

"Fight about it later, we need to go," Lot said, standing with his stack of papers.

Flynn gave her a long look before kissing her cheek. "We'll talk tonight." He followed his father from the room, hands shoved so deep in his pockets they swallowed his wrists.

"You really don't think he'll like Rogan?"

Cal snorted, standing. "Nobody likes Rogan."

"I do and so do you."

"I only like him half the time, and the fact that you do is part of the damned problem."

Kara laughed and followed Cal to the gym.

CHAPTER SIX

Intelligencer [in'telijənsər] noun

1. *Member of the Glynfyls Secret Police; an elite force of Finders tasked with the covert collection and analysis of human intelligence in support of Glynfyls' national security.*

– Excerpt from Glynfyls: A History

"The decision to found Glynfyls at such an extreme northern clime was an inspired one. Talents quickly discovered the art of shifting, binding, and fixing heat, making the brutal cold and scouring winds of the plateau a mere inconvenience as opposed to uninhabitable. The Source's Talents, and its troops, respectively, have no such provisions, resulting in an extremely limited window in which they're able to harvest our citizens with impunity."

– Lord Talos, Preceptor of History,
Academy of Glynfyls

CHAMBERS FILLED QUICKLY, the gallery above standing room only. Looked like everyone in Glynfyls without anything better to do had crammed in to gawk. The whore from this morning was front and center, batting her eyelashes at Flynn from around her lollipop.

Subtle, she was not.

He nodded to Charles and Jacques, taking his seat beside them. It'd been moved back a row, leaving the First's box empty. The speaker shuffled his papers, ready to begin.

"Very good. I hope you all had a nice lunch. The next measure up for discussion is the proposed cession of territory to the Source. Who would like to—" Riggs nodded to a Fetch seated higher up in the room. "Ah, yes, Lord Romley?"

The elderly man stood with the use of a cane, but his voice was strong. He scanned the Assembly with a stern eye. "I oppose. For those of you not versed in geography or economics, this proposal effectively annexes ninety percent of the Scot's holdings, equating to the loss of one tenth of our GNP, and their contribution to the Source's air-space tariff. None of us can afford to make up that difference, and the economic ripple would be devastating. This proposal is shameful! Uneducated at best, and treasonous at its worst!"

The speaker banged his gavel at the rumble of discussion, then pointed to Phyllis.

"I also oppose. There are some lands to the east included in this… proposal," her mouth soured, "that are currently being scouted for mining interests."

"It's those interests that make the territory of value to the Source," Julia said, as if explaining something to a toddler.

Phyllis bristled. "I'm sure. They've been keen to exploit a new source of iridium after the destruction of the Banoi Crater. What did the Dlytanese prime minister call that…? Ah, yes. Judgement from 'The hand of God.' I'm not going to question the Almighty's ruling on the matter, but you go right ahead. Personally, I find it all the more reason to oppose this legislation."

Hand of God? More like a shit ton of piss and unstable plaz. Flynn struggled to keep a straight face, his cravat abruptly tight. He missed part of what Phyllis was saying.

" …more than an isolated act of terror perpetrated by the Sons—"

"Which is why this waffling serves no purpose!" Julia cried. "You balk at every avenue. Appeasement, attack—meanwhile they're firing on our troops! If not this, then we need to make a show of force—"

Riggs cleared his throat, and they glared at him. A Finder stood, glancing between Phyllis and Julia. Shit, it was Kris's father. Did he know the Source was breeding her?

"I support it, reluctantly, if there's any chance we can keep them from abducting our children, we should take it." A few sympathetic nods peppered the room.

"That's ridiculous, Marvin." A woman turned in her chair to face him. "It just puts the Source that much closer to all our children. We close the border, and that's the end of it. I oppose, and not only for that reason. Lord Crandall, why haven't your Intelligencers arrested the animal responsible for those deaths on the plateau? My maid was telling me some poor woman was torn apart on the fifth rung last night."

Lord Crandall smoothed his goatee. "It's a complicated situation, Madame Soel, but rest assured, we should have something very soon."

He kept his gaze on the woman, but Flynn knew that last bit had been directed at him. Fucking Crandall. Asshole had been eyeing him since that Diytan comment. If Dorian hadn't kept his trap shut—

"I should hope so, the thought of that beast roaming the streets…" She shivered, pulling her wrap about her as she sat. The rest of the room was equally uneasy.

"Anyone else?" The speaker made a little motion for Flynn to stand.

Reluctantly, he did. "I oppose, for all of the reasons stated, but agree with Mistress Cree." Phyllis visibly struggled to contain herself at Julia's smirk. Flynn raised his voice. "The Source is coming. However, I'll tell you plainly, we're in more danger from ourselves right now."

"Would you care to elaborate?" Riggs asked.

Every eye trained on Flynn, and the gallery went silent. *Shit, here goes…* "As it currently stands, we're protected by several treaties. The minute we do anything to antagonize the Source… I believe it reads as 'provocation through aggression or use of talent', we lose our sovereignty, and they are legally entitled to harvest the Northern Territories and its people. You all know this, or should." Nods and mutterings spread throughout the room, and he was suddenly very glad he'd been up late reading.

"We should be pursuing legal action to address the abductions, and the border needs to be closed now. With it shut down, trade becomes their only point of leverage." Flynn resisted the urge to glance at Lot, he had no idea how that stood, other than poorly. "I would call again for the review of several proposals which directly impact the security—"

"And I would call for you to sit down." Julia drawled, as if bored with the entire process. "You've been back for less than forty-eight hours, yet you act as though you're an expert on every nuance of current law. Doesn't the Assembly canon call for a junior member to observe for the first year before putting forth frivolous proposals?"

Flynn bit back his temper. "Yeah, it does, which means six of the eight proposals I've listed should've never have been brought to the floor, let alone passed. My internship beneath Deirdre qualified me as a full member before I'd graduated from the Academy, and there's nothing on the books that prevents a member from exercising their rights after an extended absence, the submittal of proposals included."

"Perhaps there should be."

"Funny, I thought the same thing, considering your father hasn't set foot in this room since he's been elected, yet finds the time to issue a handful each week. How is Anton?"

Julia's face purpled. "I somehow very much doubt my father's health is of any interest to you, given your vileness is what struck him so low."

Bullshit. Anton Cree had been the one who introduced him to the Pony on his fifteenth birthday and paid for the whores. Flynn laughed.

"How dare you—"

"Ah, I believe we were debating the cession of the border?" Lord Riggs broke in. "If we can call a preliminary vote to see if this has the steam to go to debate? Ayes?" A few hands rose, and the secretary took count.

"Nays?" The majority of the room put their hands up.

"Abstain?" A smattering of hands.

Riggs banged the gavel. "Proposed measure fails to garner enough support for debate. Next up, we have a proposal on the allocation of funds for the Academy's new sports complex."

Flynn met Julia's eyes across the floor. There was no question that he'd just declared war.

Lot passed him a folded up newspaper. "It's in all of them, and this isn't the worst."

They'd taken another still from that fucking reel and plastered it across the front page. The story running with it wasn't any better. He tossed it to the floor.

Shit. What was he gonna do if Kara saw one of those? Flynn scribbled a quick note to French and motioned a page over to take it. His eyes met Julia's again, his resolve hardening at the contempt he saw there. He needed to take First and put an end to her bullshit.

He smirked just to piss her off. She fumed back at him. The speaker's gavel banged, ending the session for the day, and people began trickling out.

Lot sighed as he stood. "You should make an appearance in the lounge before we leave."

He followed his father to a stodgy room with dark maroon papering and bright brass accents. Flynn helped himself to some coffee, belatedly wondering if Kara smelling it on him would make her sick, or if she had to be in the room with a cup. Guess he'd find out.

It didn't take long for someone to approach them. Lord Romley tottered over on the arm of a much younger member of his House. Like the old man's voice, his handshake was surprisingly firm.

"I meant what I said, Laughlin. It's a damn shame what's been going on up here. A great deal of it could be remedied with carefully applied sanctions, but no one wants to hear it." He flicked his gaze to Lot. They'd been opponents on no few issues for as long as Flynn could remember. Shit, Romley and everyone else in the room.

Romley's focus came back to him. "You represented your House well. I'm hoping we can work together in the future. Perhaps I'll send Ryan over to get your opinion on some things; he's learning the ropes." He looked fondly at the young man steadying his elbow. Flynn smiled, remembering shadowing his mother in the same fashion.

"It's a pleasure to meet you, sir. Do you still box?"

Flynn laughed. Kid didn't look old enough to remember him before he left, never mind when he'd competed. "Not for many years."

"That's too bad. The Academy still shows your match against Hoswaith when they're trying to teach the correct technique for delivering an upper cut. I would've loved to see you demonstrate it in person."

Flynn ran a hand over his jaw. That'd been the bout that'd won him regionals a lifetime ago. "I'm afraid those days are done."

"It's not a bad thing to leave the past where it belongs." Romley nodded sagely. "Unfortunately, not everyone is of the same opinion."

Flynn winced as the man took his leave.

Phyllis glided over before anyone else could. "I'm glad to see you're back to finish our conversation. Deirdre would be so pleased that you've stepped up. She always had such high hopes for you."

Lot coughed and excused himself. Phyllis edged in closer to Flynn, slipping a round tin into his pocket. "I spoke with Bernice. These will help. One, twice a day." Her tone brooked no argument.

He wasn't about to give her one. Shit, he needed all the help he could get. "Thanks, I appreciate it."

She laughed, and several people turned. "It's like that already?"

"It is what it is."

"Well, I can't tell you how much I'm looking forward to seeing what that is. We'll all be there Sunday for tea." She gave him a quick peck on the cheek and went to join another group.

Jacques filled the space.

"Bea's amenable to what we discussed," he said with no preamble, looking nervous at the prospect.

"Yeah, ok, ah, tomorrow after lunch?" Shit, he hoped Kara was up for it.

Jacques nodded, clasping him on the shoulder and disappearing into the press.

Lot was back beside him. "Let's go. I've had enough of this crowd."

They moved towards the door, whispered conversations about the recent spate of murders rife throughout the room. Flynn kept his expression bland, feeling that rug beneath him slipping. They were intercepted at the door by an obese man in hose. His calves were bigger around than Kara's waist. Lot's face darkened, and he went to push past him.

The man moved his bulk to block their path. "A moment, Lot, please."

"What do you want, Markham?" He stared at him with open hostility.

Flynn fought to keep the surprise off his face. Only a few years older than him and never particularly fit, Kyle Markham was easily triple the size Flynn remembered. He hadn't recognized him at all… and damn, Kyle was First Fetch now? It made sense, his father had held the position prior. Flynn remembered him being ill, but hadn't thought it'd been serious—

"I need to apologize for the zoning complaint my House entered. Both of us know it's unfounded." Markham stammered, sweating profusely. He ran a pocket square the size of a bedsheet over his face. "It's the port. There was going to be an additional tariff placed on goods, and if the annexation of your lands had passed, my line would've been ruined."

The fat man licked at his lips, glancing between them. "I had to hedge my bets. I had no idea that you supported Laughlin's ascension. I would've never…"

Understanding dawned over Flynn as Markham anxiously blotted his neck. He was worried about retaliation. Flynn clasped him on the shoulder, startling him and Lot.

"You weren't the only one who was surprised," Flynn said, glancing in Julia's direction. She stood in the far corner, a dense knot of sycophants around her. He made himself grin at Markham. Christ, he'd been doing a lot of that lately. "What's done is done. Now's the time to unify in the face of what's coming. I hope you'll be a friend in the future." Flynn offered his hand to the man.

Markham paused before taking it with his damp paw. "Ah, yes. Yes, of course, I agree. We need to prepare ourselves for any impending unpleasantness. Streamlining our internal dealings and freeing up resources should be top priority. In particular, looking over mutual interests to see if we can't come to more favorable arrangements."

Flynn bit back a groan, that smile still plastered on his face. Trade was boring as fuck. "That sounds like a solid suggestion. I'm sure you and Lord Romley would be the best people to draw something up, being so versed in the subject. He had some valuable insight earlier."

Markham mopped at his forehead again, looking at Flynn in surprise. "Yes...my thoughts exactly. I'll speak with him now and get back to you. Good evening, gentlemen."

Flynn followed Lot into the hall. The whore from the gallery lounged on one of the benches, her petticoats raised to show a great deal of leg. *Fucking Glynfyls.* He jammed his hands into his pockets, striding past and ignoring his father's insolent grin. Flynn wondered if it was as irritating when it was on his own face and decided that was impossible.

"Your mother'd be proud. That was well done," he said haltingly as they stepped through the gate.

Flynn shrugged to hide his shock. "You'll have to look at what he sends over. I've never been good at that stuff."

"You should try it again, you seem to have more patience than you did."

"Just better at faking it."

"Welcome to politics. You'll do well if you can actually keep it up. I wouldn't mind being proven wrong on that count."

Taking the back-handed compliment for what it was, Flynn headed across the foyer.

French met him at the lift. "Several more missives of a delicate nature have arrived for you, sir."

"Christ, just fucking burn them and anything else delicate you come across."

The butler bowed, the approving glint in his eye far too smug. Flynn slapped the panel to close the damn door. He stared at the ceiling as the lift rose, his hand on Phyllis's tin, and his mind drifting to the whispers of murder. Breaker Business or not, she wasn't going to be able to keep a lid on what'd happened out on the plateau much longer.

———

JULIA HOOKED her hair behind her ears, pacing her study. How did Laughlin do it? The cession was the second measure he'd managed to quash just by showing up. That damned spell he'd always been able to cast was putting all of her work at risk. She was losing the Assembly. They were already turning to him when he spoke—

He'd claimed to be sober for five years. Could it be true? He certainly looked better. She frowned. It was as likely as the rest of the statements he'd made. The woman had been confirmed to be a Binder, perhaps she could heal alcoholism. Julia vaguely remembered him before the drinking and the carousing had started. Her mind tried to slide away, and she forced it back, past the hurt, gripping her temples, slick with sweat.

He'd been so very smart, kind. She'd been head over heels in love with him, along with half of Glynfyls… What if he'd come back as that man instead of the one who'd left? A wave of nausea overtook her, and she barely made it to the wastebasket.

A heavy hand fell on her collar, jerking her back. A man with round, cherubic cheeks pushed her to the floor. She struggled weakly, and he smiled, his teeth nasty little ivory nubbins.

"Titus was right, you do need a refresher."

His hands were on her temples, and everything went black.

Julia opened her eyes and smiled at the handsome face in front of her, entranced.

"That's right, lovely. You and I get on just fine. Let's take care of business, and then we can have some fun."

Yes. It was always best to get work out of the way. She settled against his hands, enjoying the moistness of his touch. There was a moment of blackness again, like the world blinked, and then everything became clearer. Her stomach settled, and she felt ever so much better.

She had purpose.

Laughlin needed to be dealt with.

She wiped her mouth and went to get up. The man put a hand on her shoulder.

"Ah, ah…give it a moment to settle, my darling."

Julia gazed into his chocolate-brown eyes. He raised her knuckles to his lips. A warmth grew between her thighs, her breath quickening.

"There you go, no other place you need to be, now is there? Let's spend some time together, shall we?" Julia smiled as his bulk pressed her to the floor, only wanting to please him.

<hr>

KARA STOOD BEFORE THE MIRROR, almost wishing she hadn't immolated the majority of her wardrobe. Not that she knew why Miriam had gone pale at the tunic and leggings she'd chosen for the meeting with the planners. That the stupid lace-paneled blouse probably wouldn't have been any better. Kara threw up her hands, stalking back into the bedroom.

Was it so bad to want Luann to like her? Ugh, it was dumb to be so nervous about it, but aside from Miriam, she was going to be the first Northern lady she'd met. Kara chewed her thumb, nauseous at the prospect. The fact that Miriam had sent her back upstairs like a child to make the reception plans herself didn't help.

Kara snagged the portfolio the woman had foisted off on her, thumbing through the photos of "proper" Introduction gowns. Every model in hideous heavy skirts, covered wrist to throat—

Flynn came into the room, his face lighting up when he saw her. Her nerves faded the moment he wrapped her up in his arms.

"Hey, beautiful." He kissed her, sliding his hands over her hips. "Before you totally distract me, here. This is for you." He held out an innocuous little tin.

"What, they only had one tiny little box in the whole store?"

Flynn laughed. "They're from Phyllis, to help with how you've been feeling. Don't worry, if they work, I'll keep you flush."

"Phyllis?"

"Uh, yeah." He riffled his hair. "Her and the other Ladies, the wives of the Firsts, will be here for tea Sunday. They were my mom's friends. You know Bernice. Phyllis's really nice, so's Evie. Alice is creepy, but she's a Carmody, one of those seers I told you about. I don't know who the Binder is; I didn't recognize their First in session."

"Why are they coming?"

"It's traditional that they approve of a match between lines. Jacques said it wasn't too bad…uh, Bea'll be here tomorrow."

Kara stared at him. "Where will you be?"

"Here," he said quickly at her tone. "With the Ladies, at least, but Bea's ok, for a Finder. Her and Jacques just wanna know if there's anything wrong…you know. An heir's a big deal." A soft smile spread across his face, hand drifting to her abdomen.

She knew.

Kara popped the lid on the tin. A dozen little jelly squares rolled in powdered sugar sat upon a rose-colored piece of parchment paper. Well, that was anticlimactic. She didn't want to, but supposed she should humor him. Kara popped one into her mouth and made a face, forcing herself swallow it.

"They gross?"

"Try one."

"No thanks…" He watched her try to suck the goo out of her molars, looking like he expected her to sprout horns. Considering her mood of late, she couldn't rule it out. "What do they taste like?"

"S'not so much a flavor as a texture." She put a hand to her throat and swayed a little, sucking goo from her teeth. Ugh, that was really unpleasant…

"You okay?" He moved to steady her, his brow knitting.

She sprang at him, knocking him back onto the floor, and sitting on him, trying to jam one of the vile things past his lips.

"What the hell!" He batted at her hands. "Fuck, Kara, these mood swings are a goddamn, prob—aghh! No, hey, come on, they're not for —aghh? Ugh!"

The look on his face was priceless as it began to dissolve.

"Don't you dare spit it out, Laughlin!" She laughed. "Eat it!"

He made the mistake of trying to chew, and she laughed harder, clapping her hands together in delight at his horror. Served him right!

He lay there on the floor for a good minute, trying to work the mess out of his molars.

"Fuck, that shit's disgusting…" He pushed up to sit, smacking his lips and glaring at her.

Tears ran down her cheeks. She couldn't stop laughing. "You'll have to thank Phyllis for me, I do feel much better."

Flynn snorted. "That's apparent. Next time I'm hiding it in cheese sauce."

She brushed a smudge of powdered sugar from the corner of his mouth and kissed him. "You really think all the trouble will be worth it?"

"Yeah." He rumbled, kissing her back. "Not a doubt in my mind."

Ugh, she wanted nothing more than to just forget about this stupid meeting with the couturier. He nuzzled at her neck, the sentiment echoing back at her. Despite how foul that jelly thing was, she felt the best she had in days.

"Come on, let's get this out of the way so I can get you into bed," he murmured, giving voice to her thoughts. She followed him to a lift at the end of the hall. He laughed at the look she gave him.

"What? I only take the stairs for effect." She swatted at his arm, the heavy door sliding shut. He tucked a lock of hair behind her ear. "Your afternoon go well?"

"Yeah, Cal's going to have the gym equipment updated, but it was nice to run for a while. I needed it." That was putting it mildly, but she'd gotten in enough miles on the treadmill to stop feeling twitchy. She'd catch up on the rest with Rogan. A smile bloomed across her face and Flynn growled, those blue motes—

"There he is!"

The lift's door had slid open, and a petite woman with a severe white-blonde updo descended upon them in a flurry of petticoats, fluttering a lace fan in front of her face. Her cosmetics were contoured to the point of caricature.

Kara's fingers ached to slap the panel and go back upstairs. She probably had something she could wear to this thing that she hadn't burnt. Flynn grimaced and nudged her ahead of him. Was he seriously hiding behind her?

"Oh, how I've missed you, Laughlin! I can't tell you how thrilled I was when Miriam asked me to dress you and the girl." She side-stepped Kara to run her hands over his shoulders and biceps. "My, you've certainly kept in shape, haven't you? Bulked up and slimmed down." She teased the tip of her fan across his cheek, biting her plumped coral lip.

He jerked away in irritation, and she laughed like it was a game. She wouldn't have if she'd felt what was coming off him.

Kara took a deep breath, resisting the urge to rip the woman's trashy face off and feed it to her.

Luann didn't spare her a glance. "This season's all about fitted breeches and tailed jackets. You'll be so very fetching in that style. Come, come, let me show you." She minced them into a parlor off the foyer where a stage of sorts had been set up. Clacking her fan against the palm of her hand, several models stood. They were all in those ugly dresses from the folio.

That wasn't happening.

Kara struggled to keep her temper, bloodlust creeping. Flynn gave her a look, and she smiled sweetly back. He pulled at his collar as if it were tight, looking away. A laugh burbled past her lips, and Luann rolled her eyes like Kara was some silly young thing she couldn't be bothered with. The couturier waved towards the models.

"Pick whichever you fancy, and Mary will take your measurements. Now, Laughlin—"

"I don't fancy any of them."

Luann turned, put out at being interrupted. "I'm sorry, dear, but if you expect to have a suitable gown in time, these are your options. Be very thankful Miriam's such a close friend, else you'd be going in whatever that is." She looked her up and down, her expression clearly conveying that she didn't just find Kara's clothes lacking.

A wave of black rage rose up at being so summarily dismissed. First by Father Benson, now Luann... Kara seethed. There wasn't a chance in hell she was going to be treated the way she'd been at the Source. Not by Luann, and not by anyone else. She fought the urge to jam the woman's fan down her throat and beat her bloody.

Flynn inhaled sharply, his hand moving to Kara's waist.

"None of these are suitable, *dear.*" She smiled sweetly, running the scenario through her mind. How satisfying would that be? Flynn's fingers tightened.

Luann arched an exaggerated brow over pursed lips. She clicked that stupid fan open, fluttering it in front of her face. "Pardon me?" Her fake eyelashes batted just as quickly.

Kara drew herself up, her bloodlust filling her with righteous fury. Flynn's arm clamped around her like a vise. "I said, no. We won't be needing your services. There's nothing here I like." She glared at the woman, leaving no question the couturier was included in that statement.

The room was silent for half a heartbeat.

"You can't possibly think—"

Kara's 'lust surged enough for the woman to step back.

"Time to go," Flynn murmured against her hair. A whisper of his scent cut through her rage, and she turned to him. His eyes trapped hers, those blue motes… She swallowed the reply burning on her tongue, letting herself be led from the room. French was waiting just outside the door.

"You're gonna need to find a new couturier." Flynn failed to smother his laugh.

"So I surmised from the ado," French said, his tone disparate with the twinkle in his eye. "I shall put the word right out. There were several earlier inquiries that Madame Miriam instructed me to ignore."

Luann swept past them, nose in the air. The room erupted into a flurry of whispers the moment she disappeared through a pale stone archway opposite the staircase. The center of it throbbed with an odd opalescent murk that made Kara's eyes go funny.

Curiosity cleared the last of the bloodlust from her veins. What was that? The couturier had just stepped into it, and was gone. Kara walked closer; she'd never seen anything like it. It was and wasn't talent, the bits of color scintillating through the captive cloud reminiscent of shifting, but not.

"What is this?" She ran her hand over the side of the arch. It was made of something cool to the touch and too smooth to be stone, its dry oiliness resonating beneath her fingertips.

"A gate," Flynn said, coming up behind her and firmly moving her hand away from the murk. "You can travel to wherever there's another one if you picture what's on the other side. It's how I get into the city and back. Come on, let's go eat. I'm starving."

"Can't just anyone come in then?"

Flynn scratched at his beard. "Yes and no… It's complicated, but Miriam's got this one keyed and there's a portcullis."

"A portcullis…" She looked back, fascinated. "What if you don't know where you're going?"

"You hope to hell someone envisions you with them when they go through. I wouldn't recommend it."

Kara laughed, stepping into the lift. "Speaking from experience?"

"Yeah, it's kind of a rite of passage up here, but that asshole Leo left me floating for a couple hours before Miriam fished me out."

"What's with you two?"

Flynn shrugged, running a hand through his hair. A piece in the back stuck up and she smiled. "Just how it's always been."

The door slid back, and he led her into the corridor with metallic-shot wallpaper. They went down the long hall and approached a vaulted doorway, his footfalls slowing. The panels were carved with swirling glyphs. Flynn stopped, chewing his bottom lip. The riotous tumult of his emotions warred against the leadenness in the air. Kara fought to take a breath, that stifling expectancy back, weighing at them.

She swallowed, trying to shake it off. "You all right?"

He ignored the question, the block on his emotions going up, hand on the door's curved handle… It swung inward silently, gloaming's pink light washing over them from beyond.

He stood in the doorway, frozen.

Kara gaped, her feet drawing her across the threshold.

It was a conservatory. The entire back wall was one impossible mosaic of glass panels set within an intricate framework of heavily patinated copper struts. Fairy lights softly lit the foliage, and others shone down from orbs, fixed in midair. Their light reflected up from the polished burl wood floor and was eaten by the shadowed walls of rough grey stone. To the left, a waterfall burbled down a tumble of scree into a clear pool. Bright flashes of koi played beneath the lilies floating on its placid surface. The ferns and lichen tracing the stones at its edge gave way to other less identifiable greenery.

Kara turned to Flynn in awe, inhaling the verdancy of the room. He'd slid down the jamb to sit on the floor, his face haunted. She went to him, kneeling at his side.

"I didn't—I thought… Shit. I don't know what I thought, but it sure as hell wasn't that he'd pay to have it fucking kept up. Goddamn that son of a bitch." He wiped a sleeve across his eyes, his voice scraping from his throat. "My mom had a thing for plants, but our growing season's so short… Lot closed up the estate when she died. I wasn't expecting it to still be like this."

"Where was she from?"

Flynn chewed his lip, a strange expression ghosting over his face. "West."

The question broke the spell. He pulled her to her feet, into the room's greenery. Past a scrolled-iron banister, the plants and the floor fell away, revealing a hidden bower.

He motioned for her to go ahead of him, down the crescent stair.

The room below nestled like a pearl. Long suede couches lined the creamy stucco walls and a fire crackled in the hearth opposite the outer glass wall. She crossed to it, looking out over the purpling twilight grounds. They were covered by a blanket of untouched snow, raised by symmetrical ridges. Ornamental gardens? They surrounded a fountain big enough to swim in. Past that, wide open fields and a dark line of trees at the horizon.

None of it was the view from his suite. "Where are your rooms from here?"

He'd taken a seat at a little bistro table set for tea, and was helping himself to a tray of sandwiches, his expression clouded.

"Past the wing to the left, all the way at the end on the other side, and one floor down."

Kara laughed. "Why so far?"

The look on his face meant it had to do with Lot. A muscle in his jaw tightened.

"Glynfyls is beautiful," she said, pulling out her chair.

He snorted, taking the innards of the roast beef on rye and mashing them onto the hard roll of salami and cheese. "This is our estate, Meddleton. Out there's the Northern Territories. The capital city's Glynfyls. It's about four hours southeast from here, and trust me, there's not one fucking thing beautiful about it."

She ran a fingertip around the gilt edge of her plate. Whatever it was called, it was surreal. "This is really all yours?"

"Ours. Yeah, I guess it is now," Flynn shrugged, taking a bite from his sandwich. "Kind of puts the coop to shame, huh?" How he could be so nonchalant about it was mind-blowing.

"You'll think it's stupid, but I wish we were still there...though Meddleton's certainly warmer." She laughed, perusing the sandwiches, and moving half a smoked salmon on pumpernickel to her plate. The food was better too.

Flynn sat back, finishing his mouthful. "Yeah, but I wish we were too."

They ate in silence for a while, and she grabbed another sandwich, ravenous. Whatever had been in that nasty bit of goo had worked wonders... Well, on her nausea at least.

"I'm sorry about all that downstairs."

He laughed. "Don't be. The look on Luann's face was priceless."

"No really, it...if I'd let her walk all over me, people'll think they can treat me that way forever. When I entered the Creche... If I don't set the tone, they will. I won't live like that anymore, but if she'd been someone important..." Kara shook her head, not wanting to cause problems. The amount of bloodlust she'd leaked was enough of one.

Rogan was going to be so disappointed. She didn't want to think about how much she'd been relying on it lately. That little voice inside her screamed that she was losing control. "I guess I just need to know when to back down."

"I wouldn't worry about it. Cal gets his way, you'll be Lady Shade." Flynn chewed. "Just don't piss off the other Firsts' wives, you'll be fine."

"If none of the Binders up here can do what I can, why did I have to renounce?"

He took his time finishing his mouthful. "The way the codes are written, men can't change their line affiliations. I think it's stupid. I'd much prefer to be Lord Binder, but there's a lot of crap like that up here that just serves to keep the same assholes in power."

Mollified, Kara poured them tea. They sat together in companionable silence, watching the stars populate the Byzantium heavens. The moon hung like a sickle on the horizon, balanced between distant mountain peaks that had hidden within the haze of day.

"All of that about Julia earlier... What don't you want me to know?"

Flynn snorted, running a hand through his hair. "Telling you kind of defeats the purpose, doesn't it?"

"It does, but you might live longer," she said sweetly.

He pushed back in his chair, his resigned dread enough to kill her appetite. "I screwed around and Julia caught me in the act, very publicly. It got ugly, and I was too plastered to remember much more than that. I'm glad I don't, honestly."

"It's in the papers, isn't it?" His eyes snapped to hers, and she laughed. "French hasn't been able to get me one since I've been up here, but I know for a fact there's a pile of them sitting on the corner of Cal's desk. After the way the press was hounding us at the station, I figured it was something like that."

"You look at them?"

"No. Should I?

"I'd prefer you didn't."

"Then I won't."

His surprised relief broke over her in a wave. "Really?"

"I don't care what you did, but I swear to that Christ of yours, Flynn, if you keep anything else from me, I'm going to beat the shit out of you."

"Yes ma'am." He laughed, that devilish grin on his face. Jerk would probably do it on purpose now. Setting his cup down, he rose, offering her his hand. "Ready to see the rest of the suite?"

"There's more?"

"Yeah, unless you wanna sleep on the floor."

They walked back upstairs and headed to the door opposite the little pond. It opened into an elegant sitting room done up in peaches and teals. The heavy furniture in a strange kind of harmony with the sheer panels of billowing lace swathing the floor to ceiling windows. Beyond that was a bedchamber and bath even more opulent than the one in his rooms.

She stood beneath an enameled reproduction of the cosmos, looking up at constellations gilded across an ombre of blues. Threads of silver traced the meridians of the sky. No fairy lights reflected in the polish of the burled floor, instead the room was lit by long spikes of alabaster set into the walls. They reminded her of rushes the way they crazed up the dark teal paper. Amidst them, frenetic points of light cast upwards, striking the stars and making them shimmer.

"How is this place real?" She ran her fingers over a settee's elaborately carved back.

Flynn rocked back on his heels with his hands jammed into his pockets. Reaching up with a shrug, he scratched his jaw. "Cal shits gold bricks. This is supposed to be ours after the Introduction, but it'd be easier if it didn't look like my mom still lived here. French said something about getting you a secretary. Tell her what you want to change."

Kara laughed, feeling his hurt through the incredulousness of that statement and wanting to take it away. She put her arms around his neck. "Change this? How would I even begin?"

"Start with the drapes. I hate pink."

"They're peach."

"Whatever." He made a show of rolling his eyes, and she laughed.

"I'm sorry I made you eat that thing."

Flynn picked her up, crossing the room, his lips soft against hers. "You're not, but you can make it up to me anyways." She laughed again as he set her on the edge of the bed, pushing her down and moving above her. He was right, she wasn't sorry in the least.

There was a knock at the door and someone tentatively cleared their throat. Flynn held Kara fast with his gaze, those blue motes churning. She licked her lips, feeling the creep of bloodlust again. Why was it so close to the surface?

"Yeah?" he growled, scenting it on her. His head dipped down, teasing her lips with his. Kara's hands were on him, not caring who was at the door. What was with her lately?

"I—I'm so sorry to, to bother you Lord Scot, sir, but, Mister French has asked me to collect the lady. Several couturiers have arrived," a very small voice stammered.

Kara pulled away from him, breathless. "Already?"

A young maid flushed scarlet and bobbed a quick curtsy at the door, her eyes averted.

"You're Lady Scot and a Binder," Flynn sighed, pushing up. "Everyone's gonna want to take your measure, no pun intended."

"Then I guess I should go down…" She stood, smoothing her hair and running her eyes over him. It was the last thing she wanted to do.

He laughed. "Shit Kara, you keep looking at me like that—"

"What? Will you keep me in bed for a week?" She gripped his lapels, lips skimming up his throat.

His hands cupped her backside. "What did I tell you about tempting me?" he rumbled.

"Ah, L-Lord Scot, Master Caliban has asked for you as well," the maid stammered.

Kara's tunic slipped over her shoulder, red bra strap peeking out. Flynn's hands on her tightened, and he dipped his head to tug on it with his teeth, beard prickling against her skin.

She let out a soft cry, fingers tangling in his hair. "Tell her to fuck off."

His head snapped up, pupils blowing outward. "We'll be down in a while."

"That's not what I told you to say." She fisted his shirt, tearing it asunder, a flurry of buttons pinged across the hardwood. The maid gasped, the door slamming shut behind her.

Flynn growled and flipped Kara over his knee. "And that's not how we speak to servants." His hand cracked down, and she yelped, springing back up and rubbing her behind.

"Ow!"

"The lesser Houses and unaffected already have enough reasons to hate us. It's important not to give them anymore. Before I left, the political climate up here was barreling toward another uprising, and that has definitely not gotten any better." He wet his lips, shrugging out of his jacket. "Take your clothes off. I'm not done with you."

She tried to bite back her smile and failed miserably. "You aren't?"

"No." His stern demeanor was belayed by the lust she was feeling from him. "Clothes, off."

Kara tongued a canine, raising her tunic over her head and tossing it to the side, her leggings following in their wake. Flynn crossed his arms over his chest, eyes riveted to her.

Her nostrils flared, smelling the heat of his skin from where he stood. She sauntered to him in her bra and panties, the subtle scratch of lace pebbling her nipples.

"That's not naked."

"You didn't say naked." She walked her fingers down his abs to tug at the waistband of his pants and glanced up at him through her lashes. "You said clothes off."

His hand shot up to fist her hair, and Kara rose to her tiptoes with a gasp. "And you're a brat. Being rude to the servants, back-talking… Do you know what happens to brats?" His nose brushed hers, and she shivered.

"N-no."

"They get punished." Those blue motes churned through his irises, and Kara's pulse ticked up.

"How are you going to punish me?"

"Ask me and find out."

She swallowed around the lump in her throat. "Punish me, Flynn. Please?"

"Take off your bra and panties, then hand them to me."

Kara quickly slipped out of them, and he set them aside.

"Mmm." His head dipped to inhale along her throat, his chest rumbling with satisfaction. He sat on the edge of the bed. "Get over my knee… Good girl." He swept her hair over her shoulder, then ran his hand down the length of her back. "Grab on to my ankle, and do not let go. You'll earn another swat every time you do."

She did as she was told, the position tilting her backside upward. His other leg moved to pin hers in place.

"Beautiful," he murmured, his fingers teasing over her lust-puffed lips to her pucker.

Kara's breath hitched, the room thick with anticipation and the scent of her desire.

The blow came without warning, and she gasped, her hands flying loose as she raised up.

Flynn chuckled, his palm rubbing the sting away. "That's one more."

She glared at him over her shoulder and draped herself back down, gripping his ankle again. The next landed on her opposite cheek. She bit back her cry, fingers tightening.

"Very good. You're blooming such a pretty pink," he crooned, rubbing at his mark. "Next time I do this, I want to see a plug winking at me from this little asshole." He spat into it, his finger rimming around the edge. Kara moaned, her hips tilting "Would you like that, baby?"

"I like everything you do to me."

"Mmm." His finger pressed into her, and she cried out at the burn of pleasure, then again when he took it away, spanking across her center. "Too bad naughty girls don't get to come."

What?! "No, I'll be good…" Another slap landed harder, reigniting his mark from before.

"No backtalk. That earned you another."

"Oh, please…" She squirmed, tears filling her eyes, fighting to keep hold of his ankle as he spanked her again, over and over, the fiery ache consuming her backside nothing compared to the emptiness burning in her core. Above her, Flynn's breath sped, feeling her need through their bond as much as she was feeling the torturous throb of his shaft.

"Good girl," he rumbled, thumb pressing against her folds, slipping through her sodden flesh to circle her clit. "You took your punishment so well. Now get dressed. People are waiting, and you need to apologize to that maid."

Kara bit the inside of her cheek. He really wasn't going to let her come? "Please, Flynn," she wept. "I'll behave, I promise."

"I know, baby. You can show me after." He pulled her into his lap and kissed away her tears. "Now be a good girl and get dressed."

Her eyes narrowed at him, and he raised a brow. She snatched up her bra and panties, along with her rest of her clothes and headed to the bathroom. Ass burning with each step, her core ached for release. What a frickin' jerk—

"No touching yourself, Kara," he called after her. "Your pleasure's mine."

"Then you should come take it," she said sweetly, about to slam the door.

His palm clapped against the oaken slab, keeping it open. "I fully intend to," his voice rumbled out, gravelly with dark promise. "But if I send you down there freshly fucked, it'll be all over the city before you make it back upstairs. Glynfyls isn't…" He bit his lip, frustration bleeding through their bond. "Certain images need to be maintained. They're hypocritical as fuck, but the alternative is worse. Just trust me on this, okay?"

Kara swallowed with a little nod, and pulled on her tunic, his muted anxiety making her own flare.

He kissed her forehead. "I'll make it up to you, I promise."

She nodded again, blinking back tears and wishing they'd never left the coop.

***

RIEGEL STRODE down the dank steps into the belly of a whale. At least, it smelled how he envisioned the innards of a leviathan would, had it washed up having died several weeks prior due to alcohol poisoning.

The more he saw of this city, the seedier and more disreputable it became. It was one of its more charming aspects. Affronted at Petra's suggestion of gainful employment, he'd worked out his gall on the whore she'd procured in one of the cleaner alleys he'd visited since then. Much of his enjoyment had been derived from the populace of this nasty little burg walking past said alley without batting an eye as she screamed. And the whore had screamed.

Prior to losing the ability to speak, she'd provided him with an interesting tidbit: it was not uncommon to find the scions of Original Houses slumming in the lower city.

Of the countless establishments to choose from, the Sailor's Pipe sounded like a promising venue to appease his handler's demand for Talents. Apparently, once a week Fetches performed some contest of skill known as "Shifting Yaw." And it seemed he hadn't been misled as to its popularity. The place was packed. Riegel's bulk ensured he had little issue cutting through the effluvia of the crowd to the end of the sticky bar. His presence in the smelly little pub creating a ripple of tension he tried not to smile at. As of yet, he appeared to be the only Breaker in here.

Riegel ordered from the slat filling tankards, a gnarled man nursing a whiskey beside him giving him the side-eye. The slat waited until Riegel'd slapped down a unit before setting one of the dented pewter mugs before him. Though it certainly didn't have the sophistication of kir, it was surprisingly palatable.

Standing head and shoulders above the rabble, Riegel took in the dimly lit watering hole with a sweeping glance of disdain. And it was most assuredly a hole. It looked like they'd shifted out the guts of an office building, then cobbled together whatever this was from bits and pieces of wrecked boats. At the far end of the room, a towering mast stood fixed in the center of a purple pad. The top of it disappeared into the shadows several stories above. The crowd congregating around it like an idol.

The gnarled man cleared his throat. "Sure you're in the right place? Don' get many of ye in here, Yaw or no…'specially not alone," he slurred, pointedly not looking at Riegel as he sipped his beverage.

Raising the tankard again, Riegel hid his sneer at the gaffer's insinuation. Well, what he could understand of it. His vernacular was appalling. The so called "cant" of the commons became so thick on the outskirts of the city it was practically unintelligible. Pathetic, really. Even subs were capable of enunciating.

"Quite. Just taking in the sights, such as they are."

The gaffer looked him up and down with a grunt before going back to his glass, muttering something about "fuckin' hillies" under his breath. A smile flitted across Riegel's lips at being mistaken for his prey.

His gaze roamed over the crowd again. Aside from the odd whore, everyone in here looked to be a Fetch. Even given the ridiculous practice of cloaking halos, they were easily identifiable with their proliferation of tattoos. What was the point of subterfuge if they were just going to advertise themselves in other ways? Even the women were covered with the barbaric things.

"Will it fill up any more than this?"

The gnarled man scratched his flaky temple, not bothering to look. "Most like."

Well, wasn't he was just a font of information.

Someone shifted in behind them, and Riegel was jostled forward, sloshing his ale onto the bar. An exceedingly lanky young man with a headful of fluffy blond curls laughed, a whore in his arms. He looked like one of those bizarre sheep from the agricultural spoke. The fumes coming off him were enough to make Riegel's eyes water and, considering the environment, that was no mean feat.

"Shite, sorry 'bout that. Molly, me love! Gimme an ale! Won me bet, and Patrick Durgan's up in Krinklebee's front window for the next hour with nary a fuckin' stitch!" He grinned broadly, the crowd around them roaring with laughter.

The slat behind the bar delivered the blond man's tankard before he'd finished speaking. Unlike the rest of them, he didn't have a tattoo in sight... Must be hidden away like those on the hill. Even with his thick cant, Riegel had the feeling this particular Fetch was exactly the kind of Talent he was looking for.

The gaffer chuckled. "How the fuck did ye pull that off?"

"Now that'd be telling." The blond man's grin widened to his ears, and he drank his ale straight off, slamming the empty tankard back onto the bar. He gave the whore a sloppy kiss, then slapped her rear. "I'll see ye later, love."

Riegel marked the sliver of red haloing her irises, advertising her vocation. She smiled up at him, sauntering off through the crowd. It'd become quite raucous in the past few minutes.

"Ye shifting t'night, Fitzy?"

"Aye, that I am. Can I spot ye another?"

"Won't say no." The gaffer tipped the last bit in his glass past his spotted lips.

Fitzy. What a stupid name. He threw some more units on the bar and tugged on a ridiculous patch of blond beard beneath his lip. Riegel had the worst urge to rip it off.

Fitzy called the slat behind the bar over again, grinning at the ugly beast like she was a beauty. She rolled her eyes, depositing two whiskeys in front of him and the gaffer. He toasted her and shot it back.

"Think she's coming 'round t'me charms." He grinned, digging into a bowl of nuts.

The old man snorted. "If ye say so. Lord knows ye've got the devil's own luck. Ye'll need it t'pry them legs open."

"What odds will ye give me?" Finally feeling Riegel's regard, Fitzy turned to face him, chomping noisily. Not a trace of halos were visible in his grey eyes, but there was a flicker of challenge.

Oh, this was going to be fun.

"Somewhat on yer mind?"

"No, not a thing." Fitzy's face tensed at Rigel's crisp enunciation. How droll. This time, Riegel didn't bother to hide his smirk.

"Eh…if you're here 'bout that job—" The Fetch's hand dropped into his pocket, fiddling with something. Not a knife, the nasty little dirk remained at his belt.

"Why don't we discuss it outside?" Riegel had no idea what he was talking about, but wasn't going to squander the opportunity. A Fetch was a Fetch, Original House or no.

Fitzy's jaw set. "Fair enough. Marl, order me up another. Shan't be long."

As far as he knew.

Riegel followed the lanky young man through the crowd and into a fetid alley. The steam from a fresh pile of malodorous debris flavored the air piquantly despite the stiff fish-laden gale coming off the docks. Riegel flipped up his collar against the wretched clime.

Fitzy appeared immune to the cold. Keeping at a healthy distance from him, his hand was back in his pocket. "Right then, now what do ye really want from me?"

The game up before it began, Riegel's mouth soured. So be it. "I'm in need of a warm body to deliver, and think yours will do quite nicely."

Riegel lunged at him, and colors ran as his fingers wrapped around the man's wiry arm.

Too late—

The wind hit Riegel like an anvil, driving the breath from his lungs. His grip loosened, falling back from the onslaught.

Fitzy shifted out of reach. "If ye make it back, I suggest ye stay the fuck out of the 'Pipe, ye shite. Try t'shanghai me again, an' I'll drop ye in the bay."

Riegel stood alone on the eastern edge of the plateau, the lights from Glynfyls a pale glow on the horizon. Grimacing, he began to jog towards them, not even his anger enough to keep him warm.

CHAPTER SEVEN

challenge [chal-inj] noun

1. *Breaker's call to engage in a contest of talent, strength, and bloodlust to establish dominance and determining their rung.*

– Excerpt from A Treatise on Talents, *Third Edition*

"Able to instinctively sense which of their brethren are a threat to their status and/or intended mate, upon majority a Breaker issues a challenge to establish their rung in the hierarchy, the result of which determines their entire future..."

– Lord Grimmight, Breaker Menot,
Glynfyls

THE ALARM WENT OFF, and Kara's eyes sprang open.

Rogan was waiting.

Flynn groaned, his beard rasping against her shoulder. "What time… Christ, it's still dark." He nuzzled at her neck, his hand running over her bare, blessedly calm, stomach. Whatever was in those horrid little jellies was worth every bit of vileness.

"Almost 4:30. I'm going to be late." He murmured something unintelligible, cupping her breast. She batted his hand away. "Rogan's downstairs, he likes to train early."

"I don't give a shit." He moved to cover her, and she pinned him on his back. His lips turned up into a lazy smile. "This works too." After making her wait last night, she'd had her way with him, and he didn't even try to struggle. Smart man. Feeling his anticipation, she smiled, leaning down to kiss him.

"Now *you* have to wait." She let him go, and he grunted, sliding his hands over her biceps.

"They ever do your stats at the Source?"

"No. Alba—Cal, didn't want anyone to know I presented anything from my sire."

"You don't talk about him."

And you don't talk about your dam. Kara bit the comment back. One of them had to start, and it wasn't going to be him. "It's complicated. Something happened when he was bonded to Nora. They keep him sedated." She sighed at his expression. "When you use bloodlust in battle, it's like adrenaline and hyperawareness meld into…" Kara drummed her fingers on his chest, unable to find the right words. "You go into an altered state…this incredible high that makes you want to beat the hell out of everything." Guilt flashed through her. "It's addictive…hard to come out of sometimes. He never did."

His fingers brushed her cheek. "You ever feel like that?"

All the time. Kara shrugged. "Cal got Rogan to try to teach me zero, so I don't—so I don't feel like I need it so much." Her stomach cramped just thinking about it. "I've been too sedentary. My muscles… I need to work them."

"Yeah? You'd call last night sedentary?"

"I'd call last night glorious, but it isn't the same."

"Then do what you gotta do, but afterwards you're mine, Lady Scot."

She got up. "I'm yours now."

Flynn grunted again, pulling a pillow over his head as she turned on a light, quickly dressing and braiding her hair. He lifted the edge to mournfully peek out at her. Toasting him with one of those putrid little jellies, she swallowed it whole and jogged to the lift.

The lights in the gym were on. The old resistance training equipment had already been cleared out, and the wooden-beamed room felt cavernous without it. A man who looked to be in his early fifties was stretching out on the matting. She jogged in and hugged him.

"Nice to finally see you up here where you belong." Rogan's smile was very white against his tan. He must've been in the Deep South. Tears pricked at her eyes. She didn't think she'd ever see him again after that fight with Cal and her leaving…

Rogan held her tight, the musk that was just him thick in her nose. His chest expanded, breathing her in the same way.

A jump of alarm came from Flynn, and she pulled back, wiping her eyes and laughing. "I'm so glad you're here, I've missed you."

His brow furrowed, fingers tracing down the side of her face. "Couldn't keep me away if you tried. You look like shit. They treating you right?"

"Gee, thanks." She stepped away from him. "Of course they are. I have everything I could possibly want." And then some.

He grunted. "Let's see how sloppy you've gotten."

She went through her forms. Flynn wandered in with a mug of coffee near the end, trying very hard to look uninterested. Having been party to his jealous anxiety lurking in the hall for the past half-hour, she did her best not to laugh at his manufactured nonchalance.

"I want you to meet Flynn."

"Ah, yes, the boy that pirated you away." Rogan glowered at him, and Flynn returned it.

"Yeah, him." She laughed. "Flynn, this is Rogan."

Neither extended a hand. Rogan looked him over more critically than she would've expected. Flynn just looked pissed. She felt like she was going to be sick. She hadn't realized how much she wanted them to like each other.

Nor the improbability of that ever happening.

Rogan grunted, dismissing him. Flynn didn't look impressed either, and those blue motes were working overtime. The Breaker turned his back on him, walking over to the mat. Flynn's knuckles popped, the hand at his side a fist.

"Your katas are disgraceful. Come, prove you're not wasting my time."

Kara gave Flynn a wide smile and left him to his coffee.

Rogan dropped into his stance. She mirrored him, and they began to circle. Her consciousness broke away, and she entered into that state of heightened awareness all Breakers had. When Rogan came at her, she could see where the punch would land. Anticipating the kick that was his follow through, she blocked. The next moment, it changed in reaction to her own jab. She was a fraction too slow, and he clipped her under the chin.

Kara shook it off, her smile widening. The bloodlust coursed through her veins, sharpening her senses, changing pain into an elixir, stimulating her need for violence. Her speed picked up, and Rogan matched her. They flew through the forms in a complicated dance.

He hesitated, and she kicked him in the gut, but didn't pull back fast enough. Rogan sent her sailing over his head. She twisted, landing lightly, then went to swipe his feet from under him. He turned and stepped into her, just missing her with a jab. Again, they circled.

Rogan put his fist against his open palm, shaking his head. Kara stepped back, his disappointment hitting harder than any blow. Her cheeks flushed with the effort it took to calm herself.

"You've been letting it get the better of you. Even if Cal hadn't told me, I can tell you're relying on it too much. Christ, I could smell it on you when you walked in here. Bloodlust's a tool, Kara, but if you're not careful, it will cut you. You've seen what it can do."

She had, and it was awful.

"You need more work and less sparring. Go, run."

Chastened, she went to the treadmill, ramping it up to the highest setting. She wouldn't cry, not in front of him. She tried to clear her mind of the last of the 'lust, legs pumping, adjusting the incline to punish herself. Rogan was right, she'd end up just like her sire.

Maxing out the machine, she wished it could go faster.

FLYNN GRIT his teeth as Rogan stalked towards him. Why the hell had that asshole just laid into Kara? What he'd just seen her do was amazing, but now it felt like she was about to fall apart.

What a fucking prick.

The Breaker was tall, able to look him directly in the eye, and jacked. His head was shaved close to his scalp except for a grey strip down the center, pulled back into a topknot. He wasn't someone anyone rational would want to piss off.

Flynn wasn't feeling particularly rational.

Rogan stood at arm's length. "How much of that you get through your bond?"

"All of it, I think."

"Think harder. I'm asking about that menace churning black. You feel it?"

"Yeah." Who the fuck was this asshole?

"Smell it?"

Flynn bristled, and the Breaker's nostrils flared, his face sour. Fuck.

"So what'd you do when it happens?"

Why the hell was he entertaining this shit? Glancing past the man, he watched Kara running full tilt on the treadmill and sighed. That's why.

"The first couple times there wasn't much I could do." He grit his teeth at the admission, bothered by it. The emotion wasn't lost on the Breaker. "But when she went after Cal, I grabbed her; she was gonna mess him up…" Flynn ran a hand over his jaw, remembering something in him answering it. Not a fucking chance he was spilling that tidbit. "That was the worst of it. With Luann she got real worked up, but it wasn't an issue when I told her it was time to go."

Rogan's eyebrows shot up in surprise. "You touched her, and you're still walking?"

"Yeah." Was this guy stupid? "I mean, it gets tense, but she always backs down. You think she'd hurt me?" The thought had never even entered his mind.

Rogan laughed, showing his very white, very straight teeth.

Flynn hated him.

"You try to touch a Breaker when they're in the midst of the bloodlust, you'll end up losing a hand, if you're lucky. If it was me? She might pull back before she killed me. I wouldn't put money on it, though." Rogan turned to watch her. He didn't seem particularly upset at the possibility.

"The Breakers up here…the line's been diluted. They have their tempers, but in the Source they've been distilled. Everything that we had in the beginning, all that fury…" He shook his head. "Make no mistake, she's a weapon. Very nice to look at…" Rogan licked his lips, slowly running his eyes over her.

Motherfucker adjusted his crotch, and Flynn wanted to put him through the wall.

Asshole sniffed, his grin bigger. "But she's not meant to be some entitled little prick's arm-candy. You try, and what you felt just now? It'll be nothing compared to what bubbles up if it's repressed." Rogan took a step forward, his smile gone.

Entitled little—a growl started in the back of Flynn's throat. He swallowed it, not about to lose his shit because of this prick. Not after the plateau with Crandall nosing up his ass.

"That was never my intention," Flynn said, not moving a fucking inch. Christ, this asshole was begging to be hit. The look in the son of a bitch's eye said he'd welcome it. Fuck him.

"Yeah, what is, Lord Scot?" Rogan moved nose-to-nose with him, spitting out the title.

Nope. Not gonna hit him. Not gonna hit him… "She's my wife."

"Subservient broodmare?"

Flynn laughed. "You've met her, right?"

"Yeah." The older man gave a faint smile, stepping back. "And I've met men like you before. Not often, but when you live as long as I have, they do crop up now and again. I'd very much like to face you out on the mats."

"I don't bout."

"What's the matter, like it too much?"

A muscle in Flynn's jaw popped, and Rogan flashed those fucking teeth of his. Asshole had no idea what the fuck he was talking about.

"Time's coming when you'll need to shit or get off the pot. I wonder how much you'll be willing to lose before you do."

Flynn's temper seared the room red, imagining that too perfect smile scattered across the floor. "I don't give a shit about any of it, except her." Which was the only reason why this asshole wasn't already in pieces.

Prick just kept grinning. "Cal said something very similar to me once. Be careful, our words have a way of coming back to haunt us."

He walked away, leaving Flynn seething. What the hell was he talking about? Christ, he needed some air. What a fucking prick.

French met him at the door. "If you have a moment, sir, Master Caliban's requested you visit his study before Assembly."

Flynn grunted, glancing back at Kara. She was his, no matter how much that asshole leered at her, but fuck, it ate at him. He stalked through the estate. Whatever name he tried to put to how he was feeling, he didn't fucking like it, but it was obvious Kara was overjoyed Rogan was here. Just made him want to beat the shit out of the asshole even more.

When he got to the office, Cal was reading the paper, headlines screaming about that murder. Christ, it had to have been a goddamned horror show if the papers were running it front page, but at least it wasn't another still of him.

His grandfather put it down as he took the chair across from him. Flynn grabbed a danish from the coffee service, fitfully ripping off a mouthful.

Cal chuckled. "You met Rogan." He poured himself a cup of coffee and sat back, rolling a cigarette. "Didn't think the two of you would hit it off. He's good people, though. If I had to name someone friend, he's it."

None of it did anything to raise Flynn's opinion of the asshole. "You gonna tell me what you lost because you wouldn't fight?" It was too early to bandy words, and the Breaker had irritated him as much as Lot ever had.

"Shithead brought that right up, did he?" Cal hissed out a stream of smoke. "He would try to use me as a cautionary tale. I'll be sure to tell him to go fuck himself next time I see him. You know the Great Incursion just about wiped out our House."

He did, but only anecdotally through Miriam. Cal never talked about the war. Flynn wet his lips, wondering how far he could push him. "You know the Overlord?"

"Better than most. Not as well as I thought." Cal looked at the cigarette between his fingers for a long moment before taking a drag. When he exhaled, the cloud of smoke hung around them like a pall.

"I lost my entire family. All nine of them. Ten, if you count the one my wife Anne was carrying. Regret's a waste of emotion. You want to keep Kara and your heir safe? You use whatever that was on that plateau to get this shit done."

Flynn returned his stare for half a second before looking away. "When I told you I'd play the part—"

"Nothing's changed." Cal pulled over a stack of paperwork, going through it.

"It's all changed."

His grandfather looked at him over the top of a report. "No, it hasn't. Not in a goddamned millennium, and it won't unless you hop to it. Get the hell out of my office. We've both got work to do."

Motherfucker.

Flynn stood, snatching the last danish and hopping the fuck to it.

***

THE PLAZ PANELS in the ceiling were too damn bright.

Marcos sat on the edge of a hard pallet, naked. There was nothing else in the concrete cube, save the drain in the center of the floor. A darkened observation window lined one wall, shadows moving behind it. Probably appetizers being served. His fingers bit into the edges of the pallet's frame.

Laurellai was in an adjoining cube. A jumble of her anger and fear pelted through their bond. Too old to be bred or work at the Olly, after this she'd either be sold or culled. The latter was the kinder option, and the more likely. Finders weren't a line that was in particularly high demand. She'd already been granted a stay of execution serving as his bellwether for the past several years. He couldn't imagine she'd be offered the opportunity to bond another retired stud.

He wished his own fate was as certain.

The portlock opened, and a girl walked in. Marcos's breath caught before reason took over. If he hadn't known better, he would've sworn it was Kara.

His gaze roamed her perfect form. She must be one of Beritram's offspring. As she got closer, the differences were apparent. A squareness to her jaw. Eyes a bit too close. The most obvious, a thin crimson line around irises so pale blue they were almost white. She stood in front of him, her pert breasts rising and falling smoothly.

If Titus's intention was to see if he'd balk at the look alike, he'd be sadly disappointed. Marcos's pulse jumped, swinging her around to bend her over the pallet. After Laurellai had whelped their required offspring, she'd forbidden him from her chambers. Not that he'd any urge to visit them. His own sense of propriety had kept him from anyone else's, though she'd indulged.

A vision of Nora filled his mind's eye, and, like all his previously delegated matings, the girl became a means to an end. He felt Laurellai similarly engaged through their bond. She wasn't enjoying herself nearly as much, and that fact pleased him more than he wanted to admit.

Regardless, her stud must've been skilled, because her pleasure built, and he let his do the same. At the moment of completion, he ripped his talent away from her, feeling only satisfied relief at the sharp termination of their bond. Nothing like the searing agony it'd been with Nora. They'd told him afterwards he'd been carried out in a half-comatose state that had lasted for weeks.

Now he just felt free.

The girl rolled over, and he stepped away. She looked profoundly bored, making no attempt to cover herself as a lab tech came in to collect Marcos's spent genetic material. He exited down the hall to the changing room, passing an open door. Laurellai sat weeping on the pallet. He found it difficult to care.

After using a decon-stall, he got dressed and went back to his office.

Nothing was where he left it. Where had Pax put his reports? He dug them out of a haphazard pile, reviewing his work. The boy had done an adequate job as far as he could tell, but Marcos prided himself in being more than just satisfactory.

Four vectors had been reassigned during his absence to maintain vigil along the length of the border, running ocean to ocean across the Northern continent. He scrutinized their sloppy positioning. Gaps in coverage from a few hundred feet to two miles sprawled between them.

His thumb worried against his first finger, recalling an errant requisition that'd crossed his desk several months ago. At the time, he'd thought Titus's off-book upgrades to existing jumps sites odd, but wasn't about to question the man's use of personal funds. Now he was certain the old Eastern trade route leading into the Northern Territories falling squarely in the center of that two mile gap wasn't accidental.

That the infrastructure upgrades supported more troops than the Source had available wasn't either. He frowned, thinking about that damned blacksite. There wasn't a doubt in his mind it existed, and Titus had ceded that knowledge purposefully, though for what reason… He hit a panel on his desk, an orb blinking into view.

His secretary's voice filtered out of the swirling orb of digital mist. "Yes, sir?"

"Cathy, can you send in some coffee? Make it a full pot, please."

"Planning on a long day, sir?"

"Is there any other kind?"

"For you, no." The woman chuckled. The orb blinked out, and she came in a few minutes later with a large carafe and some of those sweet rolls he liked. He smiled his thanks, and she left him to his work. Halfway through his first bitter cup, he was decided.

Officially, he had no way of knowing Titus's intentions.

From a purely strategical standpoint, if another satellite couldn't be requisitioned, the ones positioned needed to be moved from over the western mountains that made up a good third of the border to where they'd actually do some good. If the North was going to launch an attack, it wouldn't be from there. The jagged range rendered that precinct impassable, then dropped off into the ocean. Marcos filled out the required forms, submitting his recommendations, oddly at peace when the confirmation of receipt flashed.

It would take a few days for them to be processed and the changes implemented. Titus wouldn't be pleased, but considering the pains he'd gone to obfuscate his plans, surely the man wouldn't hold him liable for doing his job.

Marcos snorted. No, he wouldn't hold him liable. He'd cull him.

His hand was steady as he took another sip of his coffee, thinking about what he'd read over the past week. An entire city of Talents, living like subs. What would it have been like to stay bonded to Nora, to have offspring they raised?

Children. A family. He'd never know and felt cheated of it. The sudden urge to see her was overwhelming.

Opening up the communications orb again, he rang Albanach's tower. A servant answered, and after a few long moments, Nora came on the line. She was sitting in a window seat, looking lovely in a rose-colored gown. He'd interrupted her reading.

"Marcos?" Her brow smoothed at the sight of him. "I've been worried. Everything went well?"

"As well as can be expected. I was hoping you'd feel like taking a walk with me this afternoon. I hear the convention center has a pre-Surge textile exhibit…perhaps a late lunch?"

She smiled. "That sounds lovely."

"I'll collect you around noon."

"Until then."

The orb blinked out of existence. He sat staring at the void she'd filled. That confirmation of receipt still waiting for him to dismiss. Marcos absently swiped it away, his recommendations probably wouldn't even make it past Titus's desk, but if they did…

"You're imagining things…" He closed his eyes. Head crying foolish, and heart crying for it. He had. He was.

If the vectors were repositioned, it would buy time. Perhaps enough for Glynfyls to prepare.

RIEGEL STRIPPED the heavy coat off the latest Talent unfortunate enough to cross his path. They'd looked to be of a size, and he was more than willing to sacrifice style for warmth. He let the man drop face-down into the midden-filled alley and shrugged it on, shivering into the greasy fur collar, not caring about the stench. Last night's unexpected foray across the plateau and the resulting case of frostbite had cured him of any quibbles regarding fashion. He'd wear anything to cover his blackening skin and the large fluid-filled blisters plaguing his extremities.

The man was the third Talent he'd left in the dead-end alley. The other two, less hat and gloves respectively, had disappeared, and Riegel wasn't waiting around to see what became of this one. If no one came to collect, that wasn't his problem. He'd been sent to this shithole to procure, not babysit.

His gaze swept across the crazed skyline above, feeling eyes on him. They'd been following him ever since he entered the dank slum locals referred to as the Pinch. Riegel kept waiting for someone to drop on him from one of the canted rooftops. Some of the buildings were so low they were almost horizontal. Listing at unnatural fixed angles, they pressed in on the ghetto's inhabitants, forcing them to duck around and beneath their crumbling facades.

Washing hung from a low window, and he tore it down, trampling it into the frozen muck. Why anyone bothered... Everything in this filthy burg was the same dingy brown and muddled grey. A hag bundled up in rags scuttled by him through the thick clag. It was omnipresent, hanging in layered ribbons above the cobbled streets. He coughed, hacking up a congealed mass of the noisome stuff. All of the city's denizens had some degree of bronchial affliction. He wondered how long it took to contract rot-lung.

The frigid trek across the city proved to be uneventful, the building's roofs slowly regaining the sky, the air clearing a fraction. He stomped up the steps of the wretched tenement he'd been installed at and returned to the room. Petra was there, spooning up an unappetizing grey mass into her slovenly maw. Half a chicken sat in the center of the table. He sat, pulling off his pilfered gloves. A swath of skin remained with the cheap leather as a blister burst, spattering crimson ichor across the scarred tabletop. He unceremoniously divested the carcass of its leg.

Petra regarded the mess with disgust, pushing away her meal. Her mustard brown eyes took in his face, watching him gnaw at the bone. "Been bitten proper, haven't you? It's set in well and good now, will be another week before you'll know what'll slough off and what'll remain. Whatever possessed you to try to shanghai a Fetch from the 'Pipe, and you too stupid to break the temperature..."

She cackled, and Riegel wanted to break her. He wouldn't give her the satisfaction of asking what she meant. "How was I to know the lad would be so slippery? My instructions were to smash and grab. Forgive me if I did so indiscriminately." Riegel rolled his eyes, very sure his sarcasm was lost upon the foul slat. He huddled in his stolen coat, cracking the bones for their scant amount of marrow. He couldn't shake the chill that'd set into him.

She snorted, crossing her arms over her withered dugs. "You Breakers is all the same. Thinking your line's so much better than the rest. Keep on thinking it and next time it'll be a Fixer that stops your heart, maybe a Finder's knife severing your spine. Boy let you off easy. Glynfyls doesn't play by the same rules as the Source. None of them in the lower city will blink at using talent against you."

"Then I'm free of the same constraints." Not that he'd ever really abided by them to begin with, but it did allow for a bit more freedom of expression. He'd be sure to use it if he ever came across that fluffy blond pissant again.

Shaking her head in disgust, Petra stood and started throwing things into a bag. "Do yourself a favor. Stay above the fifth rung and well away from the docks. Doubt any would recognize you suffering from the 'bite the way you is, but I'd not take chances. I'm due south, so you're on your own. Rent's paid through Monday, you'll have to scrape together enough coin for the rest of your stay." She slung her bag over her shoulder. "Or not. Figure you've a week of breath left at this rate. Suggest leaving better quality than the rabble you have if you · fancy stretching that."

She pulled talent and was gone.

A week. They'd originally given him two. Picking at the chicken carcass, Riegel's gaze slid to today's paper. He pulled it over, the headlines blaring *MURDER!*

Well, wasn't this a treat…his dalliance with the whore had ousted Scot from the front page. Pity the stills really didn't capture the scene. Black and white was so dependent upon proper lighting—half the spatter had been lost.

Riegel flipped through the remaining pages, looking for any mention of Kara. The society section had an interview from a handful of couturiers gushing over her. He smirked. Comfortable enough to build a trousseau, was she? She did have a weakness for fashion. That was endemic to the Source and the one interest they shared. A smile tipped up his lips, imagining her disgust at what passed for it up here. Personally, he thought the corsets were rather fetching. He liked the way the boning popped when they were ripped off.

His stomach rumbled, that sad chicken wasn't going to suffice. Forcing the sticky leather glove back on, he left the nasty little room. There was another den of iniquity a few rungs away that sounded rather promising, and he had rent to make.

CHAPTER EIGHT

succumb [suh-kuhm] verb

1. *To permanently give into bloodlust; a berserker like madness with the single-minded desire to destroy, requiring immediate euthanasia.*

– Excerpt from A Treatise on Talents, *Third Edition*

"There is no greater satisfaction than setting your runes upon your chosen mate. More sacred than any band of gold, a Breaker's runes are a reflection of soul. So much more than the common emotional bond, it links you inextricably, allowing strength and awareness to be shared in times of crisis. It also acts as a clear warning for any would-be suitors to sod off."

– Lord Grimmight, Breaker Menot,
Glynfyls

KARA SAT at the dining room table, devouring dessert samples and flipping through the stack of couturiers' sketches. She was exhausted.

After Flynn had gone, Rogan had worked her unmercifully, and she was glad.

He was right about her letting the bloodlust take over, and without being able to achieve zero, her only recourse was physical exertion. He'd given her half an hour to eat and then expected her back. She was going to be mush by the time she had to meet that woman, Bea. Hopefully, the chocolate cake wouldn't make a reappearance when she did. No promises there, nasty jellies or not. The thought of using talent still made Kara nauseous.

She sighed, picking up another portfolio. It was becoming painfully obvious she'd wasted her time meeting with the roomful of slavering designers last night. She tossed another folder onto the reject pile, just seeing poofs and lace. The combination made her ill. There wasn't a chance she was going back to being dressed up like a doll and told what to do. She began half-heartedly leafing through the next one.

French came in and set a plate of smoked fish beside her. "Will there be anything else, my lady?"

"N—" Her hand stilled. The design beneath it was a massive departure from the rest. "Wait. Do you know who sent this?" Kara held up the portfolio.

"I believe that one is from Regina Glass."

Glass… Where had she heard that name…? "Was she the one Flynn was contracted to?"

"No. That was her younger sister, Marilla, but regardless, it has embroiled both Houses in a rather nasty legal battle."

Kara bit at her thumb, looking at the sketch. Would the woman have submitted something if she didn't want the job? An image of Tamara Hess and her gang of sycophants laughing flashed through Kara's mind. She struggled to bury the memory, along with the abject humiliation that came with it. It probably wasn't out of the question, but there was only one way to find out.

"How do I set up a meeting with her?"

French's mustache twitched. "I'd imagine you would instruct your secretary to dispatch a missive. Shall I ring for her?"

"My…uh, yes?"

He gave a curt bow and turned on his heel. Kara sat looking at the space he'd been for a moment longer before stabbing a piece of fish. Flynn had said something about a secretary, but it had happened a lot faster than she'd expected. It was like she could just snap her fingers and whatever she wanted appeared. She was tempted to try it out on something ridiculous. That cat hadn't shown up yet…

The staccato clip of smart steps came down the hallway, and a neat woman in black appeared. Kara smiled to see the tailored jacket and Mary Janes peeping from beneath her no-nonsense skirt. The woman held a clipboard to her breast and inclined her head. Her bronze hair was caught up in a simple chignon. Standing at attention, she pushed up the side of her large, dark-rimmed glasses. They magnified her kohl-lined sky-blue eyes comically, ruining the impact of her presentation.

They looked at each other, listening to the wind outside throw ice against the panes. The weather up here was as mercurial as Flynn.

"As your social standing is the highest in the room, my lady, it's your prerogative to speak first or not, depending on the message you'd like to convey. I only mention it as Master Caliban has disclosed you're unfamiliar with our societal forms. I'll assume your silence was not meant as a chastisement, however well-deserved. Allow me to introduce myself; Audrey French, delighted to be of service. I apologize for not reporting to you directly. Whilst you were otherwise engaged, I thought it best to get straight to work and have been answering your correspondence since early this morning. In the future, I'll make it a point to inform you of my arrival."

The woman's formality took Kara aback. Was this what it was going to be like up here? She'd thought French was just, well, French, but here was another…French. She laughed, kicking herself for skipping out on all those stupid etiquette lessons her mother had—

Her breath caught. Oh, Glory.

Nora had known about all of this. She'd been trying to prepare her. The long list of things Kara had railed against in favor of the gym scrolled through her mind.

Fuck.

Another laugh burbled up, but that was the only word that suited. Oh, and like the rest of the messes of late, she'd done it to herself.

Audrey's lips pursed. She pushed up the side of those wide, circular glasses again, blinking like an expectant owl. The woman must think she was nuts, sitting here giggling like a fool. Ugh… What would Nora do?

Kara smoothed her napkin in her lap, taking a deep breath and trying to channel her mother. "My apologies, Audrey. It's a pleasure to meet you. I'm sure you're very busy on my behalf and appreciate your assistance. I'd wondered if you could invite Mistress Glass to come and discuss the design she submitted." She clamped her jaw shut before she could laugh again. How pretentious she sounded! Kara slid the portfolio across the table, hoping to draw attention away from herself.

Audrey's heels clipped the checkerboard floor as she came forward, taking up the folder. Her eyebrow rose. "I would be remiss if I didn't explain the ramifications of what you're proposing. Houses Glass and Scott are currently embroiled—"

"Audrey! Is that you? Shit, last time I saw you, your hair was lime green." Flynn came into the room and scooped the woman up in a massive bear hug.

She sniffed, and he set her back on her feet. "Lord Scot." Her tone was formal, but Kara could tell she was pleased.

"God, not you too." He laughed. "So much for your music career panning out."

That won a smile, quickly swallowed. "Indeed. The Flaming Banshees haven't wailed in some time. I was elated to discover you'd returned." She looked around the room, taking in the frescoed ceiling. "I have missed Meddleton, and you." Her finger nipped up beneath her lenses, and Flynn gave her another hug.

"I'm sorry."

"Good." Audrey stepped back and, for a second, Kara thought she was going to kick him in the shins. Then her shoulders set, and she inclined her head. "I shall see to your request, my lady." She didn't exactly flee from the room, but the strike of her heels was noticeably quicker.

"What was that about?"

Flynn made a face as he rounded the table. He gave her a quick kiss and pulled out a chair. A servant hurried over with an actual meal: soup, sandwich, and fries.

"Ah, she's French's daughter. We grew up together." He tossed a fry into his mouth, laughing at her as he chewed. "Nothing like that. Audrey's like my little sister, and she's not into men."

"Is everyone so formal up here? What is that, mayonnaise?" She watched him dredge another fry in white stuff.

"Tartar sauce." He grinned at her look of horror. "I don't like ketchup, and yeah, Glynfyls is stupid formal, publicly, at least. Like I said last night, everything's about maintaining an image." He frowned, quickly stifling an old hurt from their bond.

Kara tried not to roll her eyes. Glory, she hated that. "How can you not like ketchup?"

"I dunno, it's gross. Anyways, Cal contracted Audrey to give you a run down on all the social crap up here. She was teaching etiquette at the Academy, so you're in good hands, and you don't have to worry about saying anything to her. They've been loyal to House Scot forever." He dipped his sandwich in his soup and took a sloppy bite. "What've you got her doing?" he asked around it.

Kara tried not to cringe, remembering Madame Gillibar droning on about the various degrees to which one should incline their head based upon the social stature of conversationalists present. Flynn grinned as he chewed, feeling her dread. Jerk.

"I asked her to set a meeting with Regina Glass to discuss her gown design."

Flynn choked on his bite. "Shit, Kara, didn't Audrey tell you they're suing the crap out of us for breach of contract?"

"Then why would she—"

"Who the hell knows. Politics up here… Christ, I'd feel better if you had a bodyguard in the room if you're really set on meeting with her."

She laughed. "I'm sure Rogan would love to attend a fitting."

"Not a fucking chance that's happening."

"Oh, come on, what did you really think of him?"

"He's an asshole."

"What? Why? What did he say to you?"

"It's not important. I just don't like the way he looks at you."

"The way he looks at me?"

"Yeah."

"And how is that, Flynn?"

"Like he wants to fuck you."

Kara sat staring at him, speechless, as he ate. "You're jealous."

"Of what?" He snorted, taking another bite.

"Well, let's see…" She started ticking off her fingers. "He's handsome, cultured, has some really great moves…and I've got a thing for older men."

Flynn glowered, and she laughed. His emotions weren't exactly jealousy, but were something—her breath caught. He was leaking 'lust again, but it was different… Whatever this was flushed her with heat, drawing her from her seat. She straddled him, pushing him against the back of his chair.

"You worried?" She wound her arms around his neck, skating her cheek up against his, inhaling his scent. What was that? She wanted to lick it off him, something in her rising to meet it.

Flynn gave her a sharp look, a growl rumbling in his chest. "Should I be?"

"I don't know, you've got the handsome cultured part down… Maybe I need to see those moves of yours again—"

He sent the plates behind her spinning, and she was sitting in their place before they'd shattered against the floor. His halos flared. Their clothes phased, and she gasped, trying to cover herself. They were in the middle of the dining room—

"How's that for an opener?"

"You didn't pull talent from me…"

"No, I don't need to anymore." His hand came up around her throat, and she gasped at what was in his eyes, her nakedness forgotten. "Don't play with me, Kara."

He kissed her tenderly, his thumb against her windpipe as he moved between her thighs, teasing her. Barely restrained carnality pulsed through their bond, the air thick with his scent. It set her skin ablaze, her breath coming in short, sharp bursts, legs floating around his hips, her elbows braced against the soup-sodden table linens. He licked a long line from her shoulder to her lobe.

"You're mine. Your pleasure, your pain, each one of your pretty little holes…" He kissed the shell of her ear, the prickle of his beard sending shivers up her spine. "Mine. Say it." His halos burnt with verdant fire, those blue motes churning…

"I'm yours." She wet her lips in anticipation. He teased them with his, body firm against the trembling cleft of her legs. Kara whimpered, aching and wet. He smiled, thumb dropping to strum her clit.

"You need me to fill you up, baby? Beg for my dick like a good girl."

"Please, Flynn, I need you so bad…"

He flipped her over, grinding her hip bones into the table's edge, and slapped her still-tender ass, hard. She gasped, teeth dimpling her lip as he rubbed the sting away. "Reach back and spread your cheeks. Show me where you want it."

Kara pressed her forehead to the table linens and did as she was told, panting, that darkness in her swirling.

"Mmm…" A finger slid from her folds to her pucker, her pussy weeping for him.

"Please, Flynn…" He grabbed something from the table, and a viscous liquid dribbled down her crack. "Oh!"

"You want this?" His finger breeched the tight ring of muscle, and she pushed back against it, moaning her need. He slapped her ass again and kicked her feet farther apart. "Ask me for it."

"Please!"

She cried out at the sharp burn of his thick length forcing into her backside. "That's it, fucking take it…" he groaned, pistoning into her.

Her nails scraped at the tablecloth, crying out at the sudden pain turning to pleasure, tipping back to meet him, his ferocity speaking to the darkness within her, their desire an echo.

Her, feeling him, feeling her.

Flynn wrapped her braid around his fist, pulling her against his chest. Head dipped, breath fast and hot on the nape of her neck, inhaling with a growl, scenting her wantonness. His other hand slid from her hip to delve into her folds, cock punishing her from behind.

"One knee on the table," he grunted, thrusting deeper as the new angle opened her up.

Kara bit back a scream, her nipples pebbling to tight peaks. Oh Glory, it hurt so good…

"Naughty girl," Flynn breathed in her ear, his hips working harder. "Your pain is mine. I wanna hear it." He flicked her clit, and she shrieked, her thighs dripping, sticky. His rough fingers gathered it up and jammed into her mouth. "Suck."

Kara's eyes rolled back into her head, gagging around them. He rumbled his approval and a tremor crested through her. That, the command, the smell of his lust, her body was on fire…

His hips slammed against her ass, the impact rippling through her flesh, driving her against the table. Flynn squeezed her breast, fingers pinching, teeth at her shoulder.

She offered him her throat, needing more. "Please…"

He licked up under her ear, biting her lobe. Her frustrated moan caught. She reached back, hand tangling in his hair, it wasn't enough…

"Greedy," he chuckled, railing into her. "You belong to me, Kara. Say it again."

"All of me… all of me is yours. Please, Flynn…please…"

Her fingers tightened, skin breaking beneath his teeth. She moaned in ecstasy, eyes fluttering. Their bond thrummed with it, and he laughed, reveling in her abandonment.

"It is, but that's not what I want to hear you say." He pulled out, leaving her bereft.

"I belong to you." She sobbed, turning and pulling him to her. "Please, I need you…"

His lips devoured hers, the copper-tang of her blood on his tongue. He pushed her down onto the table, moving above her. Holding her gaze, he re-sheathed himself in her flesh. She cried out, rising up as he thrust himself against her.

"Louder."

China and crystal smashed to the floor as his hips met hers, silverware pinging against the cold marble. Kara dug her nails into his lats, tearing down his sides, making him cry out with her. His hand closed around her throat.

"Again," he growled.

"I belong to you…" she gasped, head going light, vision greying into a tunnel.

"Then come for me, baby," he murmured, loosening his hold.

Everything went white with the inrush of air to her lungs. Her back arched, his mouth at her breast. Legs about his waist, her body tightened around his, cunt grasping and empty, releasing a deluge of desire over his thrusting cock. It thickened, swelling within her, and he raised up, hand heavy on her shoulder, letting out a yell—

Shattering with her.

Flynn collapsed onto his forearms, sides heaving, breath at her neck. She lay beneath him, staring at the fresco on the ceiling. Did every room have one? Nouveau swirls in shades of gray. Her gaze followed them, slowly becoming aware of the spoon digging into her shoulder blade and that she was lying in a smear of flan.

She laughed, and Flynn gently kissed her throat, his fingers sliding over the broken skin. Deep satisfaction radiated from him, echoing her own at the weeping lines of red she'd left crisscrossing his flesh.

"I want you to leave all of it," he murmured against her bruised and battered skin. "I want you to feel what we do together when you're with him. I want him to see it, to smell it, to know you're mine."

She shivered as his body left hers. Sitting up, she took his face in her hands.

"I am. I love you, Flynn. All of me is yours."

He kissed her tenderly, then pulled back, halos burning verdigris, irises swallowed by electric blue. His whole demeanor changed into something dangerous, radiating bloodlust. Kara went weak at the strength of it, gripping the edge of the table to keep upright. She wet her lips, stomach flipping with desire. Who was this man?

"And I'm yours, Kara. I'll fucking kill anyone who tries to get between us, and that prick Rogan is at the top of my list."

She staggered beneath the wave of menace, and he caught her against him. Tipping her chin up, he kissed her, lips soft, the promise of violence thick in the room. Their clothes solidified, and he ran a hand through his hair, grinning at her, his easy manner back, those blue motes hidden. What were they? Something, a half-remembered dream…she shook her head, sliding from the table weak-kneed.

"Ready?"

She blushed, looking at the mess they'd made. He laughed, his halos winking out, smushing together the scattered remains of his soggy sandwich from the corner of the table. He sat down, taking a big bite.

French cleared his throat at the door. "Ah, pardon me for intruding, sir. If you're no longer indisposed?"

What?!

Flynn got that Cheshire Cat grin, and she wanted to hit him. The jerk hadn't cloaked sound. She put a hand to her face, about to die.

After she killed him.

"Yeah, what's up?" Impossibly, his grin grew as Rogan stalked into the room. The Breaker's steps faltered, his nostrils flaring. He narrowed his eyes at Flynn, then flicked them to her.

He wasn't happy.

Flynn was.

"Assembly begins again in ten minutes, sir," French said, apparently immune to the tension.

Flynn stood, coming around the table to kiss her, brushing his fingers over the marks he'd left. "I'll see you after." He smiled, then glared at the Breaker on his way out. French cast a bland eye over the state of the dining room and followed.

Leaving her with Rogan.

"You're late."

She pushed away from the table, wiping off her greasy hands. Salad oil. Great… "Sorry, I got sidetracked."

"No, you got fucked."

"Is that a problem?" Her face burned.

"When it wastes my time, it is. You want to let everyone hear him bend you over, that's your business. I'm not up here for the entertainment."

Kara marched from the room. Why was he being such a jerk? Rogan kept pace with her back to the gym. The tension between them made her want to scream. Ugh, it was so stupid! What did he care?

"That's one hell of a bruise," he finally said. "He mark you like that often?"

She blushed again. The maid they passed wouldn't meet her eye. "Does it matter?"

His halos flared, and he ran a hand across his mouth like something was bothering him.

"He doesn't do anything I don't want him to, Rogan."

"I'm gonna guess it's after you've been around a Breaker. He always make you walk around like that when he's done?" The man's lips had condensed into a sour line.

Her face burned. "No. He's never done that before."

"Any idea why he picked today to start?"

"Do we really have to talk about this?" She threw up her hands in exasperation at his expression. "Fine. He wanted you to see it. He doesn't like you, or the way you look at me."

Rogan held the door open for her, a wide smirk spreading over his face. "Start running."

Kara got on the treadmill, fuming. She slapped it on, working up to a run. What was his problem?

FLYNN WALKED INTO CHAMBERS, reveling in the feel of Kara's irritation with Rogan. Christ, he hated that asshole. Taking the stairs down two at a time, he flipped through this afternoon's packet of papers, snorting in disgust. Useless mandates, feel-good legislation… none of which addressed any of the security concerns he'd brought up.

He sat just as Riggs banged the gavel, opening the session. There were fewer people here than this morning. Hopefully that meant his novelty was wearing off.

"Next on our agenda, Lady Everly has entered a proposal to change the definition of an Original House."

What the fuck? That hadn't been part of the papers delivered last night… Flynn flipped through his packet. It was an addendum, buried beneath a different heading.

A Binder with frazzled grey hair stood. "Thank you, Lord Riggs. I find it indecent that some of the lesser Talents are trying to pass themselves off as Original Houses. My proposal would limit the definition, banning just anyone from using the term. It's a distinct part of our heritage and shouldn't be sullied by pretenders." There was a general murmur of agreement from everyone in the room. Flynn shook his head, scanning the document. Patrician assho—His eyes widened at one of the clauses.

"Well," Riggs said brightly, "that sounds like something everyone can get behind, if there are no objections, let's bring that right up for a—"

"I have an objection," he said. "There's a sentence in here that would exclude Source Talents. That's preposterous. How are they any different from us?"

Lady Everly's mouth worked before she answered. "Their Houses have either been diluted or they're inbred."

"Are you suggesting my pedigree is less than yours because of my parentage?" The woman paled, flicking open one of those stupid fans. "I'd make the argument that our Houses are more diluted up here, and if you're worried about purity, inbreeding should be the last of your concerns." He turned to Julia. "I have to wonder at the timing of this, considering my intended entered her petition to garner a vote yesterday."

"I don't know why you feel the need to address your comments to me and as hard as it may be to believe, not everything is about you, Laughlin." People laughed and even he had to smile.

"Fair enough." He looked back up at Lady Everly. "Did you know your proposal would have this effect on Original Houses residing outside of Glynfyls?"

The woman glanced at Julia. He'd take that as a no.

"Why are none of you using legal counsel? Lord Yassir could've rattled off a dozen ramifications if you'd asked." The portly lord sitting in the far back of the Finder's section wouldn't meet his eye. Un-fucking-believable.

The speaker leaned forward. "Ah, if you're finished, Lord Scot, I believe there was a measure to be brought up for a vote?"

Disgusted, Flynn dropped down into his chair, motioning for them to proceed.

It failed by a fair margin. He shook his head, face grim as the next measure came up.

———

"YOU'RE AN ASSHOLE," Rogan said without preamble.

Cal snorted, not bothering to glance up from his paperwork. Not the first or the last time he'd hear him say that. The big Breaker strode over to the sideboard and helped himself to the good scotch. He shot it back, then grabbed the bottle and a second glass. Setting them down on the desk with a clink, he sat across from Cal.

"In general, or did you have a particular reason in mind?" He kept his face bland, pouring them both a glass. From the look Rogan was giving him, they'd need it.

"That kid's Breaker stock."

Cal pursed his lips. "Don't let him hear you say that."

"It doesn't go away just because you want it to. Christ, he's doing things instinctively, he tried to put his runes on Kara at lunch."

"Did he need to?"

Rogan shrugged, taking a sip. "I may have pushed the issue just to see what would happen."

Cal laughed. "Who's the asshole now?"

The Breaker cracked a smile at that. "She said it's happened before, but he's never made her leave his mark. If he can sense the hierarchy..." Rogan's eyes narrowed. "You knew?"

"Had my suspicions. After Deirdre died, he got a little too rough with some of the more talented Breaker girls. The last one was a talker, and it created one hell of a scandal."

"So will fucking Kara on the dining room table and leaving that mark. The room reeked of 'lust. I can guarantee there's gonna be talk after that performance. Kid needs a Menot."

"No. He needs to shake the rumors he's a twist so he can do what I need him to do. He's got Kara now—"

"Doesn't work like that. He needs someone to guide him. Being a Breaker's a lot more than hitting shit. He's a boxer, right?"

Cal reached for his tobacco pouch. "Was. A damn fine one, but he says he hasn't brawled in years, and I believe him. Flynn doesn't lie. He'll dance around if you give him the chance, but the boy's as honest as the day's long."

Rogan downed the rest of his scotch, sucking in air between his teeth. He slapped the glass on the desk for a refill, and Cal obliged. "Then he's got the honor part of it, too. Damn it, he's gonna be a problem. Trust me, you can only repress it for so long before everything bubbles up. Boy's gonna snap."

You don't say. "Kara'll level him out." Or break him. Cal lit his cigarette, thinking about the plateau.

Rogan laughed. "Fuck, Cal, what'd you bring me into? You've no idea how close she's been to succumbing. She's already got one hell of a taste for the 'lust and from what I can gather, he's pulled her off that ledge a handful of times since he's met her." Rogan itched under his man-bun with a frown. "She's breeding on top of it. That makes her more susceptible."

"Yeah, I know. That's why you're here." Cal put his feet up on his desk and blew out a cloud of smoke.

"If I couldn't teach her how to achieve zero before this, what makes you think I can do it now?"

"She's more centered since she's bonded Flynn, not so jumpy. You must've noticed."

"She's not centered, she's sliding, and if the kid can't catch her..." Rogan sipped at his drink, pensive. "You ever run his metrics?"

Cal took a drag, not wanting to answer. "Yeah." Rogan gave him a hard look. "It was a coin flip which way he was gonna land."

"Let me guess, right on the edge." Rogan shot back his drink with a laugh. "Just pick up where I left off, huh? You're a son of a bitch. He's a time bomb, Cal. A fucking ticking time bomb, and none of us has any idea what that's gonna look like if he splits."

"It won't matter if he's Overlord."

"After that last shit show?"

"You see another way to play it, let me know."

Rogan sighed. "Fine. You're the brains of this operation. I'll stay and keep an eye on them both, but the kid won't like it. If he could pull talent, there's no question he'd be challenging me. Little shit still might."

"He'll do as he's told." For now, at least.

The Breaker stood, pinning him with his storm-grey eyes. "Then you better tell him to come to terms with himself, because if he's gonna pull off this wet dream of yours, he'll need to use everything he's got."

Cal spun his glass of scotch, watching the Breaker stalk out of the room. His voice raspy when the man had gone. "That's why I called you."

CHAPTER NINE

The First Tenet
No Talent shall use their abilities to cause harm to another, neither by direct,
nor indirect means without first declaring a House War.

"A lady should at all times exude a demure confidence. You are all
responsible for maintaining the unsullied respectability of your
father's House and then your husband's. Whereas men are expected to
stray from time to time, it is a woman's duty to set a shining example
of pure thought and form for them to aspire to…"

— Lady Chatterly, Precepta of Social Graces,
Academy of Glynfyls

AUDREY HELD the lift door open, and Kara stepped off in a slim red skirt and cream blouse. She needed to look like the future Lady Scot for these dumb meetings. Whoever that was supposed to be.

Stop. It wasn't dumb if it was important to Flynn…she just didn't want to do it. Her fingers floated up to touch the scarf around her neck. The ache of the bruise there steadied her nerves. Audrey hadn't been pleased about it, giving her a very French-like expression of disapproval. It was the same one on her face as she'd surveyed Kara's remaining wardrobe, though she seemed satisfied enough with what she'd cobbled together.

Kara scratched under a bobby pin and sighed. Her hair looked lovely, but it pulled. She glanced over at the neat woman, sure she'd had the maid make it so tight on purpose.

"Do try not to fidget, my lady. Chin up, shoulders back, confidence." She pronounced the syllables in a musical staccato, rising at the end. A pep talk. Kara grimaced, she must look as miserable as she felt.

Straightening her spine, she crossed the foyer. Audrey was worse than Madame Gillibar—No. She wasn't. Kara just couldn't lock herself in the bathroom until she went away. Ugh. She knew how to do all this, so why was it so hard?

Because she hated it. Every fake, pretentious second. Why couldn't they've stayed at the farm? She had the sudden urge to rip apart her coiffure and run out across those untouched fields, Flynn at her heels, his weight bearing her to the ground, mouth hot on hers—

"Mistress Glass is just through here."

Kara blinked, hand at her throat, and gave a little nod, missing him desperately.

It doesn't mean shit to me, Kara. I'm only up here to keep you safe. I'm sure as hell not gonna make the both of us miserable while I do it.

Then why did his feelings echo hers? He didn't want any of this either.

"Are you all right, my lady?"

Kara met the woman's magnified gaze with a little laugh. "I've no choice but to be."

Audrey paused for the barest of moments before giving a curt nod. Kara smoothed a hand over her brow, squared her shoulders, and went into the room.

A heavyset blonde woman with a squint quickly rose to her feet from the taupe leather chair closest to the hearth. She had a very unfortunate nose. Kara inclined her head to the exact degree Audrey had instructed, bobby pins stabbing.

Mistress Regina Glass responded with a low curtsy, trembling hands dyed a vivid shade of blue wiping her skirts.

Kara glanced at Audrey, and the woman's eyes flicked back at her.

"Thank you so much for coming, Mistress Glass, won't you take a cup of tea?"

Regina nodded gratefully and sat after Kara had perched herself on the edge of the gold damask couch. It was as stuffy and rigid as it looked. No wonder Regina had taken a chair. She smiled vapidly at her guest. Too late to change seats now.

"I'd love a cup, thank you. Forgive me for being such a mess. I picked the wrong week to experiment with woad. I won't be able to get this blue off for a solid fortnight." She rubbed her hands together self-consciously, watching Audrey make tea. "At least the fermenting's done with, that smelled worse than the Pinch after the May rains!" Regina's laugh died at Audrey's sharp look, and she swallowed nervously. "Ah, you wanted to discuss my design?"

"Yes. I like it very much. There's a few alterations I'd make, if possible. I wanted to see what you thought."

Regina stared at her in shock, and Kara's stomach clenched, that stupid vision of Tamara Hess's smirk in her head. *I'll die if she starts laughing…* Kara fought the urge to call up a trickle of bloodlust to steady her nerves. It was a lot harder than it should've been, but she held the woman's gaze, playing the princess Cal had told her to be. She could do this.

Probably.

"You want to know what I think…" Regina glanced at Audrey as if to check she'd heard her properly. Getting no help, Regina's cup clattered onto its saucer. She put it down on the table, taking up the portfolio and glancing over the top of it at them again before squinting at Kara's notes. A cobalt finger came up to curl around her chin, her manner completely changing, a kind of assurance setting over her. Kara smiled, recognizing it. She warmed to the woman, knowing what that was like to step onto the mats and into yourself.

"I can do this, but see right here? The fabric won't fall right when you walk, never mind what it'll do on the dance floor. Lord Scot will have my head if it threw off your lines…" she murmured, sucking her bottom lip.

Threw off her lines…? Kara shot a look at Audrey, and the woman blinked back at her. Ugh, that was infuriating. "What material were you thinking?"

"Oh, that's easy," Regina laughed. "As soon as I saw your coloring, this was screaming to be done in a gold dupioni silk. It's a rich fabric that flows beautifully, with these little nubbly variegations in the weave… It's not frilly at all, you don't seem the type."

Kara fought the urge to hug the woman. "The job is yours—if you want it…" Another glance at Audrey. Was that caution in her gaze? Kara wished she would just open her stupid mouth. "Unless this unpleasantness between House Scot and House Glass prevents—"

"No!" Regina sat up straighter. "I mean, you needn't worry about it any of that. I'm quite independent of it. I want the job."

"If you're sure… " Damn Audrey's stupid blank face. "I'm glad you feel that way, because I also need to talk to you about getting myself and Flynn some proper everyday wear. I have some things for you to look at, but it's not going to be sufficient, and he has nothing appropriate."

"Seriously, me?" Regina squeaked, clapping a blue hand over her mouth. She turned an interesting shade of scalded pink.

Audrey blanched. "Perhaps it would be best to see what comes of this first project—"

"No." Kara's temper jumped. Now she had something to say? "Regina has the job, and I'd like her to bring everything she has off the rack for me to look through as soon as she's able," Kara added peevishly, hoping whatever that was would scandalize the secretary as much as Miriam.

Audrey snapped her mouth shut, noting something on her clipboard.

Turning, Kara laughed at Regina's expression before she could stop herself, and the woman returned a sheepish grin. "If that works for you?"

Regina chuckled, dabbing at her eyes. "If that works for me? Yes, yes, that works for me, I would be honored to have you as my patron."

Kara inwardly flinched at the woman's word choice, but smiled as Regina gave a great sigh, ticking off days on her cobalt fingers. Audrey's owl expression had become very pinched.

"So…six days. I'll take your measurements now, and be back with the mock-up and everything off the rack tomorrow." Her face split into a wide grin. "I'm assuming you'll want something coordinating for Lord Scot?"

"Yes," Kara said, ignoring Audrey. "I'm going to need you to come up with an alternative to tights."

FLYNN TRIED to tamp down his irritation at the debate on whether or not to replace the asphalt curbing around the courthouse with granite. The Assembly cared more about the aesthetics of the hill than they did anything else. It was sickening. Especially considering what a shithole the rest of Glynfyls was.

And to make matters worse, he kept getting flashes of upset from Kara. They were tinged with that off-feeling that meant she felt sick. He pushed her more talent, hoping it would help. She'd be meeting with Bea right about now. He ran a hand through his hair, worried.

That sick feeling from Kara increased exponentially. Flynn fought to stay seated. What the hell was going on? Every instinct was telling him to run out of there. He wiped at his brow, calming himself. French would've sent a runner if something was wrong. He put up a block, trying to focus.

A page tore down the steps, and Flynn's stomach knotted as the boy drew closer—

He handed Jacques a note.

Flynn sat back in his seat, heart thudding. *Shit.*

The amount of shuffling and low discussion behind him increased markedly. Jacques was absolutely furious. It was shocking to see the even-keeled man so incensed. The other lines gawked, and the speaker banged his gavel for order, then gave up, calling the session to an early close.

Jacques met Flynn's eye, leaving the chamber as fast as decorum would allow.

Flynn turned to Charles. "Is Bea all right?"

The smaller man stepped back with pursed lips. "You should go home."

Fuck.

Flynn pushed past the crowd, hurrying to the gate.

He stepped through to a silent house. French met him in the hall looking more collected than usual. Shit didn't bode well.

"Sir, I don't want to alarm you, but I'm afraid there's been an incident." Flynn's stomach dropped. That was Frenchese for something fucking bad had happened.

"Why didn't you send a runner?"

"Master Caliban wouldn't allow it."

Wouldn't—the room seared a scarlet so bright Flynn staggered. "Is she okay?"

"She's upstairs with Madame Miriam. I'm afraid she overexerted herself correcting Lady Martin's condition."

"Correcting…" He'd only asked—Goddamn it, he should've known better. Of course Kara would do more than just look. Flynn scrubbed at his face, opening their link wide, and feeling like a complete asshole. She was sleeping, that fucking exhaustion back in spades.

He should've been here.

"The next time *Master* Caliban tries to prevent you from doing your duty, tell him *Lord* Scot said to fuck off. I don't give a shit if I'm taking a meeting with the Almighty, Kara trumps it. What the hell happened?"

French's cheeks sucked in like he was ridiculously pleased by the directive. "From what I could glean of the situation, Lady Martin's child had been fixed in utero, preventing it from developing."

The burst of rage Flynn felt was visceral. No wonder Jacques was fucking pissed. What the hell was going on up here?

As if summoned, the man stormed through the gate.

"I'm going to kill that fucking cunt," Jacques burst out. Flynn motioned him towards the drawing room and closed the doors behind them. Jacques threw his hat on the settee, pulling his hair. Man needed a drink. "Julia's broken the First Tenet!"

"Yeah, but you need to think about Bea and your kid."

"Would you be able to?"

"No, but you've always been a lot smarter than me."

Jacques gave a sad laugh, taking the glass of whiskey Flynn held out to him. Shooting it back, he fumed. "This cannot be allowed to stand."

"Can Bea prove it was her?"

He looked into his empty glass. "Not in a court of law, but what we need right now is public opinion. I heard about what you said at the end of Assembly yesterday. I have to admit, I was a bit concerned about how that was going to play out."

"That's not a portion of my life I need to repeat. I didn't come back to make the same mistakes."

Jacques nodded, putting the empty glass down and taking a palm-sized bronze disk from his pocket. Flynn made a strangled sound at the sight of the relic. Once used by the Assembly to vote for Overlord, those disks had been kept under lock and key since the last one had fucked up. Why the hell would Jacques—

His friend raised his chin, and Flynn's mouth went dry. He knew that fucking look.

"Don't."

Jacques shook his head, rubbing his thumb over the worn metal. "She fixed my child, cursing it to a kind of half-life, and Bea—" His eyes grew glassy as he tapped the disk against his palm. "The pregnancy's progressing rapidly. No one has a clue what the fade will do to her or the child. They think she'll have it within the span of a few weeks… I've no idea if either will survive, and I'll tell you plainly if she dies, our bond will take me with her." He dashed angry tears from his eyes.

"My cousin Stephen's the most likely successor for head. We both know his politics are shit, and the Shades will be completely ineffectual. I'm heavily indebted to you after today. So much so, I'm offering you House Martin's fealty. If this takes me off the board, you'll have a leash on him, and I'll have your oath you'll put that bitch in the ground." He held the disk out to him, his eyes hard.

Flynn felt ill. "Jacques, you're upset, take some time—"

"There is none! Julia's putting the screws to all of us. Justin Hill committed suicide after she'd taken tea with his wife. He'd refused to sign over a property down by the wharf, and Julia made good on her threat of blackmail. God only knows what she had on him, but his body was cut down an hour ago. He hanged himself from the rafters, and his wife was found comatose."

Flynn put a hand out to steady himself. What was going on up here was madness—

"People are looking to you as her opposition and after today... I swear to Christ, come hell or high water, this disk guarantees you'll have House Martin's backing to give it to her. Take it Flynn. It's poor trade for what your lady's given us."

Flynn looked down at the disk. It was the last fucking thing he wanted, and Kara...goddamn it, he should've fucking been here... And he would've, if he didn't have to deal with Julia's bullshit.

He held out his hand. Jacques set the disk into his palm. It was heavier than it should've been. "I'll have the paperwork sent over." He picked his hat up off the divan. "The rest of the line knows what's happened. It's brought the matter of your nomination to a head. With Lot deposed, we can't wait for the Introduction to push your bid for First. The time is ripe for you to step up, the sooner the better."

Flynn nodded reluctantly, weighing the disk in his hand before slipping it into his pocket. He followed Jacques out, running a trembling hand over his jaw.

He needed to talk with Cal.

Jon was sitting with him in his office, going over paperwork. Flynn squeezed his uncle's shoulder as he sat in the chair next to him, wondering how medicated he was.

"I came with Shelby after I heard..." Jon's eyes had that dead-fogged look to them, answering that question. "I have to run some tests, but I'm positive Kara's deficient. She shouldn't use her talent. She'll hurt herself or the baby. The child needs to be able to draw it through you both if it's going to develop properly. She'll end up stunting its ability, or worse."

Flynn sat back in his seat, pale. Christ, that was a lot more serious than he'd thought. "I don't think she knows that. I sure as hell didn't. What the fuck does deficient mean?" Shit. She'd only used her talent because he'd asked her to. Flynn mussed his hair, feeling like even more of an asshole with that fucking disk in his pocket.

"She's not getting enough talent to support her functions and that of the baby. It happens now and then, mostly with dual Talents or when carrying multiples. Miriam needed to be supplemented. I'm assuming the rate her pregnancy is progressing is also a factor. Talents are constantly pulling incremental amounts, but she's using it up faster than she's replenishing it."

"I scoured through what the Source has on female Breakers like you asked and there's not a lot." Cal tapped the butt of his cigarette on the desk. "Whatever Titus's bred into them, he's holding out on the board; to what extent I couldn't tell you. There're no clues as to why things are moving so quickly."

Flynn grit his teeth, eyes hot. Fuck, he couldn't—Jon would take care of it. "Jacques just offered me fealty because of what she did."

His grandfather stopped in the middle of lighting his cigarette, looking at him like he'd grown another head. "And?"

"He didn't give me much choice in the matter. The paperwork'll be here tomorrow."

Flynn took the disk from his pocket and tossed it onto the desk. It landed with a metallic clunk that echoed through the room. Cal stretched out a hand, but didn't touch it. The two older men eyed it with reverence.

His grandfather took the unlit cigarette from his mouth and rolled it between his fingers. "You need to do this the traditional way."

"A blood oath?"

"Yeah."

Flynn wearily ran a hand through his hair, too tired to argue. "I'll ask French to put together a dinner for all the heads this Saturday. I'll make my bid for First then." He stood, ignoring the look of satisfaction on Cal's face. "I also told him to tell you to fuck off if you ever try to stop him from sending me word when there's something wrong with Kara. I swear to Christ, Cal, you pull that shit again, you'll regret it."

The satisfaction was gone from his grandfather's face as Flynn left the room. Good.

He slumped against the lift's wall as it rose. What the hell was he doing? Ever since he'd gotten up here, everything was moving too goddamned fast. A storm was building, and Kara…

Jesus fucking Christ. Houses hadn't pledged fealty since the Great Incursion. What was Jacques thinking? Their Houses had jockeyed for First since there had been Houses and Firsts, and with this, he'd handed all their political power to the Scots in perpetuity. Flynn couldn't even begin to wrap his head around all the implications… He hoped to hell Jacques would come to his senses, and he could give the damned thing back.

Kara was whipping up a real shit storm, all right, and she hadn't even left the house. What was gonna happen when she did?

Miriam was knitting by the hearth when he opened the door to his suite. The needles stilled in her lap. "She cannot keep doing this, Laughlin. Next time you could lose them both. It's taking more out of her than she knows, more than it should."

"Jon already spoke to me."

She nodded, collecting her knitting and leaving him with his thoughts. The fact that she hadn't berated him made everything worse, like she knew what a piece of shit he was. Washing up, he couldn't even look at himself in the mirror.

He stood over the sink, head down…that gnawing in his guts… fuck, he wanted a drink.

Serenity now.

He slipped into bed beside Kara. She made a small noise as he wrapped himself against her back, kissing her neck.

"What time is it?" she mumbled.

"Late. You overdid it." She made a noncommittal sound. He breathed her in, holding her tight and pushing more talent through their link, her and the baby taking it up greedily. "I can't lose either of you, Kara."

She said something unintelligible and fell asleep long before he did.

"YE AIN'T FROM HERE."

The shrew eyed Riegel suspiciously, reaching inside the steaming cart for whatever edible she was hawking. Her practiced hands did it quickly, flipping the lid down and cutting off the burst of heat he was attempting to savor. What was left of his frost-bitten lips pruned. He fumbled at the coins in his pocket, shooting her a foul look. His dexterity had suffered mightily with the loss of his fingertips. A wave of nostalgia for the ability to just scan his barcode overcame him.

"Only mention it on account of the 'bite," the woman nattered, plucking a bit more than exact change from his outstretched palm. "Somewhat fierce, ain't it? Ye should get yerself t'Shilo's. Pithy'll fix ye up proper, if ye've coin."

Oddly, he did. The last few Talents he'd delivered had carried surprisingly heavy purses. Something about "payday." He snatched the foil-wrapped bundle from her, a grunt escaping him as his deadened flesh registered its warmth.

"Shilo's?"

She jerked her frizzy head down the street. "Alley two down from the blue door, ye'll see the torches. Pithy ain't all on the up an' up...but he don't ask no questions." She cackled behind the back of her hand as he shambled away.

Pithy. Must be a Binder. Riegel held the bundle between his palms, soaking in its scant heat. As much as it irked him to admit it, he'd long since passed the point where he should've hunted down one of the wretched Talents, though by all accounts there were few to be had in this miserable burg. Tearing off a bit of foil, he bit into the gooey mass, his feet taking him in the direction the shrew had indicated, well aware of the possibility he was being set up to be robbed.

As he delved farther into the Pinch, that feeling of being watched returned. It'd picked up precipitously since he began delivering Talents, and he had the distinct impression it had nothing to do with his erstwhile benefactors.

The turn he was supposed to make was less of an alley and more of a fetid underpass. He ducked beneath the listing building, his shoulders scraping the clag-stained brick. He'd be damned if he bowed down to get through any part of this cesspool. A body lay prone across his path, and he kicked it aside, his boot making a satisfying thump and squelch as he passed. The body didn't make any sound at all.

Torchlight flickered through the thick haze, darker streams of greasy smoke fitfully billowing up from the sallow flames. Flakes filtered down through all of it, whether it was fly-ash or another round of snow, Riegel couldn't tell. All of it was a uniform grey and stuck to every surface like guano. He took the short flight of steps down between the sputtering brands, shouldering aside the stiff hide flap serving as a door.

The heat was a gut punch.

Riegel stumbled, the tiny foyer enveloping him in a steamy womb. A moan escaped him, warmth penetrating his dead and broken flesh, sharp needles prickling to life beneath the ravaged surface in response.

He steadied himself against the iridescent bubblegum-pink wall. From the doorway beyond, light flittered through a heavy curtain of mirrored beads and disks, disorienting him. A throbbing bass beat, the tinkle of laughter, and chime of glasses beckoned.

He pushed through the reflective strands into a room dimly lit by flickering orbs tucked into the rafters above. Sinuous trails of white smoke curled about them, filling the air with an exotic musk. It condensed into tight swirls of vapor, then rained down in a shimmering fall of pearlescent, lavender mist.

The writhing forms beneath lifted their faces in rapture before dipping them back to each other as they drubbed to the low tones beating up through the floor. It rose through the soles of Riegel's boots, matching his pulse and the flashing lights as the press of bodies seethed around him. The luster from the mist coated their sweat-slicked skin. A man met his eye as he licked it from a woman's breast, his halos blazing with a crackling storm of lights.

Another cloud burst enveloped Riegel, and he inhaled deeply; amber and herbaceous. A warmth worked outwards from his lungs, through his limbs to the forgotten ruin of his fingertips. It heightened his awareness of the bare flesh around him, drawing him further into the room, all sensation abruptly pleasant.

"Hey now, ye ain't a glim, let's pluck ye out, friend. Ye'll be here for Pithy."

Colors ran.

Riegel stood in a stark white room. He swayed, bereft of the crowd holding him up. It was dead quiet, and an examination table was situated beneath a very bright light in its center. He blinked rapidly, the coolness and clarity of the air bracing after the hedonistic den he'd just been torn from. In the far corner, a man in a white lab coat turned from a stainless steel desk, the wheels on his chair squeaking. He balanced a clipboard on one knee, his long face blank behind silvered goggles.

Pithy, Riegel presumed. The roundness of the name in his mind made him chuckle.

"Well, go on then, tell him what ye need." A small tattooed man pushed past him, and Riegel stumbled. Pithy waggled his fingers at the smaller man, and he sighed. "Them glims is having a rager upstairs, and I didn't see him come in." More waggling, and the man laughed. "Ya, straight after this." He patted the examination table, looking expectantly at Riegel. "Come on now, don't be shy! Just hop on up here, and Pithy'll cure what ails ye, quick as a tic."

Move. Pissant was asking him to move. How—ah. The horizontal slide of Riegel's lips distracted from the oblique trajectory of his legs. Forward pumping, flex and give—

Table.

The little man chuckled, moving to peer into his eyes, his expression that of begrudging interest. Dung brown irises riveted his, specks of yellow in the effluvia… What would one have to eat…

"Well, yer a queer duck an ain't never been on glimmer neither, I'd wager." He glanced back at Pithy and gave a nod. "Regardless, we ain't got all night. He need t'dry ye out, or can ye find yer tongue?"

Find his tongue? Fool. There it was, scraping at his teeth, lingering on the contours, the points… What a stupid question—No, the Fetch was alluding to sobriety, what a dreadful—Why *was* he here?

Cognizance and clarity clambered about Riegel's skull, words rolling and tucking themselves into billiards, then splitting from his grasp. He scrabbled for one of them. It oozed into his mouth, coating his tongue like treacle.

"Fros'bie." He blinked at the alien slush of his voice.

"Ye don't say." The little man grinned. "How much ye got on ye?"

On him? Riegel's lids dropped and rose. Gaze falling to his hideous shirt. The man's hands were on it, in it. Pawing. Taking. Something about that should vex… The thought flitted away into stardust at the coins catching the light… They held a secret…

"Enough t'cover, but won't be pretty. Ye can come back for that," the man said, making the enigmatic bits disappear and nodding again to Pithy.

The Binder unfolded from his chair like a grasshopper. Riegel laughed, the motion evoking a cartoon reel Albanach had played when Riegel was very young. Its soundtrack plinked through his memory as Pithy snapped on a pair of rubber gloves and turned Riegel's face to his, halos ablaze.

CHAPTER TEN

civ [siv] noun, slang

    1. *Breaker slur for civilian.*

– Excerpt from The Way of Honor

"… All female Talents are required to breed no less than twice with a stud of their Patron's discretion. (ref. Sec. 32) During the gestational period, they shall be removed from the general population and installed within the Laborium for any specialized monitoring or enhancements deemed necessary. Once relieved of offspring, breaking is to commence, and a new stud assigned…"

– Section 18, Clause 3.a

A Talent's Contractual Obligation to the Source.

ROGAN WALKED into the Marked Man and took a seat at the bar. Glynfyls was even more of a shithole than he remembered, especially on this rung. A pair of Breakers sat at the other end of the dim room playing dice. With Stonefist's army stationed at the border, the rest of the place was deserted.

Didn't stop the barkeep from taking his sweet-ass time coming over. "Yeah?"

"Tankard of dark."

The man grunted, moving to the tap. "Some advice, friend." The barkeep thumped the beer down in front of him. "I'd strongly suggest ye head up the hill t'see Lady Breakspear if ye plan on staying any longer than it takes ye t'drink this."

Rogan blew the foam from the shitty pour and took a sip. The dark was better than he remembered. "You've got a female First?"

The barkeep shrugged. The motion pulled at the scar running up the side of his neck to where his ear used to be. "After Lord Breakspear died, she stepped up. The little lord'll take it in another year or so, unless ye've got designs?"

"Not a fucking chance of that. I just want some information." He slid a stack of units across the bar. "Goes any further that I asked, and I'll be back for my money." He leaked just enough 'lust to let the man know he meant it.

The barkeep made them disappear. "Understood."

"Laughlin Scot."

"Never met the man."

"What've you heard?"

"Depends on how much you're paying me."

Rogan slid over another stack.

"Ye want the filth, then." The bartender sucked on his teeth. "Fine. He's been a right thorn in the hierarchy, I'll tell ye that. Undefeated in the ring, for the most part. Toward the end he got sloppy." He glanced over at one of the men dicing. "Jarvis went a few rounds with him before then. Scot just about took his jaw off with that uppercut of his."

The man glanced up at his name and scowled. "Son of a bitch hits harder than he's got any right to."

"Pour them another," Rogan said, throwing out a unit.

The bartender refilled their drinks and came back. "Created a hell of a lot of speculation, ye can be sure. Can't tell by looking at him now, but Jarvis weren't no slouch back in the day. Neither was the others. It were a fucking embarrassment t'the line. Can't say we was sorry t'see Scot go."

"That common knowledge?" Rogan took a long swallow and pushed his tankard at the man.

He took it to the tap, glowering. "Breaker Business is Breaker Business. Word is he don't fight no more, but I hear he's marking up his woman. One don't fall far from the other in my experience."

Rogan sourly agreed. Sure as hell didn't take long for that to leak out of Meddleton.

"There's supposed t'be a Breaker at the estate training with her, big son of a bitch from what I understand. Not from around here."

"That right?"

The man nodded, holding his gaze. "If that were the case, I could see why Lord Scot might feel the need."

"I've heard it's not the first time he's done something like that."

"Before he left?" The barkeep snorted. "No more than some rough slap and tickle. My cousin works down at the Pony, so ye can trust me when I tell ye that. Those civs up the hill are a bunch of sensitive little cunts. No, this were different. Hear tell his woman's walking 'round with everything but his runes." The barkeep scratched at his chin. "I'll be honest with ye, friend. Most of us up here couldn't give two shits if he's able t'pull. That kid's a twist or me name ain't Sirrus Fastblade, especially after what I hear he done on the plateau."

The man paused meaningfully, and Rogan dug out a few more units. They disappeared as quickly as the others.

"My buddy were on the train and ran into Scot after the crash. Man conscripted him and every other Breaker out there like he'd been born t'it. My buddy said he ain't never felt 'lust like that. Put all of 'em in the dirt. Civs was pissing their pants it were so dank. Them Sons? Man went through 'em like he were threshing wheat and not a scratch on him. My buddy saw Scot put one of 'em down, professional-like. Said the man knows what he's doing and is good at it."

"So speculate. Which rung?"

Sirrus pursed his lips. "It's been almost ten years since I laid eyes on him, so I couldn't say. But back then? If I were Billy Breakspear I wouldn't be sleeping too well. Now? From what I hear, Billy'd be in the dirt with the rest of us."

Rogan threw another stack of units on the bar and stood. He had what he came for.

THE SUN WAS SKIMMING above the tree tops when Kara woke. She went to get up, and Flynn tightened his arms around her.

"Nope, you're taking it easy today and staying in bed."

She huffed at him, but being held felt so good…until his hand slipped down to her abdomen, thumb slowly sweeping back and forth beneath her navel.

"Yesterday was my fault. I'm sorry I asked you to look at Bea. I should've known better with the way you've been feeling. Jon says you can't use your talent while you're pregnant, Kara."

Her eyes burnt. What good was she if she couldn't bind? She might as well have no identity at all. "What would you've done if I'd lost it?"

His thumb stopped its circuit. "What d'you mean?"

She lay there with her back to him, so angry she was going to be sick. At herself, at him, at this stupid thing between them—

Flynn propped himself up on his elbow. "I told you, we don't break bonds. I'd be upset, but we could have another."

"What if I didn't want to?"

"Like, ever?" He stared at her. "I don't think that's how it works."

Something in his voice stopped her from saying that with binding, that's exactly how it would work.

She might as well have. That block on his emotions slammed down. He pushed up to sit, glaring past the end of the bed, jaw set. "Can I ask why?"

She got up and snatched his shirt up off the floor, pulling it on. "Because I'm tired of being a receptacle for the next iteration's genetic code. That's what the Source wants, what Cal bred me for. I only exist so you can have—"

His bloodlust choked off her next words like a hand around her throat.

"Jesus fucking Christ! I'm gonna beat the shit out of that asshole when I see him. Why the fuck he left you down there, shit, left any fucking Talent down there—Look, you're right, to do what Cal wants me to do, I need an heir. Shit, two if you want House Jester to continue, but I don't give a shit about any of it, I told you I need a partner up here, not a fucking incubator. I want you to have my kid, my kids, because… Kara, I—"

He closed his eyes and a twisting crunch of emotion bled past the block he'd put up. Old hurt, fear, everything she knew he so desperately wanted, but never seemed to be able to say. He scrubbed at his face, then raked his hands back through his hair. His eyes were glassy when he met hers. "You ever wish on a star when you were a kid?"

She gave him a blank look.

"Up here, the first star to show on the horizon every night's the wishing star. It's actually a planet, but when I was a kid—You say this rhyme, and wish for what you want. I always wished for the same thing."

"What was it?"

He bit at his lip, his face crumpling. "If I tell anyone, it won't come true."

"I don't understand."

"If I say it, then it's real, and if it's real, it won't last. It'll be like taking the fix off those fucking roses and before I can blink it, it'll be over." He looked away, wiping his face. "It's stupid. I know it's stupid. But I still can't say it, Kara, I can't take that chance and have it ripped away."

She climbed onto the bed and pushed the hair back from his brow. "What did you say about keeping things fixed? Changeling of vanity for soul?"

"Not me…my mom. And then she died."

Kara winced, feeling like a complete jerk.

He sighed, pulling her into his arms, and sniffling. "I didn't bond you for a kid. You want to call it quits after this one, that's what we do."

She pulled back to look at him, her heart in her throat. "Really?"

"Have I ever lied to you?" She raised an eyebrow, and he grinned. "Yeah, really." He brushed his fingers over her dimple and kissed her again. "So if this is our one shot, no more talent. Jon says if there's nothing there for the baby, it won't develop properly."

She laid down against him, bewildered. "I had no idea, at the Source, breeding females don't stay with the general population. No one ever—" Kara played with his fingers, angry at all of it. "I know nothing about offspring or having one." He laughed, and she smacked him. "I'm serious, Flynn! I've never even really seen an infant. I mean, I know what they are, but juveniles just kind of appear when they're, I don't know, six, ten? How old are they when they can do stuff?" He smoothed back her bangs to kiss her forehead.

"Kara, it's gonna be fine. We'll have tons of help. You won't even have to change a diaper if you don't want to. I'm sure as hell not gonna."

She looked at him in panic. Diapers?

He opened his mouth to say something and was interrupted by a knock. "Yeah?"

French cracked the door. "Sir, I've taken the liberty of bringing your breakfast up. You've limited time if you're planning on making Assembly."

"Shit, yeah, thanks. I can't miss today." He mussed his hair with a frown and glanced between her and the clock. "If my first proposal wasn't coming up for a vote, I would. Glynfyls is a fucking mess. Tomorrow we'll have all day together, ok?"

"Promise?"

"Yeah. Trust me, it's all I've wanted since we've gotten up here."

French set a tray across her lap, then turned to tend something cooking over a thermocoil on his cart. Her stomach rumbled at her bowl; grits, smoked fish, and honey. Flynn shook his head at the combination, cutting into a ham steak.

"You really expect me to stay in bed all day?"

"I do," he said around his bite. "Just until Jon runs some tests, ok?"

She tried to swallow her revulsion, resigned to the fact his request wasn't optional. "Regina Glass is supposed to come and do a fitting."

"You really hired Reggie?" He laughed at her nod. "Cal's gonna have kittens. Fine. Have her do it in here, then right back into bed."

She mixed everything up in her bowl, feeling very alone. How did she always manage to do the wrong thing? "Did you find a kitten?"

"A bunch, actually, but they're still little. It's gonna be awhile before they can be taken from their mother."

"Why do you have to take them away? Can't they all stay in here?"

The grin on Flynn's face made her think she'd unintentionally done something dumb again. "You hear that French?"

The butler looked up from what he was making. "I did indeed, sir. I shall have Meow and her magnificent seven readied for you."

Kara laughed. "Meow?"

French gave a curt nod, filling a thin pastry with ricotta and blueberries. "I believe one of the scullion's granddaughters named the animal in question." He added it to a generous pile and placed the plate on Flynn's tray. "Would you care for a crêpe, my lady?" She shook her head, happy with her fish. "If that will be all, then, sir? You have twenty minutes."

"Yeah, thanks." The butler bowed and exited the room. Flynn busied himself with his meal, wolfing it down. She was only halfway done with hers when he laughed and kissed her shoulder. "Eight fucking cats." He threw back the covers, and was gone.

FLYNN TOOK his seat in the Assembly, surprised to see Jacques. The man gave him an affable nod, not looking inclined to take that damned disk back. Flynn sighed, at least Bea must be okay, but if he'd been in the same position, he would've stayed home. Shit, if he was in any position other than the one he was in, he'd be as far from this fucking city as possible.

He hated having to choose between his duty to his House and Kara, but if he didn't deal with this shit, a fucking Peacekeeper would be giving him a wake-up call instead of French. He needed to take First, and Jacques was right; it was time to make his move. The dinner tomorrow night needed to go off without a hitch.

Riggs banged his gavel and the session came to order.

"First item, as of noon today, the border is officially closed. We're now set to discuss penalties for infractions. Under the current proposal, an offender would be remanded to the authorities of the territory breached and prosecuted in accordance with their laws. Are there any comments before we vote?"

Flynn stood. "I have an issue with page thirty-seven, second paragraph. There's no clear definition of what's considered a breach, or proof of such. As it's currently written, I could claim I saw you wave your hat over the border, and the Source would have grounds to extradite you until my claim was proven out. It doesn't give a timetable for a trial, nor does it state when or if you'd be returned after a verdict was rendered. I don't think anyone could vote on this in good conscience with such glaring omissions."

There was a rumble of manufactured consternation. He sat, trying not to roll his eyes. Their feigned ignorance was appalling, and Julia was fucking pissed he'd called them on it. What the hell did she have on all of them?

The clamor gradually died down, and Riggs scanned the room. "Shall we take a vote to see if it has enough steam to pass?" The room resoundingly voted to let the measure die.

"Next, we have a proposal to authorize a lawsuit against the Source, on the grounds that they've abducted citizens of Glynfyls, violating several treaties." There was a rush of voices. Cal had sent the proposal out yesterday for review, along with the sanctions Markham and Romley had drawn up.

Kris's father was the first to stand. He was furious, clenching at the rail in front of him. "I vote in favor, and swear to God, if anyone stands in the way of it, I'll—"

His son, Mat, pulled him back to his seat, trying to calm him. He looked around the room defiantly. The older man had begun to weep. "House Wright supports the proposal as written."

The speaker nodded, clearing his throat to call up a vote.

"I'm against it." Julia stood, flipping through the pages. "Nowhere in this does it name any witnesses. Who are we to believe was able to get in and out of the Source, recognize Mistress Wright, and discern her alleged condition? It seems farfetched."

"That's standard practice in lawsuits of this nature for the witness's protection, Mistress Cree," Lord Merchant said from the back of the room.

"Well, I for one am not comfortable voting on such a serious measure without more information, especially when it's co-sponsored by a man with such an extensive criminal record. I'm calling for ratification by Quorum."

Shit. Julia's smug look challenged Flynn to deny it, and he fucking couldn't. The hall went silent for half a breath, then broke into chaos. Several pages ran from the room.

Riggs banged his gavel for order. "Would you like to address Mistress Cree's allegations, Lord Scot?"

Not in the fucking slightest. Flynn stood, jamming his hands into his pockets, the room fixating on him. He took a deep breath and tried to sound calmer than he felt.

"My past is a matter of public record. All of you are aware of how I comported myself before I left. Outside was less forgiving than the North." He rocked back on his heels, staring at Julia. "None of which changes the fact that the Source has been kidnapping our people and breeding them without consent. Merchant's proposal is a good one, which is why I cosponsored it. If you need to take my name off to pass it, then do it. There's no reason this needs to go to Quorum."

"But being a felon certainly speaks to your credibility, now doesn't it?"

He shrugged. "I doubt having a paper trail of my exploits radically changes anyone's perception of me." Flynn tried not to wince. That might be true, but it sure as fuck was gonna curtail his public support.

She shook the thick stack at him. "Public drunkenness, assault and battery, resisting arrest, soliciting a prostitute—"

"Again, nothing I hadn't done up here, I just didn't have anyone to bail me out."

Unable to refute him on that point, her tone became conciliatory. "I suppose you're right. We all know you're a violent sot and a lecher, but I hadn't taken you for a thief."

He'd never been picked up for that.

"I'm not sure what you're referring to," he said more sharply than intended.

She flipped through the pages, perusing them idly. Similar packets were being distributed to every sitting member.

Shit.

Flynn grabbed one, grimacing as he thumbed through it. Christ, she even had his prison medical records—"You can expect to be contacted by my lawyers for distributing this." Sue her? He was going to fucking ruin her.

She didn't seem particularly concerned. "I have it on excellent authority that you spent a great deal of your time Outside stealing cars for the Fuil."

"That right?" Flynn laughed. "I'd be very curious to know where you heard that. Perhaps from the same people who reported seeing me on a beach in Mauri. Seven years ago, I was injured in a prison riot so badly I couldn't get out of bed for a year. I can assure you the experience went a long way towards setting me on the straight and narrow."

"Answer the question, Laughlin. Have you ever stolen a car?"

"Yeah, when I was sixteen with you, Jacques, and Agnes Birch."

Jacques groaned and someone laughed. Julia looked confused, shaking her head as if to clear it. "You know that's not what I'm referring to," she huffed, trying to regain momentum. "You showed up at a trauma clinic in Greyburn last year beaten within an inch of your life. I suppose that had nothing to do with running afoul of them?"

Flynn ducked his head, forcing a smirk onto his face. "That resulted from trying to end a romantic relationship."

Julia scoffed and threw several photos into the middle of the floor. "You honestly expect us to believe a woman did that?"

Flynn ran a hand through his hair. The photos were extremely graphic. He slammed down the lid on his temper, his jaw tight. Looking away, he cleared his throat. "The knife work and the brand, yeah. The rest of it was her brother and a metal pipe."

The Assembly was silent. Julia's fingers whitened on the railing in front of her, eyes blazing, ready to go for his jugular.

"I think that's quite enough," Riggs snapped, incensed. "Lord Scot isn't on trial here. Dissemination of such intensely personal material is in extremely poor taste and violates the standards set for Assembly conduct. Shame on you, Mistress Cree, I myself will write you up for censure." Flynn looked at the kindly old man in surprise, and he wasn't the only one. Riggs doddered on, unperturbed. "I'm bringing the proposed lawsuit against the Source up for vote. Ayes? Nays? Abstain?"

The measure barely eked by, the support Flynn had enjoyed earlier in the day all but gone. The sanctions, which he deemed the more important of the two proposals, would never pass.

Shit. Cal had been right, he should've prepared for this better, though he hadn't a fucking clue how. Hearsay and speculation about his past was one thing, but having proof of all the shady shit he'd done after the scandal that'd driven him out of the city…

Every single one of these sanctimonious assholes was gonna blacklist him on principle.

The speaker banged his gavel, trying to call for order, but the damage was done. Giving up, Riggs called a half-hour recess and was immediately accosted by the Firsts of each line. Flynn tilted his head back, looking at the ceiling. Frolicking angels. He'd always hated that fresco.

Pages ran around the room with missives as members broke into animated groups. Behind him, Lot swore, thumbing through the photos. Flynn braced himself for the vitriol about to spew from the man. Wouldn't be the first time his father had eviscerated him in public. Flynn's hand reflexively floated up to his breast pocket, where he used to keep his flask. He rubbed at his chest, feeling its lack. Jesus Christ, he wanted a drink.

"What a goddamned mess." Lot slapped the pages down in disgust, got up, and left. Flynn's gaze dropped to his boots. At least that'd gone better than expected, though he was sure he'd hear about it later.

"You have to explain this one to me, Laughlin. Why exactly did you get into an altercation over chicken wings?" Klaus asked too loudly, making his way down the steps and leafing through the pages.

"Asshole kept snagging my flats."

The man laughed, delighted. Flynn stood. Blacklisted or not, he wasn't gonna let that bitch run him out of here, and he really needed a fucking cup of coffee.

Klaus followed him to the lounge. "All of this, whores, gambling... I'd say you were doing someone's bully work as well. Are you very sure you don't want to reconnect with the old crew?" The crowd around them was silent, not bothering to hide their interest.

Flynn took a sip of coffee, feeling steadier with the cup in his hands. Christ, fuck all of 'em. "You even know what all that is?" he asked, flicking the packet. "It's a hard earned lesson that cost way too much and took way too long to learn. Now that I have, I'm not gonna forget it."

Klaus rolled his eyes. "How riveting. Personal growth and all that. I can only hope that your epiphany included the importance of settling your debts." He pulled a piece of paper from his pocket and offered it to him with his first two fingers.

Flynn snatched it, glowering. Scanning the page, he snorted. Jesus fucking Christ. "Since when are you Gerrard's bill collector?"

"I'm his partner, actually," Klaus said with a coy smile. "Not too long after you took to your heels, I bought into the Pony. He was planning on speaking to you personally, but since your schedule hasn't allowed for a visit, I offered to do the job."

"The interest is astronomical."

"It's been outstanding for some time. We're open to making other arrangements." Klaus moved a ring over his knuckle suggestively. He grinned at the look Flynn gave him. "I tease. You're no fun anymore."

"So I've heard."

"Gerrard mentioned something about a bout."

Flynn's expression hardened. "I'll have the amount sent over later today."

"As you say, Lord Scot, but it's a shame...and not as if you had to keep up appearances any longer. I can assure you that after the initial shock wears off, being outed is quite liberating." He ran his eyes over him, then gave a mocking bow and left.

Flynn shoved the paper into his pocket. Everywhere he turned, his past was oozing out the crevices of this goddamned city. It was never gonna leave him alone. He ran a hand through his hair, feeling it stick out at odd angles. Christ, he couldn't catch a break.

A hand was at his elbow and he turned, trying to keep a neutral expression.

"You weren't kidding about the cars." Phyllis murmured, reaching up to smooth his hair. He batted her hand away, taking another cup of coffee. She sighed. "Oh, Laughlin. You poor boy."

What the hell? He didn't want her goddamned sympathy. "I did what I did, and I paid for it, Phyllis. As far as I'm concerned, my slate Outside's clean. It's up here that concerns me more."

"It should. We've gotten Riggs to suspend the remaining measures on the docket until Monday, but had to concede to the vote on the sanctions being taken up by Quorum. You've got forty-eight hours to win over your line and ascend to First. If you can't, we lose Crandall's support, and it all falls to her."

Flynn's stomach cramped. Forget the fingers at the rug beneath him, they'd gathered up solid fistfuls and were ready to yank it away. "I've scheduled a dinner with my line tomorrow night." What a shit show that was gonna be. He met Crandall's eye across the room.

The motherfucker tipped his hat.

"Wonderful to hear." Phyllis beamed. "I have complete faith in you, Laughlin. After all, you're Deirdre's son."

Flynn sighed, put his empty cup on a passing servant's tray, and headed to the gate.

***

CAL PUSHED BACK in his chair as Flynn slunk into his office, dragging his dick in the dirt. No doubt about it, he knew he'd fucked up. "Rough day?"

"Sure you already got an earful."

He wasn't wrong about that, though all things considered, it was less of one than Cal'd expected. "You might be surprised." He tossed a cigarette at him and started rolling another.

Flynn snorted and sat down, mussing his hair. Boy looked like a hedgehog. "She outed me."

"I saw." He motioned to a packet of papers on his desk. "Didn't know a man could get that carved up and live to tell about it once, never mind twice. That was what you looked like when you picked Kara up?"

Smiling, Flynn exhaled a fitful stream of smoke, waving out a match. "Yeah."

"You must talk one hell of a game."

"I don't know that I said much at all."

"You tell her about this?"

"Enough."

"And tomorrow?"

Flynn tipped his head back, counting ceiling tiles like he always did when he was trying to figure out how to dance around an answer. "We eat, for all the good it'll do. I didn't have enough support to move for First before this, but no one else did either, and with Jacques' pledge, and Charles being Charles, there's no other choice unless we remain without one."

French came in with a coffee service, and the boy gladly took a cup. They sat smoking, mulling over Flynn's chances. They weren't good.

"Fuck, even if she hadn't laid it all out, I don't see how I can take it. With Leeds, Morris, Gent, and Glass against me…one of them has to flip for me to get enough votes, and as it stands, all of them will block me just to be fucking spiteful, especially after this shit."

Cal grunted in agreement. If Julia hadn't prematurely benched Lot, they would've had time to gain support. He kicked himself for not believing the man was capable of eating enough crow to draw up that damn agreement with House Glass.

"It'll be what it'll be, I suggest you start praying Julia's call for a Quorum vote's enough to put the fear of God into one of them. Meantime, here are the updated terms Markham and Romley want." Cal pushed a massive folder over to him. "CliffsNotes are up top. Long story short, it's a damn fine deal."

Flynn sighed, flipping it open. His eyes widened at the note clipped to the top page. "What? Why the hell do they still want me to co-sponsor it?"

"Use your head, boy. Despite today's debacle, you're seen as the opposition to what's been going on up here. If anything, her running your name through the mud's only legitimized you as a threat to her power. You're being set up as a figurehead."

"More like a sacrificial lamb."

"Choice is yours, but I'd suggest grasping the reins they're handing you. Dinner's a good start. You get the line under you, and you'll be able to start limiting her power. Until then, Titus is gonna use her to push us into a war, and the prize he has his eye on is upstairs."

The boy bristled, the last of his cigarette crackling. He blew out a stream of smoke and flicked the butt into the fire. "Even if I somehow manage to pull this outta my ass, taking First is the last fucking thing I wanna do…"

Cal could hear the "but" and Flynn glared at him, knowing he was right, though he'd be damned before he said it. Sitting in the Assembly this past week would've shown him that there wasn't anyone else to do the job. To protect Kara, and the rest of Glynfyls by default, he had to be that man. Cal reached over and poured himself a scotch. Flynn watched the bottle intently, running a hand over his mouth.

"Neutralizing her will create a power vacuum. You're gonna need to step into it. If I was a betting man, I'd say Titus made a Hail Mary, and it fell flat with the abeyance and that bullshit about Original Houses. It's not a mistake he'll make twice. There anything else they can pin on you?"

"Shit, that reminds me." Flynn pulled a piece of paper from his pocket and tossed it on the desk.

Cal gave him a look and picked it up. "That's a tidy sum. It legit?"

"Probably."

"I'll send it by courier and have done… It is done?"

"As far as I'm concerned."

"Well, I suspect that's half of it. I've put Merchant on retainer, and I'm having him look into where we stand legally with this whole mess. Don't plan on sleeping in tomorrow, he'll be here around eight. Now, answer the goddamn question, Flynn. Is there anything else they can pin on you?"

He stood, not meeting Cal's eye. "How the fuck would I know what they're gonna do?" Jamming his hands in his pocket, he left.

That'd been a yes.

CHAPTER ELEVEN

rung [ruhng] noun

1. *Ascribed level in the hierarchy for each individual Breaker.*
2. *One of the concentric rings of streets making up the city of Glynfyls*

– Excerpt from Glynfyls: A History

"The North's rigid adherence to strict social forms and rigid traditions stems from a visceral need to preserve a culture under constant attack from those that would see its demise. After narrowly surviving annihilation not once, but thrice, the codes have become ever more important, serving as the common thread between six very different subcultures..."

– Lord Talos, Preceptor of History,
Academy of Glynfyls

KARA SAT PROPPED up in bed, feeling like she was about to hold court. Lady Martin had been insistent on seeing her, and she wasn't looking forward to it. The last thing she wanted to do was match wits with a Finder after Jon's battery of vials and swabs. Kara sighed. At least the fitting earlier with Reggie had gone well.

That had been more fun than she'd had in ages. She smiled, playing with the end of her braid and watching a pair of servants put away the last of what she'd taken "off the rack." Audrey's disapproving air over most of it hadn't stopped Kara from truly enjoying the designer's company as they went through the obscene amount of clothing she'd brought. Kara's smile grew, feeling like she might've even made a friend. It was a bizarre concept, but she'd never laughed like that with one of her peers before. Reggie's easy manner had been a welcome distraction from the tempest of emotion coming from Flynn. He'd thrown that damned block up again, but what was oozing past put Kara's stomach in a knot, and it didn't need any help.

There was a knock at the door, and Audrey came in with Lady Beangela Martin on her heels. The willowy red-haired woman was several years older than Kara, and had seemed fragile in every sense of the word until she'd met her eyes. Those were as fierce as yesterday, but the rest of her was wraith-like, her bones prominent beneath the translucence of her skin. The pale confection of silk and lace floating ethereally about her only added to the impression that she was fading along with the fix Kara had unmade.

Audrey led her to the small table set up at Kara's bedside and began to pour tea.

The elfin woman's brow creased as she looked Kara over, and she was sure hers was doing the same. "I'm sorry to bother you, but I couldn't go another moment..." She put a hand to her abdomen, the swell of it clearly visible beneath her billowy gown, like the rest of her had been sucked into it. "What you've done for House Martin, for Jacques and I... I can't thank you enough. He's offered Laughlin our fealty, and as staggering as that is, it's a man's thanks. I would offer you a woman's coin." She took the cup Audrey proffered and sat with it steaming, seemingly indecisive for all her adamance that this meeting couldn't wait.

"People always tell me I'm too blunt, but if I were in your position, I'd want to know."

Audrey opened her mouth, and Bea's pale hand flicked up, silencing her. The secretary bowed her head, deferring to the woman. Kara started to sweat.

"House Scot is doing you a disservice, however well intended. Before our initial meeting, I was asked not to broach certain subjects. Distasteful as they are, I agreed, but if Laughlin won't tell you, better it comes from someone who doesn't wish to cause you hurt or public humiliation. There are plenty of women that do after you've plucked the richest heir in Glynfyls from under their noses. More than one of them has increased their family's fortunes by exploiting his appetites and hope to do so again, if not as his wife, then as his mistress."

Kara grit her teeth against the flash of rage slicing through her, pushing Flynn's concern away. "We've spoken about it. That's not the man I know."

Bea eyed the scarf at Kara's throat. "I'd say you know that man rather intimately." She gave her head a little shake, a sad smile ghosting across her lips. "Everyone's always liked Laughlin, despite his exploits. Maybe even sometimes because of them. He's always been so charming, you just couldn't help it...until Deirdre died." She and Audrey exchanged a glance, the secretary's expression pained.

"Whether he's still a drunk and a lecher is up for debate, though from what Jacques says, I'm inclined to believe he's changed. Regardless, his past is being dredged up to weaken his claim for First, and you're being dragged through the midden with him. Your suspected origins only give them further ammunition. Women from the Source are viewed—"

"As whores," Kara finished, taking petty pleasure in making her color. Audrey looked like she was about to swallow her teeth. "And if I deny it, I suspect it would just make everyone all the more certain it's true."

"I would've put it somewhat more delicately, but yes, and if you want to get down to brass tacks, whatever occurred on your dining room table hasn't done you any favors."

Kara laughed, startling the two women. Ugh, it was like she was right back in the Creche. She let that bundle of old, wasted emotion wash over her as it unpacked itself from her psyche. All it served to do now was make her angry and a little sad. North, South, it was all the same.

"I appreciate your candor, but it could've waited. What's so important that you had to come today?"

Bea's steel-grey eyes measured her, and Kara fought the urge to pull up a whisper of 'lust. Her sense of Flynn abruptly strengthened, and the desire passed. She tried not to stare at the door over Bea's sharp shoulder.

"Other than doing what I can to sway opinion, after you're Introduced, I'll host a luncheon to bring you into society. It will show you have allies up here that aren't inconsequential—but make no mistake, Julia Cree is your enemy. I came to warn you that this dinner tomorrow night is crucial to Laughlin's success. Not a whisper of scandal can sound until they hold the vote. Until then, you need to be wary. Everything you do here will get back to the city one way or another, and Julia will use it against you. Your choice of couturier—" A soft beeping came from Bea's purse, and she frowned.

"I'm sorry, I'm supposed to take these supplements on a strict schedule… May I use your powder room?"

"Of course, Audrey, would you…?" The secretary was only too happy to usher Bea out.

A crash and Flynn's laugh sounded in the hall as the door opened. He came in carrying a basket with a ridiculously massive green bow. Small furry animals were spilling out of it, mewling pathetically. He deposited it at the foot of the bed and started picking kittens off his jacket, pulling the last from his pocket. He dropped the stripy little grey creature into her lap.

"You need to watch that one, he's sneaky."

Kara laughed at his wide grin, picking the kitten up and watching the others totter across the bed. Meow was a sleek thing with different colored splotches. She seemed quite content to lie in the basket while her brood escaped to cause mayhem. Kara turned to find Flynn looking at her with an odd expression.

"What?"

"Nothing, I just…" He dipped his head to kiss her. His fingers traced the curve of her cheek, and she pressed it to his palm.

"I missed you, too. You're back early, worried I wasn't following doctor's orders?" He got another funny look on his face, his emotions firmly blocked. She raised an eyebrow as he ran a hand through his hair.

"Ah…no. Nothing like that, Kara, I—"

"Kittens! Oh, they're so darling!"

He stood back from the bed and made a quick bow, shooting Kara a look. She shrugged. He hadn't given her enough time to tell him Bea was here, or prepare him for her appearance. He was as shocked as she had been. The woman scooped up a fluffy orange kitten that had escaped to the floor and held it to her nose. Did cats smell?

"Oh, you're so lucky, you've no idea how many times I've wished Jacques wasn't allergic!" She cuddled it against her cheek for a moment longer, then kissed the little thing between its ears and put it back in the basket. Her eyes traveled from Flynn to the clock on the bedside table. "I should go, but we'll talk soon about that luncheon." She was across the room and out the door before either of them could say another word, Audrey in her wake.

"Well, that was abrupt."

"Finders." Flynn snorted, sitting down on the bed and untying his cravat. "Luncheon?"

Kara put the grey kitten up to her nose. Oh, they did smell good. "To introduce me into society…as a thanks. Jacques offered you fealty. What does that mean?"

"It means we get House Martin's vote in Assembly, but if anyone threatens them, we're obligated to respond. It makes us responsible for them. Cal's fucking tickled about it." He chucked the bunch of navy silk onto the bedside table.

"So nothing good will come from it." He laughed and pulled off his jacket, his waistcoat following it. "You're not going back to Assembly?"

"Nope." He tossed his cufflinks onto the bureau and bounced down next to her, scattering the few remaining cats on the bed.

"Why, what happened?"

"Why does something have to happen? Maybe I just thought being here with you was more important." He picked up one of the kittens and started making faces at it, ignoring the fact she was looking at him like he was an idiot. A ridiculously appealing idiot, but still.

"Are you used to women just believing whatever load of crap falls out of your mouth?"

"Uh, yeah, for the most part." He rolled over and kissed her, then gazed into her eyes. Those blue motes churned hypnotically, throwing her off. Jerk did that on purpose.

"What are they?"

"What?"

"The blue. No one else up here has that."

His expression became guarded, and he shrugged. "My mom did."

"Why don't you talk about her?"

"I don't want to."

"Then tell me about Assembly."

"What if I have more important things to do with my lips?"

She laughed as he kissed up under her ear. "Wow, that bad, huh?"

"It wasn't good." There were inverse paw prints across the canopy above, and she giggled. How did it get up there? Flynn followed her gaze. "Bet that's the grey one."

"Bea said Julia's dredging up your past to discredit you."

Flynn rolled onto his back, tracking the kitten's progress. "I've done a lot of bad shit, Kara. Today a bunch of it came out."

"Is it going to hurt your chances for First?"

He shot her a bemused look. "I doubt it's gonna help. Why the sudden interest?" There was the sound of claws snagging fabric and an irate mewling. Flynn stood up and rescued it. It was the grey one. "Told you. He's my favorite."

"I've nothing else to do but wonder what you do all day, and of course you like the rotten one. Why would me hiring Reggie create a scandal?"

He held the little thing up to his face. It hissed, taking a swipe at him. "Aww, no, he's just misunderstood. I don't know about Regina, other than it's a mess for Cal, and you're not missing anything at Assembly, trust me."

"I'm missing you."

He sighed, sitting down and pulling her against his chest. "I miss you too." The kitten attacked his hand, and he put it on its back, scritching its tummy. "My mom used to call the blue specks pieces of her soul."

"They remind me of a kaleidovid." Her fingers slid between the buttons on his shirt, the kitten following their movement intently. She smiled. Its eyes were as big as Audrey's.

"What the hell's that?"

She laughed. "It's like a blooming light show in the psychpods. It's used to combat psychosis in some of the Breakers after maneuvers."

"I always thought they looked like a lava lamp." He dangled the end of her braid at the kitten.

"A what?" She flinched as the little thing lunged at her. "Stop that!"

Flynn laughed. "It's a tube with liquids of different densities heated by a filament. It makes these colored blobs that rise and fall. I used to have one around here somewhere. They're cool." He got up and put the kittens he could find back into their basket, moving it over to the sitting area by the hearth. She watched him kick off his boots and come back to bed.

"You're really staying?" Her arms floated up around his neck, and his lips found hers.

"Yeah."

"Then I need you to let Reggie take your measurements for your suit," He made a noise that could've been agreement, and she laughed. "Promise me, Flynn."

He nibbled at her lobe, his hand on her breast. "I'll promise you anything right now."

"I feel like I should ask for something big," she murmured, unbuttoning his shirt.

"Oh, I can give you something big."

Kara laughed, smacking him. "Can you now?"

"Mmm." He undid the knot in her scarf, letting it fall away and kissed the mark he'd left. It ached beneath his lips, his fingers busy at the ties to her blouse. "You still feel me, baby?"

She arched against him, fingers tangling in his hair. "Yes, but I'd like to feel you again."

"I can do that." He pulled her blouse over her head and threw it to the side, hand moving to cup her breast, pinching her gently through the lace of her bra. "You're so damned beautiful, Kara."

His lips were on hers, his shirt sliding back over his shoulders to join the one on the floor, her hands at his belt. His thumb glossed over her hipbone, and she shivered with pleasure as he stroked over a bruise from yesterday.

"You like that?" he murmured, nipping at her. "The reminders of what I do to you? I've been thinking about fucking you on that table all day…"

"So have I, and I've got some ideas about what I'd like to do to you now." She pushed him over, and he grinned, propping himself up half-inclined against the pillows. Eyes hungrily watching her run a hand down his torso to tease through the line of short curls leading lower. "Especially after hearing about all your would-be mistresses."

He snorted, raising his hips so she could pull off his pants. "You've got nothing to worry about."

Kara dropped them off the side of the bed, along with her own, and snagged his discarded cravat from the bedside table. "Oh, I didn't say I was worried…but they should be." She straddled him, doubling the length of silk upon itself and twisting it taught between her fists.

His pupils dilated, Adam's apple bobbing as he wet his lips. "Yeah?"

"Yeah." She smiled, leaning over to press the fabric tight against his throat. "I'm not very good at sharing." She roped it around his neck and threaded the ends through the loop, leashing him. He groaned, his cock kicking at the dampness between her legs. "You're mine, Laughlin Scot, " she whispered, brushing her lips across his and tugging the leash tight.

"Show me," he murmured back, caging her hips. She rocked above him, slicking him with her desire, a sly smile flitting over her lips. She moved down his body, tongue tracing the contours of his skin, traveling down his throat, past his collar bone, and pausing to flick at his nipple. Hands smoothing over the broad expanse of his shoulders, pecs, and abs. Inhaling along the ridge of his Adonis belt to where it V'ed, her cheek brushing the length of him.

That blackness rising inside of her, throbbing. A dark heat enflaming her core.

Glory, she wanted to make him hurt.

"Goddamn, Kara. You smell so fucking good…" Flynn groaned, hands in her hair, his legs spreading to let her kneel between them. She cupped his sac, thumb gently swirling, her tongue running the length of him to its salty-sweet tip. Tugging his leash tight, her nails scraped down the inside of his thigh as she took him into her mouth. Her throat.

Swallowing him whole.

His back arched with a low moan, fingers tightening in her hair. Their bond thrumming with lust. "Fuck, baby… you suck my cock so good…Jesus…"

Kara bobbed above him, relishing his groans of pleasure, feeling it as if it were her own, their shared passion stoking a violent need within her. His cock thickened, growing impossibly hard, his breath speeding, balls drawing up—

"No." She was atop him, leash taut, her palm catching him across the face. He rocked back, licking at his split lip, eyes blazing with carnality.

"No?" he growled with a feral smile.

"No." She arched an eyebrow in challenge. "I didn't say you could come."

His 'lust coiled around them, a heady spice of dark desire, and hers rose to meet it. Flynn's nostrils flared, and he laughed, licking at his lip again—

—and she was on her back, his weight pinning her down. The darkness in her rose up, calling for his blood, his pain… Glory, she wanted to bathe in it, to hear him scream—

His lips dusted over hers, his kisses so soft… "Goddamn, baby." He met her eyes, the emotion in them saying what he wouldn't.

He loved her.

The blackness retreated, slowly ebbing away. How could she have ever thought of hurting him? Her brow furrowed. "I love you too, Flynn."

He smiled, nudging her thighs wider with his. "And I need to make good on a promise. What was that you wanted again, something big?"

Forcing a smile, she ran her fingers through his hair and asked for the moon.

"WHAT DO you mean he sent it back?" Flynn growled around his cigarette.

"Just that," Cal said, waving at the bank note on his desk.

Flynn scratched his jaw, grimacing. Fuck. That asshole Gerrard would make this as painful as fucking possible. He looked up at those damn ceiling tiles, trying to figure out his next move.

"How's Kara?" Cal poured himself a scotch and sat back, smoking.

Flynn turned one of the smoldering cylinders between his fingers. "You actually give a shit, or you worried about one of your milestones not being met?" His grandfather raised an eyebrow, and Flynn snorted. "She's in the gym. Jon came by with the supplements he wants her on and the damn things jumpstarted her. You could've given me a heads up she's terrified of needles."

"Thought she outgrew that."

"She was probably binding it up with everything else she went through down in that hellhole. You know, you're a piece of shit."

"Tell me how you really feel."

"She's a fucking mess."

"You just said Jon's got her sorted—"

"I'm not just talking about the kid, Cal. She needs time to wrap her head around all of this shit. Christ, we both do. I get why I have to step up, but you can't expect—"

"What? You rather be up there waiting at her bedside?"

"Yeah, no fucking contest."

Cal snorted, ignoring the boot heels striking like bullets down the hall. Flynn groaned. Shit. Why the hell was Miriam on the warpath?

His grandfather pulled out his pouch with a little shake of his head. "Unbelievable. Look, you've got more important things to do than play nursemaid—"

"Did you speak to him?" Miriam clipped out, storming into the room.

"I was warming up to it." Cal sat back and started rolling another cigarette. Should've been fucking popcorn. Flynn sucked down another lungful of smoke, feeling the burn at the back of his throat.

Miriam clucked her tongue and glared at him, hands on her hips. "Laughlin, how could you?! First Father Benson, now Luann... She's one of my oldest friends!" He started counting ceiling tiles. "And, this, what is this? Smoking!"

"Firing Luann wasn't my call, but I'm sure as hell not heartbroken over it, and Christ, Miriam, I'm thirty-five years old. If I wanna smoke, I'm gonna smoke. Trust me, it's not the worst thing I've put in my mouth." He took another drag just to piss her off, and she held a handkerchief to her nose, coloring. She switched her glare to Cal like he was to blame.

The old man tried to hide a smile as he lit up. "Probably doesn't help that woman's been throwing herself at him since he hit puberty. Sure Kara wasn't amused."

"Why I can't imagine—Smoking's a disgusting, filthy habit." Miriam snapped her hankie through the air. "And as if the lawsuit wasn't bad enough, honestly, Regina Glass! What she considers designs are scandalous, and for something as important as an Introduction gown! Sakes alive, people still bring up mine in conversation, and Lady Biswert told me Regina's only client's some sultan in the Deep South; everything he buys is for his harem! No self-respecting Talent would be seen dead in her clothes—Lord help me, Laughlin James, her poor excuse for a studio's barely on the fourth rung!"

Shit, he guessed that answered Kara's question. A smile tipped up his lips, imagining her dressed as a harem girl.

"Careful Miriam, your halos are showing," Cal chuckled, pouring himself a scotch. She blushed and flicked her handkerchief at him.

"I'm not gonna tell her what to wear," Flynn sighed, hoping that would be the end of it. Wasn't fucking likely, but he could hope. "Reggie's stuff looks good."

"Oh, like you'd know." Miriam coughed. "How you stand

marinating in this… With Kara feeling better, and Jon on the mend, I'd like to have a real Meddleton dinner tonight. We need to discuss the Introduction. The font for the monogram—"

French cleared his throat in the doorway. "Forgive the intrusion, sir, but Lord Martin is in the east drawing room, and he's rather anxious. If you have a moment to spare for him?"

Flynn laughed. No fucking contest there, either. He flicked his butt into the hearth and gave Miriam a peck on the cheek, her nose crinkling.

"Six sharp, and *properly* dressed, Laughlin!"

He rolled his eyes, going to see what the next crisis was. Jacques was right where French had said he'd be, and the man looked like shit.

"Jesus Christ, can I get you anything?"

"I'll take a glass of whiskey, if you don't mind." Jacques dropped his hat onto the settee and himself beside it. Flynn went to the sideboard and poured him a stiff drink.

The man downed it and held the glass out for another.

"Bea has decided she can't abide the smell of alcohol, and it's all been relegated to the cellars. After the day I've had, I'll owe you a bottle." He took the refilled glass and slouched listlessly against the cushions.

Shit, he wasn't joking. "What's up?" Flynn asked, setting the bottle on the table in front of him.

"Well, you'll be happy to know that despite Julia's disclosure, your stance in Assembly has won quite a few of our line over…but I'm sure I don't need to tell you who isn't budging."

"Those three assholes, and Glass would've opposed me even if I'd come back Sainted."

Jacques snorted into his glass, throwing back the last of it.

"If you still hold your liquor like you used to, I'd suggest you slow down."

The other man gave a slightly hysterical laugh and ruffled his curls. "You've got a point. Christ, Flynn. I'm not here about our line. We saw Alice this morning. She sees Bea's pregnancy progressing rapidly and expects her to give birth within the next two weeks. They've scheduled putting in a feeding tube. She can't eat fast enough to keep up with the baby's growth."

"I wondered… She was here earlier to see Kara. Did Alice say they'd be all right?"

Jacques nodded, his cheeks wet. "They both should pull through, but to see the fade… God, I feel like I'm to blame." He dashed a sleeve across his face. "I'm sorry to burden you with this, but Charles…you know how he gets."

"Yeah, he's a dick." Man did emotion about as well as a bulldozer.

Jacques sniffed loudly, pulling out a pocket square. "It's good to have you back. Someday you'll understand. Soon, I should think."

Flynn chewed his lip, looking at the man that'd been his best friend for most of his life, hoping he could call him that again. "Kara was bred when I brought her up."

Jacques smiled broadly. "Then you *do* know. My God, Flynn, no wonder she was so affected using her talent—what her halos must be like!" He laughed and raised his glass at him. Flynn grinned at the gaffe, the man still couldn't hold his liquor. "That's why you're not in the Deep South."

"Yeah, it wasn't an option."

"So why not just say that? It would sway a large part of those opposing your claim, there's more than one of the older lords that doubt you've found your equal. The younger ones just doubt your ability in general."

Flynn shrugged, not in the habit of whipping it out just to satisfy curiosity. They all could wait for the Introduction. "I won't risk disclosing unless absolutely necessary. Cal thinks that as soon as it gets out she's bred, the Source will try for her."

"Then I won't say anything, as one father to another." They both shared a smile. "You leave that car of yours down at the farm?"

Flynn walked over to the sideboard and rummaged around for one of Cal's pouches. He rolled a perfectly fine cigarette when the old man wasn't critiquing him. "I wish. I haven't seen it in years. Lost it in a card game after I left." He struck a match, frowning as he inhaled.

"Your face tells me the flavor of those nasty little things hasn't improved in the last twenty years," Jacques laughed.

"No, it has not. Beggars can't be choosers, I guess."

"You do realize you're the richest man in the Northern Territories?"

Flynn snorted, blowing out a cloud of smoke. "No. It's not the easiest thing coming back to all this after so long. Last week I was lucky to find indoor plumbing. Today, I can hire a guy to cheerfully wipe my ass. It's surreal."

Jacques poured another finger of whiskey into his glass and sat back. "Give me a drag of that. Shame about the car."

"It is at that." Flynn passed him the cigarette. "Well, I know where it is, or was. I suspect I could try to buy it back."

"It'll never be the same. You're better off finding another burnt out frame to restore. Damn, these do taste like shit."

Flynn yelled over his shoulder for French.

The butler was there in less than a minute. "Sir?"

"Can you get us a couple of cigars, some coffee, and Jacques is gonna need to put something in his stomach before he leaves." French left to see it done, and Flynn sank back into his chair. Jacques was probably right about the car.

"S'good t'be the king," he slurred.

Flynn frowned, flicking his cigarette into the hearth. Said no king, ever.

TITUS THREW BACK a handful of pills, swiping through reports. These damned headaches… He attributed them entirely to the fact that his progress in the North was not proceeding as anticipated. Laughlin Scot was proving to be far more competent than previously assumed and charismatic to boot. The combination was giving him a decided edge against Julia. Titus was no longer convinced the boy's rap sheet was enough to curb his influence, but there had to be something…

He pulled up a grainy reel of the Assembly's chambers, reviewing Scot's previous performances. It didn't take long for a smile to slide across Titus's lips.

There…and there again.

It was subtle, but whenever Kara Jester's character was impugned,

Scot was a textbook example of a Breaker struggling to contain his bloodlust. Titus's smile grew. The genetics that boy must have… He couldn't help but salivate at their potential military applications.

A new approach was needed. The girl was obviously Scot's Achilles heel. Striking at her credibility would undermine his, and Titus had the perfect tool for the job. He left his office, collecting Shriver on the way. A veteran of Titus's stable, the Binder was exceptional at balancing his patients on that knife's edge of exquisite agony without allowing them the release of oblivion.

Ielle was right where Titus had left her, sporadically convulsing on the leather-clad mattress of his correction room. The artistry of her condition against the backdrop of chains and flails was evocative of Doré's *Arachne in Purgatory*. Fitting. She thought far too highly of her skills, considerable though they may be.

"Heal her just enough for her to appreciate her current state," he instructed Shriver, taking a glass of bourbon from a sub. Ielle needed to learn when to leash that wicked little tongue of hers, and the price of a good education was steep.

After several long moments, Shriver stepped back at Ielle's faint sobbing. Titus sipped at his bourbon, leisurely stripping off his clothes. The raptness of Ielle's attention on the minutia of his movements amused him. He shrugged into a thick robe and freed one of her hands from the iron headboard's leather restraints. She left it where it fell, waiting for permission to move.

Excellent.

"Would you like to finish untying yourself?"

She took a shuddering breath. "Would that please you?"

"Yes, I believe it would." He smiled, enjoying her ensuing struggle. It didn't take long for her to discover the futility of her attempts. Titus stroked her hair as she lay weeping. "Do you understand the importance of following my instructions to the letter, poppet?"

Her breathing was ragged. "Yes, sir."

"Good girl." He brushed an ebony lock from her cheek and motioned for Shriver to finish the job. The Binder's halos flared, and he left the room.

Ielle didn't move, watching Titus warily. He called for another bourbon, settling himself against the bolster beside her. She'd become adept at pleasing him, but harvesting that foul city would please him more, and he needed his cell seeded with those bots.

"I've plans for you, poppet, and it's crucial that you heed me carefully. I'm sending you to Glynfyls. I've some men I'd like you to service, and then you're to make contact with Julia. I want the Scot boy ruined. Use what you know about Kara to undermine him. She's his weakness. Exploit it."

Ielle moistened her lips. Far too eager.

"Your job is solely to instigate Scot's temper by exercising that vicious little tongue of yours and naught else. Other arrangements have been made for the girl." Ielle rolled her eyes, and Titus had to smile at her spirit. He looked forward to snuffing it.

"And my pet?" she asked, unaware of Riegel's release.

"Do as you're told, and perhaps you'll get the opportunity to play with him again." She pouted prettily, and he thought of several better uses for her lips. "Heel."

Ielle knelt before him, her face a careful blank. He'd instilled that lesson early on.

"Perform."

She moved his robe aside, taking his cock in her hand. The retracted metal studs along the length of him glistened in the flickering plaz lights. Another eager smile flitted across her lips.

Pity. He would miss her appetites. Titus's eyes closed as she bent over him, planning on enjoying her thoroughly before she left.

CHAPTER TWELVE

majority payout [məˈjôrədē ˈpāˌout] noun

1. *Funds and/or property deeded to a scion of an Original House at birth in accordance to their talent. Received on their twenty-third birthday, it is typically bestowed upon heirs once they've wed.*

– Excerpt from Glynfyls: A History

"The name 'Glynfyls' is thought to be a bastardization of 'Glen Falls'. Legend holds that the original seven Talents found an idyllic glade with a waterfall off the shores of Casmot's Bay. However, when they shifted in the buildings, the land became unstable, sinking beneath the weight of the constructs. They were able to fix the center, but the edges fell, resulting in our 'hill' and the abnormal angles of the buildings. Ironically, the feature that had led them to settle in the area suffered the worst, and is now thought to be buried somewhere beneath the Pinch."

– Lord Talos, Preceptor of History,
Academy of Glynfyls

KARA STARED BLANKLY at her cosmetic-enhanced features in the mirror. The two women behind her exchanged glances.

"Is something wrong, my lady?" Audrey asked, the maid beside her wringing her hands. She'd coifed Kara's hair into an upsweep pulled back from her face, the heavy bangs she usually hid behind tucked away, leaving her exposed. An idealized simulacrum of femininity. Especially up here.

She blinked, bowing her head, bobby pins pricking into her scalp. "I—no. It's lovely. Thank you, I'm just getting lost in the past…"

The last time she'd seen herself like this…something about another Binder. A man. Best forgotten, she was sure, but it was only a matter of time before the memory was triggered, and it washed over her. All the little things filtering back over the past week, the tiny bursts of angst, jumbles of images, random feelings of disquiet, they were becoming more vivid. Harder to ignore. The slightest brush of analogous emotion turned them from neat marbles of liquid memory to spattering bullets that bruised, leaving a mess where they'd hit.

She stood, smoothing a hand over the leather belt cinching the crystal-pleated emerald silk to her waist. The top left her shoulders bare, the front and back gathered tightly at her throat, the edges of the closely buttoned neck rising up to tickle her jaw.

Audrey had been mortified when Kara had chosen it from Reggie's "off the rack" wear. Apparently, the couturier's experimental designs were quite daring. Kara couldn't understand why, everything but her arms were covered. Well, except when she walked, but the edginess of the floor-length panels of pleated silk splitting and flowing with her steps to show flashes of leg and snakeskin stilettos was the best part. She ran her hands over her arms, something niggling about that…

"Did you want a sweater?"

Kara laughed. "No, that would spoil the effect, now wouldn't it?"

Audrey's lips pinched. She'd not so subtly suggested that effect was why Reggie was hurting for business. Kara didn't care. If she could be who she wanted, there wasn't a chance in hell she was donning a Luann special. Especially not to dine in what was supposed to be her own home.

Squaring her bared shoulders, she went downstairs. Anxiety aside, she felt the best she had in recent memory. Whatever Jon had snuck into that horrid shot had left her feeling just plain good, even if she wasn't supposed to pull talent. She fought back the temptation to bind something just to see if she could.

Her laughter rang through the foyer at French's expression when she entered, his blue eyes wide. He quickly regained his decorum with a cough.

"Ah, my apologies, my lady. I was not prepared for your entrance."

Kara swallowed the lump in her throat, her confidence deserting her. "Is it really that shocking?"

He offered her his arm, patting her hand as she took it. "I'm afraid so. Mortal women should not be so lovely, you'll make the heavens jealous."

She laughed again. "Now I know where Flynn gets his charm from." The elderly man colored, clearly pleased. He escorted her through a part of the estate she'd not been in before. "How big is this place?"

"Save for the Prydee's estate, Grynhaven, Meddleton is the largest of the ancestral homes. It has a dozen chambers suitable for dining. Madame Miriam has always preferred the Great Northern Suite. Tomorrow night's dinner will be held in the Green Dining Suite, which the former Lady Scot held an affection for."

"Did you know her well?"

"I was delighted to serve her in my capacity for close to twenty years." His tone discouraged more questions. Why didn't anyone ever want to speak about the woman?

"What's west of here?"

"A great deal of forest, mountains, and then it all ends at a vast ocean." They'd stopped before a double doorway, identical to the others they'd been passing.

"No people? Other cities?"

"Not that I'm aware of. If you'll just wait here, I'll announce you. Madame Miriam dotes on formality when in residence." He patted her hand again and went inside. Kara's gaze traveled the wide corridor. How did anyone find their way around here? More paneled walls interspersed with doors and curiosities. She glanced back over her shoulder at a suit of armor standing guard. She supposed she hadn't seen one of those before—

"Lady Kara Scot." Chairs scraped back beyond the doors.

A flash of memory, and she was eight years old. The flute she was holding dug into her sweaty palm. Her thumb worried a key, snapping it off. Anxiety washed over her as it pinged across the floor tiles… She hadn't meant to—what were they going to say, they'd know—

"Lady Kara Scot."

She started, fighting down old panic, her feet carrying her forward. It wasn't real. Well, it was, but it wasn't now—

A burst of Flynn's shock stopped her cold in the doorway. She steadied herself on the jamb, trying to find her equilibrium. His eyes locked on hers, pinning her there as he crossed the floor, the rest of the room silent.

Her cheeks flushed as he stepped close, trying to ride out the last of the anxiety from a twenty-year-old flute recital. Ugh, it was so stupid! She ran her hands over the brocade of his malachite waistcoat, the solidness of him beneath it grounding her. His fingers traced the long line of her spine through the pleated silk. Gooseflesh rose on her arms, and she shivered into him.

"Do you hate it?" She laughed as soon as the words left her mouth. Hate was definitely not what she was feeling from him.

His eyes were on the claret of her lips, and he licked his own. A smile broke across his face, and his hand cupped her cheek, thumb brushing across her dimple, firmly bringing her back to the here and now.

"Damn, woman." She glanced past him to the rest of the Scots, the men had risen from their chairs and stood watching them. Miriam looked faint. Flynn's grin just kept getting bigger. "Come on, I'm taking you out."

"What?" Her breath caught. She hadn't—"Where? I thought I had to stay—"

He laughed, the sound bouncing around the fieldstone walls of the formal room, his eyes traveling the length of her body. "Hell no. I'm showing you off. Christ, you're fucking gorgeous. Hey Graham, can I get a table at the Park Club?"

His cousin shrugged. "Sure."

"But I'm not—really? We're going to the city?" Kara shivered again, and he ran his hands over her arms.

"If we're done standing on ceremony, get rid of this rabbit food," Cal called to one of the servants. "I'll take my meat now."

"You eat those greens, Caliban!" Miriam flicked her angry gaze to Flynn. "Sit down Laughlin, we're having dinner here!"

Both he and Cal ignored her. "Damn, I wonder where that wrap my mom had ended up… You know the one I mean, French?"

"I believe so, sir. I'll be happy to fetch it from storage and meet you in the foyer."

Flynn's grin grew. He offered Kara his arm, and she took it in a daze. What was he up to?

Leo's chair screeched farther back on the floor. "Screw this, I'm tagging along. We'll grab a table and meet you there. You coming, Shel?"

Shelby looked at him like he was an idiot and shifted out. Leo and Graham were gone in another breath.

"Well, I just… Laughlin James, this isn't proper!" Miriam shrilled after them.

Flynn laughed, leading Kara back the way she'd just come.

Her heart was in her throat. "Are you sure this is a good idea?"

"Nope." He licked his lips, watching the flash of her legs between the panels of silk. He pulled up short, his hand trailing down her thigh to find the top of her stocking through a slit, and following it to her garter. "Goddamn, Kara, tell me…what color?"

She laughed, playing with his lapels. "No." He pulled her closer with a little growl. She laughed again. "You have to wait."

His lips teased hers. "What if I can't?"

"I didn't realize you had a thing for lingerie."

"I've got a thing for what's in it." He bent to kiss her, and her teeth tugged on his bottom lip. He gave a low moan, his hand moving up to cup her breast. "No bra," he murmured, pressing himself against her, those blue motes churning dangerously.

"No bra."

"I'm gonna fuck the shit out of you when we get back."

"We could just skip dinner—"

"Not a chance." He laughed, taking her hand again.

French was waiting for them in the foyer with a thick sable fur. Flynn draped it over her shoulders, fastening it with a burnished clasp. She ran a hand over the lush wrap, wishing she could see what it looked like, but from the expressions on their faces, it was a far cry from a sweater.

"Goddamn."

"Indeed, sir." French bowed and left them before the swirling portal of opalescent mist.

"One rule, you can't talk to anyone other than me and the triplets."

"Will it be like the train station?" Her mouth was dry and her stomach lurched. She took a deep breath. She could do this.

"No, we'll be above the third rung. They'll just take pictures." His halos flared, and she felt his talent settle over her. "That's to cloak the temperature and keep Finders from getting a read on you. Just hold on and make your mind a blank, ok?"

Flynn offered his arm, that wide smile on his face as her hand wrapped around his bicep. He led her into the undulating mist. It licked up around her with a cool pressure—

They were standing on a bizarre glass-encased street.

A group of women having tea at a cafe across the way took a collective gasp, and Flynn got that Cheshire Cat grin, escorting her past their dangling jaws. They weren't the only ones. Kara's palm became uncomfortably moist on his arm…but it was hard to feel meek beneath the swell of his emotion. He was loving this. She shook her head, her anxiety melting beneath his pride.

He set a leisurely pace, letting her take everything in. It kind of reminded her of the commissaries at the Source with all the little specialized shops in a row, but that's where the similarities ended. She tried not to gawk at the bright-bladed fans above, or the helter-skelter skyline beyond the glass. The people around them drew back to let them pass, the women whispering behind intricate fans like the one Luann had fluttered. Their gowns were all of the same vein; pale, flounced confections of lace and taffeta, taking up double the space they should. The women looked her up and down with a hungry kind of fascination, and at Flynn with outright hunger. Her hand tightened on his arm, remembering what Bea had said.

But as she caught their reflection in a shop window, Kara could understand their envy. The sleekness of Flynn's suit and her gown was incredibly striking amidst all the puffery; the vivid green shocking in a sea of pastels. She ran a hand over the wrap, pleased with how it complemented the ensemble. Flynn nodded smugly to everyone who met his eye, enjoying himself immensely. She was surprised to discover she was, too. A smile skimmed across her lips, he was such a jerk.

"This is the promenade. The upper rungs on this side of the bluff are all connected by tubes. Keeps the ash off everything."

Kara's eyes lingered on two ragged women on the outside of the glass, holding buckets and squeegees. Their soot-streaked, be-goggled faces followed them as they went past.

"Clinkers," he said, noting her interest. "Ah, Fetches that keep this part of the city clean. The fly-ash from the power plants cakes up pretty quick. They shift it away."

"Where—" A flash bulb went off. Several more followed, and her fingers tightened on Flynn's arm. The crowd ogling them had grown considerably. Her stomach fluttered.

"Don't worry, they won't get any closer." He rumbled softly, motioning towards a large bronze seal set into the floor.

Kara stepped onto it with him and let out a little yelp as it began to rise. She laughed, looking down over the edge. "Oh, I wasn't expecting that!"

He grinned in delight, helping her off into a different tube. She paused, looking out over the city. The moonlight reflected off a massive body of water in the distance.

"That's Casmot's Bay. Glynfyls is on its southern shore."

"That's a little piece of the ocean, right? Is the water really salty?" He got that look on his face that meant he was remembering she was from the Source. Not quite pitying, but sad. It made her want to hit something. She forced a smile instead. "What's the Park Club? That's where we're going, right?"

Flynn ran a hand through his hair. She was glad he'd stopped slicking it down. "Yeah." His grin came back, and he cleared his throat, his voice becoming affected. "It's where Glynfyls' elite goes to see and be seen." She laughed and took his arm again. "Graham bought it with his majority payout a few years ago. He's got a thing for fine dining. I'm curious to see what he's done with the place."

They strolled by more shops, the crowd a murmuration around them. The way the women gawked at him...and he completely ignored their whispers and stares, solely focused on her. Kara's throat got tight. How was he, how was any of this real?

He stopped and pulled her close. "You okay?"

She nodded. "It's just a lot."

"It's just the beginning." He kissed her brow, triggering a flurry of flashbulbs. His smile was contagious, and she couldn't help returning it. Ugh, she must look like an idiot. His arm was around her to the horrified delight of the crowd, their expressions contorted in the curves and facets of the jeweler's shop window.

"Silver or gold?"

She laughed at the way he took note of everything that even remotely caught her eye, hoping he didn't have any plans to fill a room with those tiny bright birds she'd stopped to wonder at, though she was sure the kittens would have a fine time.

"I'm not much for any of it, honestly."

She hadn't thought his grin could get any bigger, but it did.

He led her to a short ramp ending at a rounded aperture of interlocking blades. Like a portlock, but instead of rolling to the side as they approached, it spun open from the center with a burst of cool air. Her nose crinkled at the odd, sharp tinge. Beyond was a wide stone portico. Low steps rose up from the sidewalk to a set of polished brass doors between two of the columns. Panels of glass had been fixed between the others.

Thick plum curtains hid one of the sections, but the majority were pulled back to show elegantly dressed diners. They were seated in crescent-shaped booths around linen-draped tables. Flynn hadn't been kidding. The way it was situated was like some weird storefront. A man with a camera threw down his cigarette as soon as he saw them, and they were peppered with flashes of light.

Flynn ignored him, and the stares from inside as they ascended the steps. He jerked his head toward the row of cars lining the street. They were much nicer than anything she'd seen Outside. Past them, a low wall, sky, and the faint crash of waves.

"When the weather gets nicer, we can drive something in. It'll be a good way for you to learn stick."

Wait, he'd been serious about her learning to drive?

There were more flashes as they went inside. The door closed behind them with a solid thunk, kicking off a surge of frenetically whispered conversations throughout the posh room. Kara's pulse sped, feeling all the eyes. It'd been easier walking…

Flynn bent close, his nose brushing hers. He grinned as the whispering increased. "You wanna really give them something to talk about?"

She laughed, and the room went silent for a breath. Before she could reply, an oily little maître d' sidled up to them and bowed ingratiatingly.

"Lord Scot, sir! What a pleasure to see you again! We've a table waiting. May I take the lady's wrap?" He held out his hands like it wasn't optional. Kara unclipped it, letting it slide from her shoulders. Gasps sounded. Her cheeks warmed, and Flynn got that Cheshire Cat grin again.

"I—If you'll just follow me," the maître d' stammered, handing the wrap off to a woman in a high-necked blouse and a long black apron over her full skirts. Another went past laden with a silver tray of delicacies. Whatever they were smelled wonderful.

There were maybe two dozen tables, most filled. Low centerpieces of magnolia and eucalyptus surrounded softly glowing orbs. A smattering of them were fixed about the room, the diners amidst a cosmos.

Flynn motioned for her to go ahead of him, and she started down the wide aisle. A bar dominated the back of the room, the luminescent wall behind it tinting everything a subtle violet. Above was a balcony with a few more of those crescent booths. The triplets were in the center one, having drinks. Shelby waved, and Flynn returned the gesture, drawing more attention. People at the bar unabashedly swiveled to watch their progress, sipping on cocktails, and nibbling things off sticks.

None of the women showed any skin, save for their hands and keyholes of cleavage on the younger ones. Even their faces were partially covered by those stupid fans. How could they stand it? Their gazes burnt, and she resisted the urge to rub her arms.

The click of her heels through the gauntlet of Glynfyls' elite seemed very loud above their whispers and the low instrumental music. She raised her chin, wishing she had her hair to hide behind, and stupidly thankful for the subtle pressure of Flynn's hand at the small of her back.

The whispering increased the farther they got into the restaurant, sawing at her frayed nerves. When had it gotten so hot? She tried to keep her eyes on the back of the maître d's jacket, but a clang of cutlery on china drew her attention. An elderly woman caught Kara's gaze. She held a hand to her heaving breast and looked as though she were about to faint.

"Have you no shame?! What you're wearing is scandalous!"

"No, it's a Glass." Flynn grinned, not missing a beat. She made a kind of choked sound, and Kara laughed before she could help herself. The room erupted into fervent discourse, and Flynn took her hand, pushing past the stammering maître d'. He led her up a polished mahogany staircase along the far side of the room, feeling like she'd just survived round one in some surreal arena.

The balcony definitely had the best seats in the house. Up and away from the biting chatter of the main floor, only a low murmur rose up with the music. She looked past the fixed constellations of orbs, and the far wall's panels of glass, beyond the portico, to the crashing waters of the bay. They pounded against a sweeping jetty, sending gouts of spray against the stones, the arctic gale catching them up and encrusting the ocean's primal fury into crystalline bluffs of rendered white.

Kara stood, transfixed.

Flynn rested his hand on her waist. She looked up at him, trying to shake off her wonder. At some point she'd gone to the balcony's rail, and the entire restaurant was staring at her, mute. She blinked the moisture from her eyes and laughed. Ugh, she was so stupid. He kissed her temple, creating a frenzy below.

"Welcome to Glynfyls."

FLYNN TRIED to keep his eyes on the menu, but it was fucking impossible.

Goddamn, Kara was beautiful. She raised her kohl-lined eyes to his, the shimmer of emerald powder across her lids bringing out how brown they were. His mouth went dry, imagining her halos with the ensemble. Her fingers brushed against his thigh, and he gave her a warning look. She laughed at him. What a brat.

He wasn't the only one she was making drool. Everyone was salivating over just getting a glimpse of her, never mind what she actually looked like, and in that dress…every last one of the women were overblown, bejeweled peafowls in comparison. They all knew it, too, but he was positive Kara had zero idea of how the room had held its collective breath as she stood looking out at the bay. She was too perfect to be real. Christ, too perfect to be his.

But she was, and she was having his kid.

His heart swelled, and he couldn't wipe the stupid grin off his face.

"What are you ordering?" Shelby asked over the rim of her wine glass. She was the only woman tonight that hadn't eyed Kara with hostile envy. Well, maybe a little regular envy. He hoped the rest of them choked on it.

"Prime rib and oysters. You?"

"Cod special. What about you, Kara?"

Leo gave a suppressed belch before she could answer. Typical. Flynn frowned, watching him pull at his maroon cravat. It had a gaudy diamond stickpin, and he looked like he'd napped in his suit. "Doesn't anyone wanna know what I'm having?"

"Kidney pie," everyone but Kara replied. Leo shot them all a sour look and waved for another vodka.

Flynn sipped his water. "Place looks good, Graham. Who'd you get to renovate?"

"Some freak in a three-piece lime suit." Leo snorted. "Graham had to interview, then wait like two years to get on his list."

"Pierce Quinn is ridiculously selective," Shelby explained. "But the wait was worth it, it doesn't look like an old boys' club anymore."

"Paid for itself." Graham shrugged. "We've been booked solid since."

"Yeah, you're lucky he's got enough pull to get you a table," Leo said around his mouthful of bread.

"What's gillyblack?" Kara asked.

Flynn bent close to help her with the menu. Damn, she smelled good. She blushed, catching his hand as he tried to slide it farther up her leg. He grinned, loving how embarrassed she got. Leo muttered something disparaging from the other end of the table.

"Hey, nobody asked you to come." Flynn laughed. "Sorry, what did you say you felt like?" Christ, he knew what he wanted. She colored again, and he flipped his napkin into his lap. Goddamn.

"Fish, but I don't know what half of this is."

He could understand that. There were things up here that you just didn't find anywhere else. "Gillyblack's exclusive to Glynfyls. It's oily, ah kind of like mackerel, I guess."

Leo just about choked on his vodka. "Yeah, with a million unit mark-up."

"It's more akin to bluefish," Graham said, buttering a piece of bread.

Flynn shot them both a look. "Whatever, it's strong tasting. Char's like salmon but not as rich—"

"What's this?"

"Skordalia? Garlic mashed potatoes."

Graham's tsk was offended. "It's garlic with a bulky base and an emulsion of olive oil. Uro's in the kitchen tonight, most likely it's potato and almonds."

"Yeah, like I said, garlic mashed potatoes."

His cousin rolled his eyes.

Kara closed her menu. "That, with the smoked fish plate and creamed spinach."

Flynn laughed. "Really?" Christ, that sounded disgusting. He tipped up her chin and kissed her before all that went in her mouth.

A volley of flashbulbs bombarded them.

Goddamn it. There was a tussle and the press was herded out. Somebody'd made a small fortune letting them in here, and he knew for a fact the maître d' wasn't above having his palm greased. The little shit came over, apologizing profusely, and they put in their order.

"So where to after this? You taking her to the Rhineroom?" Leo asked, chomping on an olive. He was already on his third vodka.

The suggestion put a huge grin on Flynn's face. The thought of getting Kara out on the dance floor...damn. "Not tonight, but soon. Shit, I haven't gone dancing in—" A wave of Kara's dread brought him back to reality. "What?"

She was genuinely upset. "I thought Reggie was kidding...you really dance?"

He laughed. "Yeah, why would she kid?"

"Flynn's a wonderful dancer," Shelby said with a dreamy smile. "I can't wait for your Introduction. The chamber orchestra Miriam's hired out of Ifranz is divine. They played at my last competition." The look of joy on her face was almost enough to distract Flynn from Kara's panic.

"I don't...I don't dance."

They all stared at her like she was crazy.

"Of course you do. Those katas are basically the same thing—"

She bit at her thumb and gave her head a tiny shake.

Shit. She was serious.

"Hey, that's all right, she can warm the bench with me." Leo waggled his eyebrows, and Kara scooched closer to Flynn. He glowered at his cousin. Asshole raised his glass to him, then drained it.

"That's too bad." Shelby frowned. "Dancing's huge in Glynfyls."

A waiter came over with the oysters, and Flynn rubbed his hands together. Kara moved away, giving him a funny look. "What? I love these, and they're aphrodisiacs."

She laughed, making a face as he slurped one down. "Because you need one. Ugh, they look horrible."

"I'll take them any day over your weird garlic fish."

"Point taken…" Her brow furrowed. "Dancing, really?"

He shrugged, reaching for another. "It's big on the hill."

"Only if you're heir." Leo snorted. "Nobody gives a shit if us scions know the box step."

"Oh hush, Leo, that's not true," Shelby chided, her long gold ear baubles chiming softly as a waiter set a salad in front of her.

Flynn wiped his hands, chewing. Kara would look pretty with a pair of those. Were her ears pierced? He brushed a tendril of her hair away, and she smiled at him. Yeah, he should get her a pair. Gold, to match her halos. Shit, he needed to get his mom's signet from Lot— Kara's plate of smoked fish was delivered, and he made a face that broke into a grin. She couldn't pick up her fork fast enough.

Shelby smiled at her, too. "When I started competitive ballroom, I needed someone to practice with. Leo's just crabby because he's got two left feet, and Graham can't lead. Flynn's good. Not competition good, but he knows what he's doing."

Kara glanced between them. "Really?"

"Helped with my boxing footwork."

"You know," Shelby said, "I could teach you a few things. You've got to be bored…"

"I think it's a great idea, but I'll warn you, she's a taskmaster." Kara looked at him like he was full of shit, and Flynn laughed, eyes on the massive steak that'd just been delivered. Woman had no idea.

The rest of dinner came. Aside from Leo's bitching, it was the most enjoyable meal Flynn could remember having. Kara had certainly delighted in it, and the creme brûlée she was working through. What he wouldn't give to be that spoon right about now…

"You mind if I get a coffee?"

"Nope, go for it. I can't tell you how much better I feel."

It was apparent, and she'd finally relaxed, along with the rest of the restaurant, now that her novelty had worn off a bit. He ordered a cup along with a cigar. There was a murmur through the crowd below as it was delivered.

Julia walked in on a heavy set lord's arm, and the entire vibe of the room changed.

So much for relaxing.

"Shit," Leo muttered.

Graham shrugged. "She's got a standing reservation Friday nights."

"You couldn't have given me a heads up?" Flynn sighed at Kara's look. "That's Julia." He sat back and lit his cigar. Not a chance he was gonna be rushed out. Christ, he said that, but a trickle of sweat had started down his spine. Kara watched rapt as the couple was seated. Julia got her menu, then looked directly at them, far too smug for comfort.

Kara nestled back against Flynn with a cup of tea. "I thought she would've been prettier."

He laughed, sending out a fitful stream of smoke and drawing eyes. The tension in the room thrummed it was so tight. Leo muttered something, and Flynn shot him a look. If he opened his mouth, he'd beat the shit out of him.

Kara pulled Flynn's arm more firmly around her. "Who's she with?"

"Tubby down there?" Leo sneered too loudly, tipping back vodka number five. "Lord Ines. He's been trying to get her to take his bond forever. It's pathetic."

"Why can't I speak to anyone?" Kara asked.

"It's symbolic," Shelby explained. "To show the line that you'll be humble and meekly defer to your husband."

Kara laughed, drawing stares from below. Flynn didn't blame her, it was ridiculous. "And if I've no intention of doing either?" She peeked at him from beneath her lashes and there was a hint of that perfume in the air. Goddamn. Shit drove him fucking wild lately. Her fingers slid across his thigh to trace the inseam of his pant leg, and she smiled at the rumble in his chest. Woman was playing with fire and knew it.

"Whelp, I've had enough of that," Leo announced, standing. "You got the tip?"

Flynn was busy holding Kara's gaze. "Yeah, I'll—"

Leo shifted out. What an ass.

"Do you want to come back with us?" Shelby asked.

Ines' guffaw and Julia's laugh floated up from below, breaking

Kara's spell. They'd have to walk right by their table to leave. Flynn had zero doubt that'd been planned. Fuck them. He tapped the ash off his cigar, sitting back.

"Nope. We're leaving the same way we came in."

Shelby gave him one of those Miriam looks and shifted out with Graham. Flynn puffed on his cigar, his fingers teasing the lip of Kara's stocking. One of those panels of fabric had slipped to the side, and he could just make out the top. The way she was sitting he still couldn't see what color her garter was.

"Julia came knowing we were here, didn't she?"

"Probably. We're gonna have to deal with her publicly at some point. I'm sure she'll say something to try and piss me off when we leave." His fingers nudged the panels farther apart and she drew a sharp breath. "Show me?"

"You're awful, you know that?"

"It'll give me something to focus on when we leave."

She laughed. "I think you're focused on it enough."

Woman wasn't wrong. Goddamn, she was beautiful. His gaze traced the line of her jaw to the elfin point of her chin, then the red of her full lips as she tried not to smile, her dark eyes beguiling. She belonged up here and she didn't, something feral simmering just beneath the surface. He thought about her beating the shit out of that asshole Pax, then running through the forest behind the farm. That wild promise of unpredictability just sealed the fucking deal, and what he was feeling from her—

"Where do they go?"

"Hmm?"

"The pieces of your soul. I haven't seen them since we left Meddleton."

"No, you won't. Something about cities..." He looked away, shrugging.

"Too civilized. Maybe we should change that." She plucked the cigar from his lips and kissed him like she wanted to eat him. Flashbulbs blazed through his eyelids, and he didn't fucking care.

"Damn, woman." He rumbled when she pulled away. "What was that for?"

Her cheeks were flushed. "If I already have a bad reputation, I may as well do something to deserve it."

Flynn grinned, his fingers tracing the inner curve of her thigh. "That right?" He watched their progress upwards, nudging the center panel aside…

Jesus Fucking Christ, this woman—

She shivered as he met her eyes. "I didn't think we were going out."

"Give me a minute and we're going right the fuck home."

She laughed, and he swiped his cigar back from her.

Shaking his head, he flipped a stack of units onto the table, giving her some serious side-eye. She laughed again. Christ, he couldn't wipe the stupid smile off his face. He helped her out of the booth and gathered her up in his arms. His hand slid down her hip, fingertips grazing that goddamned garter. Knowing it was the only thing under her dress just made him want to see it more. Black. He bet it was black.

She looked up at him with those big eyes of hers, and God, he just—

"Thank you for dinner."

He kissed her knuckles. "The pleasure was all mine."

Taking her hand, he led her downstairs through the loaded silence of the main room, chewing his lip to keep from grinning like an idiot. That dimple was in her cheek when she glanced over at him and—

"Whore."

Kara's bloodlust spiked the air.

The heavy steak knife that'd been in Lord Ines' bloated hand bisected Julia's plate and stood quivering in the tabletop. Kara leaned in and kissed her, leaving the stark stain of her lipstick against the pallor of the stunned woman's cheek.

Flynn collected her fur from the stupefied cloak-girl like it was just another Friday night and wrapped it around Kara's shoulders. She took his arm. Ignoring the flurry of flashbulbs, and the astonished peerage, he escorted her out with a massive grin.

CAL LOOKED up from his paperwork at Kara's laugh and the low rumble of Flynn's reply in the hallway, doing a double take when they came into the room. He sat back, rubbing his eyes. They had to be playing tricks on him. For a second there…his hand smoothed down over his mustache, that brief glimmer around the two of them gone.

Christ, he'd lived too long. Had to just be the shock of seeing them both so damned happy. Radiant, if truth be told. Looked good on them. It was about time someone was, even if it wouldn't last.

Boy dropped into a chair with a shit-eating grin and pulled Kara onto his lap. She gave a little squeal as he ran his hands over her, kissing her thoroughly.

That Cal could do without. "You know, I'm sitting right here."

"I'm aware, it's the only reason she's still dressed," Flynn said, face buried in her neck. Kara was crimson, and the boy was just tickled about it. "French said you wanted to see me?"

"Yeah. Go set the board up. Maybe that'll help you keep your dick in your pants."

Boy didn't bother to come up for air. "How 'bout you just say what you've gotta say so I can put it where I want to instead?" Kara gasped, and he gave a low chuckle, getting off on it.

Cal cleared his throat, and Flynn reluctantly broke away from her, glaring at him on his way to the board. Cal joined him, casting an appreciative eye over Kara as he passed. He couldn't blame the boy, but that didn't make it any less annoying. Especially in his present state. Damn, he missed Nora and knowing their arrangement of convenience was coming to an end didn't do anything to improve his mood. *Bah, enough of that.*

"So. What'd you think of Glynfyls?" Cal asked Kara.

"More than I think of its inhabitants." She laughed, recounting what had happened at the Park Club.

Cal frowned, patting his pockets for his matches. He'd expected Flynn to be the wild card, not her. God help them all if he was the more rational of the two.

"You left them on your desk." She stood to get them.

French came in with a coffee service and a cheese plate. Boy didn't waste any time helping himself. You'd think he hadn't just racked up a second mortgage in tip at the most expensive restaurant in the Northern Territories. Cal went to ask Kara where his matches were and swallowed it quick. She'd found the packet on Flynn and was leafing through it.

Shit. His cigarette could wait. "Press there?" he asked the boy.

"Yeah, more than I would've thought."

"Good." Cal snorted at the hard look Flynn gave him. "You been reading the paper?"

A muscle in his jaw ticked. "No."

"Might wanna pick one up, even money on what gets top billing tomorrow, you two or all the disappearances."

"Disappearances?"

"Depends on which rag's reporting. Half of them are screaming murder after that nasty business a few days ago, but since the first, there's nary a corpse to be found. At least a half dozen missing persons reported every night. Intelligencers are stumped. Starting to smell like a Shade's involved. If not the one doing the deed, then cloaking whoever is. You did yourself a favor going out and being seen."

"Jesus Christ, they trying to pin that shit on me?"

"Not yet, but circumstantial evidence being what it is…"

"I wondered why you didn't say a goddamned thing when we bailed on Miriam's—" Flynn paled, his eyes on Kara. She turned another page and chewed her thumb.

"Plausible deniability outweighed social acceptability. Of course, that was before Kara got a wild hair across her ass."

She smirked, not apologetic about it in the least.

Cal shook his head, not liking where that dynamic was going. Flynn was a hell of a lot more contrite. He swallowed, glancing at her like she was wired to blow.

She turned another page.

When it was clear she was hell bent on reading the whole thing word for word, Flynn turned back to the board. They went back and forth. Boy kept missing opportunities to take his men.

Cal suspected he couldn't blame him. "You know, there's actually a style of play where the goal is entrapping the king without taking any other pieces."

Flynn moved up a rook from the lowest level. It was a dumb move and clattered as he placed it on the square. Kara had gotten to the photos. "You ever run a game like that?"

Cal captured the piece. "Only when I'm teaching arrogant little shits how to play."

"Yeah, arrogance helps." He moved his queen a few spaces over and up.

Cal's jaw dropped. *I'll be damned.* The last time he'd lost two in a row… He went to get his own damned matches. Christ, they might actually have a shot at pulling this off. "You go dark studying in a cave with an Ash'a master?"

Flynn didn't answer, his eyes on Kara. She'd rolled up the packet and was tapping it against her palm, lips pursed. He got up, and her eyes flicked to him, nailing him to the carpet. Shit, with that look on her face, Cal wasn't moving a damn muscle either. She pushed away from the desk and stood in front of the boy.

His Adam's apple bobbed. "Kara, I—"

"What did I tell you I was going to do?"

Flynn licked his lips, her hands at his buckle. The air had gone thick. "Yeah?"

"Yeah, and I'm going to need your belt."

She tugged it free, gave him one hell of a kiss, then prowled from the room.

Flynn staggered against his chair, heart pumping like he'd run a marathon. His eyes met Cal's and a massive grin split his face, then he was off, after her.

Cal grabbed the scotch from the sideboard, bringing the bottle back to his desk. Should just leave the damned thing there. He unscrewed the top, not bothering with a glass.

Rogan was right. That was not the Kara he knew.

Cal lit his cigarette, watching the smoke curl up and dissipate.

It never did last.

CHAPTER THIRTEEN

hillies [hil-is] noun, slang

1. *A lesser Talent's slur for a scion of an Original House, originating from their historical preference for the center of the city.*

– Excerpt from Glynfyls: A History

"After the Surge wiped out all previously existing technology, the Corporation unveiled the advent of plaz. However, the advances made possible by the substance came with a steep caveat: the field it emits when energized is inimical to lower life forms, resulting in the wasteland surrounding the Source. Both the Deep South and the Northern Territories have eschewed its widespread use, falling back upon traditional methods of power and/or utilizing talent based options..."

– Lord Talos, Preceptor of History,
Academy of Glynfyls

RIEGEL WHISTLED as he strode down the street, feeling toasty. He'd divested himself of the greasy fur-lined coat and picked up something more stylish around the third rung late last night. The moleskin duster wasn't as striking as he would've liked, but it was a decided step up from the rags he'd been wearing. At least the crimson scarf was jaunty. The way it matched the banded top hat was what had drawn his eye to the ensemble. The wallet that'd come with it had been a welcome surprise after that miserable Binder and his pet Fetch had so gleefully extorted every last unit from him.

It was akin to robbery given the scarring they'd left. However, aesthetics aside, Riegel did appreciate the fact that he was no longer dribbling off bits of himself in his wake. He pulled on a pair of calfskin gloves, enjoying the feel of the close-fitting leather more than the visual. Shiny and pink, the new skin reminded him of a miscarriage. He'd been assured that could be remedied for the right price, but for now, just being whole would suffice.

One of the women hurtling by in the crowd met his eye, and he smiled, tipping his hat. Her steps faltered, and his grin grew. Extremities aside, the Binder had done a fine job restoring his visage to its former glory. The bind warming his flesh was nothing to sneeze at either.

Riegel paused at a newsstand, the latest headlines blaring: *LADY AT LARGE!* Tossing the man a unit, he flipped through the paper. The society section was easily double in size today. Beside him, the stack shrinking to nothing in moments, people eagerly gobbling up the latest tidbit. He couldn't fault them. A full length photo of Kara on that ape's arm graced the front page, and she looked divine, damn her. This he would have to spend time perusing.

He folded the paper under his arm, continuing his stroll with an eye on those who passed. His eyebrow rose as a man rushed by with a brass-pommeled cane. Riegel spun on his heel, fancying himself using it as a cudgel. He quickened his step as the man turned a corner.

They'd entered a cul-de-sac. Empty barrels and shuttered stalls with brightly colored awnings lined its sides. At the far end was a rounded hatch with what looked like a portlock across it. Rising beyond was a massive brass-bound tube connected to a far-reaching network of the things sprawling across the sheer side of the hill.

His quarry approached the aperture's fanlike blades, and they spun open, then quickly closed behind him as he stepped inside.

Fascinating.

Riegel went to follow, and the entrance remained closed. What bizarre use of talent was necessary to make the thing open up?

Someone snorted behind him. "Ain't ye never seen a hillierun? Takes more than a swell's duds t'get in t'them, friend."

The area between Riegel's shoulder blades acquired that particular feeling that meant people planning him ill were about. A smile bloomed across his face as he turned. Three thugs were taking his measure. How droll.

The one with greasy red cornrows leaned over a crate, grinning at him. His scraggly goatee had been braided in trine, and a bronze bead dangled precariously from each plait. They weren't long enough to strangle him with, but would make an exquisite handhold.

"No, I'm afraid I haven't. How does it function?"

"Listen t'him all proper lawd. How do them function, Pete?" the first man asked over his shoulder.

The one with a battered tam and an overbite spoke up. "Simple-like, ye need t'be keyed."

Riegel was very sure they were playing with him. The thought of returning the favor was extremely appealing. Pity he hadn't been able to acquire that cane… "Do tell. And how would one procure one of these keys?"

The three exchanged amused glances.

"Ain't like somewhat ye stick in a door." The third one snorted nasally. "All thems with legit bid'ness gets whammied. Keeps us deplorables out, riffraff an' such as we is."

Riegel closed his eyes; their vernacular made his teeth hurt. "And what business would be considered legitimate?"

The red-head pushed back to stand. "Naught ye'd be interested in, friend."

"Are you very sure about that?"

"Positively knackers on the point, but it ain't no sorrow. Big man's asked us t'collect ye. Wallace'll get ye where ye need t'be, and first favor's always free." He smiled unpleasantly, and other two snickered.

Riegel smiled back. "Wallace, was it?"

"S'right. Just follow Pete. Stu and I'll bring up the kitty."

"Why, I'd be delighted. Lead on, my good man."

The one with the overbite adjusted his tam and started back to the main row. "Well, well, well. Now ye've gone and made me lose me bet. Figured ye for scrambled ham."

The red-head tapped the side of his nose as Riegel walked past. "Nah, he's wise t'his advantage. S'why Wallace's asking him t'visit all nice-like. That's right. Just keep following Pete. We're behind, never fear."

Riegel glanced over his shoulder as they hit the street, but the two were gone. He kept his face blank, following the battered tam through the crowd. Two blocks later, there was a hand on his back, and colors ran.

KARA LEFT THE GYM, dashing a towel across her sweat-soaked brow and mopping down her neck. The bruise at her throat ached as she went over it, and she flushed with heat, thinking about last night. The emotion echoed back from Flynn like a caress, lighting her up. Jerk. She jogged to the dining room, laughing, her dimples two-miles deep.

Happy.

She'd loved the feel of walking through the city on his arm, and his reciprocal delight that she was with him. She'd just needed time to adjust, and between what was in those jellies and Jon's shots, she'd barely registered last night's little slip… She laughed again, wondering how long Julia had scrubbed her cheek before giving up. That lipstick wasn't coming off until Kara dropped the bind.

Maybe being bred wouldn't be so bad. It was weird…but the idea of having offspring—no, a baby—was a lot more palatable now that she wasn't vomiting herself inside out.

Shelby was at the dining room table, picking at a salad and

surrounded by newsprint. She held one up as Kara came in. "You've made the front page!"

It was a good still, though black and white didn't do that gown justice. Smart steps sounded in the hallway, and Audrey came in carrying another stack. How many papers did Glynfyls have?

"Finally! We've much to discuss, my lady. Your teaser into society last night has propelled you into the forefront of things. Lord Scot has never stopped to think…" Thumping the stack onto the table, she smoothed her skirt, flustered. Kara slid the top one off the pile, this one in color.

Audrey drew herself up as if she were about to make an announcement. "You know I had my doubts about that gown, but I wouldn't be surprised if every woman in Glynfyls has one by the end of the week."

Kara stared at the secretary, sure she hadn't heard her correctly. "What?"

"Yes!" Shelby laughed, putting another page in front of her. "Read what they've been saying! Just look at how you stand out against all of them… Ugh, even me. I'm never wearing that shade of blue again." She pushed a strand of dark hair from her eyes, reviewing a photo of herself critically. "I'll have to have something new made up for the Introduction…"

Kara chewed the side of her thumb, more pleased with the expressions they'd caught on Flynn's face. Any woman who thought they had a chance with him was delusional. "Anything about Julia?"

Audrey clucked her tongue. "Only in a handful, and it's been quite watered down from word of mouth, but that in itself is no mean feat considering what they've been running—"

"Pardon the intrusion," French said at the door, "but Mistress Glass—"

Reggie pushed past him before he could finish speaking and hurtled toward Kara, wrapping her up in a massive hug.

She laughed. "Ugh, no, I'm all sweaty!"

"You could be covered in midden right now, and I wouldn't care." Reggie held her by her shoulders at arm's length, her face flushed that scalded color. "Do you have any idea what you've done? I've been flooded with requests since last night, so many, I've had to turn some away! My calendar's been booked out with consults for the next eight months solid…" She wiped her eyes, overcome. Her gaze landed on Shelby. "Oh, sorry… I didn't mean to interrupt, I just… thank you." Her face screwed up, and she left the room as quickly as she'd come.

Kara fell back into a chair, flummoxed. "What…?"

Shelby laughed. "Regina's always been a bit off. She should be a lady, but—"

"House Glass is the fourth most powerful of the Shades, however, Mistress Glass wasn't born with any measurable amount of talent," Audrey cut in. "Scions typically choose a trade in which to excel. Her failure to do so and refusal to marry has been a source of embarrassment for House Glass. Glynfyls' society isn't particularly kind to outliers." She swept a non-existent piece of lint from her sleeve, her expression momentarily brittle. "You've given Regina back some honor."

Kara looked between them in bewilderment. "I just picked a dress."

"You are no longer in the position to 'just' do anything, my lady. Case in point."

Audrey handed her one of the papers off the stack. Kara laughed at the headline: *BARBARIAN BELLE*. Beneath it was a still of her kissing Julia's cheek, knife jutting out of the table between them. The woman's expression was priceless.

"Be prepared for her response."

Kara rolled her eyes. "Everyone thinks the worst of me already."

"The sheer volume of invitations to social engagements I've been receiving since this was taken gives the lie to that statement. All of which will be declined unless they fall after the Introduction, save one."

"Oh?"

"Mmm. The Ladies will be here tomorrow for tea."

MARCOS STOOD before Titus's desk, acutely aware of the bead of sweat dribbling behind his ear to his collar. The boxes of redacted files were stacked beside him like an accusation.

Titus glowered at him over the rim of his bourbon, polishing it off, then sloppily refilling it from the bottle himself. Marcos had never seen the man in such a state.

"So, what've you learned?" Titus asked, motioning to the boxes with his glass. The contents sloshed over his hand, splattering across the desk.

The Commandant swallowed, pretending not to notice. "A great many things I was not aware of, sir."

Titus raised an eyebrow, and Marcos took it as permission to continue.

"From all accounts, the North's greatest strength lies in their combined use of talent. Historically, their battle hexes were devastating in the field. We should be training to do the same. Should our nullifying technology ever become compromised, we would be at a serious disadvantage."

"You are correct, and I've pushed the other members of the board to consider it for decades, to no avail. Do you know why?"

The Commandant remained very still. He could guess.

"That's right." Titus grinned. "The thought of you working together to slip your leashes terrifies them." He locked eyes with him. "Should I have any cause for concern, Br2?"

A whisper of Beritram's bottled bloodlust emanated from the man, and Marcos's sphincter tightened. Titus was playing with him. Did he know about the vectors? "If that were the case, I wouldn't be standing here, sir."

His Patron flashed a nasty smile. "You are correct, though it appears I have just cause to be paranoid." Marcos fought to keep his face a careful blank as the man fumbled at a stack of reports, then dashed a hand through them, scattering papers like pigeons. "I've a damned leak in my tower. Otto can't find it…though he did dig up several juicy tidbits I'd been unaware of. Not really worth the time he took with all of them, but he does enjoy his work. Here, sit for a moment, won't you?"

A sub came in with a straight-backed chair and put it in front of the desk. Marcos warily lowered himself down.

"I find myself in a quandary. Did you know I was a cunt hair away from completing my life's work last week? Then, not only do I lose the opportunity to breed Albanach's blasted Binder, I discover I've been sitting on a cuckoo's egg for the past thirty-odd years. Your offspring, it turns out, is sterile. Tell me, how is it Riegel was never culled? Do you have any idea how much paperwork is required to begin a formal inquest?"

Marcos sat very still, wishing he'd kissed Nora after dinner last night. Stupid of him. There wasn't one damned good reason why he hadn't.

Titus gripped his temples as if his head pained him tremendously. "And that fucking Scot boy! He's completely stalled my progress. It's infuriating!"

Titus slung his glass against the wall. A painting fell, the frame splintering. He rubbed a hand across his forehead again. A sub ran over to clean the mess. Another replaced his glass of bourbon. Titus took it and sat back, tilting his head to watch the woman's backside as she sopped liquor off the floor. He adjusted his crotch.

"Did you enjoy fucking that slat, Marcos?"

Startled, the Commandant sat up straighter. "I—yes, sir."

"I wondered. You never seem to enjoy the act, and after you bred that hag Laurellai, nothing. You're a Breaker, for fuck's sake! What's it been, six or seven years, and I've only watched you jack off maybe a dozen times. If I didn't have the old footage of you and that Jester woman, I would've pegged you as asexual. You're lucky the peculiarity never hindered your performance, else I'd have culled you years ago."

The Commandant's mouth went dry, the blood draining from his cheeks.

"Tell me, how goes your courtship of Albanach's whore? Have you gotten back into his sloppy seconds yet?" Titus grinned, and Marcos had the worst urge to drive his fist through the man's freckled face. His Patron raised his eyebrow, daring him to. The amount of bloodlust he was releasing grew.

Swallowing, Marcos took a deep breath, mastering himself. "Self-control is the most important skill a solider can have, sir."

Titus dissolved into laughter, wiping his eyes and waving a hand through the air. "Your next recommendation?"

"I—It would be to stage landing sites for troops. It'll take us four jumps to shift to the border and if we go on the offensive, another eight to get to the city proper. The first wave will take longer due to the lack of Fetches familiar with the territory."

Titus had gained a smirk that insinuated that wasn't the case. Marcos waited for him to elaborate. He didn't. Damn the man. That knowledge could save him a considerable amount of time and effort. He'd have to plan for both eventualities.

"And defensively?"

"Once our troops engage, the curtains, in conjunction with the standard issued nullifiers, will negate any advantage they have, allowing us to harvest at will."

"Excellent." Titus's smile widened, toasting him. "Carry on, solider!" He laughed again, the wall of holos sliding between them, each more depraved than the last. They all featured that Finder Riegel was always with.

Marcos stood, wondering what the inquest would turn up. He couldn't care less about the boy, but if it implicated Nora… Saluting sharply, he turned on his heel and left, the weight of the ax dangling over his throat redoubled.

RIEGEL LEANED back in his chair, cracking his neck. What was it with men in positions of power making people wait? He'd lost track of how many times he'd perused his paper. Enough that ogling Kara had lost its savor, which he hadn't thought possible. That flash of leg must be positively scandalizing the provincials up here. His gaze roamed over his favorite still of her, doodling over the ape's face and blacking out his eyes.

A door opened, and he was beckoned. Finally. Riegel gathered up his artwork, following a man down a low corridor into a windowless room. Wallace was considerably less imposing than Riegel had envisioned. Certainly not enough to make him wait for as long as he had. A whip thin middle-aged man with a nose ring and a plethora of tattoos, he was indistinguishable from any other Fetch up here. His left eye was covered by a jeweler's loupe. He ignored Riegel as he entered, continuing to inspect a large, blue gemstone beneath an electric lamp. The rest of the room was filled with bulky shapes beneath canvas, jumbled around the circle of light.

The thug he'd followed pointed to a chair and left, closing the door behind him. Riegel retrieved it, setting it, and himself, opposite Wallace.

He tucked his loupe into a pocket of a surprisingly high-end houndstooth waistcoat, then ran a hand across his day-old stubble. Inspecting Riegel with the same measuring gaze he'd applied to the jewel on the scrap of velvet between them.

"You've been operating without a license." The man's lack of cant was balm to Riegel's ears after having been battered by the filthy jargon for the past week. It threw him.

"Pardon me?"

"No, I don't believe I will, but you'll have an opportunity to make good. This is how things work. Rungs six through seven and the Flats are mine. You lift a fingernail from a corpse, I get a paring. My Geese have you at twenty-eight Talents, and I've yet to see a unit."

"Most were procured from rungs above that, and I was unaware there was a tariff on bodies."

"Ignorance doesn't equal impunity. You've dropped them all squarely in the Pinch, implicating my crew by proximity."

"Alas, the location was not my choice, nor can I do anything to change it." Wallace didn't look particularly surprised by the admission. Riegel had very little doubt that the man was already being compensated quite well to keep silent on the matter. He grinned, seeing how things stood. "So, how then would you like to settle up? I'm afraid I have very little capital to offer in recompense."

"I need someone broken."

Marvelous. "Well, I'll admit that does fall solidly within my skill set. Whom and how badly?"

"I'd give you some advice first."

"Oh?"

Wallace withdrew a pipe, carefully packing it. "You strike me as a man that doesn't like to leave loose ends. Most of the Talents you've dropped are of no never mind to anyone, save their wailing widows." He sat with his thumb over the bowl and met Riegel's eye. "Fitzpatrick McCreedy's the exception."

"Fitz…wait. That stringy blond pissant?"

Lighting his pipe, Wallace might've snickered. "Another's got prior claim. If you're wise, you'll leave him alone."

"I'm afraid I'm not terribly good at taking direction."

"Not even if it'll get you what you're really here for?"

Riegel's jaw tensed. "What would you know about that?"

"More than you'd think." The man wrapped his lips around his pipestem, the embers in the bowl crackling. "You're not the only one who's had something taken by a Scot. Wheels are turning, and I'd take care not to be ground beneath them. I need you to snuff a certain man, leaving no doubt a Breaker's done it. Once we're square, I'll get you keyed to the tubes."

Riegel templed his fingers, more than willing to agree to the man's terms for as long as they were convenient. Unfortunately, he sensed that Wallace was cut from the same cloth as he. Future promises held little incentive.

"That sounds acceptable, though I would ask for an additional favor… I've heard the first is free."

Wallace grinned. "It is at that."

"Well then, I'd appreciate having something delivered…"

CHAPTER FOURTEEN

Quorum [kwawr-uh m] noun

1. *An assemblage of all recognized Firsts, voting in proxy for their
   lines.*

– Excerpt from Hammond's Rules for Discourse,
Assembly Version

*"On your twenty-third birthday, you will be considered an adult and a
lord or lady in your own right. At that time, you will either enter into
or honor a pre-existing marriage contract with a Talent from your line
deemed politically advantageous to your House and your equal. Your
majority payout is to be used as seed money towards establishing your
own estates, or the continuation of those you will be ascending to..."*

*– Lady Valtroy, Academy Headmistress,
Glynfyls*

"LORD MARTIN HAS ARRIVED, SIR." French intoned.

Flynn sighed, tying his cravat, not looking forward to this clusterfuck. Having to waste the day with Cal and Merchant had been bad enough. He smoothed his waistcoat over the welts Kara had left, missing her. Damn, she'd been wild last night. He should piss her off more often.

"Kara still in the gym?"

"No, the lady is currently reviewing correspondence with Audrey. The two of you have become quite in demand."

Flynn scowled. He'd hated attending the endless social bullshit when he'd been drinking. He couldn't even imagine how much worse it was gonna be sober. "Great. Well, one shit show at a time. Let's get this circus over with."

He followed French down to the west drawing room.

Jacques stood by the fire with a bottle of wine. "I know you said you don't drink anymore, but I couldn't come empty-handed."

Flynn took the bottle with a grunt of appreciation. "No, but if I ever start again, I'll open this first. I thought we killed all of the Quillinjar Red."

"Not quite. There were a few cases in my father's personal reserve. When I got the keys on my majority, the first thing I did was set them aside."

Flynn handed the bottle to the butler. "Please put this somewhere safe." French inclined his head and left the two of them.

"So you ready for tonight? I won't lie, the line's in an uproar over yesterday, and I'm including your jaunt to the Park Club in that. What were you thinking?" Jacques laughed at Flynn's grin. "Never mind, I don't blame you, the woman's stunning. Not everyone's as understanding though, especially after that exit."

"I won't apologize for it. This, I'm not even a little ready for, but I suspect it's what needs to happen." Flynn jammed his hands into his pockets, more nervous than he should be and hoping to hell he didn't sweat through his damn jacket.

"We need a strong First, and your talent has always outstripped everyone's. There should be no question of you ascending, even with what Julia disclosed."

"Do you think they'll all come?"

"No, I don't."

"Good. To be honest, there's a few I'm praying don't."

Jacques laughed. "I can imagine—"

"My God, Flynn…"

He turned. By the look on Charles's face, you'd think the walls were covered with flayed puppies.

"This place is even more dour than I remember. Are gloomy manors in this season and no one bothered to tell me?"

Flynn took in the austere room. Bookcases lined the walls, filled with uniform tan law codices as old as Cal, and the stodgy furniture was upholstered in squeaky oxblood leather. He shrugged, Meddleton was what it was.

Charles gave a dramatic sigh and sat, raising an eyebrow as the tufted cushion protested. He ran a critical eye over Flynn. "Well, at least you've joined this century. Tell me, are those a Glass?"

Flynn glanced down at the grey pants and jacket that'd been set out for him. He hadn't given them much thought, other than noticing they fit. "Huh?"

"Ugh, you're hopeless! Haven't you picked up a paper today? Turn around so I can see."

Flynn laughed. "What? No."

"Tease. The jacket has to be. I know you didn't find a tuxedo tailcoat in a slub silk linen mixed in with those ancient castoffs from Lady Breakspear."

Flynn and Jacques looked at him like he was speaking in tongues, and Charles rolled his eyes.

"A paper? No, I've been stuck in a room with Cal and Merchant all day. I guess it's from Reggie. All of it, probably." Flynn shook his head, not caring. "Do you have any idea who's coming tonight?"

Charles looked like he was going to say something else, but let it go. "More than you'd think, if only for the curiosity factor. Meddleton hasn't been opened in over a decade, and either the heads have never been here, or they want to see how your hospitality stands up to Deirdre's. Then there's the ones that just want to watch you squirm when Peterli and Horace go at you."

Flynn grunted, expecting the last and pretty sure Charles was one of them. It was remembering the lavish dinner parties his mother had given that sent a finger of trepidation down his spine. All he'd told French was to throw something together. He ran a hand over his jaw as the man came to the door.

"Sir? Several more of your guests have arrived. I've taken the liberty of bringing them to the Green Dining Suite for appetizers, if you'd care to greet them?"

No other option, Flynn nodded and headed over. Charles made a point of trailing behind, making appreciative noises. Flynn laughed. Christ, he was glad someone was enjoying themselves.

Like most of the ground floor at the back of the estate, the Green Dining Suite's eastern wall was made entirely of glass and overlooked the gardens. The topiaries and hedges had been festooned with small lights that glowed beneath the snow. The room was full of flowers, and a sideboard had been laid out with cold appetizers. Large pocket doors were pushed back, revealing a connected smoking room. A fire crackled in its ornate marble hearth. White-gloved servants walked through, offering hot hors d'oeuvres and flutes of champagne on silver trays.

"Well, this is a pleasant surprise. I was expecting coffee and sandwiches." Charles took one of the proffered glasses, still eyeing Flynn's pants. He made a face at Jacques. "What? I'm trying to decide if I want mine with or without cuffs."

Jacques laughed and the group of men in the room turned to them.

"Laughlin," an older man said warmly, coming to shake his hand. "I see you've inherited Deirdre's flair for hospitality."

"Lord Ospre, I'm glad you were able to make it."

"Oh, I wouldn't have missed this. There should be another group right behind us. Last I knew, they were arguing with Peterli."

Flynn frowned, imagining quite clearly the cause of the argument beyond what Julia had spilled. He pushed his anger away for another time. "Yes, I'm well aware of how distasteful this must be for Lord Morris."

"As well you should." The rotund man snapped from behind him. "But I won't be cut out of this on account of a twist."

Flynn bit his tongue and gave a curt bow the man didn't bother returning.

"Where's Lot? I've a bone to pick with him about the arbitration he's done on my Eastern holdings." Morris took a heavy gold pocket watch from his waistcoat and eyed it sourly as the rest of their line filtered in around him.

"I'm afraid he's not here yet."

The man raised an eyebrow. "Left you minding the store, has he? I'm surprised they allow you to roam about without a keeper after all the scandal you've caused. Last night was shameful! I told them, a leopard can't change his spots."

Flynn had the worst urge to punch him in his bulbous nose. "Well, then it's a good thing I'm not a cat, because I can assure you, I'm not the man I was."

Morris snorted and walked to the sideboard. Flynn bit back a growl, not sorry to see the back of him, if only for a few moments.

"Laughlin." A thin, nervous man his own age walked over, tugging on his ascot. "Did I hear you say Lot wasn't here yet?"

Flynn put his hand out to shake. Looked like Greg still hadn't gotten over Lot going after him. "No, I'm not sure where he is. It's good to see you. I was surprised to hear you ascended, wasn't your older brother in line?"

Greg took Flynn's hand and shook it firmly, eyes darting about the room. "He eloped with an artist from Mauri. The marriage didn't last, but Agatha disowned him, so here I am."

Flynn wasn't surprised. Glynfyls was an unforgiving city. It was a big part of why he left.

"Pardon me, sir, but it appears all of your guests are accounted for. When would you care to begin?" Flynn gave French a blank look. "May I suggest another ten minutes?" the butler offered dryly.

"Um, yeah, that sounds fine, thank you."

"Feels like you're just playing at lord, doesn't it? I know how that is, but it gets easier." Greg clapped him on the shoulder and wandered over to another group.

Shit. Flynn took a deep breath. He was in trouble if Greg thought he was out of his depth. Christ, he knew how to do this, he just needed to dredge it back up, play the goddamned part... Lord Laughlin Scot. He straightened his lapels and snorted at the jacket.. A fucking Glass, what the hell was wrong with people? Speaking of which—He scanned the crowd. Damn it, Theo hadn't come… not that he was particularly surprised with the lawsuit, but it didn't speak well for his chances of pulling this off. The rest of his line milled about the room in groups of twos or threes. He suspected he still had to try, for what it was worth.

"Gentlemen," he said loudly enough to cut through conversation. Twenty-six heads turned to look at him. "Thank you all for coming. Dinner will be served in a few moments, shall we find our seats?"

Everyone moved to the table. French must've been going for a wow factor. The china had thick double gold rims and the flatware matched. The glasses were Abyssinian crystal and the linens snowy and crisp.

Flynn sat down at the head of the table with a small sigh. In the eight years he'd been gone, he wouldn't have been able to afford a single shrimp fork. He took a sip of water and waited for everyone to be seated. Jacques and Charles took places at either side of him.

"Morris is going to be a problem," Jacques said, pulling in his seat.

"When isn't he?" Flynn muttered from behind his water goblet. His two friends chuckled.

When everyone was settled, Flynn stood.

"Welcome to Meddleton. I'm pleased that you all could join me for dinner. I won't be coy about why I've asked you here. Our line stands leaderless, and we can't afford to continue that way. There have been some lingering questions as to my suitability for the position, and I mean to put them to rest. So please, enjoy the meal, and if there's anything you'd like to discuss, now's the time." He sat, and servants filed in with the first course, an ox tail consommé. Not his favorite, but he suspected it would impress.

"Why don't we start with your felony conviction?" Morris called from the other end of the table. "How you can possibly think anyone with your sordid history should rise to a position of such prominence—"

"Oh zip it, Peterli." Lord Daun sighed. "It's politics, not a papal seat. Laughlin was right in so far as nothing I saw in those pages was any worse than what he'd done up here. How about we have something to eat before you make everyone lose their appetite with your vitriol?"

"That doesn't excuse it! A proven pattern of malfeasance right there in black and white! I'm surprised anyone can eat after reading through those charges."

The table ignored him, returning to their earlier discussions. Flynn wondered how long the reprieve would last. He glanced at the clock across the room, wishing he was with Kara. Maybe she'd be waiting for him later in another garter…blue had been a surprise.

"Now I know that smile's not for me, Laughlin," Charles said with a sigh. Flynn coughed, coloring. "I thought as much. Since you felt the need to show her off to your advantage last night, surely you can tell us a bit about her? What has the lady been doing to occupy her time other than threatening your ex? It has to be dreadfully boring being under house arrest."

"Ah, yes and no, until recently she's been recovering from the attack. It took a lot out of her," Flynn said, a servant swapping his untouched soup for a salad.

"Jacques said as much, though I'm hard pressed to believe it given last night. I can almost understand your inclination." Flynn couldn't help the grin that spread across his face. The spry man rolled his eyes.

"Have you met her, Charles?" Lord Ospre asked from the middle of the table.

Charles puffed up, the room hanging on his response. "No, but Jacques may've seen her in the flesh. I've had to settle for the papers." He gave them a conspiratorial glance, and Flynn braced himself. Charles was going to say something sensational. The slender man picked up his glass of wine and took a sip, making everyone wait for it.

"What I can tell you, is that Laughlin is absolutely besotted."

Flynn choked on his salad. There it was. Fucking Charles.

"Besotted?" Ned gave a laugh. "What was in the papers notwithstanding, I'll believe that when I see it. The only thing Flynn's ever been in love with was his whiskey and maybe that car he used to tear around in." Several of the younger heads laughed, and Flynn cracked a smile.

"The car I'll admit to, but the bottle and I had a large falling out. As I said, I've been sober for the past five years."

"You honestly expect us to believe you haven't had a drop in all that time?" Lord Gent sneered. Several years older, Stuart had never liked him. It didn't help that his sisters did.

"It's the truth."

"Sober and besotted. Laughlin Scot."

Flynn just smiled at the man and went back to his salad.

Stuart didn't take the hint. "Jacques, did you get the same impression?"

Jacques finished chewing and took a sip of his wine before answering. "I'm afraid I haven't had the pleasure, but Bea has, and she found the lady to be exemplary. You all know what she did for us and, personally, I'd say Flynn's extremely dedicated."

"How exactly did you end up meeting this woman?"

Flynn pushed his plate away and looked at Horace. He hadn't touched his meal and was sitting with his arms crossed, scowling.

"Talent calling to talent. She'd gotten caught out in a bad storm and needed help."

Horace narrowed his eyes as servants came in with the next course, saving Flynn from whatever point he was gonna press him on. Lot followed them to the table and pulled out an empty seat, diverting Horace's attention further. "Lot, you bastard, where've you been?"

"None of your goddamned business, Horace. I don't owe you an explanation of my activities."

Flynn tried to hide his smirk by taking a bite of quail. Fucking Lot.

"No, but you owe me an explanation for that decision on my Eastern holdings," Morris grumbled loudly. Lot shoved a forkful of pilaf into his mouth, pointedly ignoring him.

"I want to hear more about what Laughlin was doing Outside."

"Exactly what would you like to know, Travis?"

"That packet only covers maybe three years. What were you doing for the rest of it?"

Flynn finished his meat, trying to buy time. "Mostly, I was figuring out who I was without everything up here."

"For five years."

"It was harder than you might think." Flynn pushed the rest of his meal away. "I built a cabin, cut and stacked a lot of wood, worked on cars for a while. Read a lot of books." He glanced at Lord Daun, and his old tutor gave him an approving nod. The majority of the room looked at him like he was speaking Greek.

"You sound like you miss it," Greg said, swirling the wine in his glass.

Flynn laughed softly, looking at all the finery on the table, thinking about his two mismatched spoons lying on the ground somewhere back at the coop. "I do. I knew who I was out there. Now I've got to figure it all out again." He took a sip of water and tapped his fingers on the table, wishing he had a cigar.

"Spare us the platitudes, Scot," Morris spat. "Aggravated assault with a deadly weapon, for God's sake! You're a thug! A convicted felon—"

"And what of it?" Lord Ospre snorted. "How's Julia any different with her strong arming and blackmail? The Hills are dead because of her! At least Laughlin's never killed anyone."

"So we should all just sit back and let Glynfyls fall to a criminal element?"

There was more than one eye-roll at that. Flynn took a shaky sip of water, wishing it was something a hell of a lot stronger. He motioned for a coffee.

"Why shouldn't we fight fire with fire?"

"Have you no pride, Ospre?! You'd give the highest honor a line can bestow to a criminal and a tw—"

"Here now, watch your words, Morris," Lord Jong growled. "Nothing's been proven on that count."

"Bah…proven. House Scot's a conglomeration of mongrels, and him bringing back some whore from the Source's done nothing to improve the situation! Snubbing a pure-blooded House, Theo dodged a bullet there. Not a bloody chance I'd offer up the fruit of my loins to that altar."

Flynn laughed into the appalled silence, fists clenched beneath the table, room tinted crimson. Morris was such a miserable piece of—

"Have you said what you came to say, Peterli?"

They both knew full well he hadn't even begun.

Flynn's grin widened, imagining tearing the man's head off. "Well, if I may interject. You've all had ample opportunity to go over my past in great detail, and I'll maintain that it changes nothing. I'm confident Lord Morris would hold the same view of my House and my suitability for First regardless if I'd come back with that papal seat Lord Ospre mentioned. The fact of the matter is, First Shade has always been determined by strength of talent, and I mean to have it."

Horace snorted from the other end of the table. "And do what with it? I agree with everything Peterli said, but beyond that, you left, abdicating your responsibilities. What's to say you won't do it again?"

The Source and all the fucking Sons about to bear down on us, you stupid motherfucker. "I don't know if you've bothered to look past our borders of late, but there's nowhere else to go. Glynfyls was founded as a refuge for Talents, but you've all let it become a barrel and are just sitting here, waiting for the Source to start shooting. What am I gonna do with it? Whatever it takes to protect my intended, and make no mistake, there's absolutely nothing I won't do. If that means sorting out the damn mess you've all made, so be it."

Eyebrows raised. Shit. He needed to calm down. His temper was getting the better of him, and those jackasses Peterli and Horace sure as hell weren't worth it.

KARA SAT ON THE FLOOR, watching the kittens tear apart a basket of lace samples Miriam had left, half-heartedly leafing through the scads of invitations that'd been delivered throughout the day. Audrey wanted her to familiarize herself with the various House crests. Inked onto heavy vellum with intricately scrolled lettering, some were so ornate she could barely read them. They gave her a funny feeling in the pit of her stomach, remembering Nora's dam, Veronica…there was something in those memories…

It was best to keep busy and not dwell on it. Kara tossed another envelope aside and reached for the last box with the most recent missives.

"Don't mix those with the others, I haven't gone through them yet," Audrey murmured, busy penning another regret. She must've written a hundred today.

"They're all so formal…what's House Scot's crest?"

"It isn't very exciting," Shelby said, handing her a sheet. She was right, it wasn't. Just *Scot* in block letters, imposed over a sash of hideous orange and blue plaid.

"What is it supposed to be?"

"It's a tartan." Shelby laughed, stretching her ink-stained fingers over her elaborately coiffed head. How she could stand to always have her hair up like that—"Horrible, isn't it?"

"It's not good."

"I'd encourage you to choose a crest for House Jester," Audrey said absently, dusting the page with pounce. Not a bit of sepia stained her fingers… *Leave the memory alone, Kara.* Glory, she was worse than a pre-pube with a scab.

She glanced at Audrey, trying not to roll her eyes at yet another thing she was being encouraged to do. She suspected she shouldn't complain, going over invitations and social niceties here was less tedious than it had been with Madame Gillibar. Despite the dryness of the subject, Kara had actually learned a lot. Enough to know that she'd made a major breach in protocol last night…though she didn't regret it, and the papers seemed far more interested in what she'd been wearing than her being seen.

She sighed, watching Shelby and Audrey with their heads together, busy doing her work for her. Kara was tempted to let them think she didn't know how to write anything but her name, very few from the Source did. She frowned at yet another preconceived notion about her. Maybe she'd ask Audrey to get her a journal.

A flash of the ones she'd written in at the Source smoldering at the bottom of a decon-stall went through her mind's eye and, for a moment, she was there again. The warm sticky wetness of her wrists, cold tile beneath her cheek, smoke searing her lungs—

Kara shook her head to clear it, rubbing at her wrists and waiting for the despondence to fade as the memory slipped in where it was supposed to be. The integration left her emotions raw and haggard.

Audrey opened up another envelope and made a face, tearing it in half and discarding it.

"Who was that from?" Kara asked, eager for some distraction.

Audrey pruned her lips, moving on to the next one. "An establishment I'd rather not mention. Lord Scot has never thought about implications. I know it must rankle to be shut up like this, but it's not for much longer. I would advise against making any more forays out."

"I still don't understand why it's so important," Kara said, leaning back against the settee and trying to shake her melancholia.

"The prohibitions are a way to gauge the quality of your breeding. Traditionally, the lines don't mix. Especially not the heirs. Lord Scot's duty was to contract a suitable bride matching his level of talent within his line."

Kara did roll her eyes at that, but could understand the last part, it was the same at the Source. Only near-culls or retired breeders of value were bonded outside their lines. Her contract to Riegel had been one of the things her peers had held against her.

"Except there wasn't anyone," Shelby said, giving Audrey a dark look. "But he should've gotten permission from Lot, then had the Introduction before bonding you."

Kara snorted, she was pretty sure she knew how that would've played out. "Is that why Father Benson was so angry with him?"

"Part of it. He's never liked Flynn, not even when we were kids."

"Taking you out...it's just not done. He's given the impression..." Audrey's lips pressed together, going back to her letter.

Kara laughed. "What, that I'm a whore?" Neither woman would meet her eyes. Kara shook her head in disgust. Flynn was right, the narrow-minded attitudes up here were ridiculous. She snatched another letter from the box—

Her stomach dropped at the spiky script. She shook so violently she could barely open it, the memory of rough hands on her shoulders, holding her down...

"Are you all right?"

A scrap of newsprint fell to her lap, torn from today's paper,

Flynn's face blackened with ink as he stared into hers, a large 'R' scrawled across them both.

Crushing it in her hand, she fled the room.

———

"TYPICALLY, Firsts have a somewhat cordial working relationship. I don't see you having that with Mistress Cree."

Flynn chewed on his cigar, trying to be patient with Lord Jong.

"She's not First; she's acting as proxy for a man who hasn't been seen in seven years. Why they don't oust Anton with a vote of no confidence—"

A stab of Kara's shock shot through him, and he blenched, gripping the table to steady himself.

What the fuck was that?

Everyone was staring at him, the servants refilling glasses loud in the loaded silence around the table.

It was Jacques who broke it. "We need to settle this, now. Quorum's been called, and we'll be locked out of the vote. I know you have your reservations, but Laughlin has the strongest claim."

"I don't believe it." Stuart snorted loudly, dandling his fork in his dessert. "We all know how strong your talent is, Jacques. He's been gone for years and could barely function before that. As far as I know, no one in this room has seen his supposed throwback ability for all the bluster. Not to mention everything in that packet." He leaned forward on his elbows. "Frankly, I'm more inclined to believe the rumors he's a twist."

Flynn barely stayed seated at the old slur. Fuck this, he was done and something was happening with Kara. Shit, why was she so upset? "You want proof, Stuart? Fine. Let's put it to rest once and for all."

Flynn pulled talent, enveloping them. His halos blazed, throwing their shadows against the wall. He let them take a good long look at them, then slapped his hands on the table and phased it. Stuart fell through it with the remaining plates and glasses, landing hard amidst the wreckage. Everyone else scrambled back in shock. Flynn dropped the phase, and Stuart's head slammed into the table's underside as he tried to scuttle away. Served the fucker right.

"Satisfied?" Flynn spat, his halos winking out. "I've made mistakes. Very public ones, and I've paid for them. I am not the man who left here. Talents are being hunted by the Source, and Kar—my intended—is at the top of their list. I will do everything in my power to keep her safe, and if that means riding roughshod over the lot of you to make that happen, I will. As of two days ago, House Martin has pledged its fealty to House Scot. I am your only option."

Lord Jong cleared his throat, watching Stuart reach over the table's edge with a shaking hand to pull himself up. "There's still the matter of an heir—"

A small cry came from the door, and Flynn's heart tore from his chest. Kara was crumpled against the jamb, her face streaked with tears. His chair fell backwards as he went to her, gathering her up in his arms and hiding her from the greedy eyes behind him.

"What's wrong? What happened? Are you hurt?" She shook her head, long locks of tangled hair rippling down her back with the motion. Audrey appeared in the hall, slowing from a run, hand pressed beneath her breast and breathing hard. "What the hell happened?!"

"She opened…a letter… I'm sorry, I didn't see…"

Kara's teeth chattered she was shaking so hard. He took her face between his hands. Jesus Christ, she was fucking terrified. Her hand pressed against his chest, clutching a scrap of newsprint. He prized it from her, and she fell against him bonelessly, as if it had been all that was keeping her upright. He caught her up like a child, and she sobbed into his neck.

Audrey knelt, gingerly picking up the scrap. She smoothed it flat against her skirt, then stood, holding it out to him, her face a careful blank.

Flynn's eyes flicked over it and the hall went scarlet. Kara's arms tightened around him as he fought to tamp down his blinding fury. "I'm gonna kill that motherfucker. Find out where it came from!" Audrey took off with it down the hall at a run.

Flynn spun to the men standing aghast at the state of the woman cradled in his arms. "The Ladies will confirm Kara is carrying my heir. We haven't announced because the Source has agents up here waiting for confirmation she's bred. That fucking note was from one of them. That's why I came back, and that's why I'm not going anywhere. Open your fucking eyes, Julia's working with them, readying a path for invasion, and I swear to God, it'll be over my dead body. Monday morning you will nominate me as First so I can put an end to it."

Kara gave a little sob, her breath hot on his neck. He held her closer to him, fighting back another wave of rage, glaring at his line. Most met his eye with the camaraderie of conviction.

He marked those who didn't.

CHAPTER FIFTEEN

slide [slīd] noun

1. *A phenomenon during breeding unique to Breaker females, during which their personalities subtly change, signaling their imminent succumbence to bloodlust.*

– Excerpt from A Treatise on Talents, *Third Edition*

"Fealty is an outdated notion harkening back to when an Overlord ruled over Glynfyls. It required a blood oath to bind the bondsman, allowing for the transference of talent between the two parties in times of great need…"

– Lord Talos, Preceptor of History,
Academy of Glynfyls

KARA BURIED her face against Flynn's shoulder, fabric heavy with her tears. She tried to make her mind a blank, to let herself be lulled by the rhythm of his stride through the estate.

Snippets of memory snowballing out from that single letter made it impossible. So much worse than the bits she'd experienced before, she was undone. She bit back a sob, feeling…ugh, what she was feeling!

Flynn changed his grip on her, and she heard a click of a stiff door handle. The temperature dipped, and must filled the air.

"Wait." He rumbled as she went to look, his hand on the back of her head. The door clicked closed and there was the hollow sound of him ascending bare stair treads. The squeak and clunk of a lid being raised and the smell of cedar. He settled her into his lap on the floor and leaned back, wrapping blankets and a fur around them. "There, now you can look."

They were in a small alcove filled with a weird green light. It softly illuminated his face as he stared out a pitched, leaded window. Her eyes followed his to the sky beyond the glass. A wide curtain of shifting green luminosity flowed across the sky. She bit back another sob, this one of awe.

"Oh, Flynn, they are real…"

Held safe against him, she watched the undulating streams of aether flickering across the heavens, unbound memories painfully reintegrating into her psyche. Her eyes were hot and puffy when the sky began to lighten behind the mountains. She turned from it and curled against his chest, his arms tightening around her.

"How much more is there?" he asked.

"Too much."

"I swear to Christ, I'm gonna fucking kill him."

She traced one of his shirt buttons, her eyes welling up. "It's not what you think, he never…"

She fumbled through emotions, needing him to know…so scared he would know…no one was ever supposed to know… *"Count the days, Kara, because when I take you, there will be no breaking."*…

"I—Riegel never—He liked to watch while Ielle—she—I did things, Flynn." A sob escaped, and she hung her head, feeling those fingers on her, the burn of Ielle's flaw…

The shame.

"Shh…we both have." He brushed her hair from her face, his hazel-green gaze guileless. "It doesn't matter. Isn't that what you told me last night? Doesn't change how I feel about you. Just makes me want to rip out the fucker's spleen and feed it to her. They're both dead, Kara. They just don't know it yet."

The softness of his lips on her brow belied his seething rage. She melted against him, and he stroked her hair, watching the green-blue curtain fade.

"Are they always like that?"

"No, sometimes they don't show for weeks, and it's too light in the summer. There's purple, yellow… My mom told me there's orange, but I've never seen it."

The pale fingers of dawn crept into the tiny space with them, the walls bare-beamed and the floor rough planking. A lone steamer trunk was flipped open not too far away, and a book lay forgotten in a corner.

"Where are we?"

Flynn ran a weary hand over his beard. "The north gable. I used to come up here a lot when I was a kid. I remember it being bigger."

That made her smile. "You had a coop even back then."

"Yeah, I guess I did."

"Why?"

He rested his head between the eaves, chewing his lip. "Because I couldn't bind my memories."

Kara looked down at her hands, still playing with that button. "When they come back… I'm there again. With them. It's everything, not just emotions. I—I feel their hands, taste—" She shivered, her voice very small. "Will you make it go away? Help me forget, just for a little while?" A tear escaped. Ugh, she just wanted to forget all of it. Feel his touch instead of theirs. "Please?"

"Jesus, Kara." His face was so sad. "You sure?"

She nodded, and he traced her jawline, his hesitation a knot in her throat. What if he said no? What if he didn't want to touch her now—A thread of her bloodlust leaked into the little attic room—Flynn's breath caught. She slipped out of her blouse, the cold air prickling her skin, smoothing her hands up over his shoulders—

He stopped them. His lips on her forehead. Her brow crumpled, another tear tracking to her chin. "Please, Flynn. Make it go away."

"Shh… No 'lust," he rumbled. "I won't…not like that."

He laid her down on the fur, shrugging out of his jacket and waistcoat, her fingers unclasping his belt. His lips were on her throat, mouth hot on the chill of her skin. She gave a soft cry as he pulled her taut nipple into his mouth, working down her sternum to her belly. He strayed to nibble on a hip bone, fingers skating between her thighs. She gasped softly as his lips followed, tongue lapping, gentle, teasing her. Hands in his hair, she arched against him, panting at the warm, moist pressure of his mouth and the roughness of his beard. He brought his fingers to her, and she couldn't bear it—

"Please…"

"Shh…" He blew lightly across her cleft, pressing her onto the fur as he kissed up her body, sliding between her thighs, rocking. His mouth on hers, she moaned against it, tasting herself and feeling their echo.

Her, feeling him, feeling her.

She lost herself, the edges of being blurred beneath sensation… There was only them. Two halves striving to become whole. Closer than before.

Flynn pushed up on his forearms, halos shimmering. Hers answered, talent plucking at them, wanting with them… The little room pulsed with it, gold and verdigris, cocooning them in power and drawing them together. Emotion and thought bled between them. Kara's breath caught, Flynn's heart stuttering in response. His deep inhalation filling her lungs.

The heat between them two-fold, feeling every aspect of their union, passion tipping…

Arching up, crying out, fingers tight around his biceps, his hips against hers, breath hot on her shoulder. Brows furrowed with the cresting of their wave, talent pulsing through them, her body tensing around his as he spent himself.

Kara panted, replete. Bewildered.

It'd never been like that before… What had changed?

Nuzzling into her neck, Flynn gave a sated rumble. "Goddamn, woman. What you do to me." He looked down at her, his eyes saying what his lips couldn't. He dipped his head and kissed her, trailing his fingers down her cheek.

"I love you, too, Flynn."

"Mmm. Say it again."

Kara laughed. "I love you."

He rolled onto his back, smiling, and pulled the quilt up over them. She snuggled under his arm. At peace. Eyes heavy, she slept.

———

TITUS LEANED against the rail of the observation deck overlooking a vast subterranean bunker, the drone of circulation fans loud in his ears. Plaz lights suspended from the extensive steel super-structure shone down upon the simulated turf below, and the formations of troops standing at the ready for deployment.

His Elites.

Before his father had stepped down, one of their most promising bitches had escaped with her unborn child. The loss of her unique ability to regenerate tissue had been a blow to their program. Titus had created the Triam to prevent such a security breach from happening again. It had also allowed for more strident experimentation outside of what was generally approved. Nuremberg. Geneva. Helsinki and Belmont. None had existed for a millennium, and he was at a loss as to why they should dictate his methods.

Here they didn't.

Located a short jump south of the Source, the Triam housed just under four hundred Breaker females in various stages of development. Scores that would never see the sky. The rest of the board had no idea they existed, nor the legions of men assembled before him. As far above Peacekeepers as they were above standard Breakers, it was a force designed for conquest.

"You've reviewed the timetable BrE2?" Titus asked the man waiting behind him.

Brix stepped to the rail, a cap shadowing the wine-colored birthmark dripping from the top of his pointed skull to his curdled lip. It was fortunate for the Goliath that the Source's beauty standards didn't apply here. "I have, and we stand ready."

"Excellent. Begin the integration. We'll advance beneath one hierarchy."

The Elite saluted. Titus rubbed the small stone set into his pinky ring and appeared back in his chambers at the Source. A fascinating technology, it completely replaced the need for a Fetch.

He sat at his desk, flipping through holos, tight-lipped. A glass of bourbon was delivered, and he took a long swallow with a handful of pills. They did little to assuage the pounding behind his eyes. The situation in the North was problematic. The closure of the border had necessitated his Fetches taking a ridiculously circuitous route to dodge the vectors monitoring for activity.

Marcos's competence had screwed him there, but this Jester gambit had to play out. The woman was priming the Commandant for something, and Titus was eager to see if his hunch was correct. If his ploy with the redacted files hadn't been enough to throw the man sufficiently off balance, then Titus was betting his recent debauched performance would. Time would tell.

It was in short supply.

He needed Ielle in the city, especially after Friday night's cat fight. The deviation from the Jester girl's documented behaviors lent itself to slide. If that were the case, it was paramount that she be removed to stasis before she succumbed, regardless of confirming her status as a breeder. He updated Barton's directives for her immediate removal. That should give Scot something to focus on other than parliamentary procedure. The boy was throwing wrenches into his plans with a shocking amount of accuracy.

"Any unsanctioned breaches to be construed as an act of war..." Titus snorted, flipping the document aside and pulling up the next one. A proposal to sue the Source. He had to admit, it was a genius legal maneuver, if they had a witness.

It irked him that he had no leads as far as that was concerned. The naming of the last Finder he'd procured, and was presently breeding, spelled out the situation too clearly not to have insider information. Otto would have to widen his search, but other than alerting him to a leak, the proposal would make no difference, regardless of its brilliance.

Come Monday, Julia would sink it with the quorum vote, then proceed to call for the Incursion. Sipping on his bourbon, he smiled, feeling things coming together.

FLYNN LAY ON THE FLOOR, watching his breath drift upward and dissipate into the ribbons of weak February sunlight teasing through the window. Kara pressed against him, her dreams tinging their bond with fear and shame, too close to his own ghosts in this room. She whimpered, and he kissed her brow, feeling that weird reverberation between them pulse.

His brow furrowed. It was their echo and not…but both were definitely getting stronger. That last time with her, Christ, he couldn't tell where he stopped and she began. He hadn't wanted to.

It was terrifying.

All that ugly he kept under lock and key, slavering to pour inside her. Not a fucking chance that was happening. He wouldn't ruin this. Her.

Kara's fingers tightened against his chest with a lance of terror, leaking 'lust. It'd become pervasive in the little room, setting him on edge. He stroked her hair. God, that she had to suffer what those motherfuckers did to her… The fact that Riegel hadn't physically raped her didn't make it any fucking better. Whatever had happened was just as bad, if not worse. Shit, she'd tried to kill herself because of it. He tamped down his rage, not wanting to wake her, but Jesus fucking Christ, when he caught up with that son of a bitch—

Yeah, he wasn't gonna kid himself. The ugly would come out, and he didn't give a shit who the fuck saw it. After last night, it didn't matter. His lack of diplomacy at the end had tanked any chance he'd had at First. Regardless of whipping his proverbial dick out for all of them, those four assholes were still gonna cock-block him. He smirked. Seeing Stuart's face when he climbed out from under the table might've been worth it.

The door opened with a sharp click.

Flynn tipped his head back and met French's gaze.

"Master Caliban has been looking for you, sir, and the Ladies will be here in a few hours for tea." He set a tray on the floor within arm's reach.

"Cal can wait, but do me a favor and ask him to have that asshole Rogan meet me in the gym tomorrow."

French's jaw inched forward a fraction as he inclined his head. Guess he didn't like the Breaker either.

Flynn snuggled back up to Kara as the man retreated. The distinct aroma of warm snickerdoodles filled the little attic, and he knew there'd be cocoa beside it. His heart constricted in his chest, thinking about all the other times French had delivered the same tray to a broken little boy in this gable…

"What do I smell?"

"French brought up cookies."

She laughed sleepily, turning to look at him. "Cookies?"

Christ, he fucking loved her. He bit the thought back, his eyes hot. Her brow creased, and she kissed him before pushing up against his chest to look.

"What kind?"

"Snickerdoodles." She gave him a blank look. "Come on, you don't have snickerdoodles at the Source?"

"Nothing called that…" She stretched out and pulled the tray closer, snagging one of them and popping a piece into her mouth. "S'like a cinnamon-y sugar cookie."

Flynn rolled his eyes as she fed him one. "No, it's a snickerdoodle."

"These your favorite?"

"Mmm, you?" He opened his mouth for another bite.

"Lemon."

"Lemon?"

She nodded, sitting up. Her hair fell around her nakedness in soft, dark waves. "Lemon anything." He propped himself up, reaching out to play with a lock. Kara picked up one of the mugs of cocoa, sipping it and looking around the little room. "Why did you bring me up here?"

He shrugged. "It's where I used to come when I was upset. I just kind of went on autopilot."

"There was a janitor's closet on level four," Kara said, staring at her cookie. "Drones are everywhere, but there are some places…bubbles.

Good and bad, I guess. They couldn't see me fall out of character, but when Riegel and Ielle found me…" He sat up so he could pull her close, wanting to beat the fuck out of them both. Kara laughed, cheeks wet again. "It's stupid, you know that's why I don't dance? I didn't want anyone touching me… I'd forgotten that…"

She burrowed back against him, and the lump in his throat thickened, not wanting to know, but having to ask. "Did Cal know?"

There was a long silence before she shook her head beneath his chin. "Nora might've suspected, but I don't think anyone knew. I never said anything."

He didn't feel the relief he'd expected. Cal should've fucking known, goddamn it. About her, fuck, about him… "Hey, none of it was your fault."

"How can you be sure?"

"I've been in the same room with the sick fuck. No one'll ever hurt you again, Kara, so help me God." He cradled her against him, his thumb brushing away her tears.

She shook her head, the tip of her nose pink. "All these memories…"

He drew her against his chest and held her as she cried.

CHAPTER SIXTEEN

imprint [im-print] verb

1. *First-hand knowledge of an item or location able to be transferred
   to others within a line allowing them to utilize their talent upon
   the target without being personally acquainted with it.*

– Excerpt from A Treatise on Talents, *Third Edition*

---

*"Though the Ladies hold no official power within the patriarchy of
Glynfyls, they are widely viewed as the fulcrum upon which power
rises and falls. Holding sway over both public and private opinion, it is
in one's best interest to ingratiate oneself with their exclusive cabal..."*

*– Lady Chatterly, Precepta of Social Graces,
Academy of Glynfyls*

MARCOS SAT AT HIS DESK, plotting a route north based on two-hundred-year-old reports and more recent first-hand accounts. He frowned at the conflicting information. The lack of vector data was frustrating. So was the inability of whomever had submitted this trash to use an odometer. He scowled. Without a Fetch's imprint, the only option that remained was to take transports up with line-of-sight jumps along the existing rail line to the city.

It was inefficient. Instead of traversing the heavily forested expanse within a span of hours, it would take days to move all of the troops up to the plateau. Titus wouldn't be happy with the delay.

The thought wasn't displeasing.

Marcos poured another cup of coffee. And once there? He fiddled with troop placement, but nothing about it felt right—

It wasn't right.

He dashed a hand through the holos, done lying to himself.

None of the self-serving military ops waged solely to increase the Corporation's global foothold were, and now here he was, strategizing the final subjugation of his own kind to line their damned pockets with the fruit of his loins.

What kind of life could he have had?

Black, white, or grey. Nothing about this one was honorable.

He stood, grabbing his hat. Told Cathy he was taking an early lunch, and went to Albanach's tower.

A sub brought him into the library. He browsed the shelves, unable to stay still. His eyes grazed over the titles, not seeing them. Little bits of art. Pressed flowers. A flat stone with splotches of paint on it. Marcos turned it over in his hands. A painfully scrawled K was on the back.

Through the window, a light dusting of snow blanketed the garden, the city beyond a conglomerate of geometric shapes and moving lights. In the far distance past the wall, a line of black hills, only visible from the highest levels of the towers. None of them had windows looking outwards.

Only in.

He'd done that enough lately, and what he saw made him ill.

"Marcos, did we have something planned?" Nora was at his elbow, her blue eyes questioning.

He gave the stone a little toss, then laid the burden down and smiled for her.

"No, I just couldn't stay away." She smiled back, and he took her hands in his, stepping forward to close the gap between them.

"Did you want to have lunch—"

He kissed her.

It all came rushing back. That unequivocal feel of her in his arms, the way she twined her arms about his neck, fingernails teasing his scalp…

And the talent.

It began as that whisper he'd felt at their picnic and built with the deepening of their kiss, his skin electrified.

This was right.

He pulled away, short of breath, searching her golden gaze, her skin ruby-tinged by the light of his, both of them afire. The wonder of it filled him, pushing out the blackness of the years bereft of her, cracking the carefully placed armor about his heart.

It fell to dust at her smile. He took a pained intake of breath, his fingers tightening against her spine.

"You still feel the same…" He brushed her hair back from her face, his throat tight. Talent thrummed around them, begging to be used.

"Was there ever any question?"

"No. Not for me. Do you want this again?"

"It's all I've ever wanted…but the hierarchy, can't ask you—"

"Fuck the hierarchy, Titus, and all the rest of them."

He kissed her as he'd dreamt of doing every night for the past thirty years. Talent surged between them, rebinding what never should've been sundered. Nora's deep contentment echoed his own.

She laughed at his gasp. "Are you surprised our bond returned?"

He shook his head, feeling complete, a piece of his soul replaced. "I'm perpetually surprised in your presence, it's one of the things I love about you…but you know they'll have already seen that surge. Titus will be furious, and my line—" He reached for his sidearm. He wouldn't be broken from her again.

Nora stopped him with a kiss. "Neither will be an issue. I lost you once, and I refuse to lose you again." She took his hand, leading him deeper into the tower.

KARA SAT with her back to the windows of an airy room of taupes, the golden midday sun streaming to either side of her. It picked up the red highlights buried in the chestnut of Flynn's messy waves, making him look entirely roguish. His outstretched fingers played with the precise spacing of his forks, like a bored kid trying to keep out of trouble.

Though she was glad he was at this stupid tea with her, she was pretty sure he was going to be about as helpful as wallpaper. He got weird whenever she asked him about the Ladies, probably because his mom had been one of them. Kara smoothed her skirts, wishing she'd worn something more forgiving than silk. She was sure the underarms of her blouse were already several shades darker than they should be.

Liveried servants filtered in, setting exactingly plated filets of honeyed salmon atop greens before them and the four women chatting amicably amongst themselves at the table.

Their ease didn't extend to Kara.

Ugh, she felt like a child sitting with them. The fact that they were here to determine the suitability of her bond to Flynn didn't help... whatever that meant. It sounded horrible, and given how suitable everyone else seemed to find her... She bit back a laugh. How did Nora always seem so poised? She would've fit in seamlessly with the stately quartet.

The servants withdrew, and the tall, auburn-haired woman began.

"Well, I can see why you've been so smug, Laughlin, she's even lovelier in person. Be a dear and introduce us." They all looked at Kara, and her cheeks burnt.

A silly grin spread across Flynn's face, and he ran a hand over his beard. "Ah, ladies, this is Kara."

"My God, check that box off—he really is smitten." The plump woman with white-blond ringlets giggled with a hand to her lips.

Bernice rolled her eyes. "I told you."

Flynn colored, and the woman tittered again. Though middle-aged, she was unquestionably cherubic with her rosy cheeks and baby-blue eyes. Her giggling cemented the impression. Of them all, Kara already liked her best.

"Oh, that is just darling! Laughlin Scot blushing like a school girl!" She poo-poohed his glare with a little wave and smiled at Kara. "I'm Evie Crandall. My Bart's First Finder."

Beside her, the svelte woman with poker-straight, raven-black hair smirked. Something about her was unsetting, the rest of them giving her just a bit more room at the table. "Smitten? He's a puppy." From her tone, she was trying to get a rise out of him, and it worked. A muscle in Flynn's jaw popped. Why would she—

Kara drew in a sharp breath, entrapped by the woman's impossibly green gaze. Her crimson-stained lips split into a coy smile as she extended a pale arm across the table. Kara hesitated before clasping her hand, and the woman's smile widened. Her grip was too cool and smooth, like a serpent's coil.

"Alice Carmody-Klein, enchanté. My husband's a Fixer and absolutely no one of consequence at the moment, but then again, neither is yours." She raised a sculpted eyebrow as if that were some great joke, and Kara resisted the urge to wipe her palm on her skirts. Carmody... where had she heard that name before?

"Oh, stop playing with the girl," Bernice chided, stabbing a tomato.

Alice pushed her plate towards Flynn. "Here, you'll want this." Her nails were enameled a shocking teal. An oversized deck of gilded cards appeared in her hand, and she began shuffling. Kara looked to Flynn for an explanation, but he was too busy glowering to notice. Make that angry wallpaper.

Evie clucked her tongue. "You'll have to excuse Alice, she'll be in a mood until whatever's in her bonnet becomes clear," she said, as if that explained everything.

"Clear as mud, if you ask me," Bernice grumbled.

Alice didn't pause her shuffling. "No one did."

Kara played with her greens, sneaking glances at them all from beneath her lashes. Her stupid 'set the tone' spiel felt more than a little hollow. She didn't have any doubts that these women would eat her if she stepped out of line, but them seeing her as—wait a minute...

She made herself meet Alice's waiting eyes. Ugh, that was creepy! "Flynn said your extra is seeing."

Her unexpectedly bright trill filled the room. "Yes, that's the easy part. It's believing that's difficult." Smirking, she began laying out cards to the exclusion of all else.

Flynn watched her warily as he ate, eyeing her abandoned plate. Everything coming through their bond reminded Kara of a petulant pre-pube. She was tempted to kick him so he would get over it.

"And I'm Phyllis Breakspear," the auburn-haired woman said before she could. "I hold the position of First Breaker in trust for my son, Billy."

"When does he make his majority?" Flynn asked. Finally.

"Three months—if all goes to plan."

Kara didn't particularly like the set of Phyllis's jaw when she said that. She dabbed her lips with a napkin and forced a smile. "Then I have you to thank for those jellies."

"The glóthach, yes, and you're very welcome. After the other night, I'd say I need to make them stronger—"

"We'll get to that in a minute." Bernice patted the manufactured brown waves of her updo and smiled, her wide mouth pulling back to her ears. "We've met informally, but I'm Bernice Markham, House Prydee by birth, Miriam's my younger sister, so that makes us kin. I'm bonded to Kyle, he's First Fetch. We're all just thrilled Laughlin's finally repent—"

"You've no Binder among you? What happened to Lady Brody?" Flynn interrupted around a mouthful. Kara glanced from Bernie's annoyed scowl to Phyllis as she answered.

"When the Sons gained access to the city several years back, Winston was caught up in the melee, and Cressida didn't survive his death. Their children were spared, but neither have met their majority. The current First's wife lacks some of the qualities we deem necessary for our little sorority—"

Bernice snorted. "Janice is a shrew."

"So are you." Alice smirked. Bernice's eyes shot daggers at her. "Never fear, Laughlin, we're expecting a suitable replacement shortly."

An icy finger went up Kara's spine.

Flynn's face hardened. "Anyone I know?"

The woman kept laying out cards like she hadn't heard him.

Evie cleared her throat. "That was a fine bit of chicanery down at the station, Laughlin. Bart can't decide if you're a genius or just incredibly arrogant. Having her sign as Lady Scot then cloaking it." She gave him a chiding glare. "Took a fair bit of finding to sort out that tangle."

He smugly popped a tomato into his mouth, and Kara shook her head. Whatever history he had with these women made him as recalcitrant as he'd been with her back at the coop. A short-lived smile tipped up her lips at that, wishing they were back there.

It wasn't missed by any of them, and met with varying degrees of censure.

Crap.

"Well, I suspect she is, Introduction or no, he's already gone and bonded her." Bernice sighed, flaking off a bite of salmon.

Evie put up a hand. "Hold that thought. I want to suss out exactly whom our Laughlin's brought home. What is it with you Scot men picking up women from exotic locales?" She shook her head, sending her curls bouncing. "So let's have it dear, what House?"

Kara glanced at Flynn as she finished chewing. "Jester."

The table went silent except for the sound of Alice's cards being snicked down, that little smirk still on her lips. Kara began to suspect it was a permanent feature.

Bernice's mouth curdled. "You really are a bitch."

"Interesting that Miriam didn't say anything," Alice retorted. "It would've served no purpose for me to tell you, but Deirdre knew all of what was, and what will be."

Kara didn't like the way the seer was looking at Flynn. He picked up Alice's discarded plate and dropped it on his empty one with a loud clink, then shoved another bite of fish into his mouth, glaring at her. He was definitely in coop mode. It only increased Alice's smugness.

"Well, I suspect that shortens this portion of the interview considerably," Evie sighed. "We'd spoken with Deirdre in length about her plans for you two, but had assumed they'd gone by the wayside, and given your reluctance at the time—"

"He claims it was the pull," Bernice cut in. Phyllis and Evie stared at her, agape. She preened. "And considering the way their energy is all woven together, I haven't any doubts."

They turned to Flynn, and he shrugged, concentrating on his plate. Their eyes flicked to Kara.

She swallowed the lump that had materialized in her throat. "I—a blizzard hit when I was on foot…he found me. I don't remember that part very well…"

Evie fell back in her chair, hand fluttering at her breast. "Oh, it's like a fairytale!"

"The question is, which one," Phyllis mused from behind her tea cup. She didn't look like she way buying any of it.

"The one with four evil stepmothers," Flynn muttered too low for them to hear.

Kara laughed and tried to play it off as a cough. Phyllis didn't buy that, either.

"Did Deirdre ever verify halos?" Evie asked, way too brightly.

Flynn started choking and grabbed up his water, crimson.

"The fact that she's bred answers that question," Phyllis said, laying her fork on her empty plate. A servant whisked it away.

"Shh, I'm trying to get a peek at Laughlin's. Just remembering them when they came in's enough to get me all hot and bothered. Lord knows what seeing them now would do." Evie bit her knuckle at him, laughing as he coughed harder, her pudgy hands clapping. Kara couldn't help smiling at his mortification. He shot her a look, and she giggled.

"Oh, Leave the boy alone, you filthy thing," Phyllis said, taking a swipe at Evie's arm.

"Come on, let me have my fun! Bart's halos aren't anything to sneeze at, but he's not what I'd call strapping. The rest of us aren't as blessed as you in that department."

Alice snapped down another card, raising an eyebrow at Evie. "Speak for yourself. I find Carl quite a delightful specimen, and I can include both his halos and personality in that statement."

"Halos aren't everything and conversation's overrated." Phyllis smiled over the rim of her tea cup. The other three laughed, and she looked way too satisfied with herself. Flynn kept shoveling food into his mouth.

Evie drummed her fingers on the table. "So, let's talk about your little outing. You do realize your reaction to Mistress Cree's slur has very clearly drawn battle lines and binding your lipstick hasn't helped."

Flynn stopped mid-chew.

Crap. Kara choked down her bite.

He ran his tongue over his teeth, pushing back in his chair. "Binding?" Those blue motes churned dangerously, and bloodlust tinged the air. Her own rose up to meet it, and he inhaled, growling—

Phyllis clucked her tongue. "Calm down, Laughlin."

His face tensed and that block on his emotions went up so fast and hard that Kara gasped. He slammed back in his chair, wood cracking, arms across his chest. The blood drained from her face. He was really mad...

"Her slip using talent isn't entirely her fault. Bloodlust affects the physiology of our line's females profoundly during pregnancy, and there's no doubt she's presenting as a breeding Breaker. The intense mood swings are only part of it. The glóthach will help."

Kara glanced from Phyllis to Flynn. He was still mad. Really mad. None of the women at the table seemed to care. "What are they?"

Phyllis pursed her lips. "Breaker Business. The codes very clearly stipulate the need to pull some modicum of talent in order to be considered such, no matter what else may present. Julia should be very glad your lipstick was the worst of it...which, aside from the pretext of ascertaining your suitability, is why we're here. The Ladies of Glynfyls have always played a role in the direction of the city and its politics. You've struck a bold move that has the potential to affect our status quo profoundly."

Kara was silent, feeling twelve years old again, being reprimanded for some infraction. She kept her face a careful blank. There was a lilac glimmer from the other side of the table, and Flynn made a disparaging noise. Evie gave a pouty little *humph*. "He's already gone and cloaked her, the devil."

"You surprised?" Bernice tsked.

"A girl can dream, can't she? Though I suspect if he's taken her into the city it's probably for the best."

"Ya think?" He chucked his napkin onto his plate, his temper dangerously short. Kara put a hand on his thigh, and he bit back whatever else he was about to say.

"That angry and she can still bring him to heel," Alice murmured, looking at her cards.

"No small feat there." Phyllis ignored Flynn's indignant growl, still watching Kara intently. "And a large part of why we've been so eager to meet you. Each of us with a preconceived notion of what Laughlin's brought to our shores, and I must admit, you don't fit what I was expecting. All I see is an exceptionally pretty, very nervous, little girl. Tell me, Kara, why did you come to Glynfyls?"

Her anxiety jumped being called out like that, and she looked around the table, wetting her lips. "Because that's where Flynn brought me. He said everywhere else Talents are hunted, and we wouldn't be safe…" Her hand floated to her abdomen, and she pulled it away, cheeks flushing. A rumble started in Flynn's chest, and he put his arm around her.

Phyllis's eyes narrowed. "Forgive me if I find it all a bit too neat."

"Then take it up with Cal." Flynn snapped back.

"Mmph. I'd believe anything if that man's involved," Evie said irritably. "If ever there was a Shade's Shade, Caliban Scot is it."

"Says the wife of a Finder's Finder."

Evie laughed. "Oh! Bart will be just tickled you think so! And don't think he doesn't know it was you who cloaked that tack on his chair, you naughty boy. Man was terrified he was going to get tetanus."

Flynn smirked, taking a cup of coffee from a servant. "Look, Kara came into all this blind. If you're looking for plots and power grabs you're barking up the wrong tree."

"There's always plots and power grabs, Laughlin," Bernice chided, waggling her spoon at him. "Intended or no, she's literally marked Julia Cree, and we want to know what she plans on doing now."

All of them looked at her, save for Alice clicking down her cards. Kara squared her shoulders, the navy silk of her blouse sticking to the sweat slicking down her back. What did they want her to tell them—

"She hasn't thought that far ahead. Neither of them have, or do." The seer swept up the deck and tapped its edge on the table, then froze. Her expression melted like wax, and the woman's almond-shaped, absinthe green eyes became distant. All at once, she was very young and incredibly ancient. Her lips parted, a voice not her own slithering from her lips.

"The best laid schemes 'o mice an' men, Gang aft agley...and forward though I canna see..."

A cloying heaviness filled the room, stifling breath. Kara's fingers found Flynn's. At the movement, Alice's head sinuously tilted in their direction, her pupils dilating to small points. Something rippled through them, and Kara thought she might pee herself.

Alice's smirk was back.

"The present only toucheth thee." Her laugh trilled out again, and the weight of the atmosphere shattered as if struck. Released from its grip, Kara slumped against the table, Flynn's hands at her shoulders. Heart thudding in her chest, she leaned into him.

Alice tapped the edge of the table with her deck thrice before secreting it away in her skirts and left the room without a backwards glance.

RIEGEL TOWELED OFF, not entirely positive he'd divested himself of the copious amount of bodily fluids he'd been spattered with. What he wouldn't give for a decon-stall. Cleansing oneself with soap and water was so very primitive. He'd have to take that into account should he decide to indulge himself again. Though Wallace had probably envisioned something akin to a hole being blown through the man's chest, Riegel thought it rather dull. What was the point, if not to enjoy himself?

And he had, leaving the mark's office splintered and splattered with portions of corpse splayed about the room. Riegel wiped the steam from the mirror and smiled at his reflection, another slash of ruby across the white of his eye. The look on the man's face as he'd vaporized his desk had been worth it, as had the opportunity to work out the resulting euphoria on what he assumed was the man's offspring. The girl hadn't been particularly appealing, but any port in a storm…

He carefully dressed himself in the garments Wallace had so thoughtfully provided, the grey moleskin beyond redemption. They would do. The jacket was a bit tighter across the shoulders than he preferred, but otherwise, he cut a dashing figure in it. He flipped through the wallet of the previous owner, making sure the card he'd been given went in his pocket beside it. Pulling his hair back into a tail, he smiled at himself again and left the miserable little room.

The city was abuzz with anticipation over tomorrow's pending Quorum vote, and Kara's threatening of some woman. He snorted, though he'd seen the infamous still of the alleged event, he had difficulty believing it. The girl was terrified of her own shadow, he'd made very sure of that… Of course, on the off-chance it was true…a smile slid across his lips, imagining her putting up a bit of resistance when they finally consummated their relationship. She'd always been such a cold fish.

And then there was his contribution to the news cycle.

He grabbed an evening edition blaring about the most recent murders and pulled a gold pocket watch from his waistcoat. *My, that was quick.* Four hours, give or take. Rumor up here spread quicker than venereal disease. The reporting was shoddy, but the photos had captured the scene exquisit—

Riegel frowned. They were lumping in his handiwork with what'd been done on the plateau before his arrival. He looked between two grainy stills and had to admit, they weren't dissimilar, but that did irk. Folding the paper up, he petulantly stuffed it beneath his arm. Pity it wasn't the sort of thing one could request a retraction for.

He fingered the card in his inner pocket. On it was a stylized image of a deer's flipped-up tail and an address, across which was scrawled a surprisingly adroit *W*. Riegel had been instructed to go to the establishment, where someone would be waiting to "whammy" him.

Not in the habit of giving names, Wallace had assured him he'd recognize the Fetch. Though the tubes didn't appear to be necessary to traverse the majority of the city, the establishments solely accessible through them catered to a decidedly higher echelon of Talent, which was exactly where Kara had landed.

Riegel headed up the hill through the seething press of bodies to the very edge of the fifth rung. Rounding a corner, he spied a sign, twin to what was emblazoned on the card.

As he entered the establishment's split swinging doors, his lips tipped up at the realization that the Whitetail was a brothel, and a lively one at that. The poorly lit room he'd come into was large, furnished to resemble someone's idea of a grand salon. Small private nooks had been created with dusky curtains and opposing couches. Most were claimed by women lounging in various stages of undress upon men whose expressions ranged from ardent appreciation to boredom. Several tables were in the back, one of which was surrounded by a crowd watching an incredibly intense card game.

Riegel stiffened at the mop of fluffy blond hair crowning one of the players. His eyes narrowed, ignoring the whore that'd come up to him and begun fiddling with his lapels. Wallace's warning abruptly made sense if that pissant was the only one that could key people for the tubes. He gritted his teeth, pushing past the whore and striding across the room.

Riegel stayed in the shadows, taking stock. The poor sot that he was standing behind held two pair, the dandy beside him a straight. A large pile of units in front of each man accounted for their grim faces. Well, four of them were grim. What had Wallace said his name was…? Fitz. He seemed more interested in the whore on his lap than the game.

"Ye gonna throw in or ogle them cards all night, Paul?" the blond man asked, his hand farther up the whore's skirt than could be considered decent, even here.

"Keep it in your fuckin' pants."

Fitz grinned at the whore. "T'is, that's me problem."

The poor sot with the two pair sighed. "Ain't the worst one ye could have. I'm out while I can still pay me rent." He threw his cards on the table and scrubbed at his face, grimacing.

Beside him, the dandy's lips twitched beneath his pencil-thin mustache. He added a unit to the stack in front of him. "Raise."

The man to his left let out a low whistle. His brow glinted damply in the rose-tinted shadows of the room. After a moment, he matched it, and asked for a card. The pissant grinned, removing his hand from the whore's nether-regions to raise and take a sip from the tankard beside him.

"S'it, I've had enough of ye lot. Call," the man to Fitz's left said, laying his cards out. He glanced from his flush to the dandy's straight and swore. "Christ, yer a shite Jonnas, another round, and I would've had that jack."

Fitz laughed. "Not a chance of that, friend." He slapped down four of a kind with that stupid grin on his face.

The dandy's hand went through his pile of units, spilling them into the center of the table. "Bah. If I hadn't won every single unit off you the other night, I'd swear you were a damn cheat, McCreedy."

The blond man pulled on that ridiculous tuft beneath his lip, unperturbed at the allegation. "Was an off night, t'be sure, but this evens us up… Ye know where t'find me if ye fancy tryin' t'get it back." He shifted up his winnings with a practiced sweep of his hand and flash of halos.

The men grunted and dispersed along with the crowd. Fitz turned his attentions to the whore on his lap, and Riegel cleared his throat. They both looked at him, and a wide grin split the pissant's face.

"Eh…ye made it back. Did ye fancy going for a swim, then?"

Riegel's mouth curdled. "I'll pass. We have business to discuss."

The man's hand strayed to his pocket, fiddling with something. He patted the whore's leg, and she stood. "Right. I'll meet ye upstairs, love." Pushing back in his chair, Fitz blew a curl from his eyes and raised up his tankard to one of the whores lurking. "Ale? Ye must be thirsty after yer walk."

Ignoring the jibe, Riegel pulled out a chair. It creaked beneath him. "I've been told you're the man to see should someone wish to gain access to the tubes."

Fitz gave no indication he'd heard him until two tankards were delivered, and the whore left. "Can't imagine who'd be saying such a thing. What yer implying ain't strictly legal."

Riegel leaned forward, looming across the table at him. He had no desire to play coy. "Wallace."

The pissant choked a little on his ale, wiping the foam from his lip as he set it down. His hand was back in his pocket. What did he have in there? "Eh…ye got somewhat, then?"

Riegel slapped the card down on the table. The young man tucked it away and glanced around the room before holding out a long-fingered hand to shake. Riegel took it, taking great pleasure in grating his bones together. There was a flash of silver from the pissant's halos.

"Right, s'done." He grimaced. "I'll take me hand back now."

A smile on his face, Riegel gave it one more squeeze, and Fitz made an agonized grunt as something popped. Glaring at him, the blond man cradled his mangled hand to his chest and shifted out.

Riegel sat back with a smile, sipping his ale. That hadn't been as satisfying as flaying him would've been, but there was a certain pleasure in knowing he was out there crippled until he could find a Binder. Riegel's eyes ran over the available occupants of the room. While he was here, he might as well take full advantage—

His gaze stopped on a man hurrying through the door. Seeing Riegel, he made a bee line to him.

"Sorry I'm late, friend." Pithy's assistant pulled out a chair and perched on the edge. "Busy day, busy day. Ye've got somewhat for me?"

Riegel's jaw tensed, his pleasure replaced by rage. He reached into his jacket. Perhaps he could salvage the situation with enough—

Standing, he flung the table across the room. The air filled with screams. Women scattered as he tore through the crowd to get upstairs. That pissant had stolen his wallet.

<hr>

"THE WHOLE SITUATION IS HIGHLY UNUSUAL." Merchant stood, sliding the pen into his pocket.

Shaking his hand, Cal had to agree. "Not gonna question it, and think I'll just sit here real quiet for the next day or so. You'll keep a tight lid on things?"

The little barrister gave him a look as he collected his coat. "Attorney-client privilege, Master Scot. You pay me very well for my discretion, and I have several children to put through the Academy. My lips are sealed and nothing will be filed until after the stipulated timeframe has passed."

Cal grunted. "Appreciate it."

Merchant tipped his bowler and left the room as Flynn came in, already puffing on a cigar. He walked right over to the Ash'a board and started setting it up. Cal poured himself some scotch and leaned back.

"How'd it go with the Ladies?"

"Tell me about the Source."

Cal took a long swallow. "What do you wanna know?"

Flynn dropped into one of the chairs, his hair a bird's nest. He chewed on his cigar for a minute, staring into the fire. "Why she doesn't want my kid."

Shit.

"Because she's got no idea what it's supposed to mean, and that's all on me." Boy looked shocked as shit at the admission. Cal shrugged. "I try to give the Talents under my purview as much normalcy as possible, but the culture that's developed down there… Breeding's become just another medical procedure. Offspring are removed, and they never see them again. Kids grow up thinking they sprang into being like little Gods, which is just how the Corporation wants it." He went to the wall safe behind his desk, riffling around until he found the cube he was looking for.

"Here."

Flynn caught it against his chest and gave him a look.

"Just play the damn thing," Cal grumbled, pouring another three fingers of scotch.

A reel flashed up from it, showing one of the Source's dormitories, and a narrator began. After a moment a pod of children dressed in whites filed in. It was propaganda prepared for the Corporation's annual shareholder's meeting. The entire thing was abhorrent. Should give Flynn a pretty good frame of reference for Kara's mindset.

Cal went back to his desk, half listening to the narrator wax poetic about the state-of-the-art monitoring and sanitary conditions their human livestock was raised in. He was surprised Flynn sat through the hour long presentation as calmly as he did. When it was over, the boy lit another cigar and sat smoking, staring into the fire. French had come in around the midway mark with a coffee service, and Flynn spun his cup on the side table.

"That property west, the one Mom left me as part of my majority payout. After the vote tomorrow, I'm taking Kara there. I don't have it all figured out yet, but depending on what we find… I'll go through the motions, Cal. Finish what I started, but I don't have enough support for First, and I never wanted head. Just give it to Graham. It won't matter who's sitting in that box if everything's being decided by Quorum."

"No, don't suppose it will." Cal pursed his lips. "I can understand the urge to skedaddle, but things being what they are with Kara—"

"Damn it, I know we can't leave until after the baby's born, I just… I need an out. An outlet. Before I do something fucking stupid." His eyes drifted towards the bottle of scotch and he ran a hand over his mouth.

"Rogan said he'll be in the gym if you decide to show up. What happens on the off-chance they vote you in?"

Flynn stood, draining his cup. He blew out a stream of smoke, his mouth curdling. "Since it's gonna take a fucking act of God to put me in that seat, I'd consider it a heavenly dispensation, and if that's the case, far be it from me to argue with our Lord and Savior." He flippantly crossed himself.

"Careful, God'll get you for that shit."

"The miracle happens, and he can add it to the fucking list." Clamping his cigar between his teeth, Flynn stalked out of the room.

Cal watched him go, pouring himself another, almost feeling bad. A snippet of an old hymn popped into his mind. *God moves in a mysterious way, His wonders to perform; He plants his footsteps in the sea, And rides upon the storm…*

Chuckling, he took a sip, certain that metaphorical storm wasn't meant to be a woman.

CHAPTER SEVENTEEN

pod [päd] noun

1. *A group of adolescent Talents assigned to a dormitory within the Creche for developmental observation and review.*

– Excerpt from A Treatise on Talents, *Third Edition*

"Leaving Talents bonded after they've fulfilled their obligation of offspring serves a practical purpose. The emotional component that a bond brings allows for an unprecedented glimpse into a Talent's state of mind. With no allegiance to each other and strident conditioning from an early age, each bellwether becomes a kind of 'thought police', ready to inform upon the other should one of them prove dissatisfied with their situation..."

– L. Merkel, Head Geneticist,
The Source

KARA WAS surprised when Flynn rolled out of bed a few minutes before the alarm went off. She pulled the covers around her, wishing things weren't awkward between them. She had no idea he'd be so upset about her using talent. That damn block was up again, and he hadn't spoken to her after the Ladies had gone, leaving without a word and not coming back to their rooms until late. When she'd tried to apologize, he just grunted and rolled over.

Once again, she'd screwed things up and had no idea how to fix them.

"Early meeting?"

"Yeah."

"Assembly?"

"Rogan."

"You don't like Rogan…"

He didn't say anything, zipping up a hoodie and grabbing a pair of sneakers from the wardrobe. There was a half hour before she was supposed to meet with Shelby. Curiosity piqued, Kara threw on some clothes and followed him from the room to the lift. Maybe something unrelated to yesterday would break the tension…

"Audrey thinks I should have a crest made up for House Jester. I was thinking something pink and flowery. Bunnies, maybe."

He grunted as they got into the lift. Kara stared at her toes, feeling like an absolute jerk.

Rogan was in the gym, running on one of the treadmills. He stopped the machine and stalked over, his jaw tight. He always knew when she was upset. Maybe she shouldn't have come—

The Breaker crossed his arms over his chest, scowling at Flynn. "Cal told me you wanted to see me. I want to hear why from you."

Flynn shoved his hands into his pockets, mouth puckering. "I need to blow off some steam and there's not any wood to chop."

"Bullshit."

"Fuck you." He took off his hoodie and tossed it on a bench.

Rogan decked him before he'd turned.

Flynn took the sucker punch a lot better than she would've expected. He spun, landing his own to Rogan's gut and following up with a vicious uppercut.

It sent him back a step, and she gasped, knowing how hard that was to do. Flynn bounced lightly on his feet, fists up. Rogan nodded in approval, wiping blood from his lip.

They traded jabs.

Kara was floored. Flynn was holding his own, but she knew that look in Rogan's eye. He threw out a kick—

Flynn side-stepped it.

How—? A cacophony of emotion flooded their link, making her realize how silent it had been before. He danced back, shaking his head, all of it disappearing again.

She concentrated on their bond. What was he doing? It wasn't the block, she could always feel whenever he was hiding something, like seeing one of the kittens under a blanket. She knew a cat was there, just not which one. Now there wasn't anything, it was a completely blank slate. She met Rogan's eyes across the mat. He raised his eyebrow at her, ducking Flynn's fist.

Kara dropped to a bench in shock.

Flynn had achieved zero. That place of calm all Breakers needed that she'd never been able to reliably call upon. She watched him spar with a new respect and no small amount of desire. Chewing her thumb, she glanced at the clock. It was time for her to go meet Shelby. The two men were completely engrossed in pummeling each other. Reluctantly, Kara left.

She trailed her fingers along the corridor's chair rail, feeling defective. She couldn't hold zero for more than a breath. How could Flynn achieve it? She laughed, running a hand down her face, just wanting to hide. How long would it take them to find her? Picking a hallway she hadn't gone down yet, she wandered, half-looking for somewhere she could wallow.

She felt a little pang. Shelby was expecting her…but everyone expected something from her up here. Might as well disappoint her, too. Kara curled up in one of the window alcoves behind heavy tapestry curtains. Outside, three pre-pubes were playing in the snow. She watched them all bundled up, digging random holes and pelting each other with the stuff. Their screams and laughter were just audible beyond the thick glass.

She tried to imagine Flynn and his cousins doing the same, sure it had ended with Leo head first in a snow bank. He'd definitely be the one putting handfuls down people's collars and deserve it. A man in a red woolen cap came out and said something, his breath spiraling out behind him. The pre-pubes stopped battering each other and turned on him, screaming like banshees. His laughter was the loudest of all as they toppled him to the ground. Kara dashed the tears from her eyes. That's what Flynn thought of when he envisioned offspring.

Not the silent lines of peers dressed in whites.

Not the sanitized dorms in rooms of two-way plex.

She sat entranced as they rolled packed orbs of snow, then balanced them precariously upon one another. What were they doing…?

"There you are."

She gave a little jump, so engrossed, she hadn't heard Flynn coming with that damn block still up. He sat beside her, smiling when he saw what she'd been looking at. He'd taken a couple big hits to the right side of his face. The bridge of his nose was split and his jaw swollen.

"You think the kittens are trouble, I hear those three are worse."

"What are they doing?"

He didn't answer, and she tore her eyes away to glance at him. His expression was so sad. Her gaze dropped to her hands, picking at a fold of her skirt.

"You've really no basis of what a family or childhood should be like, do you?"

She gave a tiny shrug, feeling defective again. "I've read—"

"It's not the same." He sighed, and his arms came around her. She melted back against him, her chest tight. "You ever play in the snow?"

"At the farm, with you." His breath tickled her neck, and she could feel his smile against her skin. "I missed you last night."

"I needed time to think. It's hard knowing you don't want our kid."

"I don't know what I want," she laughed, her eyes hot. "I don't know how I'm supposed to feel, what I'm supposed to say, do—"

Flynn wouldn't look at her. "I get it. I've been asking a lot of you. I…I spoke with Cal last night about what it's really like for Talents down there. I didn't know—"

"And now you do?" Her eyes welled up, and she tried to blink it away.

"No, not…no. Look, I've been thinking. The vote's today. Even after that damn dinner, I don't have enough support to do what Cal wants. I promised him I'd go through the motions, and then I'm out. Part of my majority payout's a property. We could go, after the baby's born. I mean, it would suck for a while, but there's an old cabin. I'm sure it's shit, but if the foundation's still sound—"

She wrapped her arms around his neck. "Really? Like another coop? You'd leave?"

"Yeah. If I can't make them see reason, I'm not gonna keep—" She kissed him, not needing to hear anymore. He winced, rocking his jaw with a laugh. "Fuck, that asshole got me good. You really hate it up here that much?"

"It's just different. Anywhere I go I'm going to have to get used to it." She ran a hand over his swollen cheek, the one that'd had the scar. "But you haven't been yourself since we crossed the border."

He sighed, looking out the window. The pre-pubes were gone, the rucked up snow and frozen monoliths all that was left of their play. He turned back to her with an unconvincing smile. "I've gotta go offer myself up for public humiliation. We'll talk more. Come on, Shelby's waiting for you." She gave him a pleading look, and he laughed, pulling her to her feet. "Sorry, you're not off the hook. I don't get my payout until after the Introduction. Three more days, we'll both survive."

Three more days. She sighed, taking his hand.

Shelby was in the ballroom turning forms to a song only she could hear. It most definitely was not a waltz, judging by her thrusting hips. Flynn raised his eyebrows and wiggled his own with a few affected steps. Kara laughed.

Shelby spun around, bright red. She hit her wristband, ending whatever she was listening to, and gave them a shy smile. "I'm competing in Latin dance this year."

Flynn kissed Kara's cheek. "Mmm, learn that next."

She swatted at him, laughing as he left the room mincing. "Have you seen Flynn box?"

"Oh, yes. When he was at the Academy, he won all kinds of competitions. Then, after Deirdre died, he started fighting at the

Pony for money." She bit her lip. "That made Miriam and Lot furious."

"What's the Pony?"

Shelby fluttered her hands, evoking shades of Miriam. "It's not nice." She'd gotten that patented Scot look when a subject was closed, and offered up an ear bud. Kara shoved the stupid thing in and let Shelby position her how she wanted. "They'll play a waltz for your first dance. All you have to do is let him lead, just relax and go with the music."

The first notes sounded, and Kara's mind drifted to what Flynn had said, the first steps easier than she'd imagined.

FLYNN ENTERED CHAMBERS, his thoughts a thousand miles away at that property. Going just felt right, but the logistics of it with a kid were gonna suck. Neither one of them knew a damn thing about babies. He riffled his hair. Until he knew what was out there, it was stupid to worry about it. He had bigger problems, one of which was eyeing him with far too much interest as he tried to pass.

"Laughlin!"

Fuck, he didn't wanna deal with this—"Klaus." The plump red-head on his arm tittered into her fan.

Klaus's eyes skated over his busted face. "I see you've been up to no good. Wonderful news! I was just telling Margot you'd be at the Pony soon. I know you got my invitation, I sent it by private messenger."

"I'm not going to the Pony."

The blond man gave an exasperated sigh. "You know Gerrard won't relent. It's one bout. I'd take the deal now, before he changes the terms."

Flynn scowled at him, but what the hell did he have to lose? After this sham of a vote, he was out. He laughed. Fuck it. Gerrard wanted a fight, he'd give him a fight.

"Fine. I'll see you Friday night."

Klaus narrowed his eyes at the sudden change of heart. "Friday."

"Friday." Flynn laughed, descending into chambers.

Lot was waiting for him. "It's about goddamned time you got here —" A chime sounded, calling members to session. His father scowled at the damage to his face. "Get your fucking head in the game." He smacked him in the chest with the agenda and took his seat.

Flynn's stomach knotted as he sat. The room filled quickly, press thronging the gallery. Everyone eager to witness the outcome of the first Quorum vote in over a century. Across the floor, Julia smirked at him, the makeup caked onto her cheek rippling. His lips spasmed into a grin, and she looked like she wanted to kill him. Christ, maybe that bit of talent had been worth it.

A runner came in just as Riggs called the meeting to order. Everyone fixated on the page crossing the floor to the lectern and handing the old man a note.

Riggs's eyebrows shot up as he read it. "Well, it seems like you're all hell bent on raising my blood pressure already. The Shades are requesting emergency precedence in response to Friday's—"

"Emergency precedence requires a majority vote, and we've agreed that this morning's measures will be decided by Quorum," Julia interrupted. Riggs frowned, but couldn't argue.

Flynn swore. Forget about wondering if he had enough votes to pull it off, he wouldn't even be able to get the matter brought up. Well, that was that. He should just leave. What the hell was the point?

"Then, ah, can I get a show of hands from the Firsts on this matter?"

Every one of them but Julia voted it through.

What the fuck? Markham and Phyllis Flynn would've banked on, but Crandall and that timid Binder, Ketsing? He was afraid to fart without Julia's say so. The tall man studiously avoided looking at her, sweating almost as much as Markham. What the hell was that about? The rest of the room was just as shocked.

"Well then… Lord Martin, if you would proceed?"

Jacques stood. "House Martin has pledged their troth to House Scot. Speaking as their bondsman, we put forth Lord Laughlin Scot's nomination for First Shade."

The Assembly exploded into a cacophony of disbelief.

Flynn couldn't help but grin at the expression on Julia's face. Damn, she was pissed!

Riggs banged on his podium for order, finally getting it after a few minutes of absolute chaos. "Do we have a second?"

Charles stood. "House Hyrro seconds the nomination and also offers their fealty."

Flynn went white as the room erupted again. Christ, he wasn't expecting—

"It was the pants." Charles leaned over to whisper.

Flynn laughed, and it was more effective in quieting the chamber than Riggs's gavel.

"We have our motion. Do we have concordance within the rest of the line?"

Here was where it all fell to shit. Flynn resisted the temptation to look behind him, chairs squeaking back as people stood.

"They're all up, except Morris," Lot murmured.

Are you fucking kidding me? He was gonna puke.

The speaker's gavel fell three times. "Enter it into the record. On this day, the Shades have elected Lord Laughlin Scot as First, with Lord Morris dissenting." The hatred in Julia's eyes was intense. Flynn gave a weak laugh. What the fuck had just happened? "Ah, would you like to address the Assembly before we proceed, Lord Scot?"

Flynn tried to form a reply and ended up just shaking his head.

The speaker shuffled his papers, tapping them square on the lectern. "Well, then, if we're quite done going off agenda? Lord Scot, if you'll take your seat, we can proceed with the Quorum vote Mistress Cree has requested. First order of business, the proposed lawsuit against the Source."

Flynn slowly stood, moving to the First's box on the floor. The rest of the morning was a blur, the other Firsts, save Julia, voted with him as a block on every measure that came up. The lawsuit and sanctions against the Source passed with little to no debate, the only voice against them hers, which was for the most part ignored. If looks could kill, he'd be splayed out like that last front page murder. The majority of the room was already buying tickets.

Christ, he hated this fucking city.

And now he was stuck.

The morning session ended, and they broke for lunch. He stood unsteadily as Charles and Jacques came over, offering congratulations.

"What the fuck just happened?" Flynn still didn't understand it, he didn't have enough votes…

Lord Glass walked over, smiling. "Laughlin."

"Sir."

"Well, you've got it. I expect you to do great things with it now."

"I…I'm sorry, sir, I don't understand. The lawsuit—"

The man's brow furrowed. "Merchant should've brought the papers yesterday. I've dropped the damned thing. Marilla couldn't be happier with the way things've played out, and Regina…" A broad smile spread across his face. "Someday you'll understand. This fashion thing of hers finally panning out is worth more to me than whatever that lawsuit would've brought in and my vote ten times over." Theo reached out to shake his hand. Flynn took it, stunned, thinking of Kara's picture plastered across every newspaper in Glynfyls.

"It's a Glass…"

"Her stuff looks good…" Jesus fucking Christ, he'd taken First because of a dress.

"Indeed. I'm going to ask her to make me up a pair of those trousers, I never did care for how breeches ride up." Theo winked at him and disappeared through the crowd.

Flynn turned to Jacques and Charles as the man left, incredulous. "Gent and Leeds stood for me?"

"They did. Between me pledging, everything at dinner, and House Glass's reversal in position, the two of them saw sense. Not to mention Horace is a hopeless romantic. Your lady is proving adept at swaying opinion."

"None of it would've happened without her. I hope this teaches you to take more care with your appearance." Charles sniffed, frowning at Flynn's jaw. "Though I won't hold my breath."

His acerbic tone cut through Flynn's daze. …*"There's always plots and power grabs"*… He shook his head. No. Kara wasn't like that…but Jesus fucking Christ! "Why'd you pledge?"

Charles took out his handkerchief and flicked it dismissively before dabbing his brow. "After what I saw at dinner, do you seriously have to ask? My God, Laughlin. I knew you were a big man, but didn't realize…"

Flynn laughed. "Sorry Charles, the lady has my heart."

He gave an indulgent sigh. "Look, you've been doing your damnedest to convince us the Source is coming. When they do, I fully intend to hide behind you. I'm fine with shedding a little blood now to earn that right. Jacques said Cal's set on being barbaric about this, though I can certainly appreciate the theater."

Flynn scratched at his beard. That wasn't the reaction he'd expected from his demonstration, but he could see where the man was coming from. Hopefully no one else did.

Jacques clasped him on the shoulder. "Go home. I'm sure Cal will want to know all about this, if Lot hasn't already given him an earful. We'll be by later to bleed on you."

They faded into the crowd, and Flynn frowned. Merchant had been in Cal's office last night. Goddamn him. That son of a bitch had known. If Cal had said something, he wouldn't have mentioned anything to Kara about that property and gotten her hopes up. What the fuck was he gonna tell her now?

Flynn made his way out of chambers, each group he passed wanting a word. After everything Julia had spilt, his popularity was surreal. He snorted. Fucking politics. Every last one of them was a criminal, and just tickled he'd been chained to the proverbial rock as a sacrifice. All he wanted to do was crawl under the damned thing. Finally through the sea of sycophants and well-wishers, he got to the hall. A hand on his arm stopped him.

"Lord Scot. I've been eager to make your acquaintance."

Fucking kill me. It was the whore from the balcony. Flynn grit his teeth as she brushed her generous bosom against his arm. He jerked it back.

"Well, you've done that, now good day." He went to move past her, and she caught his sleeve. "I'm not interested."

She pouted prettily. He probably would've found it attractive before Kara. Now it just annoyed the shit out of him.

"Oh, don't be like that, I'm sure we can come to some kind of arrangement," she purred, sidling up to him again. Several people turned to stare.

"I'd advise you to keep your distance. I'm not in the market, nor on it."

Her perfect cupid bow of a mouth smirked, and she looked him up and down like a side of beef. "So you say, but I've heard all about you. I'll be here when you change your mind."

Kara was going to kill her.

He stalked past, almost feeling sorry for the whore. He stepped through the gate to the foyer of the estate and went directly into Cal's study, collapsing into a chair.

"You're a fucking asshole."

"I get that a lot. Why now?"

"Gimme one of those cigars." His grandfather pulled two out of his desk drawer. Lot came in and took the other chair, grabbing the scotch. "You could've fucking told me, Cal."

"Didn't want to jinx it." He took the glass Lot was offering him and raised it up before taking a sip. Flynn tried to ignore the one sitting in front of him. Goddamn, he wished he had a coffee. Where was French…?

"I still can't believe you actually pulled it off after all that shit," Cal mused.

"I didn't." Flynn lit his cigar and blew out a thick cloud. "It was Kara. Theo Glass dropped the suit because taking Kara out in that dress launched Regina's career. Christ, when I told Kara she was going to whip up a shit storm, this is not what I was envisioning. What am I gonna tell her, Cal?"

"The truth, I'd imagine."

Asshole.

French came into the room and placed several folios on the edge of Cal's desk. A servant followed behind him with a coffee service and sandwiches.

"These have been arriving for the past few minutes, sir. I thought it prudent to get them to you immediately."

Cal was already sorting through them, his eyebrows rising steadily.

"I suggest you continue to let that girl wear whatever the hell she wants."

Flynn ignored the food, a sick suspicion in his gut.

"There's promises of seventeen pledges here. That's a third of the line. Merchant needs to draw up a standard form."

Flynn stared at the ceiling, not wanting to hear it. Shit. God had gotten him, all right. They couldn't leave now. Taking her to dinner, phasing in front of everyone…pure fucking hubris. Had to prove he was a big man, show her off on his arm.

Shit. Look where that'd gotten them. When was he gonna learn? He scratched at his beard, the pain in his jaw reminding him of his promise to be at the Pony. A sad laugh escaped him. Motherfucker. How was he gonna pull that off if he was First?

"There's a time and place for showmanship." Cal studied him, tapping off his ash. "Mark my words, Laughlin. This isn't going to stop here. I tasked you with uniting the line, and you've exceeded my expectations. You need to make this run in the direction you want. Instead of beating yourself up, think of it as a first step toward Overlord."

Flynn choked on his coffee, and Lot downed the untouched glass of scotch. That's what the old man had been gunning for? Jesus fucking Christ—

His father swore. "We haven't had an Overlord since the Great Incursion."

"We haven't had Houses pledge fealty since then either," Cal said, still staring at Flynn.

His stomach was a goddamned mess. He returned the old man's gaze steadily. "That's because the last Overlord couldn't protect who pledged to him. I accept those oaths, House Scot is legally bound to lend support if any of them are threatened. Most are small. It wouldn't be hard for someone to go after them to ruin us in the process."

"You're right there, Lord Scot," Cal said, completely unconcerned. "You should get 'em all tied up, regardless. There's this concept of calling in your bondsmen, boy. They're obligated to come running and lend support to whatever you deem necessary. You saw what voting as a block achieved this morning."

What he saw was a lot of responsibility. Shit, if he fucked this up—

"You're not that other guy."

Flynn chewed his lip and gave a small nod. It was time to go back for the afternoon session.

JULIA CLOSED the door to the women's powder room and locked it. She ran the water at the sink, temples throbbing, fighting to maintain her composure.

How had he pulled it off?

She'd told the entire Assembly about his sordid past, handed them copies of his rap sheet, and two days later the Shades vote him in as First after he'd brazenly paraded his paramour through the city. They were pledging to him for God's sake! It made no sense. What'd happened over the weekend to make House Glass and the others come to his side? Julia splashed her face, water mingling with frustrated tears, and slumped against the counter at the jagged pain in her head. Her knees gave out, and she slid to the floor, pawing at her purse for her tincture and draining the little bottle.

Henry.

There had to be more she could do—

She buried her face in her hands, taking ragged breaths as the pain subsided, wishing fervently Laughlin had died.

What had happened to change him so drastically? She pulled herself up, retrieving her compact, that bitch's lips a stark claret stain across her cheek. How was it no other Binder could release it? That worm Ketsing had been beside himself trying. She blotted at the damned thing, hiding what she could. Was that what had caused him to vote against her? The loss of his support had been a blow, and as much a surprise to Laughlin as her... It had to be some kind of Source witchery.

She looked through her reflection in the mirror. Collecting herself. They couldn't see her ruffled. A deep breath. She opened the door.

A tall woman was waiting outside. Julia froze at her perfect features.

"Mistress Cree, am I right?"

Julia's fragile composure left her. No, no, Titus wouldn't have—

The woman gripped her arm. "Let's take a quick trip to your estate. We have a mutual friend who's asked that you take me into your confidence, and we have much to discuss."

A chill washed over her, and the woman's smile grew. She took Julia's arm, steering her to the gate—

They were in her front hall. The woman took it in with a disdainful sniff. Julia bristled, then looked around the dim space with fresh eyes. When had things fallen into such disrepair?

"Titus is deeply concerned about what's just transpired."

Julia inhaled sharply, cobwebs forgotten. How could he already know? She trailed after the woman as she crossed into the sitting room and ran a slim white finger over the mantle. It came up black with ash. She sniffed again, rubbing her fingertips together, and sat in one of the chairs before the cold hearth. A handful of beetles scurried from beneath it into the far corners of the room. Julia colored. Why hadn't the servants been in here?

"The way you let Scot handle you, well, as intoxicating as it is to watch, he's playing for the wrong team."

Julia scowled, feeling plainer than usual and riled by the woman's condescension. She sat across from her, must rising up to tickle her nose. "I'm sorry, who are you?"

"Ielle. I wasn't informed that you were defective in any way, but I can speak slower if necessary. I'm here to advise you." She looked at her rings, turning them to catch the scant sunlight filtering through the dingy window. "Just as you grew up with that tall drink of water, I had the misfortune of being podded with Kara in the Creche. The whore you sent after him won't get anywhere. That little bitch has an uncanny ability to give men tunnel vision, no matter how appealing an alternative may be."

Julia thawed a modicum, able to relate to a woman with a grudge. "So what do you suggest?"

Ielle smirked, still playing with her rings. "That little maid from the reel, where is she?"

"Charlotte? She's probably making up the bedroom, but I don't—"

Ielle flicked her long black hair over her shoulder. "Summon her."

Julia rang a bell from the table between them. A moment later the pretty blonde woman hurried into the room. She colored at the unkept space, bobbing a quick curtsy.

"Yes, madame?"

Ielle looked her over, unimpressed. "Why did you keep her on?"

"My father—it wasn't her fault." The words felt parroted.

Charlotte winced at Ielle's laugh. "Of course not. Who would want to be bent over by a stud like that?" She wet her lips, and the maid's blush deepened. "Have her sit beside you during the afternoon session. Titus wants this stopped now. Whatever you need to do to keep Scot from garnering more support, understand?"

"He's pushing them too far, too fast. We need to back down and let things cool off for a while. If I pressure them now, they'll only run in the opposite direction."

"Your choice." Ielle flipped a dark lock of hair onto the little table.

Henry.

Julia snatched it up, cradling the scrap of her son to her bosom.

There was no choice and never had been.

CHAPTER EIGHTEEN

"Having been completely devastated by the Source's First Harvest, Glynfyls' continuance can be attributed solely to the efforts of the first Talent to hold the title of Overlord. Something of a legend, his personal details are scant, and historians still debate his motives, but whether out of vengeance or grief, his demand for a blood oath as a tribute to those fallen initiated the first mass transference of talent. This was later refined during Glynfyls' Golden Age to confer the mythical powers we associate with Overlords today..."

– Lord Talos, Preceptor of History,
Academy of Glynfyls

KARA PULLED up on the bar again, and Rogan clipped another weight around her ankles. Her consciousness fuzzed in and out of a strange reality. Most of the time, there was only the now of whatever physical task he'd set her to. Whenever she broke out of it, he made it more difficult. How he knew was beyond her.

Between him and Shelby, Kara's muscles felt like mush. She wished she could say the same about her brain. Zero continued to elude her, and Flynn's riot of emotions bleeding past that stupid block wasn't helping. Her mind refused to fall under whatever spell Rogan was trying to cast. She strained to push her shoulders past ninety-degrees. The weights fell away, and he slapped her thigh.

Kara dropped to the mat, breathing hard.

"Why did you lose it?"

"Flynn's upset." She caught the towel he threw at her and ran it across her forehead.

"Your bond's that strong?"

"Yeah, we share most of our emotions."

"That'll make it harder to achieve zero," he said, sitting on a nearby weight bench.

Kara nodded again, it'd been impossible.

"Can you shut him out?"

She laughed. "Not as well as he can block me."

"You have to learn to sink into zero. Just like your Binder training, your Breaker abilities need to be used with cold dispassion. If you don't have a place to bury the 'lust…'"

He didn't need to finish. They both knew what would happen, and the way it'd been creeping on her lately… She rubbed at the half-healed bruise at her throat. Her emotions had always been an issue until she'd learned to bind them. Fat lot of good that did her now.

Rogan's halos pulsed at her, and he grimaced, scratching under his topknot.

"What was that for?"

"That boy causes me to lose sleep."

"I love him, Rogan. I wish the two of you could get along. It's important to me."

His mouth made a thin line. "That's not going to happen until he figures out who he is."

"What do you mean?"

"You know what I mean. I'm gonna push him, Kara. You need to stay out of it."

"I—"

Rogan stood, stretching. "That's enough for today. You get twitchy, come down and run."

She stared at his back as he left, the clock on the wall well past lunch. She'd missed Flynn. He was roiling with emotions again;

something must've happened with the vote. Hers weren't very steady either after what Rogan had just said.

Kara made her way to the kitchen, shoulders and back burning. The dining room was Introduction central. After the cleaning frenzy, crates had started arriving, and a platform for the orchestra was being erected in the ballroom. She was excited, but a big part of her just wanted it to be over.

Two more days…

She asked a man in an apron for some more of those fish sandwiches and sat at the little table in the corner, limp, her head cradled in her arms. If she got twitchy…she'd be lucky if she got the energy to go upstairs. Rogan was tough, but Flynn hadn't been joking. Shelby was worse, and dancing took and an entirely different muscle set—Kara looked up at a sharp tsk to see Miriam standing there, hands on her hips. *Ugh, please don't have another seating plan…*

"All tuckered out, I see. You need to know when to call it quits. Building a baby's hard work." She dropped a folio onto the table.

Kara bit back a groan, picking it up. Wait, curtains?

"I thought maybe you'd like to start thinking about updating the bower," Miriam said, joining her at the table.

What would the coop have looked like with drapes? The thought made Kara smile. "Flynn's asked me to, but I haven't the faintest clue where to start."

"I can see how you'd be intimidated. I was afraid to change anything in our suite when Jon and I first bonded. Give it some time. Curtains here, a rug there. It'll get easier once you get used to the place. Meddleton's a lot to take in. Laughlin's never cared about that kind of thing, but I'm sure having it stuck in time isn't easy for him. I keep expecting Deirdre to walk down the hall. You know, she used to sing."

"I didn't. Flynn doesn't like talking about her."

A maid came over with a plate of smoked salmon sandwiches and a tea service. Miriam poured a cup, and Kara dug in, ravenous.

"He took losing her hard. We all did. She'd be proud of him though. Cal just told me they elected him to First."

Kara's bite turned ashy. "I didn't think he had enough votes."

"He didn't, but apparently Regina Glass convinced her father to drop his lawsuit and support Laughlin after you singlehandedly jumpstarted her career." Miriam gave her a look over the top of her glasses. "I must say, no one saw that coming. I wouldn't be surprised if you've gotten yourself an invitation to join the Ladies."

"I just picked a dress..." "...*You are no longer in the position to 'just' do anything...*" What was she going to say to Flynn? No wonder he felt so upset—

Miriam tittered. "You're much too humble. They'll be talking about this for years! What a coup for House Scot, and with so much of the line pledging—"

"But why? He doesn't want it."

"He should've thought about that before he trotted you out, flashed his colors, then phased in front of them." She shook her head, looking upward. "The arrogance of that boy is mind-boggling."

Kara's brow knit. "The way he explained it to me, isn't that kind of like showing—"

"It's exactly like that. All those men in a room trying to prove which one of them has the biggest." She frowned at Kara's laugh. "You're just as bad. I can guess what's behind that grin, Lord knows I changed the boy's diaper enough," Kara's face went crimson, and Miriam chuckled. "Oh, our Laughlin was a surprise. Only three times a child's been born between a Talent and someone unaffected, and he's a throwback to boot."

"Where did she come from?"

"Deirdre? Somewhere out west. I got the impression her people travelled around..." Miriam's brow wrinkled like something about that bothered her. She shook her head. "She'd be proud of him."

"He's afraid of the responsibility...of letting people down. Whoever he was before, he's not that person anymore."

"Good. That boy's like a son to me, but Laughlin was a philandering deadbeat with a nasty temper and a drinking problem. I could never understand why Julia put up with him, especially with my Leo so head over heels...but she never saw anyone else when Laughlin was in the room. Not that most women do. He's always been too handsome for his own good, even with that wretched thing on his face."

"Jerk knows it, too." Kara smiled wryly.

Miriam chuckled. "Yes, he does, doesn't he? The two of you are going to have beautiful babies." Kara went pale, and the older woman patted her hand. "Don't worry, you couldn't keep me away if you tried. I raised three of my own and Laughlin besides. Deirdre was always so busy with Assembly business, and Lot… Well, never mind about that. We'll work it out, that's what family does."

Kara smiled sadly, thinking of her own d—mother.

"Now, I've got to head over to the caterer's to finalize the menu. Go get some rest!"

Miriam left, and Kara dragged herself upstairs. That was it then. Flynn was First. They couldn't leave now. She laughed, ugh, she was still a menace when left to her own devices. Even when something felt right, it turned out to be wrong.

JULIA WATCHED Laughlin make his way down to the Assembly floor from her box. Everyone wanted a word with him. He stopped every few steps, shaking hands and smiling obligingly. It was a pity there weren't any babies for him to kiss.

She bit sharply through her peppermint, and Charlotte jumped at its crack. What good Ielle thought having the woman sit with her was going to do…but it wasn't like she was keeping her from the housework.

Julia tried to remember the last time she'd seen a servant other than the blonde woman, and a sharp pain lanced through her temple. Losing the thought in its wake, she dug another peppermint from her purse. The speaker pounded his gavel and session began.

The first item on the agenda was a proposal from Lady Breakspear to survey the city for siege readiness. She'd failed previously to put a similar measure through, but with the other heads voting as a block behind Laughlin, it passed. Julia didn't bother dissenting. She knew what they'd find, and it was far too late to do anything about it. All that they'd achieve would be to diminish morale. If Titus wanted them in a panic there were worse places to start.

She did frown when Lord Klein volunteered to head up the wall survey. Bonded to a seer, his wife gave Julia pause. Not even Titus's threats against Henry could persuade her to cross Alice Carmody-Klein. They had an uneasy understanding. She didn't interfere with Julia's plans, and Julia didn't try to manipulate him. Was this the end of that?

Lady Breakspear rose to speak, and Julia crunched her mint. God, she hated her. The woman began to blather on about their military capability.

"As we stand right now, we're woefully unprepared for an incursion. The cuts to funding have left our troops in a shocking state. We need to make a push to correct the deficit before it's too late."

Julia flicked her eyes at Lord Starkis. He made a face, but stood. "The problem isn't with the budget, it's with allocation."

"Have you bothered to review the numbers I've provided?" Phyllis snapped. "The clinkers out there are allotted more for scrapping tubes!"

"Regardless, the Source's troops are going to be better trained and equipped. Our advantage has always been our use of talent. We should forget about the military and focus on that."

Lady Breakspear threw up her hands. "Well, then, what's the status of the Hex training programs?" She looked at the Academy's liaison near the back of the room.

"Unfortunately, we've also been underfunded for several years," the woman stammered. "Our program now is not the same one that you or I went through."

A man across the aisle made a disparaging noise. "I'll attest to that, they're not even teaching Eli how to block properly. We've been showing him ourselves on weekends." There were more than a few nods around the room.

"So what I'm hearing is that our military is a joke, and the Academy isn't allocating its funds properly, yet we just approved a new sports complex. How did we let ourselves get to this point?" No one met Phyllis's gaze. It fell on Julia, and she failed to prevent the corners of her lips from twitching up. Her satisfaction was short lived.

Laughlin stood and everyone turned to him as if he were the rising sun. "Does it matter? We're here now and should be hearing directly from Lord Stonefist as to the status of his troops. If Hex-theory is already being taught outside of the Academy, it shouldn't be a stretch to coordinate classes including others. We're getting bogged down with problems and not focusing enough on the solutions." He rocked back on his heels, every word out of his mouth reasonable.

Julia wanted to punch him.

"Make no mistake, the Source is here, watching us and making plans. We've no time for finger-pointing. Our priorities should be actively recruiting in the city to create a larger standing militia capable of protecting the inner city, and the wall needs to be repaired—"

"Your perceived privilege is astounding!" Julia stood, gripping the railing separating her from the Assembly floor. Damn him! She needed to stop this now. "What grandiose belief grants you the right to just sweep in here after your crime spree and dictate policy? It's preposterous! You'd beggar us just trying to come up with the funding required for Lady Breakspear's proposal, never mind the rest of your—"

"Well, now, actually, each House is currently paying a considerable levy towards importing and exporting goods," Lord Markham broke in. She glared at him as he mopped his corpulent waggling chins. "With the border closed, that becomes moot. Reallocated, those funds could cover both Lady Breakspear's proposal and the recruitment for a larger militia as Lord Scot has suggested."

There were murmurs of agreement, and Julia's mouth pruned, unable to gainsay such a neat solution. She didn't dignify it with a response, focusing her ire at Laughlin. "I asked you a question; what makes you so special?"

He ran a hand across his mouth. The hall went silent, waiting.

"I'm anything but, Mistress Cree. Perhaps I just have a more objective viewpoint coming in from the outside and can see what needs to be done."

"Is it your felony conviction or jacking cars that gives you so much insight?"

Flynn gritted his teeth, and she smiled, daring him to lose his temper. He put his hands on the edge of his box, looming toward her.

"Fine, by what right am I dictating policy? There's no right about it. My intentions are strictly based on need. No one in this room has shown the fortitude necessary to stand up to what's coming for us, and I will do whatever is necessary to prevent it from swallowing us whole." His mouth was set in a grim line as he looked around the room.

"Each of you, beaten down, cowed, extorted into compliance—I refuse to sit and watch this play out!" He glared at her, and Julia's mouth went dry at the determination on his face.

"Who do I think I am? I think I'm fucking pissed you've spent the past eight years tearing down everything my mother worked for, shitting all over this city and her legacy, and I'll be damned if I let you hold the door open for the fucking Source to harvest my intended and everyone else!"

Julia stumbled back, his words like a physical blow. She wasn't the only one in the room. One of the women in the Breaker section fainted. Laughlin dropped into his chair, clenching his jaw. The Assembly sat shocked, eyeing him warily. He shook his head in disgust.

"Ah, shall we call it up for a vote, then?" Riggs doddered. "Wonderful. All in favor of implementing Lord Scot's suggestions?"

The room was a sea of hands. In pushing him, she'd lost the Assembly. Exactly what she'd said would happen.

Julia's nails dug into her palms, pain shooting through her temples at the gavel's bang, ending the session. Across the floor, Lot clapped Laughlin on the shoulder. He stood, looking miserable. What? She couldn't believe—

He didn't want it.

Damn Titus for making her push so hard. If they'd left Lot as First…she stumbled. The throbbing behind her eyes…

"Mistress, are you all right?" Charlotte asked, taking her elbow.

She nodded, the motion making her ill. The maid put her arm

around her, helping her from the chamber. "Let's get you home. I have some more of Master Otto's tincture."

Julia gritted her teeth, hoping Laughlin didn't do any more damage before she could figure out a way to counter him.

FUCK.

Flynn stood, fighting the urge to pull talent and disappear. Christ, he was batting a thousand today. Everyone but Lot was keeping a healthy distance and considering the look on Phyllis's face, he could guess why. Goddamn his temper! His father shrugged, no stranger to being treated like a pariah. Great. Just what he needed, Lot's fucking commiseration.

Flynn stalked up the steps and to the gate. He sagged crossing Meddleton's foyer, footsteps hollow on the cool marble slabs. Cal would be expecting him, and he didn't give a shit. All he wanted to do was to eat something and curl up with his wife before Jacques and Charles came to give their oaths.

The room was silent when he opened the door, save for the crackling fire. Looked like Kara had beaten him to the punch. Undressing, he slipped between the covers beside her, earning himself a swipe from the grey kitten he dislodged from his pillow. It hissed at him and disappeared to the other side of her. That one was a fucking handful.

Kara laughed softly, rolling over and popping up long enough to look at the clock before snuggling beneath his chin. Flynn breathed her in, feeling that subtle hum that started up when they were skin-to-skin.

"You're here sooner than I expected," she murmured. "I had a surprise planned so you won't hate me so much."

"Hate you?" He laughed. "No fucking chance of that."

She smiled, running her hand down his side and tipping her face up so he could kiss her. "Not even if it's my fault we have to stay? Miriam told me they voted you in. I'm so sorry, I didn't—"

"Hey, no. I lost my temper and phased that damned table. Even if Theo'd changed his vote because of everything with Regina, the rest wouldn't have without seeing that. Christ, Kara, no matter what I do, I feel like I'm being railroaded towards something, and I'll be damned if I know what it is."

"You feel it too? Like something's going to happen?"

"Yeah, and it's irritating as fuck." He dropped his face to the crown of her head, letting out a breath. "Cal wants me to try to take Overlord."

"What? I thought you said you didn't have those anymore." Her fingers teased through the line of curls below his navel, and he slid his hand down her bare back. The kitten attacked it through the blankets. Little shit.

"We don't, and people don't fucking pledge either. Doesn't seem to be stopping them from doing it though. Charles did on the goddamned Assembly floor and by the time I got back to Cal, seventeen other Shades had, too…" Christ. Maybe they wouldn't follow through. He hoped. Because that'd worked so fucking well before—

"And a few minutes ago? I don't know why you bother blocking me out, you're still a noisy neighbor."

He kissed her brow, dropping it. "Sorry, I don't realize I'm doing it half the time."

"Well, stop it. It's annoying."

"It's just—it's like there's two of me. Regular me and this other guy that comes out whenever someone pushes me. I lost it today. Told the entire Assembly that they were a bunch of fucking pussies."

She laughed. "I bet that felt good."

"I suppose. I don't… Kara, I don't know what the fuck to do. How am I gonna be what all these people think I am?" Christ, did he really give a shit? …*"every single one of those motherfuckers in the Assembly, they're all gonna burn"*… He needed to stop making epic fucking declarations when his temper was up. The only one going down in flames at the moment was him.

"I can't tell you that, but whatever it is, they've seen it in you since you've come back, just keep doing what you've been doing."

He laughed. "Great, so lose my temper and act like an arrogant prick."

"Sounds about right." Her hand had slid around his cock, and he rocked into it, a rumble building in his chest.

"And what about you, Lady Scot, what are you gonna do?"

She pushed him onto his back. "It's a surprise."

"Don't know if I'm up for any more of those today. You might have to convince me." He grinned, caging her hips as she straddled him.

Kara laughed, cheek dimpling as she stretched forward to grab something from under her pillow. She set a small rectangular box on his chest. Flynn wet his lips at her anticipation thrumming through their bond.

"What's this?" he asked, picking the box up. Something inside thunked, and his brow quirked.

She bit at her thumb, and shrugged, her eyes alight with mischief. "Open it."

Flynn sat up against the pillows and pulled the end of the blue and silver bow, glancing at her again before he lifted the lid. *Jesus fuck.* Lust coursed through him. She'd gotten a butt plug. *Where the hell…*

His throat bobbed, cock painfully hard. "Please tell me you didn't ask French to pick this up."

"Glory, no!" Kara laughed, rocking back on him. "I asked Reggie. Oh! She said we'd need this too." A little bottle of lube appeared from under the pillow.

Was she fucking—How did Regina fucking Glass know… Flynn ran a hand over his face not about to go there. "You know shit like this is basically illegal up here, right?"

Kara nodded. "That's what she said, but I guess she does a lot of work for this sultan in the Deep South… Anyway, that's why she offered to get it…and maybe some other stuff…" Her brow furrowed. "You're not mad are you?"

"What, no—I just…you've got to be careful. Otherwise it'll end up front page news." *And then the entire city will eviscerate you.* He frowned, knowing more about being a pariah that than he was gonna —wait. "What other stuff?"

She bit back a grin and shrugged again.

Flynn lifted up the blunt glass teardrop by its base and ran his thumb over the brilliant green jewel winking at its end. Shit was definitely top of the line. He needed to have a conversation with Reggie about exactly what she was designing for that sultan.

"Sooo…you want to bend over and see if it fits?"

His eyes jumped to hers. "You think this is for me?" She laughed, and he lunged at her, his body pressing hers to the mattress. "Let's get something straight; I've got plenty of kinks, but that's not one of them."

"No? I think you'd look quite fetching," she mimicked in Luann's affected simper.

Flynn laughed, kissing her. "Sorry to disappoint you, but I draw the line at tights and shoving anything in my ass."

"Mmm…" Her arms laced around his neck. "You didn't seem to have an issue with my talent up there…"

"Intangible objects don't count," he murmured, tracing her lips with the plug's smooth glass tip. "Open." He dipped the bulb in and out… "Now close…good girl. I need you to get that nice and warm." Her lips sealed around the base, his traveling down her throat, laving a long line to her collar bone, hand cupping her breast. Goddamn, her tits were fucking perfect, overflowing his hands, nipples hard little nubs against his palms. He replaced one with his mouth, sucking and stretching the pebbled tip against the roof of his mouth.

She moaned, pressing against him, her nails scraping across his scalp to tangle in his hair, Tugging just shy of painful. His hand slipped down her stomach, thumb ghosting over her hip bone to trace its angle to her bare mound. Her thighs opened for him, the scent of her lighting him the fuck up.

Christ, that perfume—her 'lust—dark and heady; his cock bucked, weeping. A rumble started in his chest, all of it bringing something out in him. A weird fucking need to dominate…

He kissed down the path his hand had taken, inhaling at the juncture of her thighs. Rasping his beard over the fleshy little pearl peeking from the top of her slit. So fucking pretty. Kara gave a muffled cry as he laved the prickle away and nosed into her, his thumbs parting her folds, licking from pucker to clit. Her hips rose, urging him deeper.

"Mmm… greedy," he murmured, taking his time. Lapping gently, rimming around her creamy core, their bond thrumming with her wantonness, her mewls of frustration music to his fucking ears. Goddamn, he loved seeing her squirm for his cock…feeling her self-control slip…

" 'Lease!"

…hearing her beg.

He reached up, and popped the plug from her mouth. "Tell me what you need, baby."

"You, please, Flynn… I-I need you…"

A smile tipped up his lips, trailing the plug down her body to her sodden core, the sheets damp beneath her. Rolling the plug in her honey, tipping it into her quivering depths. He licked her desire from his lips. "Grab behind your knees and spread your legs for me."

Jesus fuck, she was gorgeous.

He ran a hand over the perfect curve of her ass and slapped it, his hand print blooming a brilliant pink with her cry. "You've been a naughty, dirty little girl, Kara." He spanked her again, and she moaned. "What do you want me to do with this?" he asked, bringing the plug to his lips and sucking off her sweet cream.

Her pupils blew out, breath stuttering. "I-I want you to put it in my…my ass."

"Mmm…" He ran the plug over her tight little hole, growling as it contracted, hungry for invasion, back to her juicy cunt. "You're so fucking wet for me…" He pressed the tip against her pucker. "But not wet enough for this." He snagged the bottle of lube, dribbling it over her back hole and working it in with a finger. Fuck, that was hot…

"Oh Glory, please…"

Flynn chuckled, slowly breaching the tight ring of muscle with the glass bulb and working it in. Kara threw her head back, moaning, then gasped as it seated itself , her body closing in behind it.

"Good girl. Now stay just like that." He dipped his head to feast, no longer teasing, his tongue thrusting into her center, teeth nipping at her clit. Their bond thrummed with her building release, his balls begging to do the same, drawing up. His hips flexed against the sheets. Jesus fuck he wanted to be inside of her…

She cried out, tearing at his hair, thighs pressing against his ears, a deluge of her passion soaking his beard, her muscles spasming. Her release shuddering through their bond to him. Sharing her completion, her want for more.

Flynn hummed his satisfaction at hers, rising up to kiss her. "I fucking love making you rain, baby. Now you're gonna do it on my cock."

He thrust into her, eyes rolling back at the pressure from the plug running along the underside of his dick. Fuuuck... Kara captured his mouth, lapping her honey from his beard before swallowing his tongue, her nails slicing down his nape to gouge his shoulders. Her heels floated up the back of his thighs, digging in, stoking his passion. It reverberated between them, talent pricking at his skin.

"Oh, Glory...fuck me, Flynn..."

"Yeah?" He chuckled, biting up under her jaw. This fucking woman. His hand slapped against the headboard, the other above her shoulder, locking her in place beneath him. "Then hold on."

His hips pistoned into her, punishing, sac slapping against the flat base of the plug, driving into both of her tight little holes. The fucking echo between them...

Him, feeling her, feeling him.

Filling her and taking himself away. The sharp pain of him bottoming out, then the ache of his retreat. Her slick velvet clamping down around him, the flutter of her walls. Pleasure blooming from their joining, growing. Their echo all-consuming.

Her nails gouged down his lats, the slickness of his blood coating her fingers. Teeth burying themselves into the meat of his pec. She bit down hard, and he groaned in anguished ecstasy. A tingle built at the base of his spine, cock impossibly hard, balls aching for release...

"Fuck, come with me, Kara," he groaned, driving into her, dick spasming into her clenching core, filling her with his seed. She arched against him, hands gripping his ass, pulling him deeper into her, cunt milking his cock, her desire a burst of slickness dripping from between her thighs.

Their echo rife with the tumultuous aftershocks of their release. Breaths stuttered, heartbeats slowing to beat in sync. He rolled over, hissing at the scrape of linen against his shredded skin. Pulling Kara close and kissing the top of her head.

"I love you, Flynn." She traced her bite on his pec, a smile tipping up her lips, replete.

I love you, too. The thought triggered a wave of anxiety, and he held her close, kissing her head again before moving to get up. "Get some sleep, baby. I gotta go take these fucking pledges…here. Lemme take that thing out."

She made a small cry of protest at his leaving but let him pull the plug, gasping as he drew it out and curling around a pillow. "You really have to go?"

"Trust me, I don't want to." He put the plug back into its box and set it on the bedside table. "Do not let French find that."

Kara giggled sleepily. "I'll take care of it…come back soon?"

He snagged his pants up off the floor, jamming his legs in. "Yeah. This is the only place I wanna be." He buckled his belt and leaned over to give her a kiss. "I wanna see what else you had Reggie get."

She laughed and snuggled down into the blankets.

Flynn finished getting dressed and left the room, heading to Cal's study.

The old man was pleased as fucking punch when Flynn yanked out a chair across the desk from him. He sat, pulling at his goddamned cravat.

"You're doing one hell of a job, Laughlin," Cal said, rolling a cigarette. "A dozen more contracts came in while you were upstairs; two of them from Fetches. The rest were Binders… including Ketsing." Cal pushed a stack toward him to sign.

Flynn's jaw dropped. Ketsing? Christ, he supposed that wasn't that unexpected the way the man had been sweating after breaking ranks with Julia… Still, the optics of a First pledging were huge. The small hairs on the back of his neck stood up, feeling that fucking expectancy in the air.

"That must've been one hell of a speech you made in session. Five to go, and we've locked down our line—well, four. There's not a chance in hell Morris is gonna pledge."

French came in, handing Cal another bundle of papers. "Lords

Martin and Hyrro have arrived, sir, along with a number of your brethren I had not anticipated. I've moved them to the Green Dining Suite and have begun serving coffee."

Flynn closed his eyes as the butler left, tucking away the half-remembered memory of a mist-riddled forest and the mossy tumbledown cabin peeking from its edge. His stomach churned. It had to wait. A deep longing answered the thought. He picked up the fountain pen. It was leaden in his hand, and the scritch of it dragging across the page.

"So, you want to explain this shit about the Pony? Thought you said you were done."

Flynn glanced up sourly from the document he was signing. "I was. With all of it. Klaus caught me going into chambers, and I sure as hell wasn't thinking I was about to be elected to First. But I said I'd be there, not that I'd bout." He flipped through the remaining contracts in front of him. There were way too fucking many. "I've gotta figure out how to get Gerrard off my goddamn back."

"You're right about that." Cal frowned around his cigarette. "I know the type and throwing more money at him won't do it. Don't see him being particularly concerned it's illegal for Firsts to enter into any type of competition, either."

Flynn tossed the pen onto the desk and lit a cigar as he stood. "No. He won't be." He took a heavy drag, the biting smoke doing little to assuage him as he made his way through the estate to get this shit over with.

"Laughlin, a moment."

He stopped cold in the middle of the hallway. Phyllis? The fuck— His head snapped around to the music room's doors. She peered out from a crack and put a finger in front of her lips, stepping back. Flynn glanced down the empty hallway before pushing through. What the hell was she doing here?

She stood before the raised dais in the center of the room looking guilty. The door snicked closed behind him and he spun. Lot leaned against it.

"What the hell—"

"Lower your goddamned voice. They need to talk to you."

"They?"

"Yes. They," Crandall said, stepping from the shadows like the villain he fucking was. Markham was right behind him, mopping his chins. Flynn's temper spiked, and Phyllis inhaled sharply, drawing herself up.

"That's enough, Laughlin. I'm sorry for waylaying you like this, but you need to be brought up to speed without jeopardizing our work. Please, we just need you to listen…"

"Where's Ketsing?"

The corner of Crandall's mouth twitched. "Until today, we were unable to count on his support. It remains to be seen if it's legitimate. In either case, it's of no import. Yours on the other hand, is."

"Then talk fast, I've got someplace to be."

"Fair enough." Phyllis fiddled with that massive ring on her finger, not meeting his eye. "When I told you that Lot and I were the only things standing between Julia and complete control of the Assembly, it was a bit misleading. It's true as far as appearances go, but Lot, Crandall, Markham, and I have an alliance of sorts—"

"All of us recognize the need to oust Julia from power, but we've been evenly split on the means to that end and every day we've dithered, things have become increasingly convoluted. Assassination hasn't been a viable option for some time," Crandall broke in, shooting Phyllis a dirty look she ignored. He frowned, continuing.

"We've been preparing for the eventuality that we'll have to use military force. The problem being, revolutions are messy and tend to attract scavengers. Removing Julia without someone to fill the vacuum is a dicey proposition. From my intel, the Source can have a vanguard on our doorstep within a matter of hours. With the chaos her well-earned demise would bring, I've little doubt a contingent of Peacekeepers is all it would take to keep the masses subdued until crafts arrived to harvest us. However, it's become apparent it's a question of when, not if, they will arrive. Those abductions in the city are proof positive they're about to move."

"You know who's behind them?"

Crandall smirked at Flynn. "As do you. I believe your intended received a missive from him a few days ago."

Phyllis drew in another sharp breath. Goddamn it… Flynn gritted his teeth, trying to calm the fuck down. "If you know where that asshole's landed—"

"That asshole is serving a very important function at the moment," Crandall said, all fucking smug. "The press has jumped at the assumption he's responsible for the plateau, and I see no reason to dissuade them of that."

Motherfucker. Flynn rolled his cigar between his finger and thumb, feeling sick. Forget about pulling out the carpet, it was gone, and Crandall was under it with a leash. Goddamnit, he knew he'd fucked up and now this scraggly little shit had him by the balls.

Markham mopped his pocket square across his forehead, looking between the two of them. "The Fetches have been shifting in stockpiles for some time now in anticipation of the event—"

"Hold up. So you're telling me that all that shit in Assembly has been fucking theater, and you assholes have been setting me up to be a goddamned figurehead this entire time?" Flynn took a deep breath, the room tinting crimson. Phyllis made a strangled sound, and Lot crossed the room to her side. Flynn glared at him. "And you fucking knew. Cal in on this too? Why the hell isn't his boney ass in here?"

"Cal's plans are his own."

Flynn ground the cigar between his teeth, trying to keep the disbelief off his face that Lot was playing both—His father put his arm around Phyllis, and she leaned into him. The fuck—All those comments the Ladies had made at tea suddenly clicked. Christ, had everyone but him known his father was fucking Phyllis?

He laughed. "That's just great. Fine. Now what?"

"Nothing overly taxing. Just keep doing what you've been doing," Crandall said. Flynn wanted to put him through the fucking wall. "Your ability to hold Mistress Cree's attention is proving valuable. You will to continue to do so. We have measures in place to get the city on track before the Source invades, and will begin making them public. It's in your best interest to support them."

A muscle in Flynn's jaw popped. Fucking Crandall. That smug motherfucker was just cock-fucking-sure he was leashed.

"As distasteful to you as an alliance may be, our goals are aligned at present. I suggest you make the most of it while you can." The oily shit smirked.

The threat made Flynn see red again. "I want that son of a bitch solidly implicated. You point the finger at him so there's no goddamned doubt he was responsible for all of it, and then he's mine."

"I'll see what I can do." Crandall smiled and motioned to the others. Markham hurried over, and Phyllis followed after a brief word with Lot. His father stayed behind as they shifted out, hands jammed into his pockets.

Fuck. Flynn dropped onto one of the chairs ringing the dais. Without his anger buoying him up, he just felt wrung out. "You and Phyllis Breakspear." Lot blushed like a fucking school girl. "She know you're playing her and Cal?"

"Playing Cal? Don't kid yourself that the old man's in the dark about anything. Phyllis knows what she needs to know, and Crandall knows too fucking much." He looked at Flynn like he wanted to ask him something.

Whatever it was, he wasn't gonna entertain it.

He left the room.

There were at least two dozen heads milling about the Green Dining Suite. Flynn made a beeline for Ketsing and the other Binders grouped around him. The man's Adam's apple bobbed at Flynn's approach, and he reached out to shake his hand.

"Lord Scot. You'll have questions." The other Binders stood behind him, stoic. The entire goddamned line had assembled to pledge. Only six Original Houses remained native to Glynfyls. The rest had been taken early on by the Source.

"I do."

Ketsing wrung his hands. "I have a responsibility to protect my line at all costs. Prior to your arrival, our existence had been threatened unless I blindly acted in lockstep with Mistress Cree..." One of the Binders put a hand on his shoulder as his words faltered.

"You'll have to forgive Louis. He's not built for such intrigues." A much shorter man with a full beard stepped forward and bowed. "Lord Hinswich, a pleasure to meet you. Do you know what a Gordian knot is?"

"Yeah, it's an unsolvable problem, unless you've got a sword." Taking Crandall's head off his shoulders would sure as hell solve one of his.

The man chuckled. "Indeed. Well, for Binders it's a literal thing. Louis is First because none of us are able to unravel his." His halos flared and a golden mass of tangled threads appeared above his outstretched palm. "It's like a signature. I've been fiddling with it for years and can't get past what you see here. My talent's not strong enough to lift the next thread, or to follow the loose end. I still pick at it now and again, but the fact remains. After the events of Friday night, Mistress Cree went straight to Louis to have the bind removed from her cheek. The lipstick—"

"It was her knot," Louis burst out. "I couldn't even find where the thread began! She should be First, not I, I've no busi—"

"She can't be First." Flynn growled around his cigar. Goddamnit what had Alice said? Fucking seers…

Lord Hinswich put his hands up, trying to deescalate things. "Aye. We know, that's not why we're here. Louis'll continue as he has been, but we'd all pledge our troth with the understanding that more like than not, one of your babes'll be First after him. All of us have a responsibility to the continuance of our line and, frankly, after seeing what your intended is capable of, we'd be honored to add our strength to yours to keep her safe."

Add their strength—Flynn's cheeks sucked in as he smoked, trying to buy himself some time to wrap his head around what they were saying. Christ, they weren't coming as supplicants, they were coming as allies, and they weren't beholden to Crandall—

Fucking Binders and their logic!

"In that case, Lord Hinswich, I'm honored to accept." Christ, he could kiss the man. Flynn gave a sharp laugh. He had allies, and it was time to call more of them in.

CHAPTER NINETEEN

Split [split] noun

1. *A rare breeding defect seen in dual Talents with borderline metrics resulting in two distinct channels, denoted by halos that flip between the two bents.*

– Excerpt from A Treatise on Talents, *Third Edition*

"One thing historians do agree upon is that first Overlord was unsuited to the role. A militant and demanding man, once the city began to prosper, the other lines chafed beneath his rule. Unable to stomach their censure of his personal excesses, he abdicated, gaining further notoriety as the only Overlord to do so..."

– Lord Talos, Preceptor of History,
Academy of Glynfyls

"THE NUMBERS ARE ABYSMAL." Salist inspected the flute of kir in his gloved hand as if he'd discovered a turd amongst the bubbles. "If this keeps up, I may have to put off buying the province

I've been eyeing. Profits haven't been this low since that debacle in Diytan."

Nor had the temperature in the complex. Titus assumed it was playing a part in the uninspired performance of the all-male cast attempting to frolic across the stage costumed in swags of pearls. The opera-turned-burlesque house was about ten degrees shy of brisk.

"It wouldn't be nearly so dire if the board had authorized a harvest when I first floated the idea. Profitability's been on the slide for the past century, this should come as no surprise."

Titus's attention wandered to the stage below, though it didn't merit it. A chorus line of females had joined the act, the effects of the temperature much more appealing on their forms. It was the only thing about the performance that was. What he wouldn't give for a decent rendition of *La bohème* right about now.

Salist wasn't even attempting to follow the drivel below. He picked at a box of truffles on the other end of the crimson couch, his robe lined in ermine. "Agreed, but this latest business with the North's sanctions —you have to know they're all pointing the finger at you. Especially after paying through the nose for that coal shipment."

A pyrotechnic display lit the stage, sparking over a good quarter of general seating. Titus blinked at the spots occluding his vision, motioning for the sub to close the curtains at the front of his box. He'd had enough. Kasham's concept of culture was beyond tawdry, though he suspected he shouldn't have expected anything else from the jumped-up madame. "I don't see how that's my fault. Keets heads up supply. If anyone should take the blame for outsourcing issues, it's him."

Salist snorted. "As if they don't know you maneuvered him into making Glynfyls one of our biggest trading partners."

Titus took a sip of bourbon. The statement was accurate, though he'd never cop to it. He'd hoped to cut off supplies to the city, throwing them into even more of a panic when his troops descended. Instead, they'd beaten him to the punch, and the Source was left scrambling for a way to heat the sprawling facility.

"The situation is unfortunate, though you must admit, the holo of Keet's face when the shipment came in with Glynfyls' stamp on it—"

Salist laughed. "Agreed, however the rest of the board isn't as amused. The optics of liquidating assets after losing Albanach's golden goose has sent stock prices into a nose dive."

"I'm aware." Rache, the board's financial analyst, had already called half a dozen times trying to get the status of the find he'd teased her with. Layoffs in the genetics department had begun. "Getting cold feet?"

"Was that an attempt at humor?" the dark man asked wryly. "I didn't think you capable, and no, I'm eager to see if you can actually pull this off. Don't think the increase of troops at the border has gone unnoticed."

"A contract ended prematurely, and I needed to put them somewhere. Care to up our wager?"

The dark man's lips curdled, not buying it, but he didn't pursue. "Ah. You've gone mad, that explains it."

Titus pulled up a set of holos. The first was only a table of vitals, the second from Marcos's point of view, somewhere underground. "Did you know those nanobots of Orin's are sexually transmitted? I had the slat at the Commandant's breaking infect him."

Salist sat forward, reviewing that data. His breath caught as Marcos's feed swung to show the Nora Jester sleeping on a cot in the shadows. Titus smirked. His hunch that she'd been priming the Commandant for something had playing out.

"You're going after Albanach…"

Titus sipped his bourbon. "Unfortunately their escape did little to implicate the man directly, but it has highlighted his slovenly security."

"Yes, but this with the loss of the Jester girl—Why haven't you called for an inquest?"

The second holo flickered. Nora was awake.

"They've been moving through a series of bunkers and are stalled at the moment, no doubt at a loss how to proceed. She discovered my little spies before they left the facility, but hasn't been able to clear them. An hour ago I dispatched a unit of Peacekeepers. They'll have to run, or be captured."

Salist sat back, wetting his lips. "If you can prove a Northern connection, it could be construed as provocation…and if Albanach's incriminated in the process…"

"Indeed." Titus grinned.

The dark man drummed his long fingers on the arm of the couch. "You're playing a dangerous game, and I'm not just referring to bearding the old dragon. The Commandant's an exemplary tactician, and is intimately familiar with our military capabilities. On top of which, what's not to say he won't subvert any troops you send after him with bloodlust?"

"Subvert?" Titus laughed, surprising the man. "Oh no, Marcos is far too honorable to drag anyone else into his perceived disgrace, and they'll smell it on him. He's an outcast, Salist, and that lovely little pheromone you all fear? It will trigger any Breaker to shoot first and ask questions later. In the event it doesn't, the bots' extermination setting will. In either case, the Commandant was aging out. This just sped the natural progression." Titus shook out some pills. As much as he told himself that, the reality still made his head throb.

Salist grunted. "And who would you install in his place?"

"Pax has been promoted." Titus washed down the capsules with a sip of bourbon, hiding his frown. The Breaker needed to be called into account over his performance since he'd returned from the border.

Salist ran a finger across his lush lips, deep in thought. "And your progress in the North?"

"Barton's in position, and the cell on target—"

"I was alluding more to Laughlin Scot. What little news I've heard has been troubling."

"I've made arrangements to have him neutralized."

"Assassination might be more advisable at this point."

Salist wasn't wrong…any chance they'd had of the Quorum instigating war had been squandered. Titus would've given a great deal to know exactly what happened during that dinner Scot had thrown. The boy was turning into a force of nature, never mind an inconvenience. Perhaps the option shouldn't be off the table—

A sharp pain behind Titus's eye made him lose the thought. He pulled the bottle of pills again, chewing several with a mouthful of bourbon. "And lose his genetics? Perhaps you're the one who's gone mad. No, I've plans for him. So, what do you say, double or nothing?"

Salist snorted. "Since you're so determined to give me your money, I'll bite, but put it in escrow with the rest. I still think I'll have to collect from your estate… What of Riegel? You failed to mention his progress amongst all your scheming."

Titus smiled, pulling up the Breaker's feed. "I'd say Glynfyls is agreeing with him."

<hr>

"YOU, out. Your bail's been posted."

A thickset guard swung open the iron door, fondling his bully-stick. Riegel's eyebrow rose, but he wasn't about to argue. He followed the man from the squalid cell-block in much better spirits than he'd anticipated after being robbed of his opportunity to gain access to the tubes and spending the past twenty-four hours in lock-up. It was markedly similar to the Source's Klink—if you didn't take the cholera inducing, vermin-infested conditions into account. He was inclined to overlook them in light of the savory tidbit of information he'd gained from his stay.

In three days, that bearded ape would be within his reach.

Riegel grinned, signing for his meager possessions. His jacket was unceremoniously shoved through the gap between the chain-link and the battered desk top. He shrugged into it, frowning at the creases as he turned to leave.

"Ah, moment there, friend. Best not be forgetting yer summons t'appear." The uniformed man behind the desk held out a yellow slip of paper. Riegel's lips pruned, snatching it and scanning the form… released under the recognizance of a Master Eid. Hmm. Didn't ring a bell. Not that it would've mattered if it had.

The slip was in a ball over his shoulder the moment his feet hit the sidewalk.

He straightened his lapels with a crack of his neck and scanned the evening crowd. After that pissant had relieved him of his watch and wallet, an infusion of cash was needed. He set his sights on a dandy several shopfronts away and fell into step behind him.

The man stopped at a newsstand, picking up a copy of the *Post* and perusing the front page, not paying attention to his surroundings. Riegel clucked his tongue. Situational awareness was paramount in a city such as this. The carelessness of some people was appalling, especially when it extended to their person. As the man passed an alley, Riegel bum-rushed him, slamming the man's head into the clag-stained brick. It made a satisfyingly wet crack, and the poor chap collapsed into a limp pile. Riegel relieved him of his paper and wallet, then tossed him over his shoulder, and started towards the Pinch.

It really was fascinating how little attention he garnered walking down the street hefting the listless man. The few women he'd taken had created a bit more fervor, but it was never anything he couldn't talk his way out of. "Oh, she fainted dead away…" or "Had a few too many, bringing him home to the missus…" was usually enough to clear him of any suspicion. Tonight, no one batted an eye.

He found the nearest gate and traversed the three rungs and two spokes of muck-filled streets in a blink. It took considerably longer to weevil through the Pinch and drop the man in the cul-de-sac. Rifling through his pockets one last time, he left him without a backward glance. Pity there wasn't a watch. He'd become rather fond of the one the pissant had stolen.

It was a minor concern. Of more import was his lead on Scot's upcoming bout at the Painted Pony. He needed to familiarize himself with the venue.

By the time Riegel found the garishly painted carousel horse hanging from a pole, it was full dark. He strode into the establishment and a cane slapped across his chest. A man seated by the door held up three fingers, and Riegel dug out the units, looking around. The clangor of the room was egregious. Thudding music clashed with a mob screaming somewhere within its dank smoke-filled bowels.

He flipped the man his fee and continued into the murk. Card tables were staggered haphazardly throughout the room. Among them, scantily clad women undulated against poles or each other. His eyebrow rose at the pretty young men in the mix. That was a first for up here. Perhaps Glynfyls wasn't as provincial as he'd been led to believe.

Beneath an upper balcony of doors, a bar lined the far wall, every sticky seat in the place filled. It reeked of human excretion, and the air held the promise of violence. After the sterilized Corporation sponsored bordellos at the Source, the Pony was a disease-infested shithole. Riegel laughed, delighted.

A nubile blonde sidled up to him and ran a hand over his bicep. She flinched when she saw his eyes, but it didn't deter her. He bent down so she could shout into his ear.

"Looking for anything particular, han'some?"

"Yes, a fight."

Her face lit up at his vernacular, no doubt anticipating the units she could wheedle from him. Riegel pursed his lips, brushing back her bangs. He could just make out a thin crimson line around her irises.

"Betting, bouting, or bedding?" she asked, fluttering her lashes.

"That's entirely dependent upon the competition."

She licked her lips and took his hand, leading him past the scattered tables and writhing women, through a rough-cut doorway, and into a neighboring warehouse.

The noise of the mob was deafening.

He smirked, jostling his way past the tiered metal stands to the side of a large cage. What a quaint attempt at an arena. The raucous crowd stamped their feet, screaming at the two men beating each other bloody inside the barbaric chain-link structure. One of them had the clear advantage, and was soon bashing the other's head upon the rust-stained concrete. The tang of blood and sweat permeated the air, and Riegel inhaled deeply, salivating as it crossed his tongue.

He hadn't had a bout in some time and was beginning to get twitchy. After his last stint with the wretched condition, he had no desire to repeat the experience. The whore rubbed up against him, reminding him of another thing he hadn't been able to adequately work out of his system, but business first.

"Is it always like this?" he yelled to her.

She looked around at the rabid spectators, units crushed in their hands as they screamed for their favorites, and shrugged. "Ya."

Riegel smiled, becoming quite fond of what this nasty little burg had to offer. Sanitary concerns aside, this establishment in particular suited his tastes quite well.

Now to cultivate it to suit his ambition.

KARA WAS *eleven years old again, her fingers tightening on Albanach's sleeve. They left little damp ovals on the brushed silk of his jacket. She swallowed heavily, hoping he wouldn't see them.*

He smiled down at her from around his cigar and patted her sweaty hand. "It's just a party, you'll survive. Pretend you're on the mats with Rogan. It's just another kind of sparring."

She gave that stupid nervous laugh, her cheeks warming at the mention of the big Breaker. The amusement in Albanach's eyes died. He patted her hand again, looking through the doorway into the opulent ballroom.

Her entire line was out there waiting for her to be presented, then tomorrow she'd begin training at the Creche. She wasn't sure which she was dreading more. The latter she supposed, at least this humiliation would be over in a few hours. She'd be stuck in the Creche with Riegel and Ielle for the next ten years. The thought made her mouth go dry, and she ran a hand over her stomach, feeling like she was going to be sick. A thread of laughter slipped into the alcove where they waited. Tamara Hess. Kara was sure she'd been the punch line. Not for the first time, she imagined beating in her smug face. Short of that, she wanted to run back to her rooms and hide.

Albanach's hand pressed down on hers like he knew it. "Someday none of this will matter," he said softly, flicking the ash off his cigar. "Until then, keep your head down, and play the game. The moment they see you as a threat is the moment I can't protect you. That's why bumbling through this waltz matters."

He reached over and tipped up her chin. She tried to look away, ashamed, but that's what they were all out there waiting for; to see her halos and her flaw. That horrible second brown ring that marked her as a twist and made her less than every other Talent—

"Are you sure you want to do this right now?" Shelby was looking at her like she expected her to bolt. It snapped Kara back into the present. She wiped her sodden palms on her sweats and forced a smile. Ugh! After that damn note, her stupid memories had become so vivid… She scrubbed at her face.

"Sorry, I'm getting lost in the past again." She tried to bury her mortification of that waltz with Alba—Cal. It was Cal, and had happened over sixteen years ago. Get over it, Kara.

Shelby started the music again, pinching Kara whenever she looked down. Ugh, she was all feet…but after the sixth or seventh time around the room, she wasn't fumbling quite so much. She managed to make a circuit without tripping over herself and looked up to see Flynn leaning against the wall, grinning at them. Kara stumbled, her face burning.

"I don't know what you're smiling at," she said as he came over and kissed her. His right hand was awkwardly wrapped in gauze and already bleeding through.

"It's not every day I see a couple of beautiful women dancing in my bedroom."

They both rolled their eyes, and Shelby held out a hand to him.

"Come on, let's show Kara how it's done."

He took it with another grin. "It's been a long time."

The music started, and Flynn spun with her across the room. He faltered once, getting too close to a chair, but Kara was impressed. He was good. That seed of panic sprouted. She was going to look like an idiot. The music ended, and he laughed, kissing his cousin on the cheek.

She pushed him away, rubbing at the spot. "I don't know how you stand that beard, Kara."

"What do you think?" he asked, twirling Kara around.

"I think I need more practice…" she said breathlessly. Something had happened downstairs. He had an air about him that made her pulse race.

"I'll be in the ballroom at six," Shelby called over her shoulder, leaving.

The door closed, and he kissed Kara with an urgency she hadn't felt from him since the farm. His emotions were all over the place.

"What happened?"

He shook his head, burying his face in her neck and she lost herself in the feel of him.

Afterwards, she lay against his chest, listening to his heart beat. He was still a tangle.

"You ready to tell me yet?" she asked, smoothing her fingers across his pec.

"Crandall, Markham, Phyllis, and Lot all know about the plateau."

"What?" She popped up to look at him.

"They ambushed me on the way to take those oaths." He pinched the bridge of his nose. "They're blackmailing me, Kara. As long as I vote lockstep and do what they want, Crandall's orchestrated things so Riegel takes the fall for it. He's the one who's been behind all those disappearances and murders in the city."

She lowered herself back down, unsurprised at that last tidbit. The rest of it though…"What did Cal say?"

"I didn't tell him, and I'm not gonna. I didn't come back up here to have him bailing me out again." He pulled her close and kissed the top of her head. "I've gotta do this under my own steam, and I think I know how."

Kara bit at the side of her thumb. "Can I help?"

He laughed and held up his hand, wrapped in that disgusting gauze. She sat up and started unwinding it. "Can you help. You're the only reason I can do any of it. You know the entire Binder line pledged to me tonight?"

"One of them should've healed this for you." The cut was deeper than it needed to be and still oozing.

"Lord Hinswich offered, but it didn't seem right."

"It will seem even less right when it turns black and falls off," she said sweetly, smacking the panel for French.

"Yes, sir?" he intoned after the chime.

"It's me, French. Can you please find me a well-stocked triage kit before Flynn gets gangrene?" He made a face at her, and she batted her eyelashes at him.

"In anticipation of your request, I've already done so, and shall send it up with alacrity. Is there anything else?"

"Yeah, send up a steak!"

"Precut, sir?"

"Yes, into tiny bite-sized pieces," Kara laughed before he could answer. "I'll have a bowl of that spinach, please."

"Very good, my lady." There was another chime, and she dissolved into laughter.

Flynn snorted. "You shouldn't encourage him. He makes enough dick comments as it is."

"French? Aw, he's just looking out for you." She laughed again at Flynn's expression, inspecting his hand. Man, she missed her talent. "This is awful. What possessed you to make it so deep?"

"I didn't want to keep re-slicing it. There were thirty-one heads down there."

She got up to pull on a shirt. "What changed? You seem almost okay with it now."

"I wouldn't go that far, but with Crandall up my ass… I've been looking at this all wrong. The Binders told me they were pledging to add their strength to mine—to keep you safe. Every oath I take is one more House that will stand with me between you and the Source, and ultimately, if I can do what Cal wants, Crandall won't be able to touch us."

"Then you're going for it."

Flynn squeezed his fist, the wound running red. His tumult of emotion swallowed by a cresting determination. "Yeah, Kara. I don't have a choice. I've gotta take Overlord."

CHAPTER TWENTY

*Menot [*meh-**noh***] noun*

   1. *A familial mentor who guides a Breaker into manhood.*

– Excerpt from The Way of Honor

"Of the scant handful of Talents that qualified for the program, we were able to create a single split. In most cases, no matter how careful the application of stressors, the resulting influx of talent burned out their ability completely. The program was abandoned due to lack of subjects, but I'd hazard that there's no guaranteed procedure to bring a split into being…"

– L. Merkel, Head Geneticist,
The Source

FLYNN'S HEAD snapped back as another punch slipped his guard. Christ, he was out of shape. It'd only been a half-hour of this shit, and he was already winded, but he'd be damned before he asked Rogan to quit. He squared up again, keeping his center low. At some point they'd switched from straight boxing to brawling, and the Breaker kept putting him on the ground.

The asshole's foot snaked out, and Flynn batted it away, resisting the urge to use it as a lever to cripple him. Rogan frowned, making that motion he had with Kara and ending the bout. Flynn tugged his shirt over his head, mopping off sweat. Shit. He'd taken a big hit to his right cheek, and it was already swollen. Rogan stood there, taking in the marks Kara had left on him.

Suck it, asshole.

"What do you think about when you're fighting?"

"I don't."

"You don't feel anything either, do you."

It wasn't a question and he didn't answer.

"Kara feels too much. It's dangerous for her…more so now that she's breeding. You instinctively do what I've been trying to hammer into that thick skull of hers for years. Zero's a Breaker skill."

Flynn grabbed a bottle of water and glared at him, daring him to say it.

The man smirked. "So, word on the street has you at the Pony this Friday."

"Yeah." He still had no fucking clue how he was gonna pull that off and not be censured by the Assembly. He couldn't afford to lose his vote for a day, never mind the rest of the legislative session.

"You taking her?"

"Planning on it."

"You might want to rethink that…especially if she's marking you like that."

"That any of your fucking business?"

The Breaker laughed. "Yeah. You've got no idea what you're dealing with and muddling through it is gonna get you killed. Haven't you noticed she's been different?"

"As opposed to what? I've known her for all of two weeks."

Rogan grunted. "Look, kid, Breaker women get wild when they're breeding, and I'll be the first to admit it's hot as hell, but there's a fine line. Kara…" He shook his head. "Kara's one of the sweetest little girls I've ever known and way too humble to look like God's own pin-up.

All that in the city with Julia, what she's left on you—it's not like her. She's losing control."

A muscle in Flynn's jaw popped. "How the fuck would you know what she's like?"

"That any of your fucking business?"

"Yeah." The gym washed with red as he stood, nose-to-nose with the man.

Asshole grinned, and Flynn took a half a step back, a foul musk assaulting him. Jesus fucking Christ—he wiped his eyes—what the fuck—

"Get a good whiff, kid. That's bloodlust. The kind that reminds you to mind your fucking manners. What she's been leaking? It's gonna change in an eye-blink from that musky sweetness that gets your dick rock hard to something that makes you shrivel up. She'll want to put you down, and she's going to, unless you stop holding back."

The stench increased, and Flynn spat the taste from his mouth, hackles rising at the malaise of irrational fear pressing in on him with it. His pulse jumped, that blackness answering it. This motherfucker—

"That's the kind that says I'm about to put you in the ground. It's no secret what you did on the plateau. Show me."

Flynn laughed. "You're a fucking lunatic."

A blade snicked open and that otherness stirred inside him. "Don't."

The Breaker flashed that goddamned smile and lunged.

Flynn twisted, the knife scoring a line across his obliques. His fist caught the man's jaw, rocking him back, but not before he'd swept Flynn's feet from under him, putting him on the fucking ground again. That blackness heaved, rising up—Rogan was on him. They grappled, the blade inching towards his throat—motherfucker—

"GET OFF ME!" A dank cloud of rage burst forth, searing the room crimson and shooting pain through his head. Rogan's weight was gone, and Flynn gripped his temples, scrabbling for that blanket of calm to snuff it, curling up in the fetal position…

Fuck—He blinked the haze from his eyes, feeling like he was coming off a bender. His arms shook, pushing up to sit, raking his hair back. Christ, that'd fucking hurt.

Rogan squatted on the other side of the mat, blade dangling from his fingers. "How long you been seeing red?"

Since Dengshi.

"I—" He couldn't think straight, a weird pressure slowly dissipating with his rattled breath. Shit, what was the fucking point? "A couple years, maybe. Four."

The Breaker grunted. "Wouldn't hurt so bad if you'd stop trying to reel it in. Split's going to happen whether you want it to or not. You're just prolonging the inevitable."

Inevitable? What the hell was he talking about?

Rogan snorted, sheathing the blade. "What a fucking asshole. Cal's never said a goddamned word about it, has he? You're right on the line, kid. That red haze bleeding over when you're pissed? It's a secondary channel ripening, and when it does, it's either gonna amplify what you've got, or take it all out."

Flynn stared at the man, wanting to call him a liar.

He couldn't. A fucking split?

His head hung down between his knees, and he gave a sad laugh. Fucking Cal. Flynn shook his head. He should've registered when he had a chance. They found out he was a dual now, they'd hang him, and if he lost his talent? Christ, Kara—

The baby.

His mouth went dry. "How long do I have?"

Rogan shrugged. "No way to tell. I told you I've known men like you. Scant dozen since the Surge… It was different for all of 'em, but I'm guessing something bad happened four years ago to kick it off. It'll take more of the same to finish it."

Flynn's hand trembled across his mouth, the memory of blood coating his skin.

"The fact that you can achieve zero will help keep it at bay, but it's bubblegum and duct tape, kid. At some point, that channel's going to open, and I can't tell you what it's going to look like. Either way, you're gonna suck it the fuck up for her sake."

Their gazes met and Flynn stood, pulling on his shirt as he left. "I'm gonna be late."

"I'll be there Friday to keep an eye on her while you're occupied."

Flynn grunted, surprised to feel relief at that. If things fell to shit, the Breaker would get Kara out… He riffled his hair, trying to digest what the man had said. A split. Shit, that was right up there with phasing. Next there was gonna be Fetches flying around. Why not? A goddamned Pan was as likely as the rest of it.

And Cal had known.

Of course he had. What the fuck else was new.

Miriam was in the kitchen haranguing a bunch of scullions polishing silver. She scowled at his busted up face and pushed a plate of food into his hands. Shit, he wasn't in the mood for one of her lectures…talk about inevitable. He sighed, joining Leo and Graham at a table in the corner. Every other damned room had been conscripted for the Introduction.

"Where the hell have you two been?"

They exchanged glances, and Graham shrugged. The two of them looked beat.

"Work's been busy," Leo said around his mouthful of eggs.

"You smuggling in shit for Markham?"

It was his turn to shrug, and Graham answered. "Yeah. Shifting supplies from the East, and it's like eight jumps minimum. We're on a fourteen hour rotation. It's exhausting, especially when he keeps stopping to look for that stupid plaz-converter—"

Flynn fought to keep his face blank, gingerly chewing a piece of toast. He'd forgotten about that damned thing…

"Shut up. You're not even doing the heavy lifting. My channel feels like somebody bent it over a barrel." Leo eyed Flynn's face. "But at least I've still got my looks. It true you're Ponying up, or your sweetie pie give you that love tap?"

The phrase sent that old rush Flynn used to get before a fight through him. It helped him shake what Rogan had spilled. "Ponying up. You two in?"

"Shit yeah, I can stand to make some easy money."

Flynn snorted. There wasn't one damned thing easy about the situation. He finished what was on his plate and took his leave, stopping to kiss Miriam's cheek on the way out. Her scowl hadn't faded.

"One and done, Miriam."

She ran a hand down his swollen cheek. He grunted, pulling away. Her lips pinched down into that frog look. "One and done, Laughlin. I'm holding you to that."

He kissed her forehead and the dirty look was reserved for his beard this time. He scratched at it and winked, heading out the door.

Shelby and Kara were gliding across the ballroom. His eyebrows raised at her improvement from yesterday. She stumbled and shot him a black look. Christ, he was collecting those today. Laughing, he went up to get ready for Assembly.

JULIA SAT behind her desk purposefully ignoring Sylvie's pouting.

"I don't understand it." The whore petulantly twirled a curl around her finger, then brightened. "Do you think prison turned him gay?"

Julia snorted. Not in this version of reality.

"It's Kara," Ielle drawled from the chair by the fire. "I don't know what it is about her. It's not like she's anything special. Him on the other hand..."

God. She was as bad as Sylvie. "He's changed, I can't get him to lose his temper like he used to."

"Then you're not pushing the right button," Ielle said, flicking rainbows from her rings.

"And what would you suggest?" Julia snapped.

"Mmm, I've always enjoyed rumors and innuendo. There's one about Kara she never could shake..." The other women in the room perked up, and she laughed. "Thought that might get your attention. You wouldn't have noticed it up here, but her halos are double."

Revulsion crawled up Julia's throat. "She's a twist?"

"It was deemed a breeding flaw, but who's to say?"

If it was true, the Shades would revolt at the idea of him bonding her, and if he had already—

"Did you hear? He's bouting at the Pony, and the girls are in a tizzy over it. The stories they tell..." Sylvie gave a little moan. "All I can say is that man can spank me anytime he wants."

Ielle was suddenly all ears. "Really? Where's this again?"

"The Painted Pony. It's the biggest brothel in Glynfyls, fifth rung, Finder spoke. They have gambling and bouts."

"How timely you should mention it. I've been feeling the lack of stimulating companionship." Ielle flicked her eyes at Julia, and she glowered back from beneath her brows, hoping the woman would take up residence there.

"I thought you might be the type," Sylvie laughed. Her voice became conspiratorial. "He's got a preference for rough sex. They say he fucked that woman of his on the dining room table, and she was all bruised up afterwards. She's supposed to be a Binder, and he wouldn't let her heal herself!" Sylvie laughed at Ielle's expression, missing Julia's. After what that bitch had done to her, she never wanted to hear the word Binder again. "I can take you down tonight, but you'll have to find your own way back."

"Perfect. I'm curious what else they have to say about him. Unless you'd like to fill us in, Julia?"

She looked up, startled. "I—This conversation isn't fit for a woman of my station." Sniffing, she rose from her desk. "You can be certain that I was never a party to anything like that."

"Probably why he was diddling the help," Ielle said nastily. The two whores laughed.

Julia fumed. That she should be treated like this in her own home by common trollops! She gripped the lock of her son's hair in her pocket. They didn't matter. Meeting with Lord Ines before Assembly did. He was a staunch ally, regardless of his motives. Julia huffed from their cackling to the gate and into the Assembly hall.

Session didn't start for another half-hour, allowing her plenty of time to peruse the agenda a page handed her. She flipped through it, strolling to the lounge for her morning cup of—the third sheet stopped her dead in the doorway. She slumped against the jamb.

The entire Binder line had pledged.

Her fingertips rose to her cheek, the powder beneath them incensing her. She snatched them away, her hand balling into a fist. That twisted bitch... Ielle was right. Laughlin had never cared about his own reputation, but he'd already threatened Klaus over that woman's.

Julia would ruin her with it.

Her eyes returned to the agenda, scanning the list of Houses he'd bamboozled into pledging. Aside from the Binders, the rest were Shades, save two. Both of them weaker Fetch Houses. She snorted. No surprise there. Thanks to Miriam's Prydee connections, the Scots were overly cozy with the line, his—A burning pain seared behind her eyes and she stumbled, losing the thought.

"Are you all right, mistress?" A servant took her arm, helping her to a chair and then coming back with a cup of tea.

"Thank you…would you send a runner back to my estate? My maid has something for my headaches." The man gave an odd, rolling blink before bowing and leaving to do as she'd requested.

Julia sipped her tea. Earl Grey. A single cube of sugar sat on the bottom and a slice of lemon at its side. Just how she liked it. What had she been thinking about? Temples throbbing, she riffled through the stack of papers again. How were the Firsts taking members of their lines pledging fealty to another? Perhaps that angle would bear fruit. Personal attacks on the man were getting her nowhere.

"Mistress Cree." Lord Ines' silky voice sounded over her shoulder.

She tried to keep the disgust off her face, unable to manage a smile. "Lord Ines. You'll forgive me if I don't get up. I've one of my headaches. A runner's just gone for my tincture."

"Please, Julia, call me Hansel." He pursed his lips in sympathy. "I do wish you'd let one of the Binders take a look at you. They did wonders with my Annabelle's migraines when she was still with us."

Her revulsion at the suggestion was so strong she was almost sick all over his shoes, her head lolling back.

"Oh my. Are you sure you should be in session today?"

The arrival of a page saved her from having to answer. She took the vial and poured a jot into her tea, drinking the mixture straight off. The effect was immediate.

Julia had purpose.

She sat up to see Laughlin cross the lounge's doorway. Assembly must be about to start. He always cut things close. She handed her empty cup to the page and allowed Lord Ines to help her to her feet. After a moment of dizziness, she let go of his arm and walked into chambers. Her eyes narrowed seeing the man in Lady Breakspear's box. What was Stonefist doing here? After the way his last appearance ended, she'd thought she'd seen the last of the Breaker general.

The speaker banged his gavel as soon as Julia was seated. "Good morning. First on the agenda, Lord Markham has a status of our proposed finances."

He stood, wiping at his face with a thick handkerchief. "I'll be brief, there's a complete accounting of funds in your packets. After consulting with Lord Stonefist, at our current income levels it looks like we can support the recruitment and training of an additional ten thousand men…" He went on to speak for some time about the actual numbers.

It was not brief.

"Are we really going to do this?" Lord Ines peevishly interrupted as Markham referred them to yet another spreadsheet. "Why in the world are we increasing funding for a force that's woefully inadequate?"

Stonefist rose from his seat, and the room quieted, eager for a repeat performance of him frothing at the mouth. "Because as it stands, the curtains they've erected have negated our ability to shift out of the Northern Territories. They've trapped us like rats, and if we rely solely on talent, we'll be sitting ducks when they advance. As of yet, they haven't figured out how to do the same to a bullet. The more men we have to pull a trigger, the better."

Ines rolled his eyes, waving a bloated hand. "Scare tactics."

Laughlin cleared his throat, and the room turned to him. Julia scowled. The thought of anyone bonding a twist made her physically ill. His perversions knew no bounds.

"It's not scare tactics, it's the truth. The Source's Breakers are genetically engineered to be elite soldiers. Even without talent, one of them is worth at least ten men and last I heard, they have a standing force of just under twelve thousand—"

"Super soldiers?" Julia sneered. "That's ridiculous. Next you'll have us believing in phasing and Pans."

The Shades all developed smirks. "If you doubt the Source's ability to create, what did you call them…? Super soldiers? You're a fool, or willfully ignorant of the facts. I can personally attest to how vicious their Peacekeepers are. Hell, you've all seen the pictures, however, the same technology that limits us does the same to them. You should be very grateful for that."

"Grateful?! How can you possibly—"

Laughlin raised his voice to cut over the din his comments had created. "Our advantages are that Source Talents aren't trained to use their abilities together, and they need our genetics. For that, they have to take us alive."

The Assembly quieted, somewhat mollified. Stonefist stood again. "I've warned you that the Source was upgrading their infrastructure to move large numbers of men north. As of Sunday, there's been an influx of troops. Not the standard Breakers Titus sends up to keep us on our toes, Peacekeepers. Everything I've been warning you about is coming to a head, and if I had to guess, he'll move against us in the next few weeks, if not days."

The room went still.

Riggs cleared his throat, looking pale. "Ah, if no one has anything else," Riggs banged his gavel, preempting any replies. "Enjoy your lunches."

Julia stayed seated, watching the crowd mill about. Currents of people swirled around Laughlin, bearing him up and out of the room. Many of them the same sycophants that had been licking her shoes last week. The ebb and flow of power in this city was fickle and fleeting, more often than not steered by rumor.

She smiled to herself. It was time to start one.

BARTON BUSIED himself bussing tables in the Assembly's lounge, listening to Lord Scot speak to another group of people. The man was incredibly charismatic. They all smiled and shook his hand, falling under his spell of confident competence, whispering Overlord in the Assembly's halls, the city's streets. Warmly. Wanting… Wanton.

Scot was of consequence. So few were.

Barton could feel Scot drawing people to him. Their need to get close, to possess a part of him, sublimate it into themselves and share in the glow.

His tongue flicked over his lips, tasting power.

No. He concentrated on collecting cups and plates. Occupying his hands. Fingers. Mustn't bite.

Not yet, and not Scot.

His target was Kara Jester.

He carried the tub of dishes to the kitchen, his day at an end. Untied his apron and folded it precisely before slipping it into his messenger bag. Donned his jacket, buttoning it up two-thirds of the way, then positioned the strap of his bag over his head cross-wise, resting it against his left hip. All as it should be.

Barton left the building at an amble, enjoying his freedom before he returned to the Source with the girl. The crowd jostled him along. Unnoticed. A no one in the middle of a million other inconsequential lumps of animated flesh. He dodged antiquated cars spewing noxious exhaust, air thick with it and the smoke of coal-burning hearths. Ash from the power plants raining down. Still preferable to the Source's sanitized streets. There you couldn't even find gum on the sidewalk.

Here you might find a body part.

He smiled at the odds of that, ducking his head and pressing on, down the main row spoking out from the city's center, into one of the densely packed trade districts. The upper rungs of this one were home to the designers, all of them in a frenzy of late. On the lowest, tanneries and sweat-shops. Barton had taken rooms at the midpoint, above the brothel where most of Glynfyls' aspiring models earned their rent. His choice of lodging was deliberate.

The Painted Pony had the distinction of catering to hillies and commons alike. The quality of the whores and the stakes of the games reflected this. Given Scot's outstanding debt, it also meant he would land there, sooner or later.

The girl would be alone when he did.

A vessel. Vulnerable.

His victim.

Barton pulled his finger from his mouth, swishing the tang of copper over his tongue. It washed away the memory of "other" from the plateau. That had tasted of death.

His.

Extra caution was needed.

He nodded to the bouncer at the door and went to the window to give his report. The new tally of times Sylvie had been turned down went up on the board. Barton collected his fee, then shifted into his seedy little room.

Bed, table, chair. Nothing differentiated it from any other in the city, save the pitch of the canted floor. The furniture had legs here, albeit uneven.

He took off the messenger bag, then his coat, hanging each onto its own peg. His uniform came off next. He inspected it, shifting a smear of danish from a sleeve, and draped it across a chair, his carefully folded apron shaken out and laid atop it. Creases wouldn't do.

He stood in the weak patch of sunlight at the window, naked. It did little to illuminate the tattoos mottling his flesh. Days were too short. His art was suffering.

He reached for the box on the table, taking out a small needle, a bottle of ink, and a head shot of the Jester girl.

His focus.

She was also of consequence.

So few were. Two together less so.

He dipped his needle in ink. A high-pitched buzzing filled the room, his talent vibrating the implement rapidly as it drew across his inner thigh.

The natural light faded.

Barton wiped at his work, pleased with how the outline of Kara's cheek had come out. It nestled amongst the others he'd been sent after. He opened a bottle of gin and splashed his efforts, hissing at the sting.

Her smiling face looked up at him, and his fingers drifted to his open lips.

It wouldn't be long now.

KARA JOGGED down the sweeping staircase to the east drawing room. It had taken her way too long to figure out where Audrey was telling her Reggie had set up. Stupid, pretentious…she was in the little purple room off the foyer. Why couldn't Audrey just say that? Calling everything by colors was so much easier.

When she got there, the furniture had been pushed against the walls, making way for a low platform in the center of the room, full-length mirrors cupping around it. Reggie was sprawled in one of the armchairs next to a changing screen. Yawning, she motioned to a box.

"Are you okay?"

The blonde woman laughed. "I'm so far beyond okay, it's not even a dot in the rearview. God, Kara. I never dreamed that I'd be this busy. I've had to take on people just to keep up. I swear it's harder training them than just doing it myself…" She pinched the bridge of her nose. "Go on, open it."

Kara raised the box's lid with a murmur of appreciation and ran her fingers over the gown. It was gorgeous. She pulled it out and held it against herself, listening to Reggie chatter.

"Not that I'm complaining! To think, a week ago I was questioning my life choices… Anyway, this should be the last fitting before the Introduction. God, I can't believe it's in two days. Here, let me help you."

The gown was sleeveless, the bodice just kissing her collar bones, then cascading to the floor. Subtle darts cinched her bust and waist, but the focal point was its back. Well, lack of back. It left her bare from nape to just shy of scandalous. Kara laughed. After her outing, she probably wanted to rethink that. Below the plunge, it hugged her hips, then trailed out behind her. Flynn was going to have to deal with the tiny bit of talent required to keep the whole thing in place.

The door creaked, and Audrey peeked in. "Pardon the intrusion, my lady, but Lord Scot is on his way, and I'd hoped to take a moment to review your schedule…" She looked Kara up and down as Reggie tucked and pinned. "I must say, that gown is stunning. I've never seen anything like it."

Kara beamed, rather pleased with it herself. "Thank you. Reggie's amazing."

"I can't take much credit, she'd make a burlap sack look good." The couturier stood with a hand at the small of her back. "That should do it."

Kara went behind the screen to change. "I have something on my schedule?" She hoped it wasn't with Miriam. Who cared what china pattern they used? It was enough to make her miss the partitioned stainless-steel trays at the Creche.

"Invitations have been sent out for the luncheon Lady Martin's holding in your honor next week. It's being touted as the event of the season—"

"After you went out the other night, all of them want a Glass," Reggie laughed with a little shake of her head. "The whole district's lost their collective mind."

Audrey gave a brittle smile. "I think it wise, with that and the Introduction so close, to review some specific etiquette pertaining to the events. When you've finished, I'll meet you in the southern parlor."

"Where?"

Her secretary's lips twitched. "The taupe room where you had tea with the Ladies."

Right. Kara ran a hand over her stomach as Audrey left, the memory making her nauseous.

"Is it safe?" Flynn's voice rumbled from the doorway.

She laughed at his caution. The weird customs up here...he hadn't even wanted to hear about her dress. She couldn't wait to see his face when he found out it wasn't one of the white poofy nightmares in those folios Miriam had left her. "You're fine."

He walked in with a sandwich and kissed her cheek, smelling of mustard. Kara's brow knit. Rogan had done a number on his face. Maybe that's why Flynn had been so angry earlier.

"I got twenty minutes, you sure we gotta do this now?"

"Unless you want to stand up there nude," she said, relieving him of his pastrami.

Reggie snickered and handed him a box. He shot her a look, taking it behind the screen. After a great deal of fumbling and grunting, he walked out pulling at the regency-style cravat, less than enthusiastic about it.

Kara blew him a kiss.

He sighed stoically, getting up on the platform and shrugging into the jacket. He tugged at the lapels, a grin splitting his face. "Looks good."

"You're a fine sight better than good..." Reggie muttered, making a few marks on the jacket and hem of his pants.

Kara had to agree. He looked amazing, and the jerk knew it. "Yes, you should wear your cravats like that all the time."

Flynn's grin soured, and she laughed. He went to change while she worked out the last of the details with Reggie.

"I'll be here Thursday, two hours before." She loaded the last box onto a wheeled cart and wiped her blue palms over her skirt. "Nothing should need any alterations, but...God, I'm so nervous you'd think it was my Introduction!"

Kara smiled, glad she wasn't the only one with heartburn. She saw the couturier out and came back to find Flynn on the couch eating his sandwich. She sat beside him and put a hand to his swollen jaw.

"This looks awful. You either have a Binder heal it before Thursday, or I will."

His eyebrow rose. "Yes, ma'am. Anything else I should do before then?"

"I'm sure I'll think of something," she laughed. "Assembly go okay?"

"If suicidal ignorance is okay, then yeah. I got into an argument about whether or not Peacekeepers were really a thing. No one in that damned room save Stonefist has any idea of what they can do."

"What?" He had to be kidding.

"I know, they're fucking idiots. If any of them saw a Peacekeeper in action, they'd shit themselves. Maybe Cal can get his hands on a training holo..."

Kara bit at her thumb. "There aren't any. He tried before Rogan came to the tower, everything's redacted."

Flynn grunted, wolfing down the last of his lunch. He glanced at the clock and sighed. "Well, then I guess I'll go yell at them some more. Your petition to be added to the rolls is coming up this afternoon. Julia will sink it if she can."

They stood, and she ran her fingers through his hair, trying to make it less of a bird's nest.

"Two more days and I can go with you."

He took her hand, kissing its palm. "Mmm, only after you dance with me."

A knot of apprehension clunked down in her stomach, and he laughed on his way out the door. Jerk. "Good luck," she called after him.

He grunted and was out of sight. Kara sat back down on the couch. Two more days.

CHAPTER TWENTY-ONE

breeding Breaker [brē-diŋ brā-kər] noun

1. *Term for a Breaker female during the gestational period inclusive of their severe mood swings, tendency to leak bloodlust, and heightened need for violence. It is not uncommon for a female to succumb during this period, necessitating her mate to remain by her side.*

– Excerpt from The Way of Honor

"Although all of the lines have their individual traditions and mysteries, Breakers are a society unto themselves. They are the most clannish of the lines, though Shades come close."

– Lord Grey, Preceptor of Talent Studies,
Academy of Glynfyls

RIEGEL SAT at the edge of the sagging mattress, pulling his hair back into a tail. The whore behind him didn't move much at all, but that was to be expected. Her performance had been adequate, though uninspired. He sighed, an uncomfortable longing for Ielle niggling at him.

The thought of getting his hands on that ape dispelled it. In two more days, Scot would Introduce Kara to his line, whatever that was about. Of more importance, he'd be here afterwards. What a supreme pleasure it would be slaughtering him before thousands, and if he touted her out to witness his demise… Well then, Riegel rather liked the idea of consummating his dominion over her next to Scot's corpse. Good humor restored, he left the room.

The midday crowd at the Pony was considerably more subdued, though the odor of the place was not. Spilled beer and sex hung dankly in the air, along with the subtle aroma of the not too distant tanneries. He descended the sticky steps, avoiding the handrail.

The second story windows along the front of the building let in claggy streaks of light to fall upon the denizens below. Several men crowded around a table playing cards, a haze of smoke above them. One dandled a whore on his knee, but the others were intent on the game. The rest of the tables were empty, chairs flashing their upended legs atop them. A boy with a mop swabbed at a slick of vomit.

The barkeep was nowhere in sight, only a single man seated at the long, scarred slab of oak. Riegel frowned, pushing past the scattered tables to the window where bets were placed. A whore was behind the chain-link, jaw working as she played with a lock of hair.

Her dull eyes brightened as he approached. She snapped her gum and smiled. "Can I help ye, han'some?"

Riegel pursed his lips, considering it. The thickness of the crimson rings about her irises promised she'd be more sport than the slat he'd left upstairs, and her curves were considerably more pronounced. A decade ago, she'd probably been a tasty morsel.

She'd been ridden hard and put away wet since.

"I've business to conduct first. Who's the proprietor of this establishment?"

The stupid trull looked at him blankly and Riegel rubbed a temple. "I want to see who's in charge," he said, speaking slowly.

"Oh! Gerrard's busy with a liquor delivery out back, getting ready for Friday. Ye here for the big fight? Flynn's bouting." The excitement in her voice was nauseating.

"So I hear. You sound like you know him."

She preened, playing with a long lock of chestnut hair. It was one of her more redeeming features. "I were his favorite. He'd always ask for me, name's Melanie." She attempted to look coy. "Ye could do the same."

"Fascinating. Tell me, who's the man you're pitting him against?" That blank look again. "Who is Scot fighting?"

She tittered behind her hand, far too old for the gesture. "Ye hillies an' yer airs… Gerrard ain't said nothin' official yet, but for a ten-spot, mayhap I could introduce ye to a friend of mine brought up special for the weekend…"

He parsed the units onto the counter, and she swept them up into her rumpled kirtle, smiling as she stood. One of her molars was absent. That pang for Ielle reared again. He ached to bend the courtesan over and wrap his hands around that slender neck—

The whore was at his elbow, and he obligingly offered his arm. She took it, fondling his bicep. "Sure ye ain't interested in seeing how ye measure up to Lord Scot?"

Riegel's burst of fury at the suggestion sent her back a step. He smiled, her fear far more arousing than her attempts at seduction. "I'm more interested in meeting your friend."

She jerked her head towards the bar. "Trammel's over there." The dark man seated at it was shoveling gruel into his mouth.

Riegel strode past her and leaned against the scarred wood at his side. "Good afternoon, I hear you're slated to fight Lord Scot."

The man paused mid-chew, looking him over. Riegel did the same. He was a big, brute, hair shaved close with the kind of muscles subs only acquired through chemical means.

"What's it to you?" He took another bite, narrowing his eyes.

"I'm going to take your place."

The man smiled, spinning on his stool to face him. "Yeah? And what makes you think that?"

Riegel set a thick stack of units on the bar. The cards had been good to him last night, and to the man he'd jumped in the alley. "The law of averages. Now, you can take the money and leave, or I can beat you bloody and keep it. Either way, I'll be fighting Lord Scot."

Trammel picked a bit of something from between his teeth. Before he could reply, an ugly little bald man came out from the back. Trammel's lips sealed at the newcomer's approach. Neither looked pleased.

"Who're you and why're you laying out cash on my bar?"

His bar. Between that and Trammel's reaction, this must be Gerrard. Excellent. Riegel smiled winningly at him. "I was just explaining to Master Trammel that I'll be fighting Lord Scot and offered him recompense to acquiesce, or, and I much prefer this option, I can hurt him. A lot."

Gerrard flipped through the stack of units, unimpressed. He tossed them back onto the bar, meeting Riegel's eyes. "You some kind of Breaker? I thought Stonefist conscripted the whole damned line."

"I'm currently an independent agent."

The bald man snorted. "Scot's got a reputation up here. I don't know you from boo, but that ain't to say I ain't open to the idea."

"What would it take to persuade you?"

"Beat Trammel, you're in."

The dark man sighed, taking one last look at the stack of units as he stood. Given his girth, he was somewhat shorter than Riegel had anticipated, but that was of no matter. He followed them into the warehouse, the room's cavernous hush odd after last night. He hung his jacket on a bolt projecting from one of the steel beams supporting the cage. Trammel was already inside, loosening up. Riegel popped his knuckles and entered. The gate shuddered behind him, and he inhaled, breathing the redolent violence of the space.

"No talent, no weapons. Either puts you on the street," Gerrard said, hitting a buzzer. "It ends when one of you don't get up."

Riegel let the large fool circle him, then close in. He took an uppercut and a jab in quick succession. Trammel danced back. Riegel opened his arms wide, welcoming more. The man's lips went flat, and he rushed him, hitting him in the gut twice, stoking Riegel's 'lust.

He let the black fury fill him and cold-cocked the man.

Trammel went flying and landed in a heap against the side of the cage.

He didn't get back up. How disappointing.

Riegel smoothed his shirt sleeves, fighting to quell his rage. He exited the cage and retrieved his jacket. The bald man met him and held out a hand. Riegel took care not to crush it in his own.

"Name's Gerrard, and you are…?"

"Your ringer," he answered curtly, trying to tamp down the urge to damage someone.

Gerrard pursed his lips, looking him over. "What d'you got against Scot?"

"He stole something from me."

"Fair enough. You can take Trammel's room upstairs. Girls and booze you pay for, up front. My take on the match's seventy-five percent."

Riegel slapped his stack of units at Gerrard's chest, shrugging at the outrageous terms, none of it was important. "Fine. Send me that brunette, Melanie."

His ambitions in motion, he was eager to see exactly how he measured up against Lord Scot.

FLYNN GOT to chambers as the doors were closing. He slipped through, dusting the crumbs off his jacket and ran a hand over his beard. The whispering and poorly concealed conversation had jumped with his arrival. Shit. Did he have mustard on him? Kara would've said something…

Riggs pounded his gavel to start, and Flynn sat, trying to pay attention as another trade issue was brought up. He sighed, mussing his hair and glanced at Julia's box. She had Charlotte with her again.

The little blonde woman smiled shyly at him. He kept his face neutral, pissed Julia would drag her into this. And at himself. Like he needed the reminder he was an asshole.

Riggs called for debate. Shit, he didn't even have the right page open. Flynn waited for someone else to stand. A man in the back began to give his opposition. A few more chimed in, and it didn't have enough support to go to vote.

The next measure was the addition of Kara's House to the Assembly roles. There was a flurry of excitement when Riggs named House Jester, especially from the Binder's section.

Lord Ines stood and opposed it, bringing it to the floor for discussion. Flynn's temper thrummed as the man talked.

"… and seems premature in light of recent rumors. Why create a vote now?" There were far too many nods of agreement.

A sinking feeling started in Flynn's gut. What the fuck had Julia dug up? He pulled zero. This wasn't gonna go well. "What rumors?"

Ines flushed, the rest of the Assembly on tenterhooks. "That your intended's talent is tainted."

Flynn laughed, and the entire room drew back, his reaction the last thing they'd expected. "Are you serious?" Jesus fucking Christ. Looking around chambers, every single one of them believed it, and the Binders—Shit. They were fucking pissed. Kara's talent was the sole reason they'd pledged, if they thought she was a twist… He was gonna have to address it.

Motherfucker.

Flynn's gaze landed on Julia. "You really wanna go there?"

"Is it true?"

His palm itched to slap the disgust off her face.

The Assembly waited.

Flynn shook his head, gripping that blanket of calm. Next they'd want her fucking bra size. "Fine. As distasteful as it is to have to address my intended's halos publicly, it appears I don't have a choice. They're outlined in the same dark brown as her irises. The Source deemed it a breeding flaw, but if you're aware of a talent that presents like that, I'd love to know. I'm sure the Source would, too."

There was a flurry at the impropriety of his disclosure, the room bursting into excited whispers. He knew for a fact half of them would still spread the rumor as gospel. Patrician assholes. Flynn went to sit and another Fixer stood.

"Twist or not, I don't see the point in adding House Jester to the rolls if she's abdicating in a few days. Legally, she won't be able to speak for them. It's an empty vote."

The speaker turned to Flynn and he straightened back up.

"The claim has been entered to be held in trust for our second child." A murmur ran through chambers. "As the last member of her House, our contract stipulates that they become House Jester's heir, ensuring its continuance—"

"Then this should wait until a suitable child actually exists."

Flynn glared at Julia, biting back the first thing that came to his lips. "Establishing House Jester now allows for funds to be put towards its future stability and creates additional income for our current efforts, essentially doubling the amount I'm paying into Glynfyls' coffers. I'd have thought that would be something you could support."

There were a few chuckles, and she narrowed her eyes. "I don't see how that's the Assembly's issue, waiting—"

"Until when?" Christ, he was tired of dealing with her forked-tongue. "Conception, birth, or majority? Where on that slippery slope do you wanna get off? First the Original House bullshit, and now this. Attacking my intended's talent and putting me in a position where I have to refute it publicly goes beyond the pale! Why are you so desperate to prevent Kara's House from having a vote?"

Julia's face went scarlet at his familiar referral, and there were several murmurs at his breach of protocol. She took a moment to collect herself. The rest of the Assembly was salivating at the drama playing out. "Regardless of the purity of her talent, given the probability that any resulting child will be unsuitable for either role—"

"That's a House Matter. Nothing prevents a dual Talent from becoming heir, only from holding public office—"

"It's still premature to extend a vote to a woman whose House, and therefore breeding capabilities, are unknown, as are your own. The leap of faith you've weaseled from your line to garner you First is unconscionable!"

He laughed, smiling down into his beard. She was really trying to bait him into saying something he'd regret. Fuck her. Too many people already knew about Kara's pregnancy. He'd be damned if she forced him into announcing it. Julia opened her mouth, and he steamrolled over whatever she was about to spew.

"Her pedigree is tattooed on her wrist. You all know Source Talents unable to breed are culled. So what you're essentially calling into question is my virility. You of all people can attest to that, and can assure you all of my diligence."

Julia's face contorted. Several people gasped and others snickered, one woman laughing out loud. He retook his seat, done with their shit.

Riggs looked around the room. "Any further discussion? Well, then, let's have a vote." It eked by. Flynn grit his teeth, keeping a firm hold on zero. Imagining Kara beating the shit out of Julia helped. Fuck every last one of the bigoted pricks.

"Very good, House Jester will be added to the rolls, effective immediately." The gavel dropped. "Now, that's quite enough for today, I'll see you all tomorrow."

Assembly dismissed, people milled about, their discussions animated. Fingers picked something off Flynn's shoulder. He turned to find Klaus holding a long dark hair up to the light. He smirked and let it fall.

"You always did have a thing for brunettes. Personally, I like redheads, but you knew that. The blonds were our even split," he said, looking at the whore in the balcony. Christ, her dress was cut so low you could almost see her navel. She waved, and Flynn scowled.

"If I were you, I'd just fuck her and satisfy her curiosity. Once was usually enough. At least, that's how it used to work." Klaus grinned at his expression.

"What d'you want?"

"Just checking in. This little appointment to First isn't going to sully our plans for Friday, is it?"

Flynn scratched his beard, wincing at the bruise. "I said I'd be there. Who'd you get?"

"You didn't hear it from me, but Gerrard's lined up a gentleman by the name of Trammel. I suggest you work on covering that right side, he's got one hell of a hook."

Flynn grunted, pushing past him and out of chambers. Goddamn it, how the fuck was he gonna—

A slender woman blocked his path, and he bit back a groan. Jesus Christ, he couldn't catch a fucking break.

"Laughlin," Natalia purred, extending her hand to him.

He returned a curt bow over it. Motherfucker. He also couldn't afford to insult her, as much as he'd like to. Her father was head of one of the more powerful Breaker Houses and already hated him.

The details of their dalliance were fuzzy, but the aftermath wasn't. Cal had paid the man an obscene sum not to kill him, and Flynn had become a regular at the Pony. Natalia was out of her fucking mind if she thought he'd want to get involved with her again.

"What can I do for you?" He tried not to let his irritation show.

Apparently he was too successful.

She wet her lips, playing with one of those frilly little fans. Damn, she wore shitty perfume. "I thought I spelled that out quite clearly in my notes."

"Whatever you, or anyone else sent, has been burned unopened, and will continue to be."

Natalia stepped closer, mouing. "Don't tease, I'm sorry for how things fell out between us. It's your last night as a free man. I'll do that thing you like—"

Goddamn, her perfume was awful. He coughed, gagging on it and took a step back. "I've no desire to stray from my intended."

She tapped the fan against her lips. "Really? Have you said those three little words?"

Flynn colored.

"Mmm, I thought as much." She smirked. "Forgive me if I don't believe it. Once her novelty wears off, I'll be happy to remind you of what a real woman can do."

Flynn laughed. A real woman. Bitch had no idea. "I'll let her know that. The two of you can work it out. Excuse me, I'm late for a meeting." He was still laughing when he stepped through the gate and into Meddleton's foyer.

KARA STORMED down the hall to get ready for Shelby to humiliate her in the ballroom. Ugh! She was so done with all of, of this! Audrey's stupid etiquette review had been more like a primer on how to imitate cardboard. *"You can be whoever you want Kara…but be vague. Nothing about the Source, or your duality… It will be a formal event, perhaps an outfit a bit more reserved? The House matriarchs will be there, you don't want to offend their sensibilities—"*

Yes. Yes, she did. All of them could go take a—

The lift doors opened, and Flynn stepped out in a roiling cloud of some bitch's perfume with a grin on his face.

That blackness in her surged up, and his head snapped around, inhaling, eyes wide.

Her fists were in his lapels.

She jacked him up against the wall, some stupid vase toppling from its pedestal and shattering. A rumble was in his chest and his 'lust licked out, answering hers.

"Who is she?!"

"What? I don't—"

"Bullshit! I smell her all over you!" Another burst of blackness rose up, her grip on him tightening, control slipping away…

He laughed.

She decked him. He went sprawling, taking down a bookcase as he fell. That rumble in his chest became a growl in his throat. His 'lust twined with hers, straining against it, stoking her fury… Oh, the blackness of it…

"Kara, calm down, it's not like that—goddamn it!"

His hands were on her shoulders, and she pivoted, driving her fist into his gut. He grunted, slamming her against their bedroom door. The latch gave, and they fell through.

She hit the floor with him on top of her. Her leg bent to knee him, and he twisted his hips.

"Then what the fuck is it like!"

"Natalia came on to me after Assembly, I didn't fucking touch her!"

"Natalia?" Kara flipped him onto his back with a burst of rage, pinning his arms above his head. She glared at him, nose-to-nose. "Who the fuck is Natalia?!"

"Nobody, I—Christ, Kara, she's an old fucking mistake that's too stupid to know it's done! I swear to fucking God, I—" His jaw tensed, his emotions cutting through the blackness of her rage. She pulled up short, feeling the truth of them—

What was she doing?

Flynn's arms slipped from her grip to wrap around her. He tucked a lock of hair behind her ear, voice ragged. "There's only you, Kara. It'll only ever be you."

She closed her eyes, the last of the darkness retreating from his light. What was wrong with her? She'd wanted to kill him…like, literally. Her breath tripped over a sob, and he pulled her into his lap, stroking her hair.

"Shh, it's okay. We're okay."

"Ugh, I'm so sorry, Flynn—I…I'm having trouble controlling my 'lust." She sniffed. His poor eye was swelling shut. "I didn't mean… I'm stuck in this house, Audrey's constantly preaching about how I should behave, then you come back with that damned grin, smelling like some whore—"

"I was imagining you beating the shit out of her." He kissed the top of her head. "She stopped me in the hall as I was leaving… I-I've been getting notes from her and some of the others since I've been back. French burns them, unopened. She wanted to know why I haven't answered."

A bolt of rage went through her. "So the whole time I've been being preached to on how not to give offense, you've been getting notes from those same women who think I'm a whore, trying to sleep with you." Ugh, her head hurt, and she felt sick. The hypocrisy of it… "What did you say?"

"That I never read them and wasn't interested. She didn't believe me, and I told her to take it up with you."

Kara laughed. "You did?"

"Yeah." He smiled. "Trust me, I'd love to see you kick her ass. So would Cal. Whatever she told her father happened between us cost him a couple mil."

"Bea said women took advantage of being with you—"

He snorted. "I wasn't exactly innocent, Kara, but it didn't help that

I was too lit to remember most of it. If they said something happened, I just assumed it did. So did everyone else."

"Maybe it wasn't true."

"It was true enough."

"I'm sorry."

"Not your fault."

She traced the side of his face. "This is."

"I'll let you make it up to me."

"Make it up to you? You were keeping things from me again!"

"You're right, I should know better." He looked at her deadpan, then wet his lips, that Cheshire Cat grin blooming over his face. "What're you gonna do about it?"

Ugh, he was such a jerk! She bit back a smile. "What do you want me to do?"

"You should beat the shit out of me again."

She laughed, her fingers at his buttons, his chest, pushing his shirt from his shoulders. She traced the clawed lines patterning them, a wave of heat going through her.

His shirt was on the floor. She raised her arms and he lifted hers over her head, lips grazing across her skin, the twin crescents at her throat. Her head tipped back, his hand at her breast, teasing through the fabric of her bra. She tangled her fingers in his hair…

"Then take your pants off and get on your knees."

He smiled against her skin, beard sweeping at the line of wet kisses to her ear. Their bond thrummed with his eagerness. "Yes, ma'am."

She slid out of her sweats, eyes running over him as he knelt before her. Her Adonis. Glory, he was a beautiful man. "You're mine, Laughlin Scot." She toed his knees farther apart and slid her foot up the inside of his thigh, brushing against his rigid cock. "Say it."

"I'm yours." He groaned, her leg in his hands, leaning into her. His mouth hot, fingers questing… Kara made herself step back, tipping up his chin, voice husky.

"Shh…don't touch."

She curled her fingers through his messy waves, her other hand sliding across his shoulders, her body moving down his to rest her shins upon his thighs. Those blue motes churned through his irises, his breath coming fast. She kissed along his jaw, softly. Slowly. Reaching down to cup and stroke, thumb swirling the dew of his anticipation… She brought it to her lips, salt and the musky darkness of his arousal.

His pupils dilated, desire thickening the air. The way he smelled… She pushed her own down, not done. That blackness from before…she wanted to feel him hurt first. Her mouth was on his skin, traveling lower. Pec, to ribs, to abs. The crease of his thigh. He rocked towards her, his head back, Adam's apple bobbing. Expectant. She sat back on her heels and pulled the belt from his pants, snapping it between her hands.

His breath caught, and he bit at his lip. Eagerness tinged with trepidation. The taste of it stoked her 'lust, and it redoubled. Their bond churned with blackness. She trailed the leather over his shoulder, moving behind him. He shivered, a light sheen of sweat skin prickling his skin.

"Is this what you want?"

"Yeah." She could hear the excitement in his voice. *Jerk.*

"Tell me how many."

"Eight." His voice was ragged with need, and her own breath sped, the air heavy with 'lust, her skin aflame, she bent, lips brushing the shell of his ear.

"Stroke your cock, and count."

He let out a strangled groan.

She flicked the tail of the belt at him, and he cried out. The echo of his pleasure inciting hers. She shivered, the tips of her breasts tightening, flicking it again, white blazes turning red, his desire her own, building, burning…

"Four…" he grunted out, his balance wavering beneath the assault.

The stripes across his broad back bloomed and wept, crimson smears spattering as she lashed him, crisscrossing his flesh. Her core throbbed, echoing the building fire from the rough passage of his palm across his rigid cock, its crown an angry red, slick with need. Their bond thrummed with her hunger for his pain and his need for punishment.

"Seven…" his voice hitched, the crack of the last blow twining with his bellow. Sweat dripped down his brow, breath coming fast.

Kara dropped down before him, pulling his hand from his cock, kissing up his thigh—

"Please, Kara…oh, God, please…"

His hands were buried in her hair, back arching as she took him in her mouth. A deluge of carnality swept them up and there was nothing but their echo.

Her, feeling him, feeling her.

Sensation blurred, time slipping. She was above him, her forehead to his, lips insistent when they met through sharp intakes of breath, the light of her halos gilding him in gold. Talent plucking at them… wanting… She bit his lip, overcome. His chest rumbled, tongue licking his blood from her mouth.

"Goddamn, I fucking love you."

She laughed, her cheeks wet. "Say it again."

"I love you, Kara Scot. Only you, always you…"

He flipped her onto her back, the sweeping echo of his passion cresting, casting her upon breakers of verdigris and electric blue as he thrust. She cried out, her body feeding off his, taking everything he gave. Sublimating his soul and offering hers in turn. Talent filled her like a vessel, the damage to his face receding, a god reborn as they shared a moment in eternity.

"I love you too, Flynn," she whispered, all of that blackness gone. "Was that so hard?"

He sighed. "It was too easy."

"I'm still here."

"Shh. Don't jinx it." He kissed her, and she smiled, tracing his lip.

"That bite left a scar."

"Yeah?" He fingered his lip.

"What do you think that is?"

"The talent? I dunno and don't care. You're better since it's been happening."

He caught her back up in his arms, and she reveled in the hum between them, wanting to just stay there, with him… "Ugh, Shelby's going to be mad I'm so late."

Flynn shrugged, nuzzling at her. "I'll tell her it's my fault. I needed that, you. It grounds me. All this shit with the Assembly…feeling your marks remind me why I'm doing all of this."

"They help me, too," she said, winding her arms around his neck and kissing him.

"You keep this up, and you're going to really be late." Flynn rumbled, his hands sliding down to cup her rear. He gave it a little slap and sat up, mussing his hair. "I've gotta see people, too."

She ran her hand over the ripple of welts across his back, remembering the lash marks that'd scarred it. Had he loved that woman, too? The darkness in Kara stirred. "Who?"

"Binders. Julia started the rumor you're a twist. I had to refute it on the fucking Assembly floor."

Kara paled as he dressed. "What did you say?"

"That the Source deemed it a breeding flaw, but I need to do damage control." She pulled on her sweats and bit at her thumb. He took it from her lips. "Hey, it'll be fine. Nobody's ever heard of a talent that presents brown. I'll get it sorted and then I gotta to check in with somebody who might be able to keep an eye on Crandall for me."

He didn't look thrilled about the prospect, his emotions a mess. She took his hand, both reluctant as they left the bedroom.

Shelby was pissed. She rolled her eyes as soon as she saw Flynn.

"It's my fault, we had to work some stuff out."

Him grinning wasn't selling it.

"Whatever, you owe me a dance. Get into position, it'll be easier for her if she's used to your frame."

Kara cringed, but Flynn just grinned wider, taking hold of her waist. Music started playing through the room's speakers. It went smoother than yesterday, but that wasn't saying much. Kara grimaced. Ugh, she was going to make a fool of herself… She stumbled, losing the rhythm.

He laughed, spinning her around and setting her back onto her feet. The music ended, and he kissed her. "I gotta go, I'll be back for dinner."

"I want her on time tomorrow, Laughlin." He waved over his shoulder and was gone. Shelby turned to her. "I know it doesn't feel like it, but you're really progressing nicely. You have amazing muscle memory. If you'd stop thinking about what you're doing, I bet the steps would come naturally."

Kara sighed, trying to concentrate on the music and letting everything go. After the whole flute debacle she wasn't a big fan of classical...but after being with Flynn, it was surprisingly easy to float... The room fuzzed, and it was just her and the notes, moving...

She stopped, throwing Shelby off balance.

It was almost the same thing Rogan was trying to get her to do.

Shelby gave her a funny look and restarted the piece.

Kara laughed. Zero state. She'd almost had it.

She let the music fill her, and everything fell away. She could feel Flynn's irritation about something, but didn't let it touch her, floating on the music, just letting her body do what she'd been practicing.

The piece ended, and Shelby stared at her like she'd grown another head. "That was... unexpected. I don't think you're going to have any issues with the waltz... What just happened?"

"The music, I don't know. Something just clicked."

Shelby's brow furrowed. "Once more, then let's try a variation."

Kara grinned, eager to learn everything Shelby could teach her.

CHAPTER TWENTY-TWO

"More than a cost-savings measure, the mandatory practice of culling Talents at age sixty is a humane alternative to caring for an aging population no longer able to serve in the capacity of their prime. In particular, aging out for Breakers is a traumatic event. Left to their own devices, when cast from their rung and out of the hierarchy, most succumb. Preemptive euthanasia prevents collateral damage, and with the ability to document every aspect of their lives, the up-and-coming generations of Talents need not be subjected to the fallacy of their wisdom. One only need to access the applicable holo to benefit from past experience without the taint of rogue ideologies…"

– L. Merkel, Head Geneticist,
The Source

"THEY'RE PLAYING WITH US."

Marcos crouched beside Nora, his sidearm drawn, breath clouding in the dim flicker of the plaz lantern. Nothing moved at the other end of the tunnel, but it was only a matter of time before the squad advanced. Seven minutes, to be exact. After that mess in Tombago, Marcos had been the one to update the protocol for gaining intel by routing guerrilla combatants, and Beta squad was following it to the letter. The sloppy advance allowing them to escape had been textbook. Collins's crack about how Nora's ass looked in jeans hadn't been.

The Breaker parroting Marcos's words spoken hours earlier had been a warning.

Most of the Source's tech he had intimate knowledge of, stemming from all the damned in-field repairs it required, but this… Whatever Titus had infected them with wasn't anything like Marcos had seen before. He cursed himself for playing into the man's hand. Courting Nora, the breaking… He'd been a Trojan horse to get inside Albanach's tower.

And expendable.

Marcos grimaced, holstering his piece. It hurt more than it should. He'd had four years left, damn it, and it didn't make sense, not with the incursion looming. He scrubbed over the grit covering his face, too tired to make sense of it. It'd been too long since they'd slept…ate. Nora wouldn't be able to sustain much more of this.

"I'm assuming the tech's come back."

"I've tried, but they replicate too quickly to clear with my talent." She sagged against the tunnel wall, twisting her ring, jeans and parka filthy. "It reminds me of that gift the Hilkari envoy sent Albanach."

Marcos scowled. How that swarm of kill-bots had ever gotten past security still bothered him. Now was a hell of a time to be thinking about—

Wait. Would it work internally?

Her eyes were resolute. They both knew if it didn't, there was no moving forward.

"I remember."

At his nod, they opened their channels, flooding the bond between them with talent.

The tech sprang into view, a nebulous roiling cloud. She bound one of the tiny invaders for him to inspect. Some kind of nano-biotech. The net of force they'd created to deal with the kill-bots wouldn't be enough, but maybe…

"Condense the weave."

She shrank it into a finer mesh, and he charged it with the equivalent of an EMP. The precision in which he could wield his talent had always set him apart from other Breakers, but he'd never attempted anything like this… If he screwed up…

The captured bot fizzled into ions.

It would work, or fry them. Maybe both. His physiology was altered enough to withstand the pulse, but Nora's…

His eyes met hers again. At the other end of the tunnel the squad was advancing.

"I trust you, Marcos."

She pulsed the weave over them, his talent lighting it up in a burst of crimson and gold. A wave of nausea hit, and he steadied himself against the wall. Nora fell to the ground, seizing.

He grabbed her and the lantern, already running, and threw a blast of talent over his shoulder at the tunnel's ceiling. It collapsed, thick clouds of grit and debris shooting past them, obscuring everything but the bubble of brown they ran in. Nora gagged, pressing her face against his chest.

"Where am I going?!"

"Straight, second left, then the first right. There's a hatch…" She coughed, pulling talent with a little cry. Nothing happened. Damn it. "We need to make the truck stop ten miles due east. A Fetch should be waiting. Put me down!"

"The hell I am. That burst did a number on you, and this is what I'm built for. I'll get us there, then you get us north." He hiked her up higher, her arms tightening around his neck. "Did we miss any of them?"

"I don't think so, but without understanding how we were infected in the first place—"

"It was the girl. Titus was far too smug about that damned breaking, I assumed it was because she was one of Beritram's, but I'd guarantee they're sexually transmitted." His lips twitched feeling Nora's displeasure.

"We haven't been intimate yet."

"Oh, I don't know. That was one hell of a kiss." He felt her smile and held her closer. A break in the tunnel was coming up. Marcos put on another burst of speed. The sooner they got north, the better.

FLYNN SAT in a dimly lit room, watching the fire burn low in the hearth. The desk covered with coded missives was at odds with the scattered toys casting long shadows across the floor. Devoid of bookcases, framed pictures done in a child's hand hung upon the walls.

What the hell was he doing?

That prick Rogan was right about Kara, and if he was right about splitting… Flynn fidgeted in the chair, shirt scraping the welts across his back. Fuck. He could feel it—had felt it.

He was on borrowed time.

Unless he could take Overlord. If it worked the way the histories said, he'd be imbued with all six talents, and no one would know.

Christ, he'd know.

And Cal had always known. There wasn't a doubt in Flynn's mind that's why the asshole was pushing for this. A Shade's Shade. If that wasn't the fucking truth. Bastard had to be coming in his pants at the idea of skating this past everybody.

Flynn gritted his teeth. Goddamn, he hated being maneuvered by the old man. He stared at the far wall's jumble of pictures. Vague representations of animals and flowers, stick figures and hearts. Uneven words scrawled in crayon.

I lov u dady.

He bit at the scar crescenting his lip, wanting the same. A family. A real one, not some broken-ass dysfunctional shit show like he'd grown up in. Christ, he'd dance to whatever tune Cal was piping to get it…to be able to say he loved them… like he'd said to Kara. His guts churned, praying that hadn't been a mistake.

Please, God, don't take her away—

The door on the far side of the room opened, and a blond man came in. He stopped short, running a hand over his smirk. "I was wondering when you'd show up."

Flynn glowered at him. Christ, he didn't wanna be here. "Trust me, it's not a social visit, but things being what they are—"

Dorian barked out that braying laugh of his. Jackass. "Yes. There is that, now isn't there?" He closed the door and crossed the thick carpet with a pronounced limp. "I'm assuming you haven't come to reminisce."

"And I'm assuming you haven't disclosed."

Dorian moved a doll from a wing-backed chair and sat. "I gave my word I wouldn't, though if I'd known what that silence would be worth at the present moment, I never would've agreed. I'll tell you flat out, Crandall knows he never got the full story of what happened in Diytan."

Flynn glared at him. "He's not gonna."

Dorian's lips curved into a calculating smile, playing with the toy. "Your resurrection has already put him on the scent. Coming here is tweaking his nose. You must want something desperately." Jackass was just fucking tickled at the prospect.

"Yeah. I wanna know what that weaselly shit is up to."

Dorian laughed. "Short of world domination, I couldn't tell you. Our Houses aren't particularly close."

"Is the rest of your line?"

Dorian's lips pursed, gloved fingers smoothing the doll's dress as he set it aside. "House Crandall holds us all with an iron fist. Whatever they have on you pales in comparison to the generations of deviance and misdeeds that've been collected on the rest of us. The current Lord Crandall has a devilish flair for using it to game the system in his favor. You've been lucky. Julia's regurgitation of your past and that bit today was rather ham-handed. He would have used it much more effectively."

Flynn grunted. "You don't have any ins with the Intelligencers?"

"I didn't say that..." He tapped on the arm of his chair. "But if he's got you over a barrel, I don't know that I want to disturb him while he's having his fun."

"You're full of shit."

The jackass brayed. "I might be persuaded for the right coin... You've gained a great deal of influence in a remarkably short amount of time. I'll hazard a guess that Crandall is responsible for some of that. No one has prospered of late, and Mistress Cree's preoccupation with you is to his benefit. My eye is on what comes next."

Shit, Flynn didn't like the sound of that. "Next?"

"After seeing what you're capable of, I have no doubt that you'll take Overlord. Once you do, I want a place at the table."

"Mind if I smoke?"

"I do."

Flynn lit a cigar. "A place at the table. What exactly are you gunning for?"

"As you may have noticed, I'm not the man I was, to use your popular phrase. You were right in thinking I'd pissed someone off. Our line's politics…" He shrugged.

"House War?"

"Nothing so neat. I'll spare you the details, but the same accident that gave me this damned leg…" He took off a glove and held up an extensively scarred hand. "Car bomb. I'd just collected my daughter from lessons. She fared far worse than I." He'd picked the doll back up, his lips a white line.

Christ, maybe Kara—no. Dangling that carrot was a dick move. "I'm sorry, but I don't see how—"

"You don't do you?" Dorian rapped his knuckles on the arm of the chair. "A large part of a Finder's talent relies on probability. Julia, Crandall, anyone I've ever come across has a set methodology. All of that," he waved at his desk, "intel to predict who will move what where next, and plans to counter or aide. You and that lady of yours don't fit a pattern of intent. What you want is very rarely what you do, except when it is, and in that case, my God, Scot, you destroyed—"

"Careful."

Dorian sat back. "I want a part of it. Your squad was the only one that didn't lose a man in that crater. Whatever spell you cast to do that and then walk away… I want the same for my House. For that, and only that, I'll gladly stick my nose up Crandall's skirts."

Flynn just looked at him. How the fuck was he supposed to— "Dorian, I can't promise—"

"Of course not." He went to riffle through the papers on his desk. "Nor can I. Either one of us could be dead tomorrow, although I sincerely doubt that in your case… Ah, there it is." He held a blade out to him, hilt first. "Short of sealing our pact with gillyblack, I'd pledge you my troth. I've a copy of the standard form somewhere around here, but suggest you wait to file it... along with several others I have reason to believe will back your bid given the same assurances."

Flynn exhaled a long line of smoke, watching it swirl around the little doll.

"Yeah. I can do that."

———

IELLE STROLLED DOWN the street arm-in-arm with Sylvie, enjoying the scandalized looks and low whistles. They were a striking pair, and she'd always filled out a corset better than most. The fact wasn't lost upon the whore. The courtesan looked like she was rethinking taking her out. Ielle snuggled closer and blew a kiss at some lout's perverse suggestion, tempted to show him how it was done.

Whether by accident or design, Titus hadn't sent her up with any meds, and she was dying for a man. The Breakers she'd serviced when she'd first arrived had been a treat, but she'd been warned to stay away after. Not that she'd be able to find them again in that nasty warren of tunnels. Hopefully, this little soiree would be just what she needed. There was no way she was spending all her time roaming around that decrepit manor of Julia's. Half of it wasn't even heated and there were old vermin nests in the mattress of the room she'd been given.

Sylvie turned into one of the listing buildings, the malaise of cheap alcohol, sweaty men, and sex slapping Ielle in the face.

Her smile became radiant.

"The Pony gets a cut if you plan on working the room," Sylvie yelled into her ear before disappearing through the crowd. The place was packed with people of questionable character and the undercurrent of violence was palpable.

Ielle drank it all in. If she'd been wearing any, her panties would've been soaked. A man sitting by the door collecting money watched her out of the corner of his eye with unveiled hunger. She sauntered over and fingered his collar.

"What's a girl got to do to get a job around here?"

"The boss. Ye can come see me after, love."

"You'd better introduce me then."

He put his fingers in his mouth and sent a piercing whistle through the clamor. A dark-skinned woman in a diaphanous blue nightie approached, looking Ielle over with the same eye as the man at the door.

"Ye here for work?"

"No, I'm here for fun."

The whore laughed. "Won't get much of that, but yer timing's good. Gerrard's looking t'add some girls for the fight. Flynn always could draw a crowd."

"Did you know him?"

"More than once." She smirked, leading Ielle through the haphazardly placed card tables and groups of men. Scantily clad women lounged on every surface and gyrated against poles. It was nothing like the white viewing stalls at the Olly. Her pulse quickened at the garishness of it all.

"Is he everything they say?"

The whore laughed. "And then some. Ye'll have t'get in line t'find out, but don't worry, he takes us in pairs. If he picks ye for one of 'em, make sure you put up a fight. He likes it when ye act like ye don't."

Hmm. Domination fantasy. Those were always fun. "He's into rape-play?"

"Nah, just Breaker slap and tickle. All them is like that, but Flynn always made us ask 'fore he did aught, getting permission-like, which is more than I can say for the rest of 'em." She brought Ielle into another building and pushed through the screaming crowd. Men inside a large cage were beating each other bloody. Ielle licked her lips, thighs slick with desire. The whore's fingers grabbed her wrist, pulling her along.

A curtained doorway in the back led into a dimly lit room. Women were draped over low couches and pillows, smoking sear from a long silver pipe, men scattered between them. One was snoring in the corner, shirt open and belt undone, a whore going through his pockets. The dark woman knocked on a door. A gruff voice answered, and she pushed it open, speaking to someone within. She gestured, stepping aside, and Ielle entered, the door snicking shut behind her.

The rugs and furniture were of much better quality than the rest of the place merited. The portly man behind the desk fit right in. He motioned for her to take a chair, then steepled his fingers in front of his lips as she sauntered towards him.

"Crystal says you're looking for work, so this is how it is. I don't care what walks through that door. You take him upstairs, do what he wants, how he wants, and make sure he leaves smiling. I get half the take."

"Anything he wants?"

Gerrard looked her up and down again. "Yeah, and them hillies are gonna ask for some depraved shit. That gonna be a problem?"

"Oh no," she laughed. "Depravity is my specialty."

He leaned back and rubbed a hand across his jaw. "Yeah? Show me."

CHAPTER TWENTY-THREE

House Matter [hous madər] *noun*

1. *A sensitive subject relating to the inter-workings of an Original House not open to discussion or criticism.*

– Excerpt from Glynfyls: A History

"Fixers and Fetches, able to freeze and translocate matter respectively, have a more understated rivalry. Known for their fastidious and steadfast natures, Fixers view their duality as little more than modern day pirates, holding their 'shifty' ethics in disdain. Fetches, in turn perceive their Fixers with a kind of pity for having to endure such intensely boring existences..."

– Lord Talos, Preceptor of History,
Academy of Glynfyls

THE ALARM WENT OFF and Kara grinned, springing up to get dressed.

Flynn groaned, pulling a pillow over his head. "Why are you up so early? Christ, Rogan's not even down there yet. Come back to bed."

"I asked him to come earlier so I can practice more with Shelby."

He peeked out. "Since when are you excited about that?"

"Since I found zero."

"Wait, that's what that was yesterday?" He rolled onto his side, propping himself on an elbow.

"Yep. Something about the music…" Kara shrugged, going over to him. Glory, she loved it when he looked all soft and muzzy. She ran her fingers through his hair, and he pulled her down, nuzzling at her.

"Change your mind?"

"Mmm, I'd crawl right back in there if you didn't look so good on the dance floor." She took his hand in hers, frowning. The bandage was gross again. "Everything go well last night?"

"I had to invite the Binders to the Introduction, but yeah, I guess. Eight Finders pledged on the condition Crandall doesn't find out. Apparently I'm not the only one who thinks he's a dick. Where are you—"

She brought the triage kit back from the bathroom. He winced as she cleaned out the crusty mess. "Those medical records from the packet Julia spread around…" Ugh, the cut was disgusting. On anyone else it would be an infected mess. "You should be dead. Twice. They don't make sense, Flynn. Even if a Peacekeeper had sustained those injuries, they wouldn't be able to regenerate tissue. When I healed your knee, it was just a ligament tear. The scans show the joint crushed."

He chewed his lip, watching her re-bandage his palm. "I dunno what to say. I've always healed quick."

Kara snorted. "There's quick and there's impossible. You'd be the latter, unless it's talent related… Who was the Breaker?"

"It's not something—" He squirmed and gave a sigh. "Cal's wife, I think. She died when I was really young. Pretty much all I remember about her are these stories she used to tell about Valkyries, and him pitching a fit because she wouldn't let a Binder touch her."

"Sounds familiar. Valkyries, like handmaidens of Odin?"

"No, they used to be these elite female Breakers way back when that would kick ass so the Breaker Alpha didn't have to or something. And I let you touch me plenty. In fact, I think you should do it more."

"Maybe if you stuck around I would… That must've been something to see. Female Breakers only fight exhibitions in the Source. They're too valuable to send out on maneuvers…speaking of fights, you want to tell me about this bout at the Pony?"

He gave a strangled laugh, scratching at his jaw. "You heard about that?"

"A bunch of servants were talking. Shelby won't tell me anything."

"Yeah, I bet. Essentially, the Pony's a whore house. I spent a lot of time there." She raised an eyebrow, feeling a whisper of 'lust. He wet his lips, his tongue lingering on the crescent scar and looking her up and down. "Lot cut me off after my mom died. I'd do bouts to pay rent, my tab. When I left Glynfyls, I didn't settle up. I tried to a few days ago and, they sent my money back, want me to fight instead."

"You going to?"

"If I do, the Assembly will censure me…but I gave my word I'd be there." He shrugged. "I haven't figured it out yet."

"I want to go."

He grinned. "I was hoping you would. It'll give you a chance to practice zero." Her eyes narrowed, and he colored. "I guess a lot of the girls I, uh, knew, are still there. You gotta promise not to damage any of them, okay?"

"I'm a medic, Laughlin. I'll bring my kit," she said sweetly, downing one of those jellies. She hadn't thought it possible, but this new batch was even more disgusting than the first. "See you tonight!" Grinning at his expression, she jogged from the room.

Rogan was in the gym, spinning his staff in a complicated kata.

"I want to spar." His lips pursed at the request, and she laughed, surprising him. "Please?"

He jerked his head at another staff against the wall. "First whisper of 'lust, you're done."

She grabbed it, squaring up with the waltz running through her mind. Shelby had taken her through it so many times, she could hear the music as if it were playing in the room. Rogan advanced, and she floated, her responses faster, lines cleaner.

A smile spread over his face. He pressed her harder and harder until neither one of them was holding back, their forms a blur—

He was on the mat, the butt of her staff against his throat. She stepped away, panting…but not because of the 'lust. She'd never moved so fast—that had been amazing!

Rogan got up, grinning ear to ear, and hugged her. "It's about goddamned time! Good on you! What changed?"

She matched his smile with her own. "I learned how to dance."

"Yeah? Show me what you got." He retrieved his staff and held it up.

Grinning, she attacked.

FLYNN SAT IN HIS BOX, resisting the urge to close his eyes. The late night with the Finders had kicked his ass. Stonefist droning on with his troop readiness report wasn't helping. He was supposed to be some kind of military genius, but Christ, he was fucking boring…

Lot kicked his chair, and Flynn's eyes flew open.

Shit. He changed position, trying to focus.

"…brick and mortar is compromised in several sections. Until that's addressed, the functionality of the shield is moot."

"Ah, Lord Klein, I believe you've completed the wall survey?" Riggs asked.

A dark-haired man stood, flipping through a notebook. "There are approximately fourteen breaches. Three of them I'd consider major, six moderate, and four minor." He stopped to consult his notes again.

"That's only thirteen, Carl!"

He shot a nasty look over his shoulder. "I know that, Peter. The last one you can drive a damn tank through, I was saving it for later." He turned to face the Assembly again, clearing his throat. "With your approval, most can be repaired by the end of the week. The largest requires more material than we have on hand, granite in particular. The Engineering Guild has stressed that the wall's composition remains consistent, which necessitates using the quarries north of Loshwaitz. For those of you unfamiliar, that's where the Source fired on our troops last week. Extracting what's required will be problematic, to say the least." There was a hum of concern.

Flynn stood. "That's the seventh rung, right? What's up against the wall?"

"It is..." Klein riffled through his notebook. "Derelict buildings, shops, a few factories...and a newer housing development in the north."

Flynn sucked in air between his teeth. This was gonna go over like a fart in church. "Everything within a couple hundred feet of the wall needs to be razed. That should give you plenty to work with."

The room went silent, then erupted into chaos.

"How can you defend a wall you can't see?" Flynn's rumble cut through the din. "Everything down there's a mess, Fetches can't shift material into a breach they don't know exists, and there aren't enough Binders to ward the walls from breaking...and just so we're clear, that's inside of the wall as well as outside."

"That equates to an entire rung!"

Flynn shrugged, inciting another moment of collective panic. He ran a hand across his face, sitting. He was too tired for this shit.

"You're going to run into issues." A matronly woman he didn't recognize had stood. "Since rumors of another incursion began, people have been leaving the Flats and squatting in those buildings. We need to have a plan for the populace before wantonly destroying housing or they'll riot. The mood is tense as it is."

Lord Klein cleared his throat. "In either case, I'll survey for potential for material. If a Fetch would be so kind as to accompany me, I can have that by this afternoon."

Wait, what? Flynn did a double take. A Fixer asking for a Fetch's help? Even odder, Markham readily promised his assistance. Well, that fucking stank of Crandall...

"This is ridiculous! Resurrecting the shield wall... Next someone will suggest maintaining House armies. How can we be so sure anything's coming? We've been rushing to implement these measures like the Source is marching as we speak—"

"Are you deaf as well as stupid, Ines?" Stonefist snapped. "Without that wall, we won't be able to fend off an attack. Those people squatting? Evict them. If it's not repaired by the time troops get here, you won't have a couple hundred displaced people, we'll all be in nullified chains heading south. Pull your head out of your ass, man! Scot's got the right of it!" The Breaker ignored the room gasping at his coarse vernacular and gave Flynn an approving nod.

Markham stood. As hard as it was to believe, the big man seemed to be sweating even more than usual. "Ah…I may have a solution. I think Lady Henshaw would agree, plenty would leave if given the opportunity. With the railway down, they have none. If the moratorium on shifting was lifted, the Fetches can facilitate."

"I thought Stonefist said we were trapped here like rats!" a Fixer called out.

"Ah, yes, well, in regard to those nullified curtains…" Markham mopped his chins. "There are certain, ah, avenues still available to transport goods and people."

Holy shit! Flynn swallowed a laugh. Markham was all but admitting to smuggling on the Assembly floor. A murmur went through the room.

"Yes, you all heard me correctly." The fat man snapped, pulling himself up straighter. "As First Fetch, I'm disclosing our capabilities for the good of Glynfyls, even those others may consider unsavory. Regardless of any potential backlash, we've been utilizing our talent to stockpile supplies, food chief among them. There is absolutely no reason for panic—"

"And just where are all of those supplies being stored?" Julia interrupted.

Markham looked at her a long moment, sweat dripping down his face. His eyes flicked over Crandall and swung to Flynn.

Shit. His throat bobbed, feeling the set up. This wasn't gonna end well.

The fat man blotted his forehead. "I'm afraid I'm unable to disclose that, Madame Cree. As a matter of public safety, supplies will be shifted to a centralized location for distribution when the time comes. Until then, you'll just have to take me at my word."

Julia sprang to her feet, incensed. "That's preposterous! You've been handing us tally sheets for the past week showing hundreds of thousands of units being funneled through what you've just all but admitted are smugglers! Now you're saying you can't show us anything tangible? How are we to know our funds are being well spent? There's zero accountability!"

Markham licked his lips, glancing at Flynn again. He grit his teeth, resisting the urge to glare at Crandall. What the fuck were they trying to pin on him?

"It's not that he can't show us, Madame Cree. It's that he can't show you." Lord Klein stood, straightening his lapels. "I'm calling for a vote of no confidence."

Holy shit! Flynn could smell blood in the water. The room held its breath as Riggs banged his gavel to call the vote. With the exception of Ines and one other lord, every House voted against her. Flynn laughed, and her eyes snapped to him, murderous. Fucking Crandall. The little man smoothed his mustache, pleased as fucking punch Flynn was gonna take the heat for this.

Another Fixer stood. "House Clay puts forth a motion to nominate Lord Klein as First."

"Do we have a second?" Riggs asked, obviously expecting one.

"House Gates seconds the nomination."

"We have our motion. Do we have concordance within the rest of the line?"

They all stood, less the two. Julia's face was purple.

The speaker's gavel fell. "Enter it into the record. On this day, the Fixer line has elected Lord Klein as First. Dissenting vote from Lord Ines and Wu, Lord Cree absent." Riggs shuffled his papers and tapped them on the desk. "Lord Klein, do you have anything to say before we get back to the agenda?"

"Yes." He walked down the steps to the Fixer's box. "First and foremost, madame, I speak for our entire line when I say quite plainly, get out."

He held the gate open for her. Flynn couldn't help but grin at Julia's expression. She grabbed her stack of papers, nose in the air as she climbed several steps to sit beside Ines. Klein stepped into the box and gripped its railing, addressing the room again.

"Secondly, I want to thank Lord Scot."

Huh? Across the floor, Crandall's brow furrowed. Whatever was coming, it wasn't part of his script. Flynn started sweating.

"He's right. Not one of us has had enough backbone to stand for the common good. We've been so busy trying to protect our own little slices, we've lost the bigger picture. His return has been a sorely needed wake-up call, and after much deliberation, with the exceptions of Houses Cree, Ines, and Wu, the rest of us are publicly offering fealty to House Scot." A shocked silence stretched and dissolved into pandemonium.

Flynn rocked back in his chair. *What the fuck?* The only thing keeping him upright was the split second of surprise that'd crossed Crandall's face. Asshole didn't know everything.

Flynn clenched his fist, the slice across his palm aching. With the Fixers, he'd have over a third of the Assembly...and half of the Quorum vote.

Julia had gone limp, Ines' doughy arm around her. Lord Klein remained standing, putting his fist to his heart and bowing to Flynn.

A vassal's salute to the Overlord.

The clamor stilled. Waiting.

Jesus fucking Christ.

Flynn scrubbed a hand over his beard before standing and returning the gesture.

Formally declaring his intent.

This was what he wanted, right?

He sat, feeling about a thousand years older than before he'd stood.

"Anything else?" Riggs chirped cheerfully. "Wonderful, I think that's quite enough for this morning." He banged his gavel and people started to mill about, their excited whispers filling the room with a festival air. Flynn slumped. What the fuck had just happened?

Lot smacked the back of his head. "Feel sorry for yourself later, boy. You're still on the clock."

Asshole. Flynn mussed his hair, slapping a smile on his face, and stood to shake Lord Klein's hand. Behind him, Julia stared daggers at them both.

Klein grinned. "Mad enough to shit nails, isn't she? I couldn't care less, but I would've thought you'd be happier to have twenty-seven Houses pledge in one fell swoop. We needed to make a bold statement of solidarity after her besmirching the honor of our line. I won't take credit for the salute at the end, that and the publicity was Alice's idea."

Fucking seers—"It's a lot of responsibility, Lord Klein. I don't take it lightly."

"Please, it's Carl, and that's why you've got it. I meant what I said. My line, all of us, have been led astray for too long. I wanted to step up when they asked before, but Alice counseled against it. When Crandall recently approached me...I couldn't say no. I'm ashamed I didn't do what was right sooner."

Shit, Flynn knew what that felt like.

"But enough with regrets. I wanted to talk to you about the walls. That group from the Engineering Guild was looking at the old cups. Lady Mayfield mentioned you'd tinkered with them in the past, and wanted to discuss some advance with you, but I'm sure she hasn't gotten around to sending a missive."

Flynn shared a smile with the man, time had no meaning when Jesse was working on a project. "I'll make it a point to get down there, and I know what you mean. There's quite a bit I still need to set right up here."

"Rumor has it some of that's at the Pony?" Carl asked, raising an eyebrow.

"Yeah, unfortunately. Certain parties are refusing to take my money."

"I've seen you fight, Laughlin. I'd imagine they'll make a hell of a lot more getting you in the ring, but you can't mean to go through with it..."

The crowd listening to their conversation pressed closer.

"I gave my word I'd be there, even if that means letting whoever they've lined up pummel me."

The man ran a critical eye over him, unconvinced. "I suppose that would be a loophole...though it's difficult to believe that's how things will play out. I wish I could go, but Alice would skin me alive. Your intended has to be an extremely understanding woman."

"Actually, she's looking forward to coming."

"You're joking!" The crowd around them roiled with gleeful incredulity.

"Not in the least."

The man scrambled to pick his jaw up off the floor. "Well, good luck then—Oh, one last thing, Alice wanted me to extend an invitation to your intended. She's going trap shooting next week in preparation for the upcoming Nationals."

"Trap shooting?"

"Oh yes, she's quite the dead-eye. You should see the trophies she's won. She's quite the competitor. Does your intended shoot?"

"Ah, yeah, she does. I'll pass it along." His brow knit. Why wouldn't Alice just—

Fucking seers.

Carl chuckled. "I won't ask, but I figured she was up to something. I'm looking forward to working with you."

He shook the man's hand again, a grin blooming across his face. "Same. Now if you'll excuse me, I've gotta go see a woman about some pants." Laughing at the expression on Carl's face, Flynn made his way out of chambers.

Lot kept stride with him, scowling. "I hope you know what the hell you're doing. Half the goddamn city was already gonna turn out, now it's gonna be even more of a shit show."

"I need to take care of this, and Kara wants to get out of the house—"

"Laughlin!" Klaus intercepted them at the door. "What's this I hear, you're bringing your intended to the Pony? I must say, it's not the kind of clientele we encourage… Unless you're planning on letting me entertain her while you're otherwise engaged?" He made a rude gesture Flynn ignored.

"Quite the contrary, Klaus. I thought I'd do you a favor and bring her to lend some respectability to your establishment." He grinned. "For old times' sake. Lot was just mentioning half of Glynfyls will be there, I believe I've just guaranteed the other. I hope you're able to accommodate. I'm assuming we can use the back entrance?"

Klaus narrowed his eyes. "You can."

Flynn clapped him on the shoulder, and the gaunt man stumbled. "Wonderful, we'll see you Friday."

Lot gave him a look as they walked to the gate, and Flynn's grin widened, hoping Reggie could do what he wanted in time.

THE HISS AND bite of conversation in the room washed over Julia as the session was dismissed for lunch. The stares and half-whispered vitriol barely cut through the thudding in her ears and rising nausea. She swallowed, her mouth dry, panic speeding her pulse.

Henry.

Lord Klein crossed the floor to the Shade's box. Her eyes bored into the back of his head, wanting to put a bullet through it. She would ruin him. Both of them—

Henry.

Her fingers went to her throat. Oh God, what was she going to do?

A moist hand took her elbow. "Come, Julia. May I escort you to the gate? It's been a trying morning."

She fought the urge to shrug Ines off, unable to afford losing his support. Forcing herself to smile, she inclined her head, eyes still drilling into Klein. How dare they! All her work, her sacrifice—

Ines led her from the room, oblivious to the murderous stares that followed them out.

Julia returned them.

The anger holding her together gave out as she crossed through the gate, and her feet hit the dusty granite slab of her foyer. She crumpled, her wracking sobs becoming violent heaves of watery bile.

No one came.

Her temples throbbed to splitting. Flashes across her mind's eye. Tiny explosions of memory. Where was everyone? Her father, the servants…she'd had dogs. Two of them, little spaniels… Her cheek pressed into the gritty stone, body jerking, all of it a weird disassociated montage, images of her little boy, when she'd held him. And him, he was there with her, that grin of his—

Agony burst inside her skull, and she screamed—

It went black. Warm and velvet. A womb, salt-tinged, a low drubbing in her ears.

No, it was the ocean's surf, a warm sea breeze caressing her skin… The pain had gone, if she'd ever really known it. Had it been real? Golden light enveloped her, and she felt such peace… A comfort she hadn't known since she was a child…

"You did right to bring her here, the damage is substantial." A woman's voice.

"Mother…?"

Dry fingers stroked her temples. "That's right, child. Mother is here."

Julia tried to open her eyes and the glow intensified, streamers of light wrapping and weaving. She was borne away by it, voices just tickling the edges of her consciousness.

"How long?"

"You're ever impatient, Otto. You can bring her back her in a day, perhaps two. I need to rebuild her psyche, I've warned you about leaving too many scraps of memory."

Julia's brow furrowed, and Mother hushed her, warmth where there should be…something…

The man grunted, sullen. "Yes, Mother."

"I'm assuming you're taking more care with Titus."

"Yes, but I've had to coddle him, your latest directive involving Marcos is at cross-purposes with his core compulsion."

"I'm well aware, but I wouldn't have been able to pry Nora Jester out of that tower with any less of a carrot. She has to be in Glynfyls for what's to come. The line up there isn't strong enough to do what I need them to."

"But to lose access to his genetics—"

"We're past that phase. Cal's been priming that grandson of his to be Overlord since he was born, and his goal is coming to fruition. Without a strong Binder in Glynfyls, he won't be able to go through with the Investiture. A pregnancy will prevent the girl from filling the role."

Julia's brow crumpled. A vision of caressing her own belly, strong hands sliding with hers…golden light surrounded the memory, pressing inwards. The image fragmented, and a new one resolved from the shards.

Her purpose.

"That's right child, now listen to Mother…"

TITUS SPUN the cylinder of his revolver. "Tell me about the border op."

The Breaker standing on the other side of the desk tensed, the glisten of sweat at his temple. "On January twenty—"

Click.

Hmm. Pity.

"No, no, no." Titus spun the revolver's cylinder again and waved the weapon at the man. "I know what your report says, Br2. I want to hear what it doesn't."

Pax's stance wavered, uncomfortable being addressed by his new rung. Titus sited a kneecap, wanting an explanation. The Breaker's recalcitrance was vexing.

"Is that a direct order, sir?"

"Is that a—" He rubbed a temple, missing Marcos's competence. It had not been inherited by his offspring. Frowning, Titus pulled the trigger again.

Click.

Vexed, he loaded the rest of the cylinder. Perhaps competence was a learned behavior.

"A subset of my squad and I came into contact with the fugitives, sir."

"Go on."

"She…she bested me, sir." The man's throat bobbed.

A bullet tore into it, his shoulder, and the afore sited kneecap. He hit the granite floor, gore spattering.

"Keep him breathing, then get out."

Shriver stepped from the shadows, pulling talent to attended the man. Titus grimaced at the pain lancing through his head, throwing the revolver onto his desk, and grabbing his pills, the cap flinging from his fingers, capsules scattering across his desk. He cursed, sweeping up a handful and chewing them like candy, his temples threatening to erupt.

By the time Shriver departed, the throbbing behind Titus's eyes had receded to a manageable level. Pax lay curled on the floor, emitting a satisfying wheeze.

It was the only thing about today that was, though that fight at the Pony on Friday had the potential to improve his mood. Titus called for a bourbon, pulling up several holos. Riegel had exceeded his expectations in that regard, but couldn't be allowed to end the man. Titus planned on enacting his kill-switch after Scot was beaten bloody. The boy's genetics were too important to lose, and Riegel had served his purpose.

Stemming from the Breaker's feed, a network of others had begun populating the background. All drudges at this point, but that would change. The whores he'd infected with Orin's nanobots were industrious, and with every intimacy, Titus's awareness of the city's inner workings tentacled outwards.

Unfortunately, despite Orin's assurances talent wouldn't be able to eradicate the little spies, the feeds for Nora and Marcos remained dead, the last five minutes on a loop. How the two of them had learned to use their talent in tandem was troubling, and the subtle jump of Marcos's ability at the end… That had to be something Albanach had bred into the Jesters, which went a long way towards explaining the magnitude of the voids at the border and Riegel's disparate levels of talent. The board would be livid that the trait hadn't been documented and exploited accordingly.

If it could be proven.

Titus tapped his fingers on the desk. Causation and correlation. Still not enough to hang the old dragon, but it was another twist of hemp to add to the rope. He slapped a panel on his desk, calling up a communications orb. "Send Brix in."

The Goliath entered, his leg jerking as he passed Pax's crumpled form like he wanted to kick him. He'd get his chance.

Titus sat back, sipping his bourbon. "Status?"

"Unchanged. Troops are positioned, at the ready. Curtains have the mutts caged."

"Mmm. About that. Today that bloated Fetch admitted to smuggling. Any idea where they could be procuring supplies from? I thought your people were watching for upticks in trade."

Brix's mouth hardened. "They are. Someone must have stockpiles they're selling off. I'll get on it…" He rubbed at the edge of the birthmark discoloring his face.

"Yes…?"

"I need to look at the satellites. They shouldn't be able to shift out without the vectors picking them up, and even if a Shade's working with them, the distances don't make sense."

"Do whatever you need to do to shut it down." Titus pursed his lips. "How have your integration efforts gone?"

Brix snorted, hawking something up and spitting it at Pax. "Quickly. One of my Elites has command of each squad, with reserves of real troops to show them how it's done."

"Excellent. Take Pax with you and educate him, won't you? Ostensively, he's to maintain the Commandant's position as head of our forces, but you have command."

The ugly man saluted sharply and dragged Pax from the room by his collar. Titus smiled into his bourbon, though the rest of his reports gave him little reason to.

Julia's dramatic ousting from power hadn't been unforeseen, but it had been a surprise that it had come at Lord Klein's hands. The man's about face, taking up the mantle of First and his subsequent speech to the Assembly was worrying. If nothing else, Julia had been very successful dividing them into warring Houses only concerned with their own survival. Scot's ability to inspire patriotism was yet another unexpected issue. At this late juncture, Titus would've thought it too late for them to pull together cohesively, but Scot seemed to delight in defying his predictions—

A notification flashed beneath the running line of requests for status from Rache. The board would see that soon enough… Ah. Ielle was checking in. He scanned the whore's report, his ire at her disobeying him by venturing into the city dissipating. Titus tapped his lips, the edges curving upwards. She was a delightfully nasty piece of work. Pity she'd most likely be dead before he retrieved her. He sent back a quick reply, sanctioning her suggestions with a caveat, and setting her loose.

ROGAN KICKED a beer can across the cavern, sending it skittering into the shadows. It hit with a dull metallic clunk that echoed through the space. A moment later it crunched beneath a boot. A tall auburn-haired woman wearing a black mourning ribbon and Valkyrie's leathers came into the glow of his flame.

With a name like Phyllis Breakspear, she was more of a looker than he'd expected. The leathers he hadn't expected at all. She probably didn't have a fucking clue what they'd meant. "If you don't mind, I'd prefer more light for this meeting."

He grunted, pulling talent and igniting the long troughs of oil lining the chamber. Flames ran up the shale walls, illuminating low tiers of stone dropping to the football field of sand they surrounded.

She toed a burnt-out fire pit. Several dozen cans littered around it. "Looks like there's some cleaning to do before the moot."

Rogan sat, lazing back on his elbows. "You called one?"

"I had no choice, and rumors of the Alpha Prime's return aren't helping the situation."

He snorted. If she was trying to guilt him into something by using that title, it wasn't gonna work. "I'd say it's your alliance with that Intelligencer that isn't helping."

Her spine straightened. "That alliance is all that's keeping—"

"Bullshit. There's a rogue out there and you're not handling it. That's not an issue of an alliance. That's Breaker Business." Which, up until now, he'd stayed well fucking clear of, goddamn it. It pissed him off he had to be here at all.

"You're right, it is. And after Friday, it will be sorted."

"Friday." Rogan sucked in his cheeks, leaning forward with a sick suspicion burning in his gut as to just how far she'd gotten into bed with Crandall. There wasn't one damn reason that fuck from the Source was still breathing unless he was bait. Rogan spat. God, he hated fucking politics. "You're setting the kid up."

She flushed, but didn't break his gaze. "I am in an untenable situation. Our line has been without a true Alpha since my husband's death. My son, Billy, will ascend, but doesn't gain his majority for another three months. Stonefist has been all but exiled to the border, leaving me to protect our interests as First. The hierarchy is all that's keeping our troops from open revolt, and after what Laughlin did on the plateau, the line is asking questions that threaten—"

"Why isn't he at the border?"

Her brow crinkled. "Laughlin?"

"Your son."

Phyllis pursed her lips, the skin pinching into furrows around them.

Rogan snorted. "Hell, I'd be asking questions too, because it sounds like the only thing Flynn is threatening is your boy's rung." He grinned at the way her halos had started to sparkle, inhaling the musk coming off her. Not bad for a woman a couple pages past prime. Might be worth pissing her off enough to take a swing at him…

"The matter needs to be resolved. The commons don't care that Laughlin can't pull and with you acting as his Menot—"

Rogan held his palms up. "There's no bond between us."

"Oh, there's blood there."

He ran a hand across his mouth at the allusion to his family…what was left of it. If she delved any further into that subject, he'd be the one swinging. "Kid's too smart to be baited into a fight."

"I think once he sees his opponent, being smart will count for very little. You have to understand, I don't hold Laughlin any ill will, but—"

"The Intelligencer wants him gone, and little Billy's destiny is at stake." Rogan grinned at her puff of 'lust and sent back one of his own.

She shivered. "Laughlin was intended to be a decoy. He's becoming a threat."

Woman had no goddamned idea how true that statement was. "And if he wins the bout?"

Her gaze was steady as it met his. "I don't believe that will happen."

He laughed, rising to his feet. Sand crunched beneath his boots as he stalked toward her. "You've sanctioned his death?"

"I-I've done nothing." Her throat bobbed. " 'A man's destiny is fraught with peril.' "

"And 'assassination is an abhorrent tool of a coward.' Don't quote the fucking Way to me." Christ he'd written half that shit down when he was plastered, and the rest he'd bastardized from Tolkien. "If he gets in that ring, there will be no interference…and FYI, if that rogue Breaker does manage to put the kid down, Kara will return the favor. What will you do then, Phyllis?"

Her eyes narrowed. "I very much doubt that in her present condition—"

Rogan laughed. "In her present condition. God, none of you up here remember where you come from do you?" He spat to the side. "Those first two incursions… I've seen Breaker females on the battle field give birth, then rise up to eviscerate the enemy, babe strapped to their breasts. Your physiology's designed for combat, and pregnancy has never been a determent. Believe me when I say it isn't for Kara. There will be no interference."

"Are you speaking as Rogan Firestorm, or as the Alpha Prime, first Overlord of Glynfyls?" Her nostrils flared at what he was leaking.

Rogan scowled. "Is there a difference?"

"Not in my mind. Both of them abdicated their responsibilities. Would you challenge to get them back?" She'd drawn herself up, 'lust coiling, broadcasting her status as Alpha Female—

All it broadcasted was her lack. It was fucking endemic up here. Rogan snorted. "There's not a chance in hell I'm stepping into this shit any more than I already have, but why not you, Phyllis? You or your boy? You want a resolution? Man the fuck up and face the kid."

He laughed at her expression, the sound bouncing around the chamber and intensifying until she winced. "The problem's not with the commons, or the hierarchy. Shit, it ain't even with the kid. Problem is, and has always been, with you and your kind. Original Houses, just a bunch of privileged aristocratic assholes too worried about their own fucking perceived honor to do the right thing."

He spat to the side and prowled around her, looking her up and down. She'd tensed… fight or flight? Rogan grinned, stopping at her shoulder and skating his nose up the side of her throat, lips just brushing the shell of her ear. He felt her tremble, and his 'lust jumped in response.

"You earn those leathers, or they just part of some elite girl's club you can snub each other over?" A muscle in her jaw popped, and his grin grew. "Yeah? Show me what you've got."

Rogan dropped into his stance, and she hesitated before doing the same. He let her throw a couple punches before putting her on the ground. She got back up and came at him again.

Once, twice. The third time she fell and lay panting.

He clucked his tongue, pulling his knife and crouching beside her, slicing the winged patches from her vest. Phyllis's eyes went glassy, her mouth set in a down-curved line.

"The problem with living so long is that everything turns to shit. Loses purpose, gets corrupted. Breakers were the sword of Glynfyls, Original Houses first into the fray. Your little Billy sitting on his ass eating bonbons is a fucking disgrace. So was your performance just now. No wonder they're all champing at the bit for the kid to challenge…and you know what, Phyllis?" Rogan smiled, and she shivered, her eyes closing as he traced a knuckle down her cheek. "Talent or no, if he wanted it, he'd have it already."

She swallowed. "The codes specify—"

"I don't give a flying fuck what they specify, and considering what's coming at us, neither should you." He stood, cradling the wings he'd removed from her vest in his hand.

Trying not to think about when they'd meant more.

"And on that note, after Kara's Introduction, you will act as her Bane."

Phyllis sat up, laughing. "Is that why you asked me here?" She sighed, wrists on her knees. "There's three months until I can step down, Firestorm. Unless you know something I don't?"

"Like you said, after Friday that should be sorted." No way the kid was gonna be able to keep a lid on things when he saw Riegel waiting in that cage.

"Will you tell Laughlin?" she asked.

"Nope." Phyllis cocked her head and Rogan laughed, tucking the wings into his pocket. "I'm up here solely for Kara's benefit, and if that means keeping that asshole alive, you better believe I will, but I'm sure as hell not gonna do it by bubble-wrapping him."

CHAPTER TWENTY-FOUR

stay of arms [stā əv ärmz] *noun*

1. *A call from Alpha for all Breakers to stand down from any and all forms of conflict.*

– Excerpt from The Way of Honor

"The final duality consisting of Breakers and Binders, respectively able to cohere and explode matter apart, is a complex one. Breakers are almost a race unto themselves, not well understood by any of the other lines. Their volatile personalities and appetites are an anathema to the placid and logical Binders. However, unlike the other dualities, they have a distinct symbiosis, especially in times of crisis…"

– Lord Talos, Preceptor of History,
Academy of Glynfyls

FLYNN TOOK his seat in chambers, unable to wipe the smile off his face. Kara was gonna shit when she saw what he was getting her. Several people smiled back at him. He wasn't the only one in a good mood. The entire room felt lighter. He was sure that could be directly attributed to Julia's absence. Someone told a joke behind him and there was a ripple of laughter.

Riggs smacked his gavel and the room quieted. "Well, then. Let's get right to it. Lord Markham, you have an update on the embargo?"

The large man stood, wiping under his chins. "To be brief, it's resulted in a surplus of funds after forcing the Source to go through a subsidiary of ours for coal. I'm afraid they were gouged quite badly on the price." His expression belied the statement. "A full accounting of the windfall is included in your packets."

Flynn flipped to the tally sheet. *Whoa.* It was considerably more than he would've expected. An appreciative murmur spread through the room.

"I'll also mention that as of this morning, the deficit of arms has been resolved. If recruitment goes as Stonefist anticipates, we'll be in good shape on that front." Markham sat, a pleased look on his face.

"Which brings us back to the wall," Klein said, standing. "The preliminary assessment proves Lord Scot correct. It's impossible to see the outer base with all of the encroaching shanties and temporary structures. The brick and mortar buildings should provide us with the materials we need—"

"And the interior?" Lady Henshaw asked.

He flipped to another page in his notebook. "Ah, that will be more challenging. Essentially, the first street of the seventh rung needs to go." An agitated murmur rippled through the room, and her mouth set into a grim line. "The housing complex in the north is of particular concern, and trees will need to be cleared along the eastern edge of Chase Park."

Flynn snorted at someone's crack about displacing thugs and sear-junkies. They weren't wrong. Even he'd avoided that part of the city in his younger years, and there was no way it'd improved. Someone suggested they leave it and let the Source take their chances.

Riggs cleared his throat, stopping the banter. "Well, I think that's enough information to decide whether or not we'd like to pursue this course of action. Shall we vote on, ah, demolition, I suspect is the appropriate term?" The room fidgeted beneath the sweep of his gaze.

Christ, the chicken shits were gonna sink it—

Flynn stood, shaking his head at the collective sigh of relief. It wasn't gonna last, those buildings needed to go. His fist clenched at his side, wound throbbing.

"House Scot calls on its bondsmen to vote in favor of securing the wall for repairs." Jaws dropped, then snapped shut as he met their eyes. They'd all known what they were getting into when they pledged, but being slapped in the face with the fact that he had the Shade, Binder, and Fixer votes at his beck and call couldn't be easy to swallow. Shit, he had a hard time choking it down.

Across the floor, Phyllis stood.

"The Breakers also vote in favor of the measure."

"As do the Finders," Crandall said a heartbeat later.

Riggs looked at him, as surprised as Flynn if the altitude of his eyebrows was any indication.

The room turned to Markham. He swallowed, mopping his brow. "Well, I suspect I'd be remiss if I didn't make it a proper Quorum. Fetches vote in favor."

A Quorum…and Flynn had half of it.

Motherfucker. It was for Kara. What needed to happen. He still felt sick.

Riggs's gavel dropped and they took their seats, that heavy expectancy in the air again… "Next on the agenda, oh…ah, if we can clear the gallery for this, please…"

A general outcry came from the press above as they were herded out, cameras flashing. The upper doors boomed shut.

"Now then, Lord Crandall has an update on the murders."

Flynn's mouth went dry, his agita at pushing the vote through, gone. He resisted the urge to pull at his cravat as the weasely little shit stood, his smile far too smug. Somehow, this was gonna fuck him.

"Yes. We've a witness." The uproar was immediate. "After taking his deposition, I've elected to have him join us to answer what questions he can. If you would be so kind, Lord Markham?"

The fat man gave him a look, clearly not as excited about the prospect as Crandall was. "I may be a moment." Frowning, he shifted out.

"While we wait, I need to impress upon you the need for discretion, as this is an active investigation."

Flynn snorted, between excluding the press and that statement, the man had just guaranteed a special edition with this on the front page by tea. He already felt sorry for the poor son of a bitch they were gonna drag—

"Hey! Lay off! I were just—shite."

Markham had reappeared, his hand clamped firmly around the arm of some skinny commoner barely out of his teens, if that. He had the messiest mop of blond curls Flynn had ever—No, something about that rang a bell…

"Are you serious, Crandall? This is your witness?"

The kid's shoulders slumped in abject misery.

"I suggest you give him the opportunity to answer your questions."

"Why? We won't be able to understand them!"

The room broke into nasty laughter, and the kid tried to bolt.

Markham's hand tightened on his arm. "Enough! Whether you like it or not, Fitzpatrick's blood is as blue as yours. The fact that an attempt was made on his person should only reinforce the fact that while this monster is roaming our streets, none of us are safe!"

That quieted down the worst of it, but people still weren't taking it very seriously. Who the fuck was this kid? Markham gave him a little shake, and the kid reached up to pull at his lip—no, he had a fucking soul patch. Flynn tried to bite back his smile. The rest of the Assembly was less amused.

"Go on, Fitzpatrick. Tell them what you told me." The kid scowled at Markham, and the big man gave an exasperated sigh. "Sooner begun, sooner done."

Fitzpatrick glared at him then dropped his gaze, mumbling. "Breaker were at the Pipe. Talked like a hill—eh…all proper—"

"You should try it sometime!"

Markham glared at the cat-caller and said something in the kid's ear when he tried to bolt again.

Fitzpatrick's eyes narrowed. "Yer a right shite." Markham sighed, and the kid looked like he wanted to spit. "Fine. Thought he wanted somewhat else, went t'talk, and the shite tried t'shanghai me. Said he were looking for bodies t'deliver. Shifted him t'the plateau and left him lonesome."

Christ, his cant was thick, he sounded straight outta the Pinch. It took everyone a minute to process what the hell he'd said. When Flynn did, his pulse jumped. "A Breaker? What'd he look like?"

The kid shrugged. "Big as ye. Blond, clean shaven. Eyes was off." Something about that made him real uncomfortable.

"Off how?"

"Like his halos was bleeding. Slashed red 'cross the whites."

A woman tsked. "I find it very difficult to believe that you've been unable to find a man fitting that description, Lord Crandall. Especially with the lion's share of Breakers at the border."

"Despite our best attempts, he remains elusive. It's a big city, Lady Ellerbee, I can assure you, we've been utilizing all of our resources."

"Do you suspect a Shade's involved?"

"I'm afraid I can't rule anything out at this point."

That fucking prick. Flynn's jaw popped. Crandall had solidly implicated Riegel all right, then left plenty of fucking room for him to hang right beside him.

"I don't see how that proves anything—"

"He's not done, Lord Wu. Go on, Fitzpatrick, what happened then?"

"Two days later, I'm playing card's at the 'Tail, and the shite sits down at me table. Wants me t'whammy him. S'why I went t'Markham." He glared at the fat man, and Flynn couldn't blame him.

"What in God's name is he talking about?"

"The suspect wanted Fitzpatrick to key him to the tubes."

That got the Assembly's attention.

People started shouting, and the kid cringed back. "I ain't done a damned thing!"

"That'll be a first," someone laughed.

Flynn turned to Lot. "Who the hell is this kid?"

"Denis McCreedy's boy. He's even more of a fuck-up than you."

Denis Mc—oh shit. The Dock Uprising. No wonder he didn't wanna be here. Flynn stood.

"Let him finish!" The room settled. "Why'd he ask you?"

The kid pushed a lock of that chin-length poof behind his ear. Shit, yeah, Flynn could see it now. He looked just like his dad, except for that wide Prydee mouth. He shoved a hand in his pocket, fiddling with something. "Eh, dunno."

"Like we can't guess," someone sneered.

"I didn'a do it. Cleaned him out instead."

Flynn laughed, and the kid glanced at him in surprise. He almost smiled.

"What did he—"

"I think he said he stole something."

"Yes, and it's fortuitous he did," Crandall broke in. "The wallet belonged to the accountant on the fourth rung who'd been murdered earlier in the day, his blood still tacky on the units. We'd already ascertained a Breaker was responsible, but thanks to Fitzpatrick, we have a description of the man, and proof placing him at the murder. You should also be aware of one more thing. The suspect had a barcode tattooed on his wrist."

The room erupted, all of them well aware of the implications.

Riggs banged the gavel for order and finally gave up, the room a cacophony of voices. Flynn jumped the rail of the box and crossed the floor to Markham before the kid could escape. Close up, he didn't look nearly so young and smelled like a still. He'd probably be tall enough to look him in the eye if he wasn't so hunched over.

Markham smiled nervously. "Lord Scot, ah, you probably don't remember him, but this is my nephew, Fitzpatrick McCreedy."

"No, I'm afraid I don't." He held out his hand for the kid to shake. "I remember your dad, though. He was a good man. Wish there were more like him."

The kid met his eyes in surprise. His were weird, the irises shattered. No wonder whatever was going on with Riegel's eyes had freaked him out. His grip was a hell of a lot more assertive than the rest of him. "Ya. Thanks. S'Fitz."

"Can you tell me anything else—"

Carl was at his shoulder. "Laughlin, sorry, I don't mean to interrupt, but after conscripting our votes, my line wants to get the paperwork and oath done as soon as possible. Are you free in an hour or so?"

Flynn ran a hand through his hair and sighed. "Yeah, I should be able to get everything set up for then."

"Splendid. We'll see you in an hour."

He turned back to talk to Fitz, but the kid was gone. Markham gave him an apologetic shrug. "Fitzpatrick isn't particularly comfortable on the hill. If you'd like, I can try to set a meeting elsewhere…?"

Flynn snorted. "Wonder why. What the hell happened to him? His father—"

"It's a long, unpleasant tale I'd rather not get into."

"I'll bet. Yeah, if you can pin the kid down, I'd like to talk to him."

"Will do." They shook, and Flynn made his way out of chambers, his palm already throbbing. He glanced down to see how bad it was bleeding through, and a woman stepped into his path. He grabbed her shoulders, spinning her to the side so he wouldn't trample her. Her back struck the wall, and she brushed back an ebony curtain of hair with a gasp, her considerable bosom heaving as she smiled up at him. His hands sprang from her shoulders like he'd been burnt.

Motherfucker. It was Miss January.

Ielle.

The hallway seared red, and he threw up zero, his pulse racing. Fuck! Her almond eyes widened, and she licked her lips, tongue lingering at the tip of a canine. The unveiled interest and whispering around them ticked up a notch.

Flynn leaned into that blanket of calm. Christ, the last thing he needed was to be seen threatening a woman with Crandall's noose waiting for him. He had to be smart about this and play the fucking part.

"My apologies, madame." The words tasted like bile.

"I'll let you make it up to me," she said, her mouth caressing the words like they were a very different part of his body. He had a decidedly inverse reaction, ignoring the hand she held out to him. Her smile brightened, and she stepped closer. "I'm new to the city and would love a tour."

"I'm sure you'll find someone more than happy to assist you. If you'll excuse me." All these fucking people needed to get the hell out of his way. She was up against him, inhaling. Her pupils dilated, and she smiled beatifically at him, her fingers at his belt.

Zero buckled and the press lessened around them in response. He scrabbled for it, fighting back the tint bleeding across his vision. "Don't fucking touch me—"

"What will you do if I disobey?"

He'd make an exception to his rule.

Flynn grimaced, seeing her innards splattered across the marble as he pushed past her, feeling her eyes on him all the way to the gate. Christ, he needed a shower. That pretty packaging was covering something decidedly not.

CAL DROPPED his cloak and sat frowning at where the communications orb had hovered a second ago. Even with the emergency board meeting over the North's embargo, and the shit show it'd made of the Source's share prices, things were too quiet on that front. He'd expected the board to have filed a grievance against him by now.

Titus was up to something, and whatever it was, the man deemed it worth losing the Commandant over. With the imminent war looming, that threw up one hell of a red flag. Why he hadn't let the rest of the board know Marcos had jumped ship with Nora... It was time to buy some favors. Most would be amiable to taking his money, but Orin would be a pain in the ass. He always was.

Cal pulled out his pouch of tobacco, his fingers going through the motions. He didn't have a choice. Nora's last message bothered him. It bothered him more that she'd missed the rendezvous. He prayed to God she made the next one—

Someone knocked on the door. "Yeah?"

It opened and Flynn poked his head in. "Busy? French says you've been holed up in here all day."

"Perpetually. What d'you want?"

Flynn opened the door enough for the butler to wheel in his coffee service, a massive stack of papers on the shelf beneath. He started off-loading it onto the desk. Boy ran a hand through his damp hair and sighed. "Not me. Them. Fixers ousted Julia, then turned around and pledged as a block. They'll be here for the oath in a half-hour."

"Where would you like them to wait, sir?"

"Ah, stick them in the Green Dining Suite and give them something to chew on."

"As you wish." The man left, and Flynn flopped down into a chair across from Cal with a cup of coffee.

"Sounds like I missed quite the show. Gimme the CliffsNotes while you're signing."

Boy snorted and grabbed a pen, launching into a summary of the day's theater as he worked through the pile.

Lord above, Cal didn't miss a damned thing about being in that room, and Ielle showing up was an issue. He lit his cigarette. What the hell was Titus up to? He'd just bought the courtesan for an exorbitant sum. Pissing all that away by sending her up here didn't make any goddamned sense...but neither did the rest of the shit he'd been pulling lately. It was enough to give Cal heartburn.

"With everything you just spilled, and Riegel in the city, I don't think taking Kara to the Pony's the wisest move."

Flynn tossed down the pen and grabbed a danish. "I hope the sick fuck shows. I'm taking Leo—shit, that reminds me." He grubbed around in his pocket and tossed a data chip onto the desk.

"What's that?"

"You tell me. It was in a plaz converter the asshole was way too hot to get his hands on."

Two of them were as fractious as cats in a bag. "I'm gonna assume there's a story behind that, but I'm more intent on addressing this Pony shit."

"Worst case, that dick Rogan said he'd be there."

Cal stowed the regulated tech, having to admit that the Breaker was one hell of an insurance policy. Still... "You remember the oath you took when your halos came in?" Flynn looked at him like he was an idiot. "Ever break it?"

"Once."

"You sure?"

"Yeah, and still feel like shit about it, thanks for asking."

"Then how about you repeat it back to me."

"Are you—'On my life, on my honor. None but mine own line shall see my power. None but mine own people shall see my use of talent. To keep us hidden, to keep us safe. So I swear.' "

"You might want to think about what that means."

Flynn took another bite. "If it's important, you might wanna just tell me. I've got a lot going on, and riddles are being relegated to the back of the bus."

Cal reached for his scotch. Boy had him there. "That oath was instituted to keep the Source in the dark, not to isolate us from the other lines, or the rest of our people. I suggest you be circumspect about it, but if you get into a tight spot at the Pony, don't be afraid to use what you've got."

"Un-fucking-believable." Flynn shook his head, scowling. "You recommend doing that before or after I split?"

Cal sucked air through his teeth, knowing exactly who he could thank for letting that slip. "Asshole's lips are flappier than a blown-out whore's."

The quip fell flat, Flynn's jaw popping as he counted tiles. Shit. "Were you gonna tell me?"

"You take Overlord, it won't matter."

"They'll fucking hang me and bury the rest of you."

"Split's not a twist. Codes are written calling out Talents with dual-ringed halos. Split's only have the one."

"That's a hell of a technicality—"

"Merchant's one hell of a lawyer."

"I'll make sure to tell the mob that when they're waving their pitchforks." The boy snorted. "Shit…that reminds me, I had to invite the Binders to the Introduction—"

Cal choked on his drag. "Miriam's gonna have a goddamned

coronary, but I suspect it was the right call… I'll tell her it was my idea, otherwise Kara won't have anybody to stand up there with."

French cleared his throat at the door. "Sir, Lord Klein is here."

"You mind if I do this here?"

Cal shrugged, reaching for his bottle. He'd rather not, but seemed like something the boy needed his blessing on. Flynn slid a tactical knife from his pocket. It was the one from the plateau. Probably some guilt-ridden reason he was using the damned thing for this. Cal wasn't gonna ask. He drank his scotch instead.

Klein came in as Flynn unwrapped the bandage from his hand and sliced open the gory mess. Wincing, he handed the blade to him. Man was a hell of a lot more judicious with his cut. They shook, each sending out a tiny thread of talent, creating a dormant link between them.

Flynn looked the man in the eyes when he did, and Klein stepped back in surprise.

"M-my liege," he stammered, bowing his head with his hand over his heart.

Cal upended the bottle.

Flynn bowed back, and the next man came in. It took close to an hour to get through them all, and by the end, the boy's palm looked like burger. He wrapped it up again, and Cal snorted. Kara was gonna have a fit when she saw it.

His grandson turned at the sound. "That how it's done?"

"Yeah." He lit a cigar. "Now get out. I got work to do."

Flynn shot him an injured glare and left the room. Cal ran a hand over his face. Jesus fucking Christ. Yeah, that was how it was done. Now he was gonna pray like hell Nora got here in time so the boy could do the rest.

KARA GRITTED HER TEETH, feeling Flynn's hand throb through their bond. How was that even possible? If this stupid lift didn't go any faster—Her thumb worried the handle of the triage kit. She was going to kill him if an infection didn't first. Stupid oath, stupid fealty, ugh, stupid men!

The door opened and she ran over, intercepting him as he came from Cal's office into the foyer. She felt his shock at seeing her, and he opened his mouth to say something.

She pushed him down onto the steps hard enough to make him grunt as he landed. "Don't even!" She dropped the kit and snatched his hand, unwrapping the nasty bandage with a cry. "I swear you do this just to piss me off. It doesn't need to be a half inch deep, ugh, you're just begging for sepsis..." She glared at him, his face a mixture of mortified amusement. He grinned, mussing his hair. "You're such a jerk! I'm binding the damned thing!"

"Wait, Kara—"

Her halos flashed, and a healthy pink scar lay where the mangled flesh had been.

He cringed, standing. "I'd Introduce you all, but it's still a bit premature."

The blood drained from Kara's face, and he chuckled, kissing the top of her head. She peeked over her shoulder, at least two dozen men stood by the gate, gaping at her. One of the older ones looked like he was about to fall over. Oh no...had they seen—she went beet red and Flynn got that Cheshire Cat grin.

She burrowed against his chest. "Did they see my halos?"

He chuckled. "It's not your halos, what are you wearing?"

"I—" She looked down at the shapeless white shift. "What? Shelby wanted me to wear a long dress to practice in. This was all I had."

"It's also entirely transparent when you're backlit, and you cast one hell of a shadow." He pulled her against him, addressing the men. "I think this is where I say goodnight to all of you. I'll see you in the morning at session."

There were stunned nods, and they resumed filing through the gate with a flurry of hushed conversation. Flynn dipped his head and kissed her like they were already gone.

"You look beautiful," he murmured, breaking away.

She scowled. "I didn't know it was see-through, and I didn't know they were here. Good news is, I don't think I'm going to totally embarrass you on the dance floor."

"Yeah?" He took her by the waist and twirled her around the foyer. She laughed, following his lead back to the lift. He slapped the button and kissed her again, his hands sliding with the dress's fabric. "I think you're right, but nothing you do embarrasses me."

"Not even flashing my colors in front of a bunch of old guys you work with?"

He laughed. "Not even that. I really like this dress."

"I really like that you really like this dress." They got into the lift.

"Mmm, but you're not gonna like what I have to tell you."

She raised an eyebrow as they went into their suite. Most of it had been packed up and moved into the bower. She looked around; it was weird thinking this was their last night in here. The little grey cat zipped by, taking a swipe at Flynn and hissing.

"Christ, he's a jealous little shit."

"Aw, no, he's just misunderstood." She laughed, picking the kitten up and cuddling him. "What do you have to tell me?"

"Ielle was at Assembly."

Kara blanched, dropping into one of the chairs by the fire. "You're sure?"

"Miss January."

She felt like she was going to throw up. "That's why you were so angry earlier..."

"Yeah. She stopped me in the hall, but I don't think she knows I recognized her. You've got no idea how hard it was not to put that bitch through a wall—Hey, it's okay. Come here, I'm not gonna let her anywhere near you." He moved her onto his lap, earning another hiss from the kitten. "Christ, he's a dick—Miriam has the estate warded, and Cal's got Rogan working security. Nothing's getting in here. You're safe."

She trembled against him, his anger lancing through her terror. Ugh, she needed to get past it. He was right. They couldn't hurt her anymore... Her head said that, but the rest of her wanted to lock herself in the bathroom. The kitten purred up under her chin, and she laughed, stroking him. Ugh, she was so stupid... "I know. I'm sorry, I just… I can't get around it, shut it off…the two of them… They terrify me."

"It's completely understandable, Kara. There's nothing wrong with feeling things." He smoothed her hair back and kissed her forehead. His fierce protectiveness flowed through their bond, soothing her. "They fingered Riegel as the murderer they're looking for. Had some kid ID him during Assembly."

"Do they know where he is?"

"Crandall says he can't find him, but that's bullshit. He's gotta be one of the only Breakers in the city, and the kid said his eyes are all messed up like his halos are bleeding—"

Kara's stomach clenched. "His halos are bleeding?"

"Yeah. Red slashed through the white the kid said."

"He's got a boost."

"A what?"

She chewed her thumb. "A boost. The bleeding halos are a side effect. It's tech they were trying to develop to increase a Talent's ability, but it never got clearance. It distorts a subject's channel, turns them into a conduit. At some point, he's going to lose control—"

"Ow!" Flynn pulled his hand away from the kitten. "You're telling me he's a fucking bomb?"

She nodded.

Flynn laughed. "Great. You know what, for the next couple of days, that's not my goddamned problem. Hopefully he's standing in the seventh fucking rung when he goes, preferably after Ielle asks him to show her around."

"Wait, she hit on you?" A jolt of bloodlust tempered her fear.

"Don't worry, she's not my type," he teased, giving her that grin of his.

"Oh really, and what is your type, Laughlin?"

"I've always had a thing for gorgeous brunettes, one in particular."

"That's a good answer."

"I thought so. It's even true. You name this little monster yet?"

Kara looked down at the cat. She'd sent the others back to the kitchen, but he seemed to want to stay. "No. It never occurred to me."

"No wonder he's all pissy. You should."

"What would you name him?"

"I dunno. Something to fit his personality."

She rolled her eyes. "I'm not naming my cat Jealous Monster Dick."

Flynn laughed. "Miriam would love that. Something to think about."

Something to think about. Kara sighed, settling back against him and playing with the kitten. There always was, and with the Introduction tomorrow, names were preferable to the rest of it.

BARTON NURSED HIS ALE, riveted by the altercation out on the street. He'd spent his day off roaming the city and gathering intel. The makeup of the crowds had changed drastically in the past twenty-four hours. Proclamations had been posted decreeing the moratorium on shifting lifted, and anyone with another place to go, was. Fetch stations had lines of people that went on for blocks, a one bag per person limit strictly enforced. A brisk trade had started up around the piles of belongings people hadn't been able to take. As had the debate over what fit the definition of a bag. Two constables were clubbing a man who'd argued a bit too ardently that his trawling net did.

Entertaining, but not of great import.

The Breakers coming back were.

Not all of them, but the heads and heirs of Houses, both Original and lesser, had been trickling into the city for the past few days. It was curious. Barton had claimed a table at the Marked Man, his bland demeanor rendering him and his ale forgotten in a shadowy corner of the bar. That wouldn't last when Otto joined him, but for now, he sat all but invisible, listening to the two graybeards at the table next to his.

"Me money's on Scot. After them rumors, I got no doubts."

The one with a cloudy eye grunted. "Then ye going t'the moot tomorrow?"

"Nah, no point in it." The other took a slug of ale. "Them hillies ain't gonna see sense, but I'll tell ye true, push come to shove, man I'm following ain't by the name of Breakspear."

"Ye'll not be the only one, and the rest ain't gonna have no choice. Ye hear about that closed session t'day?"

"Aye. Intelligencer's full of shite. The son of a bitch McCreedy fingered broke me grand baby's arm two night's past at the Pony, and us on a stay of arms…else I'd put a bullet in the rogue meself." He spat. "Fuckin' hillie games."

"Bastards is probably hoping he'll put Scot down. 'Tween time he spent down here before he left, and what he said in chambers today, ain't no way them's gonna let him keep his seat."

"That so?"

"Shook McCreedy's hand, and said he wished more men were like his da."

The spitter took a long pull of ale. "That ain't gonna end well, God rest Denis's soul."

"Aye. Nor is Scot bringing his woman."

"Hear tell she can handle herself, but yer right, Pony ain't no place for a lady…"

The chair across from Barton scraped back, and Otto plunked down into it with an ale. The graybeards moved to the bar. Barton gnawed on a finger, blinking at the Binder.

Dark shadows rimmed the man's eyes like a clown's over those bright red cheeks. "Your move. She'll be in the city, and I can promise you he'll be occupied."

Barton's halos pulsed, and he pulled his fingers from his lips, tasting death…but that's all he'd tasted since using his talent on the plateau. He took a sip of ale, washing it away. "Pony will be tricky timing. Can't be sure."

Otto threw back his tankard. "Of course not. Nothing else has gone smoothly, why start now? Anything else to report?"

Barton gnawed a cuticle. "Breakers coming in from the border. Moot's tomorrow."

"Do you know why?"

"Something about Scot. What he did."

Otto rolled his eyes, finishing his tankard as he stood. "Well, there's a news flash. Who isn't talking about what that blasted man's done or about to do. If that's all, I need to get back to Titus."

Barton shook his head and Otto left.

Laughlin Scot. They were saluting him as Overlord. His star ascendent. Barton sat for several minutes longer after Otto had left. His halos glowed a sickly prune, the flavor of graveyard midden slicking his tongue, and the base of his neck itching where Titus's detonator was implanted.

Both he and Scot of consequence.

Barton was of none.

CHAPTER TWENTY-FIVE

"Bloodlust is a tool. In its purest form, it heightens awareness and increases physical responses to danger. Sensed as a pheromone, you'll learn how to use it as a warning, a challenge, and during mating rituals. Like any good tool, it has a sharp edge. Mishandle it, and it will cut you. Therefore, it's critical to also develop zero; a place of perfect calm within you in which to sheath it. Unlike bloodlust, zero removes everything but what's in front of you at that moment, allowing you to act unencumbered by emotion..."

– Lord Grimmight, Breaker Menot,
Glynfyls

THE ALARM WENT OFF and Flynn tightened his arm around Kara, pulling her back against his chest. They'd spent the entire evening together and sure as hell had made the most of it. Christ, he wouldn't mind making some more of it right now. He nuzzled into the hollow behind her ear and she laughed, trying to wriggle away.

"I'm not letting you up," he murmured. "It's not even light out."

"You're so lazy in the mornings, though I suppose I should give you a pass today." Her excitement flitted through their bond, and he chuckled. She was like a kid on Christmas.

"Excited about tonight?"

She rolled over, laughing. "Not as excited about what after tonight means. Are you going to be back early?"

"Yeah, we have the afternoon and tomorrow off."

He kissed her throat, and she took a sharp breath, his hands running down her back and over her hip. Moving her leg over his. Her heel slid up the back of his thigh, fingers in his hair.

"Christ, I can't get enough of you." His lips were on hers, tongues—

A knock on the door. Kara laughed. Goddamn. "What?!"

"Sir, you asked me to remind you to review the penalty clauses for the border before session."

Kara nipped at his chin, the devil in her eyes. This fucking woman —he pushed up to get out of bed. She watched him, trailing her fingers down her sternum, lips still bee-stung from last night—

Fuck it.

The penalty clauses didn't get reviewed.

An hour later, he chewed on a croissant, hair still damp, flipping through paperwork as he walked from the gate and into the Assembly hall. Lord Klein fell into step with him.

"My God, Laughlin, last night—"

Flynn laughed. "You don't know the half of it, Carl."

"Forgive me if I try to imagine. Don't tell Alice."

"I'm sure she already knows."

"That would explain the look I got when I came home." They laughed, making their way to their boxes.

Lot came in a moment after Flynn sat. "How the hell did the entire Fixer faction end up getting an eyeful of Kara?"

"She ran into the foyer to heal my hand and didn't see them. I didn't introduce her."

His father grunted, sitting back. "That's the only thing that's saving you from being called out. Thank God you can let her loose after tomorrow."

He was probably gonna want to rethink that.

The speaker called the session to order. Julia was conspicuously absent again. Flynn couldn't help but feel like that wasn't necessarily a good thing. Not knowing what the hell she was up to made him nervous.

"Well, thanks to the auspicious occasion of Lord Scot's nuptials, we have a short day. Congratulations, Laughlin, I'm looking forward to meeting your lady." Someone snickered and Flynn couldn't wipe the stupid smile off his face. "Now, on to the agenda. Lord Klein, you've been very busy, I hear?"

"Yes. With the scope of the job before us and the time constraints, some of the Firsts thought it best to get started and met after session yesterday."

Flynn cocked an eyebrow. They had, huh? News to him…

Carl continued. "With the moratorium on shifting lifted, the population Lady Henshaw was concerned about has drastically reduced and continues to dwindle. We've cleared the eastern quadrant of the wall, and in light of her concerns, some of the smaller, sound structures that were encroaching have been shifted and fixed elsewhere. I hope that suits?"

The older woman nodded, but obviously wasn't satisfied. Flynn snorted. Whatever. He would've blown all of it up.

"Did you have something to add, Lord Scot?" Riggs asked.

Shit. "Ah, I was just thinking that anything unsound could be utilized to fashion a defensive berm around the Flats. We'll want to hold them on the plateau, avoiding street to street fighting for as long as possible. Stonefist would know more about it than me."

Carl made a note. "Sounds like a solid suggestion. I'll see what he says."

"Yes, Lord Patton?" Riggs asked at the man's waggling fingers.

"I'm just curious where Laughlin's picked up all of this fascinating insight. I don't recall military strategy being taught at the Academy." Klaus's comment was met with a few laughs, but most of them turned to Flynn, wanting to know the same thing.

"At one point, I had a lot of time on my hands to read. I can also tell you all about the reformation of the Church of England, but it doesn't seem as pertinent." The French Revolution did, but drawing parallels wasn't gonna do him any favors.

Klaus rolled his eyes. Fuck him.

"If there's nothing else...next on the agenda, Lady Spantz wanted to relay the status of the volunteers supplementing the Academy's curriculum by teaching Hex-theory."

A frazzled woman stood, rubbing her palms against her skirt. "Training has been going very well, we've had a surprising number of volunteers, if bake sales are anything to go by. Our current ratio is two instructors per Hex, and overall it seems to be quite effective. Many of our recent graduates have also come back to observe or take part."

The satisfaction on Lady Breakspear's face was apparent from across the room.

"Any questions on that? No? Well then." He looked over the tops of his glasses at the sheet in front of him. "Our last item of the day is the updated language for the penalty phase of the border legislation, discussion?"

A debate followed giving Flynn the impression it'd been rewritten satisfactorily. He voted for it, hoping it wouldn't screw him.

"Wonderful. Measure passes. Now, I feel like we're leaving things in a good place, and many of you have an Introduction to prepare for, so I'll see you all on Monday morning." Riggs banged his gavel, dismissing them for the weekend.

"The reformation, really?" Lot asked.

"I didn't have a lot of options at one point. Pretty interesting stuff, actually." Flynn stood and stretched, wishing every day could be as short. "So, were you at that meeting?"

His father's shoulders bunched. "One of us had to be. You were occupied."

"Yeah," Flynn grinned. "I was. You can fill me in later."

Lot muttered something about the Introduction and left. Flynn was surprised to see Charles behind him, getting up to do the same.

"Where have you been?"

He rolled his eyes. "Dealing with a House Matter. I can't believe how much I've missed! It figures as soon as I'm called away, you start having fun."

"I don't know that I'd go that far. You bringing Bryan tonight?"

"He'd murder me in my sleep if I didn't. Wait until you see how dashing he looks in his suit, it was outrageously expensive, not that you appreciate that kind of thing. Unfortunately, I can't stay and educate you, I'm due at the salon, and you could use a trim." He spun on his two-inch heels and left.

Fucking Charles. Flynn smiled into his beard and made his way to the lounge to grab a cup of coffee. Klaus sidled up to him, tipping a flask into his own cup. Flynn snorted. The man was wearing a gilt-leather codpiece.

"What? With the short day, I opined casual attire wouldn't be a faux-pas. They really are remarkably comfortable. I can only imagine how fetching you'd look in one."

"I'll pass, thanks."

"To each his own. So, your lady, she does know that the Pony is a pleasure salon?"

Flynn took a sip of coffee. "Actually, I told her it was a whore house."

Klaus took a large swallow from his own cup. "Yes, well, I suppose that does sum it up." He gave Flynn an odd look. "She's fine with accompanying you to such an establishment?"

"She's looking forward to it."

"If I didn't know you better, I'd say you were full of shit. That said, I'd wager there's a rather large omission somewhere in that statement."

Flynn shrugged. "We'll be there, which is all you have to worry about."

"If only that were the case. The girls aren't happy about your plus one. I can't guarantee their good behavior."

"I wouldn't expect you to. Nor can I guarantee my lady's. She's a bit possessive."

"I seem to remember you having that effect on women before you left, and it didn't stop you from sampling the buffet," Klaus said, abandoning the pretense of his coffee and tipping back the flask.

"I didn't have a woman like this before."

"I've heard she's a magnificent creature, even with her flaw. You nervous?"

"What? No. I'm never nervous before a bout."

Klaus smirked. "I meant about the Introduction. That was your second coffee, and you're having a civil conversation with me."

Flynn looked down into the dregs of his cup and laughed. "That obvious, huh?"

"At one point I knew you quite well. Sobriety isn't the equivalent of a lobotomy, though this impending gelding may be. You should go and get it over with. The anticipation is always the worst part. One quick slice and it's over."

Flynn snorted, looking at his palm. If only that were true.

* * *

KARA CUPPED HER FIST, bowing to Rogan with one eye on the clock. "Are you coming tonight?"

"Nope, I've got a set of encyclopedias that need alphabetizing." She glared at him, and he shrugged. "Dentist had an opening to fit my root canal in?"

"You're such a jerk!" she laughed. "Really? You're not coming?"

"In case you haven't noticed, this kind of stuff's not exactly my scene, but I'll tell you what, I'll check in with you before you head on down the aisle. Make sure you haven't changed your mind."

Kara rolled her eyes and left him, jogging up to the bower. She needed to get cleaned up and only had a half-hour before Reggie was due to arrive. Servants were everywhere, putting the final touches on decorations and polishing anything that could hold a sheen.

She ran into Flynn on his way out of the master suite. It was still too new to think it of as their bedroom. He was shirtless, loaded down with a bunch of boxes. "What are all those?"

"Clothes. Shower's yours. Reggie came early with someone to do your hair and face. I'll have a tray sent up, you missed lunch." He kissed her cheek, smelling like soap and something spicy.

Kara pulled him down for a kiss, her fingers tracing over the marks she'd left on him. She nipped his lip as he broke away.

"That's not nice, Kara," he said, glancing at the clock.

"I like this aftershave," she murmured, nipping at him again. "You should put the boxes down."

Miriam cleared her throat behind them, and he laughed. "Laughlin Scot, you leave that girl alone, you're making everyone late!"

"It's not me you gotta worry about," he said with his Cheshire Cat grin. "You better go shower." He kissed Kara again, and she headed to the bathroom, Miriam giving him an earful about the marks striating over him as he left. Kara's face burned, but a big part of her liked that everyone was getting an eyeful of what they did together. It seemed important.

After her shower, a roomful of women were waiting for her, and she was abruptly the center of a whirlwind.

When they were done, she didn't recognize herself. Her hair was piled high on her head, woven through with gold ribbons. Her makeup made her look...like Nora. Regal, somehow. She felt a pang, missing her.

Despite Reggie's fears, the dress didn't need any altering. Flowing modestly to the floor in the front, it dropped low enough to see the dimples beside her tailbone in the back. Shelby came in as Reggie stepped back, admiring her work. Kara blinked back tears. She didn't —she pressed her lips together, then laughed at the look they were giving her.

"Sorry, I just...even at the Source's fêtes... I've never looked like this. I don't—it doesn't feel real. I mean, I don't, I can't—"

Reggie took her by the shoulders. "You can and you're gonna. Now knock it off before you mess your makeup."

"It's because you're happy, Kara," Shelby said. "Are you ready to show your halos? That's the worst part for everybody up here."

Kara laughed, dabbing at her eyes. "Yes, go ahead."

"From all that is hidden, all shall be revealed." Shelby blushed, pulling talent. "Oh! They're so beautiful!" Her own were a striking lime green ringed with silver. Kara stared. She was a twist? Flynn hadn't said anything... Shelby looked away, pushing a lock of dark hair behind her ear.

"You all done in here yet? Everybody's waiting—" Miriam stopped dead in the doorway swathed in a silver satin gown, hair blazing red with a fresh dye job. Her pewter halos shone through her glasses from across the room. Kara gaped at her, she was easily one of the most powerful Fetches she'd ever seen.

Miriam clucked her tongue, coming over. "Well, it's not traditional, but at least it's more modest than the last one." Kara bit back a smile as the woman sighed, crossing herself. Reggie was behind her trying not to laugh. "You remember all your responses? Then let's get on with it, from all that is hidden, all shall be revealed." Her halos flashed and colors ran.

They stood in the foyer, Rogan and Cal sharing a bottle on the steps. Glowing orbs studded the air above and twinkled in falls of silk garlanding the walls. A hum of voices came from the ballroom. Kara stiffened, the sudden urge to bolt washing over her—

Flynn.

She felt him in there, so nervous it made her stomach flip. She smiled, he probably looked like a hedgehog. A burst of excitement echoed between them, and she laughed. Cal came over, so dignified in his three piece suit and ascot. His wide olive halos matched it exactly.

"I've got her from here, Miriam. You go on in and get things started," he said, putting an arm around Kara as the older woman shifted away. His fingers hit skin, and his bushy eyebrows rose, taking in the back of the dress. "I'm gonna wager she didn't see that." Kara laughed again, and the old man shook his head.

Rogan's finger made a spinning motion, and she turned obligingly. He gave a low whistle. "Engine's running, sure you don't want to cut out?"

Cal shot him a look, and the Breaker shrugged, upending the bottle.

"You outshine your mother by a mile tonight," Cal said, snuffing his cigar in a topiary.

She rolled her eyes, not believing a word. Notes from a string quartet drifted into the foyer, and her pulse sped—

"Asshole doesn't deserve you." Rogan stood and tromped off down the hall. Her brow crinkled as she watched him go, and Cal gave her shoulder a quick squeeze.

"Never mind him. I need your head in the game. It's important you play the princess when you walk in there. You sure as hell look the part."

Kara nodded, straightening her spine. She could do this.

"That's the ticket. Remind 'em you're a Jester, damn it."

Her stomach roiled as they started in, her fingers tightening on his sleeve, leaving little ovals of—Kara took a deep breath. No. This wasn't then. She checked her posture again, raising her chin just so, looking without seeing. Being the princess—

And almost lost it when she stepped into the room. Hundreds of people stared back at her… There were so many—

Flynn.

His eyes caught hers across the sea of people, his emotions bearing her back up.

He stood on a low dais, striking in his chocolate-brown trousers and a matching Mandarin-collared jacket. His build lent the ensemble a military air. The cravat of iridescent copper verdigris was tied intricately at his throat, his halos blazing.

His grin was beyond Cheshire, and she laughed, returning it. Cal cleared his throat, and she wiped the emotion from her face. It was hard with the tumult she was leaving in her wake as the crowd caught sight of her back—

And then she was before him, Flynn's hand taking hers, lifting her to the dais.

Lot stepped forward, holding an ancient Bible in his hands, his halos a thread of spring green. "Who gives this woman to us for safe keeping?"

"I, Caliban, patriarch of House Scot, son of Randolf and Hannah, in surety for House Jester."

"Who is this woman who would join House Scot?"

"Kara, daughter of Nora Jester, First Binder, and Beritram, Br1, Alpha Breaker." The last of that left a sour taste in her mouth, quickly swallowed. Murmurs came from the crowd at the disclosure of her duality.

"Who takes responsibility for this woman while in House Scot?"

"I, Laughlin, head of House Scot, and First Shade, son of Adlothian and Deirdre, claim her as wife."

"Are there any that would oppose such a bonding?"

"Fuck 'em if they do," Flynn rumbled softly. She bit back a laugh at Lot's glare.

He raised his voice again. "Kara, daughter of Nora and Beritram, do you renounce your House to join us in ours?"

Another burst of bile. "I, Kara Jester, renounce my House to become Kara Scot."

"Then add your name to ours and be welcomed."

Flynn knelt down, and Lot rested the Bible across his shoulders. Kara's fingers trembled as she signed the ancient page. Lot took the book back, and Flynn stood, slipping a pair of signets from his pocket and handing her one.

He slid the other onto her finger, and she did the same for him, then held out her palm. Lot nicked it with a small blade, then Flynn's. She laced her fingers through his, the wounds pressing together. Lot was speaking again, but it was lost in that hum between them—

Flynn wasn't paying attention either. He pulled her close, those motes churning. His nose brushing hers. "You know."

"I do."

He kissed her like they were the only ones in the room, skating his fingers down her bare back, rumbling with surprised pleasure. She melted against him, her arms around his neck.

Lot cleared his throat. Twice.

Flynn pulled away with that rakish grin, and Kara blushed scarlet. They turned to face the room and after a hesitant start, the crowd clapped three times. Then they lined up by House in front of the dais. Flynn's grin didn't fade an iota throughout the tedious introduction of every last one of them. After what seemed like hours, the Houses stepped back into their original places and Flynn cleared his throat.

"Kara Scot, née Jester, is now bound to me by blood and name. From all that was hidden, all is now revealed. She is of House Scot and Shade."

"She is of House Scot and Shade." The crowd intoned, bowing their heads.

"This is Kara Scot. This is my wife!" Flynn caught her up in his arms again, and she laughed. When he set her back down, every halo in the room had been extinguished, and a few Houses had disappeared. The rest milled about as servants entered with trays of food and drink.

Flynn touched her cheek, and his own halos winked out with hers. He spun her around, and swore. "No wonder everyone was having a fit."

"You like it?" she asked, beaming at him.

"Of course he likes it," Cal said, lighting his cigarette beside the dais. "We all saw how much, now knock it off." Flynn grinned at him, unrepentant, his fingertips leaving a trail of prickles down her spine. Cal shook his head. "Binders have just come in, they're over there by the musicians."

There weren't very many of them. It looked like maybe six small Houses. Flynn gave her a squeeze, and they made their way over.

A tall man stepped forward at their approach, bowing low. "Lord Scot, Thank you for inviting us. I apologize for doubting—" The man frowned at the sharp jab of an elbow from the woman at his side.

"Enough of that vile rumor, Louis." A severe woman at his side made a perfunctory curtsy. "Well, go on, introduce us."

"Lady Janice and Lord Louis Ketsing, First of our line in Glynfyls." He took Kara's hand and brushed his lips across her knuckles. Janice stiffened, flipping open one of those fans. The other women behind her did the same, like they were all connected by some bizarre hive-mind.

Kara ran a hand down her stomach, feeling their censure. What had she done? "I-I'm so very happy to meet you."

Louis inclined his head. "And we, you—"

Janice snapped her fan shut, and the man's smile faltered. "I want to see the binds you used to heal the damage in those photos—what Louis? I've no desire to wait the better part of the year once she's bred." The woman's sparse lips thinned further. "I doubt it will take long."

Kara took a step back, Flynn's arm wrapping around her waist. He grinned. "Nope, no time at all if I have anything to say about it." The woman's fan snapped back up, and there were gasps from the others. He turned to Louis. "If you'll excuse us?"

"Of course, Lord Scot." The poor man winced, gripping Janice's arm as they escaped.

Flynn steered Kara to the dance floor.

"What was that?" No wonder the Ladies hadn't included her at their table, the woman was awful, and the rest of them…

"A green-eyed monster rearing its ugly head. Ready to dance?"

The orchestra started up a waltz as he led her onto the parquet floor. The space was magical, a glade amongst citrus trees festooned in fairy lights. Flynn's face was aglow with delight after the first few stanzas. They glided across the floor, nothing else in the universe but the two of them and the music…

Kara was startled when it stopped. He rested his forehead against hers, smiling.

"Another?"

She nodded, wishing she could spend the entire night in his arms.

TITUS SIPPED HIS BOURBON, eyeing the latest nanobot feed to go live. Another sub. Though the man and the rest of his ilk were of no interest genetically, they provided an unprecedented indication of the city's temperament, in particular, the unrest amongst the outer rungs.

If he was unable to topple the city from the top, he'd rot it from beneath them.

His cell had been very successful agitating the populace, especially after the demolition order went into effect. As of now, it was exclusively subs fleeing, and Titus was more than content to let the wheat separate itself from the chaff.

Of the handful of lesser metropolises scattered about the Northern Territories, all but Riesdale had a solidly established chapter of Sons. That's where Talents would shift when they began evacuating—

Brix stalked into his office, a smirk across his ugly face.

"You have something for me?"

"Ocean freighters. They've been using them as jump points to move supplies."

"And?"

"They won't be anymore."

"Excellent. See that it remains that way." The Breaker saluted and left.

Titus tapped his lips, pleased. Hoarding and price gouging was on the uptick, with the poorer sections of the city already seeing a spike in bread prices. With supplies well and truly cut off, it was only a matter of time before panic ensued. His cell would guarantee that, and Scot's lavish party tonight was already creating a backlash with the lower rungs. Titus smirked. Perhaps he should have a plan in place to send up troops under the guise of a humanitarian effort. The thought made him chuckle. Wouldn't that be rich?

Another feed popped up, Riegel infecting a whore. This one was of decent quality, or had been before he'd dislocated her jaw. The boost was making him unstable faster than anticipated. It was a good thing Scot was slated to be at that dismal little brothel tomorrow night. The last time Riegel looked into the mirror the scoring in his eyes had been severe. Once his halos bled into cataracts he'd be on borrowed time, and at this rate, he wouldn't last the week.

Nor would Ielle. Titus had been banking on her libido overruling his instructions, but her choice to debase herself at the same venue Riegel had established himself at was unfortunate. Titus had no illusions as to how that reunion would end. Still, she was doing an admirable job at spreading his little spies.

He pulled her feed closer, watching her ride the corpulent man beneath her. Given what the man was packing, Titus had difficulty believing her enthusiasm.

A holo chimed, and a visual of a lavish ballroom sprang into view. Ah. It was about time his operative began transmitting. Titus's eyebrows rose at the glass-paned walls and multitiered crystal chandeliers illuminating the aristocracy below.

Servants bearing silver platters threaded through the sumptuously dressed crowd. It seemed the rumors of the Scot's vast fortune were well-founded. All spoils for the coming war.

By far the largest man in the room, Laughlin was easy to pick out. Titus zoomed in on him and the Jester girl, pausing mid-sip.

She was absolutely breathtaking. That veneer of timidity she'd portrayed in holos had been shed, an aura of confidence bolstering her appeal a hundred-fold. The need to possess her seared through him. The way she gazed up at Scot with those adoring eyes—

And he back at her.

Titus tapped the side of his bourbon, pensive. A nasty smile contorted his lips. Perhaps all was not lost with the Assembly. He composed a change of directive to Barton, ordering him to leave breadcrumbs when he removed her. The more public her abduction, the better. The man wouldn't like it, but Titus didn't care.

Wherever she went, Scot would follow.

IELLE RAPPED on the door of the apartment, eager for it to open. Suppression meds well out of her system, her body was frantic to be bred. It had translated into a work ethic that'd delighted that nasty little man Gerrard, especially with the influx of customers anticipating the fight. If this door ever opened, it would make over a dozen johns tonight.

None of them had been anything to write home about.

Although certainly degrading enough to suit her tastes, her recent liaisons had lacked that delicious shiver of fear… She sighed, flipping her hair over her shoulder. *What I wouldn't give for a decent lay…* A smile slid across her lips, thinking of Riegel kenneled in whatever hole Titus had stuffed him in. Glynfyls' men were weak sauce in comparison…but this one held promise.

Trammel had run through three of Gerrard's girls in rapid succession and had treated none of them gently. They said he was a hulking brute of a man, and he'd ruined two of them for the next few weeks. If he wasn't slated to fight tomorrow, Gerrard would've thrown him out after he dislocated Melanie's jaw, never mind Keely's arm… though in Ielle's opinion, it was the whore master's own fault for keeping his ringer under lock and key for the past few days. The poor man must be all pent up… She licked her lips just thinking about it.

Ielle went to knock again, and the door swung open. She walked in and it shut behind her, the bolt sliding home. Like the others, he'd requested she not look at him or speak. She sauntered to the window, feeling his eyes on her. A pair of large hands, knuckles thick with bloodied scabs encircled her waist.

Ielle smiled, scraping her nails across them and making them weep. His fingers tightened, digging in painfully. She gasped, his erection pressing into her back. He lifted a hand and pointed to a scarf lying on the sill. Ielle picked it up and handed it to him over her shoulder, whimpering as he tightened it painfully across her eyes.

A finger ran down the ties of her corset, then yanked the sides apart. Her breath caught as the boning popped, cheap satin shredding. It hit the floor and those hands were on the wispy muslin of her under-gown, then rending the buttons from her skirt. It pooled about her ankles.

His fist gripped her hair, tilting her head. Lips and teeth along her throat. Ielle shuddered, her body afire with need. He pulled the tie of her under-gown, and it fell away, leaving her nude in the chilly little room.

The rough callouses of his hands tore across her skin, a sudden blow catching her across the temple. She fell to the floor, tasting blood. He ground her cheek into the floor boards, mounting her from behind. Ielle moaned ecstatically. Finally—

Something sharp pricked her buttock.

Her throat constricted, robbing her of her pleasure, furious gurgles passing her lips, limbs leaden as he took his. Ielle raged—all that anticipation for this? She'd never been a fan of necro-play, though she'd done it enough. Bored, she waited for him to finish.

A laugh. Familiar…

He pulled her up against his chest and yanked off the blindfold. Her head lolled as he softly kissed her cheek, hefting her onto the stained mattress.

"You're right darling, it is a pity you can't scream."

Riegel.

Her bowels released, and he tsked. "A side effect of the paralytic, but you know all about that, don't you?" He sat, moving her head into his lap and gently stroking her hair.

Oh, Rie… her heart constricted. Something was very wrong with his eyes…

"I didn't expect you here, but when one of the others described the new girl whoring… I knew you were asking to be punished. I never could deny you, and you know you have to pay for what you've done, my love. I think you'll enjoy most of it. I know I will." He lifted her up, tenderly kissing away her tears.

Ielle's shiver of fear bloomed to terror.

ANOTHER DANCE ENDED, and Flynn laughed, running a thumb over Kara's dimple and kissing her. Damn. She was fucking perfect.

And she was his.

"You know we're going to have to talk to people at some point," she said breathlessly.

"Yeah. Miriam's been glaring at me for the past half-hour, but I'd rather be out here."

Kara laughed. "Me too, but these shoes are killing me."

"Take 'em off."

"Can I?"

He knelt down and slid one off, rubbing her instep. "You can do whatever your ladyship wants."

"I'm not going to argue." She kicked off the other, and he grabbed them, standing. "I never would've figured you for a dancer back at the coop."

Flynn snorted. "At the coop I could barely—"

"Do you mind if I borrow him, Kara?" Shelby asked, materializing out of the crowd. "They're going to play a foxtrot."

"Not at all, I want to see this."

He handed Kara her shoes and took his cousin by the hand. The music started, Shelby moving like liquid, pinching his arm to correct him. He grinned, not caring—*Oops.* He messed up a turn, and she glared at him. Flynn laughed. He'd forgotten how pissed she got. The piece ended, and Shelby washed her hands of him, a red-headed man claiming her for the rest of the set. Miriam was beside Kara, frowning as she watched them samba.

"Who is that guy?" he asked his aunt. "He's good."

"I should hope so, she's been partnered to Paul for the past year." Miriam eyed Flynn critically. "You're a bit rusty, but not too bad."

"Wait—Paul Morris?" She had to be fucking kidding.

Her mouth pinched down into frog-mode. "Leave it alone, Laughlin."

Shelby's face was radiant. Christ, that wasn't gonna end well. A grin split his at Paul's expression. No, it wasn't. Peterli Morris had to be shitting nails his son was cozying up to Shelby.

"What's there to eat?" Flynn waved over a servant carrying a tray of canapés, loading as many as he could onto a napkin.

"Good Lord, Laughlin, those are appetizers, not the meal! Everything's laid out in the dining room!" His aunt's gaze darted around as if to see if anyone had noticed him take half the tray.

He shrugged, chewing. Mmm. Shrimp something. It was well past midnight, and most of the guests left had taken liberal advantage of the open bar. He doubted if any of them would care if they had seen.

Miriam shooed him toward the doorway. He rolled his eyes, offering Kara his arm. Even with the thinner crowd, it took forever to cross the room. Christ, maybe because of that. Each group they passed wanted to offer congratulations that digressed into personal anecdotes.

Charles approached, interrupting another lady's lengthy description of her wedding gown. Thank God. "Laughlin, you remember Bryan." The Breaker at his side bowed, his extremely well-tailored aubergine suit popping against his burnished skin.

Flynn returned it, and Kara inclined her head to them both. "Of course, I was surprised you didn't bring him up to be introduced."

"We had quite a tiff about it on the way over, I can assure you. I told him you wouldn't have an issue with it, but he's such a traditionalist." Charles huffed. Bryan rolled his eyes.

"Well, let me present you to my wife, Kara. Kara, this is Bryan, Charles's partner."

"Lovely to meet you both." She smiled, taking his hand.

"I'm supposed to give you Jacques' regrets; they have Bea on strict bedrest. The only way she'd stay home was if he did, too. She's furious about it." He eyed Flynn critically. "I certainly would be, missing you all dolled up like this." Bryan gave him a look, and Charles laughed. "Mistress Glass designed his suit as well, and I have to say, I'm very pleased with her work. I'm seriously considering jumping ship on Aimes."

Bryan smoothed his lapels with obvious satisfaction. "She's got a good eye, and it's refreshing to see someone thinking outside the box up here. Have you read Tyndall's recent essays on the stagnation of our culture? They're—"

"Exceedingly boring," Charles interrupted.

"No, I'm afraid I haven't had much time for reading anything outside of proposals. He still publishing in *The Quarterly*?" Flynn asked, ignoring Charles's moue.

"No, they censured him a few years back, he's at a limited press now. I'll send you what I have. Really thought provoking stuff."

"I'd appreciate that, I always liked his work." Flynn's stomach growled, and Charles sighed.

"I swear Laughlin, you eat more than a Breaker. We won't keep you, I know how testy you get when you miss a meal. Besides, I need to get Bryan on the dance floor for at least one waltz." The larger man bit back a smile as they walked away.

"They seem nice. Why didn't he come up?"

"Bryan's a common and their bond isn't recognized by our line. They met when he was working security at some event Charles's House was hosting. It was a huge scandal, I dunno, twenty years ago or so."

"Oh… Why didn't you tell me about Shelby?"

"Not my place to. She's really sensitive about it." How the hell she got partnered with Lord Morris's son… Flynn pulled Kara into his arms, spinning her down the hallway to the dining room. She laughed, and he stopped to kiss her, fingers finding that stretch of skin…

"I do like the dress. You're lucky I'm not a jealous man."

Kara raised an eyebrow. "Oh, really?"

"Well, not very jealous." He amended, kissing her again. A finger dipped below where the fabric ended. She gasped against his lips, his body responding. This fucking woman—

"Another hour or so, boy." Cal's acid tone cut through the air. "Now, move it, you're gumming up the works."

Flynn shot him a look. If he wanted to kiss his wife, he was gonna kiss his wife, especially tonight. The old man made a shooing motion, and they proceeded him into the dining room.

A buffet spanning two walls had been set up. Flynn filled his plate as high as it would go, smiling at Kara's mound of smoked fish. They sat, and he started slapping his gleanings between dinner rolls.

"I'm pretty sure you're going to have to unhinge your jaws to eat that," Kara said wryly.

Waggling his eyebrows, he took a huge bite just for her. Cal snorted, taking a seat.

Leo ambled over with a snifter of brandy. "Quite the party, Laughlin." He plopped down beside Cal, pie-eyed.

Shit. His cousin was either an absolute bastard when he was drunk or your best friend… Flynn relaxed an iota, spotting Miriam headed their way. Leo was less likely to be a dick when she was around.

Which still meant it was pretty likely.

"Thank your mother, Arileo, she set it all up."

"Thanks, Ma." Leo raised his glass to her as she bustled over to their table, brows knit.

"Have you had anything to eat, Leo?"

He laughed. "Fruits and grain."

"Why do you use Flynn's full name, but not Leo and Graham's?" Kara asked.

"Because he was always gonna be First, and that's what his mother named him. My boys can afford to be familiar. Laughlin needs to set a proper precedent."

Leo drained his glass. "Yeah, Laughlin's the one everyone needs to be impressed with."

Ah, shit. They were getting the bastard.

"Well, they certainly seem to be. Four more Fetch Houses have asked to pledge."

Flynn choked down his mouthful. Christ.

"Try to act a little less miserable about it. It's time to grab the reins, boy."

He shot his grandfather a sour look. Easier said than done with Markham in Crandall's back pocket, and that weaselly shit just waiting for him to fuck up.

"Well, isn't that a pretty package wrapped with a bow. Like fucking everything else, you get Glynfyls delivered on a silver platter, and it's not good enough," Leo sneered. "But hey, why stop at Overlord? Pretty soon it'll be King Scot. Just watch him around the help, Kara. He has a tendency to fuck them before you've left the room, just ask Julia. Or wait, you can see the reel."

The room seared crimson, and Flynn lunged across the table, just missing the motherfucker's collar before he shifted away. He gripped his temples, soaked in sweat and swearing. He ignored Kara's hand on his heaving back, dashing his plate across the table and stalking to the windows, trying to pull up zero to quash the haze—sparks of scarlet danced across his vision—

Goddamn that motherfucking prick!

In the window's reflection, people made a hasty exit from the room. He pinched the bridge of his nose, regulating his breathing. The pain slowly dissipated, but a weird burn remained. His stomach knotted, pretty sure he knew what that meant.

He was running out of time.

"That boy's a bastard when he drinks, Miriam," Cal said, taking a drag of his cigarette like they'd just been discussing the weather. She stared at her hands, pale.

Flynn turned away from the window, pulling at his hair. Forget about the rest of tonight, that shit show was gonna be front page news, and Kara—

He met her eyes, and his anger drained out of him, leaving him tired and more than a little sad. He walked over and brushed a hand across her cheek. She pressed it to his palm, then stood without a word and led him upstairs to the bower.

He sat on the stones at the lip of the pool, watching the fish weave beneath the lilies.

"Tell me what just happened."

"Leo—"

"No, with you. What did I just feel, Flynn?"

He grimaced. "It's that red haze I told you about. Rogan says I'm a split. Every time I lose my temper, I dunno. Some bullshit about another channel—"

"I'm pulling talent, and you're going to sit there and let me."

"Kara—" Shit. The look on her face… "Yeah, okay."

Her halos glimmered. "It's not bullshit. Does it hurt?"

"It'll hurt more when they fucking lynch me for being a twist. He said pulling zero will slow it down, but that it's gonna happen…" He bit at his lip, unable to meet her eyes.

"What else?"

"I-I could lose my talent. I don't know what that would do to us… the baby… Christ, I've been trying not to think about it at all. If I can take Overlord first—shit, Kara. I don't know what to do. There's not anything *to* fucking do."

She chewed on her thumb. "I could bind it."

His eyes jumped to hers. Was she serious?

"I can see where it just tore, Flynn. It's not going to take much for the rest to go…"

He wet his lips. "Would it take a lot of talent?"

Kara shook her head. "More finesse than anything. When Talents got brought into the Infirmary, sometimes we had to bind their channels to stop them from reflexively pulling during a procedure. I mean, it's not like you're going to be able to flip out like that again, but it'll withstand an initial knee-jerk reaction." She rolled her eyes when he hesitated. "With all the jellies and shots I've been taking, I feel fine. Trust me, I don't want to exhaust myself either. I swear I won't overdo it."

Flynn raked a hand through his hair. It was a goddamned band-aid, but if it would buy him time… "Okay. Do it."

Her halos flared, and a pressure eased that he hadn't realized he'd been feeling. That weird burn disappeared with it. She tipped his chin. "You call up zero as soon as you feel that haze coming on. The bind isn't meant to hold more than a few seconds." He nodded. "Ready for a test?"

"A test?"

"Yeah, tell me about the reel."

Fuck. He was hoping she'd give him a pass on that, but the look in her face said that wasn't happening. "Leo—I don't know who took it or how he got ahold of it, but he was the one who showed it to me afterwards." Christ, thinking about it still made him wanna puke.

"Do you think it was him?"

Flynn shrugged. "Not that he'll admit."

Kara sat beside him, frowning. He slumped, head hanging toward his knees. Goddamn, he was a fuck up. "I'm assuming everyone's seen it?" He nodded. "Was that what was in the papers?"

"Yeah. Stills. Recaps. Christ, Kara, I didn't—I don't want you to think of me like that."

She sighed, smoothing her dress over her knees. "When you said you spoke with Cal about how things were at the Source… I was afraid you'd seen holos of me. How I was."

"No. It was some shareholder's thing."

She nodded, rubbing his back. "Neither of us are the same person, and I think… I think that's the best way to look at it. I was a sad, scared girl, and you were lost, Flynn. They can't hurt us with it unless we let them, and I'm tired of hurting. I want to be happy." She put a hand to her abdomen. "I want us to be happy."

His chest got tight. "You really mean that?"

"Yeah, I think I do…but full disclosure, I did use talent tonight. This dress won't stay up without it."

He gathered her up into his arms. "What did I tell you I was gonna do if you pulled again?"

"Mmm, I think keeping that reel from me cancels it out, but I'll let you spank me if it makes you feel better." He laughed, and she trailed a hand down his cheek. "You were really going to kill Leo."

Flynn sighed, not proud of that slip. "He brings out the worst in me. He's always been pissed Jon stepped down as heir in favor of Lot. If he hadn't, Graham would probably be head by now."

"That doesn't make any sense. Graham doesn't seem to care and would be lousy at it."

"You're not wrong, Leo's just…ambitious, I guess. More Prydee than Scot. I dunno. I gave up trying to figure out how the hell his mind works a long time ago. I'm sorry I lost it like that…" His teeth worried his lip. "Kara, if I lose my talent, our bond—"

"Shh…I don't care. I didn't go into this thinking you were talented. I'd miss our echo, but it's you I love, not your cloak. Besides, it's stupid to worry about this right now, and if you want my professional opinion, that's not going to happen."

"Really?"

"Would I lie to you?"

He snorted. "I hope all that didn't ruin the night for you."

"Your cousin's a jerk. He hits on me shamelessly when you're not around."

"Seriously? If I catch him bothering you, I'll beat the shit out of him."

"I thought you said you weren't jealous?"

"I said I wasn't very jealous." Kissing her fiercely, he swept her up in his arms and carried her into the bedroom.

CHAPTER TWENTY-SIX

Valkyrie [ˈval-k(ə-)rē] noun

1. *One of the nine warrior handmaidens of the Alpha Prime, known for their viciousness in battle, often exceeding that of their male counterparts.*

– Excerpt from The Way of Honor

"The shield wall was created by the original seven Talents, and like the gates, the secret to its creation has been lost to time. Once capable of repelling invasion by physical and talent-based means, less reliable accounts also allude to its dubious ability to phase the city and its populace. Now completely defunct, all that remains is the crumbling edifice surrounding the inner city, an eyesore as opposed to a mythical defense..."

– Lord Talos, Preceptor of History,
Academy of Glynfyls

THEY SAT IN THE BOWER, finishing a leisurely brunch after spending the morning in bed. That was something Kara could get used to. She smiled, glancing up through her lashes at Flynn. He was frowning, scanning through the long list of Introduction gifts that had been delivered with their meal. He tossed the sheets onto the table.

"More fealty pledges. Shit, I don't want this." He laughed sourly, digging the heels of his hands into his eyes. "I don't want any of this."

She came around the table and kneaded his shoulders.

Sighing, he leaned back against her. "Cal must be doing a jig right now. I get that people are looking for someone to take charge, but why the hell does it have to be me?"

"Maybe they all see you like I do, extremely capable." She moved to the base of his neck, his hair just curling over her fingers. She gave it a little tug and kissed his ear.

"Mmm. Must be why they didn't invite me to that planning meeting." He finished his coffee. "Fuck 'em. Ready for your first day of freedom? I thought we'd start with a quick trip into the city."

"I'm ready to do anything that gets me out of this house."

He offered her his arm, laughing. They went downstairs, collecting heavy boots and thick jackets, then stepped through the gate and out onto a crowded city street.

She recoiled against him at the crush of people, the quiet of Meddleton abruptly replaced by the clash and din of humanity. Flynn grunted at the teeming street, cars clogging the center of the avenue.

"I don't remember this part of town being so busy…huh. Come on, we're only about a block from the Guild." A stiff breeze riffled his hair, and he raked it back, muttering something about his beanie.

Kara moved under his arm, there were far more people out here than she was comfortable with and the buildings… She eyed them listing above, long ropes of laundry hanging like pennants from windows caked with frozen grey slop and long spears of ice.

Flynn squeezed her shoulder, pulling her close. "Weird, right? Don't worry, they're all fixed, you'll get used to it, and the smell."

She didn't see that happening. It was so different than the Source… she shivered against him. Traffic started to move through the slushy street, a passing car sending out a huge cloud of exhaust. She coughed, the air was thick enough to chew.

A group of people stepped back, watching them pass. Flynn tensed, meeting one of the men's eyes with a nod. The man continued to stare. Kara colored, her eyes dropping to the grimy sidewalk. Everything was a uniform shade of squalor.

The people hurrying by were bundled in rough woolens of the same hue, their expressions strained. Flynn stopped at a steaming cart, speaking with a man in an apron. A woman came along, dragging a screaming child by his ear. No one seemed to notice him thrashing against her. She cuffed him, and Kara lost them in the press. He'd been so little—

"Here." Flynn handed her a crumpled paper bag. Her fingers pulled back at its heat, and he laughed. "They cool quick, try one." He reached in and popped a bunch of the nuclear little missiles into his mouth, crunching.

Kara pinched one out, dubious, but he was right. About the temperature at least. The spice on it lit her up. She fanned at her mouth, and he laughed again.

"Spiced nuts. You can't get them like this anywhere else."

"Wonder why." Glory, she'd started to sweat—he handed her a paper cup and she took a long swallow of cider. That was really good. "You keep those. I'll keep this." He grinned, chomping another handful.

They walked on, and Flynn took her up the steps of a squat building. He opened the door, her heart leaping at his smile. Whatever the Guild was, he was really excited about it.

The walls inside were a dingy tan and a light in the hallway flickered like a strobe, the linoleum worn down to the subfloor in places. The door chunked shut behind them, a faint hum audible with the noise from the street cut off. He took her hand, their boots echoing down a dim hallway to a set of double doors. He grabbed a couple pairs of clear glasses from a bin.

"Safety first." The low hum increased as they entered a large factory space. A man operating a vehicle with prongs zipped by, and other people milled about purposefully. The sloped floor was marked with colored lines bringing them below ground.

"Stay in the blue ones," Flynn said, noticing her gaze. "The others are for the machine operators or test areas like that one there."

A large glass cube was in the middle of the mayhem. Several people with clipboards stood around it, observing what was going on inside, which didn't look like much of anything.

A very thin gray-haired woman came over when she saw them. "Laughlin! Sorry I missed you at Assembly, but I couldn't tear myself away."

"I'd expect nothing else." He grinned, giving her a quick hug. "Lord Klein said you've made some progress?"

"Yes, go have a look. Giles can get you up to speed. You must be the new Lady Scot." She offered her hand, Flynn wandering over to talk to one of the men. "Jesse Mayfield, proctor of Glynfyls' Engineering Guild. It's a pleasure to meet you."

"Please, call me Kara… I'm sorry, but he didn't tell me why—"

"No. He wouldn't." Jesse's smile faltered. "Laughlin's always been far too humble about his intellect. We've missed him, and I'm excited to pick your brain as well. Come, tell me if any of this seems familiar to you." She took Kara's arm and walked her over to the cube.

"We've been experimenting with crystals at different voltages. This morning Jonas made a blip." She laughed. "I know it doesn't sound very exciting, but trust me, it's a big deal."

A large piece of masonry was in the center of the cube, the middle of it bored out to form a cup. A crystal was fixed in its center. Kara chewed her thumb, no idea what she was looking at.

"It's part of the shield wall," Flynn said, returning to her side. "Our histories say it worked kind of like a nullifier, but was talent based. During the Great Incursion most of the city was destroyed, and no one's been able to figure out how it's functioned since."

"I don't know how I can help, I've never worked with structural binds."

"Our Binders can't detect any of the old weaves. Are you able to?" Jesse asked.

"I—" Kara caught Flynn's eye, and he shrugged. Really?

"Just look."

She couldn't help her cheeks from dimpling as she pulled talent. Ugh, it felt so good to be useful again... Faint lines of gossamer webbed around where they'd situated the crystal. No wonder the Binders couldn't see them, they barely existed.

"Yeah...they're there, it looks like the crystal sat in a matrix..." Kara frowned. The structure was completely foreign. What was it supposed to do? "Can I have a piece of paper?"

Jesse handed her a clipboard, and Kara sat, sketching out what she was seeing. The rest of them launched into a discussion using technical jargon that might have well been in a different language. Flynn spoke it fluently, and they were all intent on his comments. She smiled, concentrating on her sketch.

Above the stone, binds wove into a sphere of twelve threads, equidistant apart. Below they were all mangled, but had run throughout the material at some point. She tapped her lip with the pencil. It kind of reminded her of a lung reconstruction she'd seen Nora do. The top part at least.

"I think the bind around the crystal was meant to move, like flex beyond the confines of the stone, outward. Fixing would stop it from doing that."

"Interesting theory. Those crystals are supposed to vibrate, but we've been going on the assumption that the cup channels the force downward. Can you recreate it?" Jesse asked, taking the clipboard back.

"I—"

"Not today." Flynn helped Kara up. "Giles will have to use the sketch. We've gotta get ready for our big date."

"Oh yes, the bout's tonight isn't it? I didn't mean to keep you so long, but, well, you know how it goes." She shook his hand again. "It's so good to have you back. I hope we see both of you again soon."

They took their leave. When they got back up to street level, Kara was surprised to see it was well past noon. Her nose crinkled. The wind had kicked up, bringing a horrendous funk with it.

"That's the Pinch. Just wait until spring." Flynn laughed. "So what did you think?"

"I think you're quite the Renaissance man, Laughlin Scot. Jesse seems nice."

He smiled down into his beard, like he was pleased by her answer. "She is, and driven. If anyone can figure out how those things are supposed to work, it's her." He chewed his lower lip. "If she can't, we're in trouble. Up until the Great Incursion, it kept the Source at bay for like six hundred years."

"How did they get past it?"

Flynn shrugged. "Nothing about that time's real well documented, but for whatever reason it didn't go up. Some people think that's on the Overlord, but I can't imagine he was that incompetent."

They stepped through the gate and into Meddleton's foyer.

Cal was waiting for them.

"Do you know why the shield wall wasn't deployed during the Great Incursion?"

He glared at her. "Somebody defaced a bunch of cups, and the whole thing fell to shit. In my office, now." Kara's jaw dropped as he stalked off. What the heck had that been about?

Flynn kissed the top of her head. "Sore subject. I'm surprised he answered at all. Let's go see why else he's pissed."

They walked in as Cal seated himself behind his desk. "Leo's gone dark, and the other two can't find him. Little bastard's hanging us both out to dry. He was supposed to make a run for me, and I don't want you going tonight without a Fetch you can rely on—"

"That motherfucker. I'm having problems thinking of anyone off the top of my head, you got any ideas?" Flynn asked, pulling zero. Kara covertly eyed his channel. The combination of talent and technique was working well together.

"Graham's been dating a Fetch. He left a while ago to see if she'd be willing." Flynn looked poleaxed, and Cal chuckled. "Boy might not have swagger, but he's got game. Your cousin's one hell of a poet."

Flynn burst out laughing. "The only poetry of his I've ever heard was a raunchy limerick once when he was drunk."

What? Graham? Kara didn't know if him being drunk or raunchy shocked her more. She shot Flynn a disbelieving look.

He grinned. "True story."

"I was appealing to your lowbrow sense of humor." Graham walked in and took a seat by the fire. "Celine'll meet us here at eight. She's looking forward to doing some empirical research. I gave her the imprint of the back entrance."

Flynn blinked at him. Empirical research at a whore house?

"And that other thing I asked you about?" Cal snapped, lighting a cigarette.

Graham scratched at his temple. "The distance is a problem. Commons can't make it in single jump, and I don't have an imprint of anything else that can get us around the curtains."

"Goddamn it, I needed a Fetch down there hours ago!" He slammed one of his desk drawers shut and raked a hand through his hair. Kara pressed closer to Flynn. She'd never seen Alban—Cal—so riled.

"What about that Fitz kid? He's Original House, and your cousin, isn't he?"

"Yes, he is," Cal said, brightening at Flynn's suggestion. Graham looked like he wanted to crawl into a hole. "Find him, and whatever Markham's paying you to move goods, triple it. I need that job done, pronto." Graham looked like he was gonna protest, but Cal's expression shut it down quick. He slunk out of the room, muttering.

Kara looked between the two of them. "Why's he upset about it?"

"House Matter," Cal said, pouring himself a glass of scotch. "I still think this bout is a damned fool move, boy."

"Won't be the first or the last. That it?" Cal grunted, waving a hand at him, and Flynn grinned at her. "Come on, I got you something." He tugged her from the room, his face lit up with excitement.

Kara laughed, following him into the lift. "What else could I possibly want?"

He waggled his eyebrows and took off running toward the bower as soon as the doors opened back up. She caught him in the bedroom, digging in his closet. He pulled out one of Reggie's boxes.

"Up here it's traditional to exchange gifts after the ceremony—"

"I know, I have something for you, too."

"You do?"

"Yes." She laughed at his expression and retrieved a much smaller box from under the cushion in the kitten's basket. "Hiss has been keeping it safe."

"Hiss? Well, that sure as hell fits—" He held the box out to her.

"No. You first. Don't make me sic him on you."

"Freaking cat is always stealing my thunder," he grumbled, tearing at the paper… His fingers shook as he pulled out his beanie. It didn't look as good as it would've if she'd bound it, but it was a far cry from where it had been. You could actually tell they were wolves howling along the brim. "How did you…"

"Miriam helped me. She shifted the yarn back into place and showed me how to stitch it—No! Don't look at that part, I messed up, and it's lumpy."

"No…it's perfect. Thank you Kara, I—" He rubbed his thumb over her work, then dashed a hand over his eyes and laughed. "Christ. Your turn. Open it. No, come on, I'm fine. Open it."

She lifted the lid and pushed back the paper. What—?

"I know you said it's different down South, but up here, female Breakers fight alongside the men, and you are definitely as fierce as the Valkyries in my grandmother's stories. They had a kind of uniform. All I could remember was something about 'winged leathers of night,' but Reggie dug up a description. She said this is pretty close."

Kara pulled out the inky leather pants and stood, holding them against herself. They'd ride low, and were studded with pockets and buckles.

"Tell me you don't hate them."

"Hate them?" The top was a riff on a flak vest. She ran her hand across it, filled with a weird longing. "No, it's seriously bad-ass, but there's no way I can wear this to tea with the Ladies—"

"No, but you can wear it to bout in."

"To bout…?" Was he serious? She searched his face.

"Tonight, at the Pony. I gave my word I'd be there, but Firsts can't enter into competitions. There's nothing that prevents their wives from it, though… I mean, if you wanted to."

"I've never fought in an arena." Her pulse jumped at the thought of a real competition.

"There's gonna be a big crowd. You okay with that?"

She bit her lip. "I think so. It's different when I'm on the mats. I never needed to worry about hiding who I was there. But Audrey—you really want everyone to know? What will people say?"

"Kara, I don't give a flying fuck about what anyone says, it's a part of who you are…" His mouth twisted. "I'm not gonna keep you on a shelf."

She bowled him over, wrapping her arms around his neck and kissing him, his amusement at her excitement coloring their bond. She laughed. He was really ok with her Breaker abilities!

"Damn, woman." He grinned, running his thumb across her dimple. "Two things, Gerrard can't know this is a set up, and I need a promise out of you. I was serious about practicing zero, and Rogan will be there, so we'll both know if you slip."

"I won't. I got a handle on it." Her brow furrowed at that look he got… "What else?"

"It's just—You were right about setting the tone. We've gotta send a message to anyone who's tempted to cash in on our past."

She batted her lashes at him. "Like with those women still sending you notes?"

His eyes narrowed. "You're not—"

"Reading them?" She tried to look scandalized. "No…but Audrey's been compiling a list of authors for me."

Flynn laughed. "Full disclosure, French has got a running list of the assholes sending you shit, too, and some of those, I do read."

She gaped at him. Men were sending—"Anything good?"

He reached for her. "Nothing I can't do better."

"You sure about that?"

His hand tangled in her hair, fisting. The subtle scent of his bloodlust tinged the air as his lips teased hers. "That a challenge?"

"You want it to be?" Kara's pulse sped, her thighs clenching.

"Oh baby, you got no idea…" His halos flared, phasing their clothes, and he was on his back, lifting her to straddle his face. Flynn's hand cracked down across her ass, and Kara cried out, gripping the headboard as he feasted. She rocked above him, head falling back, her long hair dusting over his chest.

Strong fingers dug into her hips, keeping her in place as she writhed above him. She tilted back, hand gripping this rigid cock. "Please Flynn… I want it in my mouth…"

"Want what, baby?" he murmured against her slick core, lapping.

"Your cock. Please…"

"Mmm." He flipped her around, and she squealed. "Take it. Whoever comes first loses."

"Wha—oh!" she gasped, his face burying between her cheeks…

Kara gripped his wide shaft, tongue rimming around the crown, the rumble of his moan sending tremors through her body. She tongued his slit, lapping at the salty musk of his arousal, then sucking him through taut lips. *Whoever comes first, huh?*

Flynn paused, his hands tightening on her hips, fingers dimpling her flesh with a muffled "Fuck…" then his pace increased, fingers at her clit, circling to pinch.

She cried out around his cock, bucking back against him, the echo of their mutual pleasure increasing the stakes in their game. Her mouth descended again, drawing him into the back of her throat a hand reaching to caress his sac, and he growled, a hand slapping down on her ass.

Kara laughed, his dick kicking against her tongue, and pulled the barest threat of talent…

He groaned, driving himself deep, cock throbbing… salt and seed spurted, filling her mouth. She drank it down, lapping it from his softening flesh—

"You're a fucking cheat!" He pulled her off him and whipped her around over his knee, spanking her. "The fuck did I say about you using talent?"

She laughed again, squirming. "You're just mad because I won!"

"Lies." Flynn threw her onto the bed, covering her, the light in his eyes belaying his stern expression. "Now I've got to punish you."

"Mmm… I guess you do."

His lips teased hers, Fingers threaded to clasp her hands in his, drawing her arms up over her head. "Do you have any idea how much I fucking love you?" he murmured, those blue motes churning through his irises.

Their bond thrummed with the emotion. Filling her. Filling him. Leaving no room for doubt.

"Yes," she said kissing him. "But I wouldn't mind a demonstration."

"I dunno. I thought I told you naughty girls don't get to come."

She pretended to pout. "You like me naughty."

"I like you anyway I can get you," he breathed, releasing her arms, lips at the hollow beneath her ear. "But no more talent."

"No more talent," she sighed, her hips moving to meet his hand. He swirled his fingers through her wetness, re-stoking the flames of her desire, delving deep and scissoring. She rode his hand, his mouth capturing her breast, and chased bliss.

MARCOS CRADLED NORA AGAINST HIM, brow furrowing at the raggedness of her breath. Frying those bots had done something to her, and it was getting worse. The flight from the tunnels and the trek through knee-high snow drifts and biting wind hadn't helped. Sitting on their asses beneath the false floor of a defunct garage for the past three days was just insult to injury.

It was also unsustainable.

The beeper on his watch went off, and he patted her cheek. Glory, she was burning up. "Rise and shine, beautiful."

Her eyelids fluttered. "Are they here?"

"No. You need to take some more of these damned things." For all the good they were doing. He handed her two more of the little white pills and held a bottle of water to her cracked lips. She finished what was left, and he tossed the empty into the corner with the others. If this damned Fetch didn't show up soon—Nora started coughing, and he didn't want to consider the alternative.

"Someone will come," she rasped when she'd caught her breath.

"That's what I'm worried about. We can't stay here. You need medical attention, and we've all but tapped this hole's cache of supplies. There's got to be somewhere—"

"There's not..." she wheezed. "Have faith, Marcos."

He grimaced. The only things he had faith in were his gun and that the sun would rise tomorrow, whether or not they'd be here to see it. He brushed back her fever-damp hair. To lose her like this—

"—I swear t'fuckin' Christ, ye Prydee shite!"

"Please, stop talking."

Footsteps above. Marcos eased his sidearm into his hand… The hatch lifted, and he sited on a skinny, dark-haired man.

The blond kid behind him laughed. "Aye, shoot him! One less of the—"

"Shut up!" The dark-haired one snapped over his shoulder. He turned back to them, exasperated. "Albanach sent us. You ready?"

"See Marcos…faith."

He frowned, less than impressed at their would-be saviors, but holstered his piece and lifted Nora up. "She's ill." The blond man shouldered the other out of the way, taking her. Marcos hefted himself up beside them.

"Shite, she's more'n ill, she needs a Binder," the blond kid muttered, his brow drawing together.

The dark-haired one scoffed. "Miriam can—"

"Nah, ain't a chance in hell I'm turning her over t'that harpy." Nora made a noise that could've been agreement. "Energy work ain't gonna cut it. Woman needs healing proper. Pithy'll set her straight."

"Pithy?!" The dark-haired man looked like the suggestion was akin to KP duty.

"Ye got a problem with that, Grantham? Common or no, man's got more talent in his little toe than all them hillies combined." The two of them glared at each other.

Marcos shouldered between them, cradling Nora's limp form against him again. She'd lapsed back into a fitful slumber.

Grantham stuck his finger in the other's face. "This is on you, Fitzpatrick."

"S'Fitz, ye shite."

"Whoever you are, let's go," Marcos growled.

The Fetch's halos flared and colors ran.

They stood in a cramped bubblegum pink room, a curtain of

mirrored disks flashing across a doorway. Grantham snorted in disgust, and Fitz shot him back a look of the same.

"Wait here." He pushed through the curtain, music thumping from the room beyond, the distinct tinge of intoxicants with it. It was preferable to the painfully cold draft at Marcos's back cutting down from the stairwell. He edged closer, furtive voices just beyond the curtain.

"Ye know he don't take hillies."

"She ain't one, and the man owes me—" Fitz shot back.

"Ye'd spend it on this?"

"She's in a bad way, Trick. Just take her in."

"Yer a bleeding heart for the ladies, Fitz, and that favor ain't gonna be enough—" There was the clink of a heavy purse being passed, then a sigh. "Right." A little man covered in tattoos pushed through the curtain. Trick, presumably. "Well, well, well. What've we got?" His brow furrowed at Nora. "She's in a bad way, sure enough. Not t'worry, Pithy'll cure what ails her. But certain types ain't encouraged and that ain't negotiable." His eyes flicked to Grantham.

"This is on you," he said again, glowering at Fitz. A pre-pube grunt was more intimidating.

"Aye, and me paycheck dependent on delivering. Fuck off, ye shite."

Grantham tromped up the stairwell and was gone.

"Now that we're among friends, shall we?" Trick's halos flared and colors ran.

They were in a sterile while room with an examination table beneath a bright light. Marcos blinked, his fingers itching for his sidearm. The similarities to the Source were uncanny…right down to the drain in the center of the floor.

Trick patted the table. "Why don't ye get her settled whilst I go fetch the good doctor." He shifted out before anyone could object.

Marcos laid Nora down, wiping the sweat from her brow with his sleeve. It left streaks of dirt in its wake. He tamped down the surge of 'lust her condition incited, glancing at the blond man leaning against the wall. He'd taken an odd coin from his pocket and was flipping it.

"What took you so long to get us?"

"Eh? Weren't me. I'm just fillin' in."

Marcos grunted. "Thank you, then. I owe you a debt."

Fitz shrugged, shoving his hands in his pockets.

"Well, he ain't happy about it, but he'll take a look." Trick had shifted back in with a tall, lean man in a lab coat. He approached the table slowly, his expression unreadable behind silvered goggles. His head moved up and down Nora's frame, then he reached out, turning over her wrist and exposing part of the barcode beneath the jacket's cuff. He stepped back, making a series of motions with his hands.

"Ye serious?" The tattooed Fetch gaped. "I don—right, right." He dug out a purse and threw it at Fitz. "Says yer money's no good, and ye can save yer favor."

Marcos's leaked 'lust. "He won't heal her?"

The little Fetch laughed. "Oh, Pithy's gonna heal her all right. Just ye wait."

Golden light leaked from around the Binder's goggles, one of his long-fingered hands on Nora's face. The fevered flush to her skin faded, and she took an unencumbered breath, falling into a natural sleep. Pithy's halos snuffed out, but his hand remained, fingers stroking her cheek. Marcos reached for his sidearm, a growl escaping him, and the Binder stepped back, his hands raised in supplication, and a barcode on his wrist.

FLYNN PACED THE FOYER, smoking one of Cal's big black cigars. Kara had asked Reggie over and the two of them had kicked him out of the bower well over an hour ago. He was more nervous than he wanted to admit. Feeling her emotions as they walked through the city... The crowd at the Pony was gonna be a hell of a lot worse and if she couldn't pull this off—

Shit, if *he* couldn't pull this off. Holding zero while she bouted was gonna be hard enough, never mind letting Trammel beat the shit out of him. As far as Plan B went it sucked, but it was all he had. At least from what he'd been able to dig up on the guy, it wouldn't take long. Man had been special-ops in Huran, which was about as close as an unaffected could get to a Northern Breaker, and if he was juicing, he was probably better—

The lift pinged, and the two women came into the foyer, laughing. The designer gave Kara a hug and disappeared through the gate. The outfit he'd gotten her was only visible from the knees down, the rest covered up by a shapeless oatmeal sweater.

"It fit ok?"

"You'll have to wait and see." Her claret-tinted lips smirked, sweeping her eyes over him. "Informal Lord Scot?"

"Huh? Oh, yeah, I guess." He'd ditched the jacket and cravat for a Henley.

"Little tight, isn't it?"

"You callin' me fat?"

She laughed. "No, I'm calling you a tease."

Flynn snuffed his cigar. "You say that like I don't know what you're wearing under there."

Her eyes got a mischievous glint. "Do you?" She did up the bottom button on his shirt.

"I thought you weren't jealous."

"You thought wrong," she said sweetly.

Christ, it got him when she did that. He kissed her, then met her eyes. "You gonna be able to do this?"

"Yes, but you better believe you're making it up to me—"

Graham shifted into the foyer with a petite tattooed woman on his arm. She was a looker, but sure as hell wasn't Original House inked up like that. Miriam must be shitting a brick.

The woman stepped forward, ignoring Flynn and sticking her hand out for Kara to shake. "How do you do, Lady Scot? Celine Esmov. Graham's told me so much about you, I feel like we're already friends." Flynn's eyebrow raised. She was a ballsy little thing, and no common, even with all those tats.

"It's Kara, please. Graham said you were coming to do empirical research?"

Celine laughed and turned to boop his nose. "He's got such a sense of humor."

Flynn scraped his jaw up off the floor at the way they were looking at each other. What the—shit, guess he'd been wrong about his cousin not being into women. "Are you ready for this?" he asked, pulling Kara close.

"Are you?"

"We'll find out."

She smoothed her hands up his chest. "It'll be what it will be. Worst case, we go west."

A profound longing shot through him, and his heart swelled. God, he loved her—Kara raised her face to be kissed, and he obliged. Graham cleared his throat after a long minute.

"Sorry," Flynn muttered, not sorry.

"Don't apologize for my sake." Celine smirked. "Graham warned me about your predilection for inappropriate public displays of affection."

What? His predilection for—Kara laughed at him. God, she was a brat.

"Ready then?" Celine asked. "We're already later than fashionable."

"Yeah." Where the hell did Graham find this chick?

Her halos flashed and colors ran.

They stood in a dank basement. A set of stairs led up through the floor of the room above, noise from a raucous crowd and bass-heavy music pounding down. Goddamn, he never wanted to set foot in this cesspool again… Flynn riffled his hair, knowing what was waiting for him at the top of those steps.

He pulled zero. *Christ, don't let me fuck this up.*

"We'll meet you at the cage," Graham said, heading up with Celine.

Kara squeezed Flynn's hand, and he forced a smile. Time to get this shit over with.

As soon as his shoulders cleared the hatch, the room was a mass of squealing women. They surrounded him in various stages of undress, pushing to get close. He lost his grip on Kara and a surge of blackness roiled from her. It sent a ripple through his hold on zero. Shit—

"Ladies! Please, I'm a married man…" He held his hand out to Kara, and she took it like a queen. Christ, an ice queen. All but the most brazen of them fell back.

Melanie was one of them.

She stayed close to his side, playing with a long chestnut lock and looking Kara up and down with a sneer. Man, she'd hit the wall hard. She had to be what, close to forty now, but looked at least ten years older. Her jaw was heavily bruised and the powder she'd used to cover it made it look worse.

"I didn't think ye liked 'em with somewhat already shoved up their arse."

The other whores snickered and Kara got that sweet little smile…

Shit.

"No, it's blown-out diseased cunts he objects to."

Flynn laughed before he could stop himself. He put his arm around Kara's waist, her 'lust slicing through the malaise of their perfume. This was going bad, fast. "If you'll excuse us, I have business to attend to."

Melanie moved out of their way, still sizing Kara up. She flicked her hair over her shoulder, brushing an old scar at her throat.

Motherfucker. Kara stiffened, that blackness speeding through their bond. Melanie tensed in response, her nostrils flaring—Kara's hand was at her throat—

The scar and the bruise darkening Melanie's face disappeared.

"There." Kara simpered, tucking a stray lock behind the whore's ear. "Now you don't look so used."

Melanie was fucking livid.

Kara batted those damned lashes of hers and pushed past, leaving Flynn to catch up. His throat bobbed, hurrying after her. Jesus fucking—

"Kara—"

"Later," she growled, rapping on the office door. A gruff voice yelled at them to enter.

The office was more lavishly appointed than Flynn remembered. Klaus's influence, he was sure. The man sitting behind the desk was the same. Doughy and as bald as a peeled egg. Fuck. It was showtime.

"Gerrard." Flynn flipped a fat envelope onto the desk, trying to regain his equilibrium. Kara had stomped over to look at a painting on the wall, her emotions throwing him for a loop. Christ, had she really called Melanie a cunt? He didn't have to fake his smile. "I'm here, and there's what I owe you. I'm done with the Pony."

The man grinned back, ignoring the envelope. "Too bad the Pony's not done with you. Klaus told you I don't want your money. I've got a house full of people waiting to see a bout. One night, your debt's paid."

Flynn sat, glancing at Kara. She shot him a dirty look, still seething. Goddamn it—

Gerrard looked between them. "How's married life?"

"In the shitter for about the past five minutes. Look, it's not my only problem. Other than my legal obligations as First, I've been out of it for too long. I go in that cage, I'm gonna get my ass kicked so fast it won't even be a show, and that's gonna blow back on you."

Gerrard snorted. "Bullshit."

"Up until two weeks ago, I could barely walk without a cane, and I haven't bouted in over six years. I'm not even close to what I—"

A burst of frenzied yelling cut him off as Klaus sauntered into the room. He closed the door with a salacious smile oozing across his face and approached Kara. "Well, if it isn't Laughlin and his Lady Scot. The pleasure is all—"

"Mine," she said, offering him her hand with a radiant smile. "Please, call me Kara. Flynn's told me so much about you."

The fuck?! All he'd said was that motherf—ah. That's how she was gonna fucking play this, huh? Flynn gritted his teeth, trying to sink further into zero while Klaus ogled her.

"Rather warm, aren't you?" he asked, running a finger down her sleeve. She glanced over at Flynn and a growl rose up in his chest.

"I am. Hot, in fact." She pulled the fucking sweater up over her head, prowled over, and dropped it into his lap. "Try not to mark it."

Gerrard's and Klaus's tongues were on the ground, and as pissed as Flynn was, Reggie needed a raise. Jesus fucking Christ, Kara was smokin'. She went over to the bar and popped a chip of ice between those claret lips of hers. Her eyebrow raised at him, sucking on the damned thing, and it was like she was whispering in his ear, *What are you gonna do about it?*

Goddamn, he was gonna—

Gerrard cleared his throat. "Pour me a vodka while you're over there, doll. So, Klaus, Flynn here tells me he ain't gonna be able to fight. What d'you think?"

The blond man ran a hand over his pointy little goatee, still watching Kara. She crossed the room with Gerrard's drink and leaned over the desk to give it to him.

That fucking does it—She pushed back to sit on Flynn's knee and started playing with his hair. This fucking woman—Christ, the 'lust coming off her…he couldn't think straight…

"I think if we don't have a fight, we'll have a couple thousand people looking for blood." Klaus threw back whatever was in his glass and poured himself another.

"He goes down as quick as he's saying we will, too."

"So let me do it," Kara said, jolting Flynn out of his daze. Shit, she was keeping it together a hell of a lot better than he was if all this had been a hook… He needed to play his part.

"No. You made your fucking point, Kara—"

"Now hold on," Gerrard said, his obvious interest at odds with his tone, "she's supposed to be half Breaker, ain't she? How about seven to one."

"Looks like more than half to me," Klaus muttered into his drink.

"Not a fucking chance." Christ, she had them eating out of her hand… *"There's always plots and power grabs"*… She was gonna make one hell of a Lady Shade…

Kara smiled at the whore master. "You were giving Flynn five-to-one, I want ten, fifteen and I'll draw it out into the show you want."

How the hell had she—shit, he bet that's why she'd had Reggie over.

Gerrard rubbed his bald head, considering.

"I'll tell you exactly what kind of show I want to see, and I'd very much like to participate in the performance," Klaus said, leering. Gerrard raised his eyebrows, not disagreeing.

Flynn scrabbled to hold zero. "She's my wife, not one of your pox-ridden whores. You'll give her fifteen or we walk."

Gerrard's smile was predatory. "There's the Flynn I remember. Agreed."

They shook on it. Flynn sat back, running a hand through his hair, trying to calm down. He and Kara were gonna have a long talk after this. "So, I hear you brought some guy up from the south, Trammel?"

Gerrard waved the name away. "This other guy showed up outta nowhere and took him out with a single punch. Big Breaker with fucked-up eyes. He'll be thrilled with you, son of a bitch likes to beat on women. Give me a minute while I go prime the crowd."

That motherfucker was here? Kara's eyes went huge, her tawny skin fear-bleached to bone. Flynn fought to keep his hold on zero.

Klaus clucked his tongue. "I hope she's better at blocking her right side than you are." He threw back the rest of his drink and followed Gerrard out, the door closing behind them with an ominous click.

"I'M GONNA KILL THAT MOTHERFUCKER."

Kara put her hands on Flynn's chest, pushing him back into the chair. "No."

"What d'you mean, no? I told you I was—"

She shook her head, her pulse pounding in her ears. Riegel was here! She swallowed the sick rising in her throat. It had been inevitable. He would never let her go. He'd told her as much. "No, you can't. You have to stay calm, and I have to do this." The truth was bitter on her tongue. She couldn't run any farther than she had, and there was nowhere left to go.

"What? Kara, I'm not gonna let him touch you again."

She swallowed her fear. She could do this. She needed to do this. "No. I have to end it. I can't—I'm tired of being that sad, scared girl, of letting him hurt me. This is…it's something I need to do." She pushed her hair back and took a deep breath.

I can do this.

"Kara, I—" His teeth gritted down, and she could feel his struggle, but he nodded. "Fine. But I'm phasing the baby, and I swear to fucking Christ, if it starts to go sideways, I'm ripping that fucker's heart out regardless of whether you've got closure, and I don't give a fuck if I split doing it." His halos bloomed verdigris and an odd there-but-not feeling spread through her midriff and up through her torso. "I don't put a goddamned thing past that sick fuck. If he tries to pull something like back at the coop, he's gonna be shit out of luck."

She nodded, smoothing her hands over her stomach and stood. The pressure felt weird, her internals numb.

Flynn snorted, eyeing her with a shake of his head. "Damn, you look fierce."

She smirked, despite feeling like she was going to throw up. "Good thing you're not very jealous."

"We're gonna have a serious discussion about you fucking playing with me like that."

"Sure, we can talk about how many whores you've marked when we do."

He colored, scowling at her. "Christ, let's get this shit show over with."

They left the office, the roar of the crowd drowning out the music from before. Flynn took her hand, leading her across the room they'd come up in, to a curtained doorway. Beyond it, the crowd was rabid. She peeked out into a warehouse, wall to wall with people. In the center of them was a big cage. Gerrard was in the middle of it, warming up the crowd.

Riegel stood with his back to her, beside him.

Her mouth went dry.

"Just say the word, Kara. You don't have to do this."

"Yes, I do."

Flynn sighed, cupping her cheek, his thumb running over it. "Then after you, my lady."

He stepped past the curtain, holding it aside with a little bow. Gerrard caught sight of him and grinned, making a sweeping gesture in their direction. Kara stalked forward, pulling her hair back to braid. The crowd parted before her, their leering cries fading into chamber music.

RIEGEL SHOT BACK a tumbler of cheap scotch as they dragged the body of his last opponent from the ring. He'd managed not to kill anyone, but it was a close thing. The ape was late, and Riegel's temper dangerously short. Gerrard made his way through the crowd and Riegel cracked his knuckles.

"There's been a change—"

Riegel growled, and the man put his hands up.

"Listen, I told you to go easy on those guys. Now no one's betting against you. Ain't no profit in pitting you against a civ, but this wife of Scot's is supposedly part Breaker. I need you to make it look like an even match. Let her get in a few hits before you damage her too bad."

Riegel started laughing, the crowd around him going silent.

"Yeah, I figured you'd like the chance to beat on another woman," Gerrard said dryly, raising up his bullhorn. "Make it look good."

He turned to address the crowd. "After seeing what my champion has done to all of these sorry sacks of shit, I've decided that for the good of our fair city to let the Lord Scot pick his own Breaker to face mine." The crowd erupted into boos and hisses, flinging streams of profanity and garbage at the man. He held up his hand until they settled enough to listen.

"I think the substitution will more than make up for your disappointment!" Gerrard flung out his arm towards the back of the room. The ape stood beside the curtain. His eyes locked with Riegel's. A massive grin split the Breaker's face. Oh, this was going to be marvelous!

"Tonight's featured bout: My ringer vs. the Lady Scot!" The crowd exploded into hysteria as Kara burst out and stalked to the cage, Scot trailing in her wake.

She'd changed since Riegel had last seen her, moving like a Breaker instead of a mouse.

His pants tightened in anticipation of the beating he was going to give her. First Ielle and now Kara offering herself up for punishment. Perhaps there really was such a thing as divine providence—she paused before the gate, kissing that ape with more passion than Riegel had believed her capable of. The man's hands roamed over her tight little body. When she finally broke away, Scot glared at him again, the crowd wild.

Riegel grinned back. "Was that a kiss goodbye? You're about to watch me do a great deal more than that to her, coward." Scot took a step forward, jaw clenched, and Kara put a hand on his chest. He stood down in deference to her.

What a pussy letting a woman bench him. Riegel spat. He'd been looking forward to ripping off Scot's balls and shoving them down his throat, but apparently they'd already been removed.

Kara stepped into the cage. Riegel's pulse raced, vision wavering beneath his surging 'lust. He licked across his teeth, his smile widening at the fear he smelt coming off her. Gerrard came between them.

"No talent, no weapons. This is strictly hand to hand until one of you doesn't get back up. You break the rules, you lose, understood?"

Kara nodded, and Gerrard slapped Riegel, turning his face to look at him. He nodded, barely restraining himself from sending the man through the chain-link. Gerrard frowned and stepped outside, locking the gate after him.

The buzzer sounded.

Riegel lunged forward, and Kara slipped from his reach, landing a punch to his kidney. He grunted and spun to face her, swinging at her head. She ducked, her fist clipping him in the jaw. Riegel spat red, backhanding her.

She flew back against the cage. He smiled, her ears would be ringing from that one. She pushed off, coming at him and sweeping his feet from under him. He landed badly, and she stomped on his kneecap before he could recover. Riegel howled, favoring his other leg as he sprang up, glowering. Kara had never been in the arena, but she certainly fought like a Breaker.

He wouldn't underestimate her again.

CHAPTER TWENTY-SEVEN

leathers - [lĕTH'ərz] noun

1. *The traditional uniform of a Valkyrie, earned through trial by combat and adorned with wings indicating their status within the elite group.*

– Excerpt from The Way of Honor

"The hierarchy stems from the Alpha Prime, first of our line born in the fires of the Surge. He drew us from its madness and set our feet upon the Way of Honor, harnessing the darkness to serve something greater than our own ambitions. Thrice the harbinger of a coming harvest and once to claim a mate, each return he is asked if he would challenge and take up his rightful place..."

– Lord Grimmight, Breaker Menot,
Glynfyls

FLYNN GRIPPED the side of the cage, watching Kara and Riegel trade blows. His hold on zero was tenuous, that black rage boiling beneath the blanket of calm. He dug his fingers into the chain-link, trying to ground himself with the pain.

Klaus came up to stand by his side, nursing his gin. "Your omission, I'm assuming?"

"And yours." Flynn growled, not taking his eyes off the two of them. "Why didn't you tell me Gerrard hired that fucking monster?" Shit, if he'd known, he never would have involved her in this, fuck whatever closure she thought she needed. He tamped down a burst of rage as Riegel delivered one hell of a gut shot. Christ, his phase better fucking work. What the hell had he been thinking?

"Can she do it?"

Flynn tore his eyes away, needing the distraction. "You still taking bets?"

"We are."

"Put everything I owe the Pony on her to win."

"That's a tidy sum."

Flynn's attention snapped back to the cage at Riegel's bellow. Kara had landed a nasty combo. He was losing his temper and getting sloppy. Asshole had probably assumed she'd be an easy win. Flynn couldn't feel anything from Kara. He raked at his hair, praying she could stay in zero. If she lost it, there was no way he was gonna be able to hold.

"What were the house odds?"

"Ten-to-one. That lady of yours is going to make me quite a bit of money if she wins."

Flynn raised an eyebrow. "You, not Gerrard?"

Klaus shrugged, finishing his gin and calling for another. "Gerrard bet on the Breaker. Who wouldn't? Look at him. He's destroyed everyone he's gone against."

"Why didn't you?"

"I was at The Park Club. Standard Breakers don't move that fast and considering her origins…well, let's just say I found the potential for gain too tempting to dismiss. But I am curious, how is it you both know that behemoth?" He rolled his eyes. "Oh, come now, Laughlin. By your reactions, that much was plain."

"The Source sent him after her. He's dangerous, Klaus."

He took his drink from a scantily clad woman. "I can't say I'm surprised. Even without Crandall's description circulating, there's been a curious lack of vermin for the past few days. If I had to guess, I'd say it's quite possible this is live-streaming to them now."

Fuck. Kara recoiled from a jab, and Flynn's fingers tightened in the chain-link, her eye swelling shut. That was gonna be problematic, although Riegel wasn't in any better shape. The left side of his face was a pulpy ruin and gore spattered across his torso as she dodged his fists.

"She's in trouble, isn't she?" Graham asked woodenly.

Flynn started. Where the fuck had he come from? "Not yet…" but it was getting pretty fucking dicey. He squeezed at the fencing, fingers oozing where it'd cut into his hands.

Riegel grabbed her around the shoulders, pinning her against him. Flynn's teeth popped. The Breaker whispered something in her ear and licked up the side of her face, grinding against her backside.

A surge of rage went through Flynn, amplified by her own. The pressure her bind had relieved began to press in on him, and he scrabbled to find zero again, his breath coming fast—

It was sucked out of him, and he staggered against the fencing, abruptly weak. What the—

Riegel was airborne, the crowd exploding into a frenzy.

He careened into the chain-link, metal clashing, and lay in a heap before slowly getting up, the knee Kara had stomped threatening to buckle. His right arm hung limply at his side.

"Holy shit," Klaus gaped.

Flynn tried to shake off whatever the hell had just happened, his heart thudding in his ears. What the fuck? How the hell had she'd managed to throw—*Shit*. He pulled at his beard, trying to calm down. That blackness still churned down their bond, inciting his. What had he said to her? If she couldn't maintain zero…

Flynn raked at his hair, mouth dry. "Double my bet."

"Done."

Riegel knew he'd rattled her. The asshole grinned, spitting out a mouthful of blood, and rammed his shoulder into one of the I-beams ringing the cage. He bellowed again, sending out a cloud of rancid menace and went at her, both arms working. It wasn't anything like what Flynn had smelt coming off Pax or Rogan. This was corrupt. Unclean. Flynn bit back a growl, fighting the blackness inside him trying to answer it, the primal need to put a sick animal down, remembering what Kara had said about her father.

"COULD this be any more of a tangle? Tell me I didn't just see that."

Rogan glanced at Phyllis, softened by shadow, perched on the crate beside him. She'd left the evidence of her wings being torn from her vest. Wearing her shame. Spoke more highly of her than anything else had. He tipped back his bottle of tequila, scanning the frenzied crowd, eyes landing on the kid.

Goddamn Cal for not getting him a Menot.

"In my experience there's no upper limit to a cluster fuck, and you most assuredly did." Shit, every Breaker in the fucking room had seen them share strength, and where the hell Kara had gotten leathers from… Instead of patches across her collar bones, wings were etched into the back of her vest, the pattern continuing down the backside of her pants like she was some kind of avenging angel.

He adjusted his jeans. She sure as hell fit the brief.

"You said you were here for her…did you intend for her to be your mate?"

Kara drove Riegel against the cage again, then doubled him up with a gut punch.

"I fuck, Phyllis, I don't mate." Rogan took another swig from his bottle. "What was the outcome of the moot?"

She swallowed her shock at his reply. "W-we walk the Way. No talent, no further discussion."

He grunted, that couldn't be sitting well, and at this point they were splitting already split hairs. God help her if there were any lawyers in their line. It was impossible to pull strength without some transference of talent—

His nose twitched, the malaise of decay threading through the room, prickling the small hairs at the back of his neck. Breaker by

Breaker the others picked up on it, stepping back to ring the margins of the warehouse.

Standing vigil.

Riegel was on the verge of succumbing and they all knew what came next.

"Will she be able to put him down?"

Rogan took another pull of tequila, eyes catching furtive movement beneath the bleachers on the other side of the room. He smacked the bottle against Phyllis's chest.

"Hold this."

THAT FUCKING CUNT! They circled, and Riegel lunged unsteadily, trying to grapple with Kara again. He sent out another cloud of 'lust. She ignored it, flipping over him and taking him backwards, slamming his head against the concrete. The crowd roared, pressing in on the cage, its clang as loud as their clamor. She followed up with a mean cross. Stars exploded across his vision, his nose crunching beneath her fist. He rolled into a crouch, coughing out a mouthful of gore, sight doubling.

Rage burnt through what was left of his rational thought. He breathed in the fury, reveling in the chaos licking at him. His world narrowed to the bitch in front of him. She should be on the floor beneath him, not standing above. He was going to beat the shit out of her and fuck whatever was left after he aborted Scot's brat.

Riegel's face set in a rictus grin. He threw himself at her, pinning her against the chain-link, teeth tearing at her neck and sucking at the wound. Kara screamed, her knee slamming into his groin. He stumbled back, retching. She followed, her heel cracking his head to the side. He spun, hitting the floor, her boot stomping down where his throat had been a second before. She regrouped, kicking him in the stomach as he tried to crawl away. Spots flecked before his eyes—

The dank darkness of 'lust rose up, and he embraced it.

"GOT YOU."

Titus crowed at the feed from the Jester girl's perspective, her vitals streaming to his private servers as the nanobots infected their new host through Riegel's bite. He couldn't believe his luck at Scot's shocking decision to allow her to take his place…that is, if he had any say in the matter. The way she was manhandling Riegel, Titus had little doubt that she was an Alpha bitch. Scot would be at her mercy.

He sipped his bourbon, scanning the numbers with half an eye, unable to gain confirmation on several key metrics. Curious, but there would be plenty of time to mine the data later. Right now he was enthralled with her performance.

How had Albanach polished such a gem? Titus chuckled at the limited possibilities. Though remarkably quick studies, even his Elites required intense instruction to program their reflexes. The girl's skill bespoke years of training, and her technique was decidedly that of a Breaker.

Of the Northern persuasion.

The rope to hang Albanach had become a noose.

Riegel's feed alarmed, and Titus frowned. Damn it. He'd hoped for this to play out longer, but the man's level of bloodlust had become dangerously high. The only thing that would stop him now was a bullet to the brain. The charge at the base of his skull would perform the same task admirably.

Titus typed in his code to end the man and sent it.

Nothing happened.

He typed it in again, rocketing forward and sending a similar command through the bots.

Riegel got to his feet, readying to spring at the woman.

Why wasn't it working?!

Titus pulled random feeds, all of them going dark at his command, hosts exterminated—

The Breaker's fail-safes had been negated.

He fell back into his chair, hand raking his scalp.

Watching it play out.

KARA JUMPED BACK at Riegel's snarl, barely managing to keep him off her.

He'd succumbed.

She buried her visceral stab of fear in zero until just facts remained.

Riegel was going to kill her unless she put him down, and she needed to do it fast. Pain was only going to fuel his 'lust. The longer this went on, the more frenzied he'd become.

She gritted her teeth and ran towards him, flipping onto his back and getting him in a chokehold—

Bad idea.

He hurtled backwards, slamming her into an I-beam. The crowd screamed for her blood, as much an animal as he. She fell, hitting the concrete hard, breath jolted from her, head ringing as she tried to crawl away. Riegel laughed, kicking her in the ribs and flipping her onto her back. Pain stabbed through her side. He was on her, wrenching her arms above her head. She screamed, straining against him.

He thrust his tongue into her mouth.

A dark maelstrom of crimson-laced rage stormed through her from Flynn, entwining with the blackness in her, his fury electrifying her with strength like the last time Riegel had gotten ahold of her.

But this time, Kara didn't just use it, she took it in.

She bit down, teeth severing flesh, her legs finding purchase, hoisting him from her. Riegel shrieked, scrabbling back. She spat the hunk of fetid meat at him, trembling with what she'd just taken from Flynn. She wiped at her chin. Riegel crouched on the other side of the ring, his grin scarlet.

"It's gonna be sweet fucking you, Kara," he lisped, and came at her again.

FLYNN BLINKED, forehead pressed into the chain-link, light-headed and seeing spots.

What the fuck had just happened?

Christ, that building pressure—he'd almost lost it, and then everything had been sucked out of him again—his rage, concern, all of it was all gone, leaving him in a bizarre kind of zen.

"My God, Laughlin, what is that woman like in bed?"

Flynn shook his head, Klaus's voice attenuated, the crowd...all of it slowed and dissociated like he was underwater. Beyond the fencing, Kara's mouth was smeared with Riegel's blood. Bets were flying as to who would die first and how, the house giving odds on all of it.

Flynn was filled with the calm certainty it was gonna be Riegel. Whatever had just happened had super-charged her. He lunged at her midsection, and she brought up her knee, clipping his jaw hard enough to hear his teeth crash together despite the screaming crowd. She cupped her hands, slamming them down over his ears. He fell back, shaking his head. Kara hit his weak knee again, and it collapsed under him. He howled, struggling to make it work, but it wouldn't bear his weight. She kicked his other leg from under him, and he fell, trying to grab her. Her boot found the side of the head, and she danced away.

Flynn's brow knit, the atmosphere in the room changing. Static jumped from the chain-link—

The crowd's cries turned to screams, scrambling from the cage. Klaus grabbed his sleeve, cowering. "Shit, he's pulling talent!"

Flynn blinked. Facts clicking.

"You're telling me he's a fucking bomb?"

His halos blazed, phasing through the cage to Kara. He swept her behind a shield, turning to the crippled Breaker, everything around him moving like stop-motion.

Riegel's halos erupted crimson, eye sockets decaying into twin maws of raw force.

Flynn's talent met it, the shockwave shaking the district. The crowd screamed, people knocked from their feet, scrambling from the clash of forces. He pressed forward, his cloak scintillating and sparking with the talent it was phasing. Ozone seared his nostrils, the air dense, that zen cracking away, the darkness welling up until a single, cold fact remained.

That motherfucker was his.

BARTON STOOD BENEATH THE BLEACHERS. The Breakers ringing the room gave him pause. Between them, the crowd seethed in an incoherent mass, fighting each other to gain the lone exit at the far side of the room. Too frenzied to work together to remove the twisted metal of the collapsed stands from their path, they trampled and buffeted one another in an infinite loop of violent futility.

Amusing, but of no importance.

Scot was.

Somehow, the man had rendered the cage insubstantial, exploding from the sidelines to put himself between Kara and Riegel faster than Barton could credit. What he was seeing now—

Mmm. He gnawed a finger. Ozone crackling at the back of his throat. He didn't know what he was seeing. It also gave him pause. But Scot wasn't his target.

Kara was behind him, slack-jawed at the show of power raining down around her in iridescent waves of eerily silent force.

Disoriented. Distracted. Delicious.

But not defenseless.

Barton slid the blow gun from his sleeve and fitted a dart, his tongue flicking across his lips as he raised the weapon—

A prickle of warning flared up his spine.

He pulled talent, shifting several feet away and sending the dart through the space he'd just occupied. It struck a fleeing whore's back. She fell mid-stride and was crushed by the crowd.

Barton's breath hissed out, scanning the writhing masses for anomalies. His halos flared and the distinct musk of Breaker coated his tongue. He found him above, stalking him from the bleachers. Barton shifted to the far side of the room just in time to see a big man with a topknot drop down to where he'd been. A moment later and he reappeared, searching the crowd. His eyes unerringly landed on him, halos flaring.

Barton shifted to one of the many rooms he had scattered throughout the city, sliding the blowgun back into his sleeve, this window of opportunity gone.

Another would open.

KARA STOOD ROOTED, every hair on her body electrified. Waves of phased talent broke around her, the air saturated with power. Flynn fought for traction at the apex of his shield, boots skidding back, negating every hard won step towards Riegel's seizing form. The Breaker's body arched from the concrete, more raw force than any Talent could channel exploding from his body.

Her hand went to her torn throat, the nothingness she felt from Flynn crumbling beneath the onslaught. The bind on his channel fraying.

The darkness in him rising.

She went to pull talent, and it answered from the air around her, the crushing immediacy of it bringing her to her knees. It wanted, crashing against her, insistent—too much, too fast—

Kara cried out, wrestling to regulate the flow and bolster her bind. Flynn's channel pulsed an angry crimson and a cloud of bloodlust dank with menace roiled from him, knocking her prone. Panting, her palms scraped the ground, sweat slicking her skin.

If he couldn't contain this—himself—they would all die.

She threw her channel wide, binding the talent scattering from his phase and letting it roar through her back to him—a scream bursting from her lips.

The burn! She couldn't—

I can. For him. Glory… Save him…please…

Something behind the talent answered, wrapping her in golden light, and she surrendered.

FLYNN GRIT HIS TEETH, phasing the waves of destruction Riegel was unleashing, fighting for that last goddamned step to get to the man.

To his corpse.

Fuck, he was gonna be a corpse. Him and everyone else in the goddamned city.

Flynn strained to get closer, feeling Kara behind him, pushing him talent—Jesus fucking Christ too much talent—she screamed—

The bind on his channel dissolved.

No. No, No, NO…

"KARA!"

Searing pain cut through his temples, driving him to the floor, talent burning through him. His temper spiked, the room becoming a crimson midnight. Breaker talent filled him. The overwhelming desire to destroy devoured rational thought. He shook with rage, and his shield buckled, the force erupting from Riegel skidding him backwards—

"Use it!" Kara screamed.

She was alive.

He wrestled with his fury, needing to keep her that way. If using Breaker talent was the way to do it, so fucking be it.

Flynn slammed down a hand, anchoring himself in fractured concrete. A cresting wave of strength coursed through him, and he rode it, pushing it into his shield. Feet beneath him, he barreled forward, the edges of his cloak flaring crimson.

He rammed it over Riegel, cutting off the torrent of power and severing the Breaker's channel. His body collapsed, juddering against the concrete.

Why the fuck wasn't he dead?

Flynn dropped to a knee beside him, jerking the man's head around to look at him.

Bloodied sockets stared back, weeping with the distinct sheen of plaz. He growled, Klaus had been right. This piece of shit was loaded with tech.

And that meant Titus.

He hoped the son of a bitch was still watching.

"You want a war, motherfucker? Try it, and I don't give a shit who the fuck you send up, I swear to Christ, they'll meet the same end as this sorry sack of shit, and then I'm coming for you."

Flynn phased his fist through Riegel's chest and tore out the

Breaker's heart, flinging it down beside the corpse as he stood. He dropped talent, staggering. Kara was beside him, pushing up under his arm. He drew her close, breathing her in. Thank fucking God—

"Are you okay?"

She nodded, her wounds healed. How the hell—

"Yes…all that talent, I—I'm fine, but look at them, Flynn…"

Startled, he raised his head. The room had been so quiet, he'd thought them alone. The warehouse was in shambles, the crowd from earlier wide-eyed and huddling on its knees.

Afraid.

Flynn's stomach cramped. They'd seen him split—Christ, did it matter anymore? He scrubbed at his face, then swore, wiping a bloody hand on his jeans.

He couldn't catch a goddamned break.

The crowd watched him, mute.

"Jesus, get up."

A scarred man with greying hair stood and met his eye. Shit. He'd been with that squad of Breakers out on the plateau. He thumped his fist over his heart.

"As ye will, Over-lawd Scot."

Fuck, that wasn't what he—At the margins of the room a line of Breakers rose, thumping their fists over their hearts, the rest of the crowd rising and following suit. Kara looked up at him, and he took a deep breath.

So much for him not making epic fucking declarations.

***

TITUS SAT STUNNED at what he'd just witnessed.

How the hell was any of it possible?

His gaze drifted from the crowd's troubling obeisance to the metrics collected before Riegel's demise. The talent the boy had negated… Titus tore at his hair, temples throbbing.

Phasing. How had such a powerful ability been relegated to a footnote in the archives?

He called for a bourbon, upending the last of his pills and

crunching on them, certain it was Albanach's doing. A jump in logic perhaps, but the evidence against the man was mounting to near titanic proportions.

Titus's eyes snapped to the Jester girl's feed, her missing vitals abruptly populating. He'd been right about the slide—he chuckled, abruptly knowing exactly where that gravid Breaker bitch his father had lost wound up. The girl was roughly eight weeks bred, signaling that her Elite genome had found another's in Laughlin Scot. It was rather impressive she'd made it through tonight without succumbing, but it was borrowed time. Her Binder genes would only buy her so much.

Her metrics were equally impressive, and what she'd channeled to Scot at the end... Titus brought up the last data points from Marcos and Nora. They were similar enough to correlate causation. The ability to share talent was definitely something Albanach had bred into his Binders. A smile slid across Titus's lips. The board would be furious.

It was time to make his move against the old dragon.

Scot dipped his head to kiss the girl and another holo sprang into being above Titus's desk.

He pulled it closer, brow furrowed at the metrics, then sorted through the tables, cackling. It was even better than he'd suspected. The man was a split. Both Shade and Elite Breaker DNA in equal parts, with something...other. Titus had never seen anything like it.

Not in a human, at least.

He sat back in his chair, bourbon washing away his pooling saliva.

"You want a war, motherfucker?"

The boy had no idea...

"… From all that is hidden, all shall be revealed, waters pull back from the shore, leaving the detritus of the sea exposed. Gulls circle, scrambling to pick before the wave hurtling toward them crashes in, behind it a leviathan to swallow the world…"

– Excerpt from the dream journals of House Carmody

MOTHER TICKED through the multitudes of consciousness bound to her by shimmering golden cords. Webbing out around the globe, tonight they all trembled.

A short, ugly man, alone in a shack crouched over a cathode tube.

In the Deep South, a woman, fingers pressed to an ear piece, reel flickering against a building in downtown Heswait. The crowd around her as rapt as she.

A child clutching a battered stuffed bear.

They weren't alone in their fear.

This is what they can do. What they will do. He said he's coming… For who?

Mother saw through their eyes, a wraith in their minds, subtly twisting emotion. The tide of trepidation churning to one of anger.

Then of action.

The night filled with the screams of enslaved Talents across the

Deep South, slain by their masters. Rabid mobs surrounded the homes of those who didn't display the mutilated corpses, whole families torn to pieces for harboring the monsters.

Riots spread.

Feeds blinked out and were re-established, the Corporation unable to pull enough strings for a media blackout. Injunctions served and ignored, speculation rampant as to their involvement, the world remembering what they'd done in Diytan, the massacre in Tombago—

Mother's head tilted a fraction at the scuff of leather on stone.

"I'd ask if you're aware of recent events, but I already know the answer." Otto's petulance bounced around the bare stone chamber, allowing her to echolocate him like a bat. He huffed up the hundred steps of her inner sanctum to the dais where she lounged on a low chaise. "I'd be surprised if there are any Talents left alive outside of the Northern Continent by the time the sun rises. The blowback on the Source is going to be problematic."

"For some." Mother swallowed a smile. The board was going to throw Titus to the wolves and he'd drag Cal into the pit with him while events unfolded.

Otto pinched the bridge of his nose, no doubt frustrated at his inability to see all the levels of the board or the threads binding the pieces. His lack stirred a delighted disgust in her bosom. He took a breath. "I'm more concerned with Scot. The man is dangerous."

"He needs to be." Mother smiled to herself. Her halos and one of the shards adorning the golden band encircling her forehead glowed softly.

A petite woman entered the room, the faceted amethyst at the center of her dusky brow casting the same soft light. Bits and baubles woven into her long braids chimed pleasantly, their echoes tinging about the chamber.

Julia was at her side, staring blankly ahead. Her hair was done up in the same complicated plaits and threaded with small beads. The style wasn't nearly as appealing on her as it was on Elize...but it mattered little. It was the message it carried. A clumsy threat, perhaps, but Cal would recognize his wife's aesthetic and be reminded of the rules to their game, lest he become tempted to break them. Mother turned to Otto.

"Julia's been primed, but is brittle. I don't expect her to last long. Make the most of her while she does."

Otto's smirk was repellent. He came forward, stroking the back of his bloated hand over the girl's cheek. His halos flared, reading her directives, and chuckled. "I'm assuming you'd like me to take care of the corroborating evidence?"

Mother was unable to hide her distaste. "You are an expert in such matters." He grinned at her, the energy about him an ugly pulse of maroon. His father's son. Mother flicked her fingers, dismissing him. He grasped Julia's arm, and they disappeared.

Elize stood mute as Mother settled herself against the chaise's cushions, waiting for Enoch to join them. It didn't take long. He was never far from his twin. Begrudgingly, he separated himself from the shadows. Of all Mother's thralls, his leash chafed the most.

"They'll make Scot Overlord after that."

"Perhaps." She smiled at his rancor, running a finger over the amethysts at her brow. They both flinched as if the reminder of her dominion had been physical.

In some ways, it was.

"Do you find any other outcome more likely?"

Enoch pursed his lips, amethyst halos flaring around shockingly blue irises. "Ultimately, no, but a concerning tangent is forming. I would suggest—"

"There is always the rise and fall of potentialities, your job is to watch and wait for my leave to act on them should it become necessary." He grunted, and she smiled, tasting his resentment. "I've promised you your revenge, and you'll have it soon enough. Now go, I've wild Talents to hunt."

The twins shared a glance and left. Mother leaned back, returning to those caught up in the golden web of her talent and imposing her will upon them. Sons and Daughters of the Messiah, afroth at the coming of the promised sign, their long awaited call to arms.

The leviathan rising from the deep.

Judgement day was at hand.

GLYNFYLS WAS BURNING.

Flynn stared out the window of the Assembly Hall, overlooking the eastern spokes of the city. Beyond the wavy glass, the rising sun was a crimson smear across the smoke-streaked horizon. Below, the clamor of an angry mob rioted through the streets.

They were pissed.

How the hell a cluster fuck of this magnitude had gotten kicked off last night—he scrubbed at his face. Shit. He knew exactly how.

His hand rose and talent the color of old blood flickered between his fingers, sparking off and singeing the carpet. He scuffed it out with his boot, jaw clenching. After the past few weeks of trying to play the goddamned part, he'd fucking split when he put Riegel down and, caught in a catch twenty-fucking-two, the entire city had seen him do it.

But if he hadn't, the boost the Breaker was rigged with would've blown Glynfyls to shit. Flynn sighed. Instead of the city, everything he'd worked for had gone with Riegel into the hereafter. Christ, Julia and Lord Morris must be having a fucking field day with this. Both of them would be in chambers now, smug as shit, lambasting the room with big fat I-told-you-so's…

God, he was gonna puke. Dual-Talents couldn't hold office, and he'd used both a Shade's talent to phaze away the blast, and a shit ton of Breaker ability, publicly. He'd saved the city only to hand it over to Julia, and she'd pass it right on to Titus.

His eyes closed, seeing it all play out. Legally, he was screwed. The Shades were gonna abjure him from his seat on the Assembly. Lords Klein and Ketsing, the Fixer and Binder Firsts that'd pledged their line's fealty to him, would pull their support. Then Crandall would bury him. He's gleefully drive the last nail into Flynn's coffin by tying him to the Sons that'd been slaughtered out on the plateau.

And as for Phyllis and Markham? Neither one of them was gonna do a fucking thing. No, check that. Markham would mop the sweat from his brow when they came at Flynn with a rope to hang him. Couple of minutes swinging, then done deal, Flynn'd be in a box and they'd be back to business as usual.

Until Titus sent in his troops and Peacekeepers harvested the lot of them.

"I wish I was a fucking twist, then I wouldn't have to pretend..."

Of all the wishes he'd ever made, it figured that would be the one granted. God had to love fucking with him.

Kara pushed up under his arm. "We can tell them it was me—"

"No. I won't lie about it." They'd gone over this. If Merchant couldn't get him off, he'd cloak them at Meddleton until the baby was born, then head west. Disappear. He'd done it before, he could do it again. He kissed the top of Kara's head, wrapping his arms around her.

"You should try and sleep."

She laughed, the strain of the past twenty-four hours etched across her brow. Once the adrenaline from the bout last night at the Pony had faded, Riegel's death had triggered a cascade of memories. Each one left her more brittle than the last, and that damned talent debilitation plaguing her pregnancy was back. Add to it being locked up in this goddamned conference room without any idea of what was going on other than one hell of a shit show...

Christ. What a fucking mess.

The door opened and Merchant hustled in, looking grim. His suit was rumpled and his grey-streaked hair awry. A servant came in after him and set a coffee service and two plates of eggs on the conference table. Flynn's stomach growled. Damn, he could go for—Kara turned to his chest, pale with nausea. Goddamn it, he needed to get her home.

"Take it away, please."

The woman looked at him in surprise, then wet her lips, glancing at Merchant. She pulled a scrap of paper from the napkin, holding it out with trembling fingers, and flashed her colors. Thin rings of fuchsia pulsed around her irises. It was the signal Flynn and Dorian had agreed upon for when the Finder had turned something up on Crandall.

Flynn took it from her, and she bobbed a curtsy, fist to heart. Vassal to Overlord. He snorted, like that was gonna fucking happen—his temper spiked at the contents of the note, and it smoldered where he gripped it. Damn it—His anger was too close. Too easy to pull from. All this time, is that what that constant simmering rage had been? Talent just waiting to come out?

"I suggest you cloak this conversation." Merchant frowned, tossing a newspaper onto the table. "They're attempting to charge you with inciting the commons."

Flynn's jaw dropped, note forgotten. *That's not*—His halos flared verdigris, cloaking them. "But they all saw—"

"A great deal of talent being used. As evidenced by that front page still and multiple reels. You haven't developed concentric halos. By definition, a twist evidences a dual-halo, and without a second ring around your irises, you cannot be considered as such. Additionally, without confirmation from the Breaker line as to whom was doing what, any and all charges are unsubstantiated, and will be treated as libel and or slander. Now, I suggest we focus on the matter at hand." He snapped open his briefcase.

"The matter at—are you serious?" He—there was no way—how was this not about him splitting? Was Merchant seriously getting him off on semantics? Shit, Cal had said he was good, but no one could be that good.

The little barrister tapped a folio of papers square. "The Assembly's charges are predicated upon legislation enacted in response to the Dock Uprising, however, the reels clearly establish that it was your arrest, not the fight, nor your actions afterwards, that sparked tensions."

Flynn's mind struggled to shift gears. The Dock Uprising? Those riots had gone on for months, and half the city had burnt down. That's what was going on outside? Jesus Christ, what the fuck had he done?

Aside from saving all their asses. A manic laugh burbled from his lips.

Merchant wasn't amused. "Breakers called conclave, the city's up in arms over your detainment, and Assembly's been in session since you were brought here. If you didn't have half their oaths, your head would already be on a pike."

Flynn dropped into a chair. Out of the frying pan and into the fire. Either way, he was toast. Kara sat beside him, picking up the paper as Merchant continued.

"To further complicate matters, the international press has been running with the story and the Sons of the Messiah have officially declared jihad. There are riots all over the Deep South. Anti-Talent sentiment is at an all-time high."

Kara slid the front page over. *THE MAN WHO WOULD BE KING* was printed in bold block letters over a still of him, halos blazing, holding up Riegel's heart. The inset was of her, mouth painted crimson with the Breaker's blood. She took his hand, as pale as he felt. They looked like fucking psychopaths.

"It gets worse. The Source has filed paperwork to enact the Harvest Clause, citing your threats of retaliation last night as provocation through aggression."

Flynn laughed—shit, Merchant was serious.

"We've filed a counter suit," the barrister continued, "and given the precedence set by Banoi and Tombago—"

"What did Cal say?"

Merchant pursed his lips. "I've been unable to get in touch with Master Scot."

Flynn stared at him. Where the f—"You got a cigar?"

"I—no."

He grunted, running a hand over his beard. If they were gonna try to screw him with this…shit. Borrowed or not, it gave him time. He needed to play this out. "Fine. I fucked up. I'll stay as long as I need to, but none of it has to do with Kara—"

"What? No. I'm staying with you."

"You're past due for your shot." He ran a hand down her cheek, neither one of them able to pretend that creeping exhaustion wasn't edging in again. She wouldn't look at him.

"The lady has medical needs?" Merchant glanced between them and sighed. "I'm not going to lie. Legally, they can't hold you with what they've presented, but this isn't going to play out in court. The next one will. I haven't raised objection because we're fighting an uphill battle against public opinion. You need to be seen as cooperative. If you have something to disclose…please. Help me, help you." His eyes flicked to the note.

Flynn bit the scar on his lip. Christ, he had to trust someone, and Cal was putting Merchant's kids through school. There were worse reasons to be loyal.

"Three days ago, they had Riegel in police custody. He was released under the recognizance of a Master Eid. I can't prove it, but I damned well know Crandall let him walk. He let that fight happen, all this fallout is on him." Flynn's temper jumped again, his fingertips sparking. He snuffed them in his fist. Asshole had probably hoped the Breaker would kill him.

"I'd encourage you to keep the fact you know the Breaker's name to yourself." The little barrister took off his glasses, rubbing a cloth over the lenses. "As far as Master Eid is concerned, I'm assuming he doesn't exist, and no one knows anything about the alleged incarceration."

"You would be correct."

"God, I hate politics." Merchant could say that shit again. He replaced his glasses, looking even more dour than when he'd come into the room. "And the lady?"

Flynn bit at his lip. "We haven't announced, but she's pregnant, and is suffering from a talent deficiency. There's a regimen she's got to follow." Kara chewed her thumb, and he could feel her annoyance through their bond. Too damned bad. She was gonna end up on bedrest otherwise.

Merchant took a seat. "You do realize how ludicrous that sounds, given her performance in the ring last night?"

Flynn's temper spiked, and she put a hand on his leg. He gritted his teeth, that weird burst of strength he'd felt during the bout coursing through him with his anger. Christ, he had to keep it together…

"I don't give a shit how it sounds. The ladies will confirm she's carrying my heir, and Jon's got her fucking labs if you need to enter an exhibit—"

Feet pelted down the hall. Shouting. Glass shattered somewhere in the building, and the sounds of the angry mob grew louder. The door flung open. Markham stood there panting. It wasn't a good look on the First Fetch.

"Quickly, the commons have breached the main doors!"

Flynn grabbed Kara and bolted to the big man, Merchant already at his side—

Colors ran.

Markham shifted them to the center of chambers. The massive doors were barricaded, and a contingent of Fixers stood by them, halos blazing bronze, holding them shut with their talent. Others held the gallery entrances, the white marble awash in the metallic glow. Pounding and rabid cries came from beyond them. What the hell—

Riggs cleared his throat. The speaker sat at his lectern in lavender striped pajamas and a robe. Was he wearing bunny slip—

"Lord Scot. If you'd take your seat so we can begin?"

Something big hit the doors, the boom reverberating through the hall. The light from the Fixer's halos flared brighter. Flynn swallowed, directing Kara to his box. Nothing about this was gonna end well. Merchant took the chair Lot usually occupied. His father was in the seats above, scowling.

Dawn bled through the tall windows, spiking across the chamber and highlighting the empty Breaker section. Kara's anxiety was on overdrive, bleeding through their bond to fuel Flynn's. She stumbled, and he caught her elbow, moving the chair from beside Merchant next to his, its legs scraping too loudly against the marble. Flynn's heart thudded in his ears. He took his seat and her hand again, kissing her trembling knuckles. She wasn't doing well, jumping as Riggs banged his gavel. The call to order echoed over the booms coming from outside the room, the swelling clamor from the mob ratcheting up everyone's tension.

"I call this special session to order. Well, then, Laughlin. Would you care to explain yourself?" the elderly man asked.

He bit back a no, running a hand over his beard. "For what?"

"Everything last night!"

Right. That. Flynn took a deep breath and stood, shoving his hands into his pockets. Christ, he needed to calm down…"When I returned to Glynfyls, certain individuals refused to let me settle a debt I'd incurred before leaving. The bout last night was how they insisted payment be made. Given the prohibition against Firsts entering into any form of competition, Lady Scot graciously stepped up in my place."

A wrenching squeal and another boom came from the doors. Were there Breakers out there? Phyllis's pinched face glaring at him from the crowd last night flashed before his eyes. Damn, there might be—

Lord Klein's halos flared, his talent bolstering the other Fixers. "Goddamn it, Markham! Can't you control your line?"

"My line—" The fat man mopped at his brow. "The Fetches, ah, I— I'm afraid things are a bit strained at the moment, and keeping the public from these proceedings—"

"Then we should expedite them," Crandall said, stroking his greasy little goatee far too calmly. Flynn grit his teeth. Yep. Asshole was about to bury him. "If you would continue, Lord Riggs?"

The speaker scanned the page in front of him. "Laughlin's brought up a point Lord Ketsing requested clarification on."

"Yes." The Binder First said, wringing his hands. "We were led to believe that Lady Scot was a Binder. After last night—" He licked his lips, about to make an accusation he wouldn't be able to take back.

Flynn's temper surged with Kara's dread. If her called her a fucking twist… Why couldn't they leave her out of this? "Her halos were witnessed by the entirety of my line during her Introduction, what other proof—"

"Can I speak?"

She'd come up beside him. His surprise cut through his barely contained rage.

"Yeah." Flynn glared around the room, daring someone to say otherwise. She was terrified, but had raised that elfin chin… Goddamn, he loved her. Her fingers tightened on his sleeve, keeping him at her side.

"My genetics are both Binder and Breaker, my progenitors First of their lines at the Source." She held out her wrist, baring the barcode tattoo from beneath her sleeve. "I'm more than happy to provide the metrics proving my Binder genes ascendent. Though registered as a duality, I was slated to replace my d—my mother as First Binder when she aged out."

The room broke into scandalized outcry at the public disclosure of her duality. Since she only presented Binder talent, it wasn't the same as being a twist, but all these assholes would consider her bloodline tainted. Didn't matter that she had more talent in her pinky than all of them put together. God, he hated this fucking city.

The Binder section erupted into fervent discussion. Between her declaration and him splitting, the odds any of their children being a pureblooded talent were slim to none. He didn't give a shit, but they would. Their line's pledge of fealty had been predicated on the possibility of a Jester heir ascending to hold the position of First Binder one day.

So much for that. House Scot was probably shit out of luck, too. Flynn knew he was, but what the hell else was new?

Riggs banged his gavel. "If we can hold discussion to the end? Lady Scot is not here to defend her pedigree, although the clarification is appreciated." He smiled, motioning for her to sit and turned back to Flynn. "If you would finish with your version of events?"

He gritted his teeth. His version of events. Like they hadn't all seen it. "What's there to tell? I contained the blast and severed the Breaker's channel. Look, the Source is coming. Last night proves that they have people here, preparing the way for a harvest—"

Lord Ines stood, and Flynn broke off, surprised Julia wasn't at the man's side…or anywhere else in the room. Why wasn't she here? You'd think she would've been first up to tear his throat out.

"And you've done that for them, haven't you? They've entered a lawsuit—"

"And in doing so, admitted their guilt. I didn't name names, and if I hadn't acted, Glynfyls would be a smoking pit!"

"It's not far off now," Crandall said dryly.

"Maybe you should've thought of that before you had me detained."

"I wouldn't have had to detain you, if you hadn't usurped the prerogatives of the individual lines by taking the oaths of the commons."

Flynn's brows knit. The oaths of the commons…he hadn't done that. Though, he could see how it'd be assumed he had, given the way with those Breakers last night and the Finder earlier had saluted him as Overlord… Fucking hell. His knuckles popped, wanting to put his fist through that weaselly little Finder's—"Why shouldn't I? Original Houses were given authority over those less talented in exchange for our protection—"

"Which is the purview of their duly elected Firsts!"

Flynn riffled his hair, jaw clenched. That was the pretense they were trying to hang him with? Of all the patronizing fucking—"So let me get this straight, Original Houses are free to pledge as they see fit, but the commons need permission." Crandall tried to backpedal and Flynn wasn't gonna let him. "As per the codes, commons enjoy the same liberties we do, less the ability to vote. If this was such a damning issue on principle, why wasn't it brought up when lines other than Shades began pledging?"

Crandall's lips pursed, and Flynn laughed, wanting to pummel the pompous prick. The rest of the room fidgeted, the noise from the mob calling them on their bullshit. Something hit one of the windows, and several woman shrieked, moving closer to the floor.

Flynn laughed. "Fine, I'll play along with your elitist hypocrisy. You wanna split hairs, Crandall? None of the Breakers swore, and I wasn't approached by any Finders last night. I hold the oaths of the Fixer and Binder Firsts, which gives me carte blanche over their lines in addition to my own. All that out there? Your doing, not mine."

There was another outcry over that, and Flynn didn't give a shit. It was fact, and they'd all lined up willingly to pledge. He dropped into his seat. Jesus fucking Christ—

"Point of law," Merchant chimed in. "Lord Scot is correct that there is nothing legally preventing him from taking the oath of any citizen of the Northern Territories, regardless of their affinity."

"Nothing other than him being a goddamned twist!" Morris's irate voice boomed from behind them.

Fuck. A growl rumbled through Flynn's chest at Kara's flinch, not surprised that odious prick was gonna try to whip up even more of a shit storm.

The room went still.

"Any speculation as to my client's talent—"

"Speculation? Bah! I've said it before and I'll say it again, man's a mongrel! We all saw what happened, why he's not in chains—"

"Yes. We all saw what happened, and today's front page." Markham stood, mopping at his chins. He glanced at Crandall and then at Lord Klein. His head was bowed, dark hair falling across his face. The rest of the Fixers weren't doing so hot either. How much talent outside those doors were they trying to mitigate? "I see no evidence of Laughlin being a twist, and given the current situation, the Fetches would like to pledge—"

The fuck?!

"Are you serious, Markham?!" Morris frothed into the room's stunned silence.

"I shouldn't have to remind you of the last time the lower spokes revolted. Whether you realize it or not, that whole sordid affair only served to further engrain the commons's dissatisfaction with the status quo. Tonight was just the spark that lit the tinder. Listen to them out there! We can't afford another strike, especially not now, and swearing fealty to a man capable of what I saw last night seems prudent."

The uproar was immediate.

"Let them strike!"

"How dare they threaten—"

"Prudent! What we saw was murder!" Morris blustered above it all. "Scot admitted to severing the man's channel! That Breaker should've been held for questioning instead of being silenced with the same savagery evidenced on the plateau! Crandall couldn't rule out a

Shade's involvement, and I'd bet Scot killed him to stop from being fingered as an accomplice!"

The room erupted again, and Kara's head whipped around, her bloodlust churning black through their bond. Flynn's own rose up to meet it. Shit, that was gonna be a problem—

"That's a lie! Riegel was fitted with a boost. The tech negates a Finder's talent—"

The clamor died, everyone staring at her. Behind them, Merchant made a pained sound, and Kara's hand rose to her throat.

"Riegel," Crandall drawled, standing and straightening his lapels. "You knew him personally, Lady Scot?" he asked the question staring at Flynn.

Fucker already knew. Kara slumped against him, and Flynn tamped down the urge to blast the man to hell. "That's a House Matter. You should be more concerned that he was a common Source Breaker, not a Peacekeeper. Twelve thousand of which are gonna be storming our walls, and all of you are playing into their goddamned hands. The chaos out there? Shit, you don't think they know about it? Forget about spies kicking around, that Breaker was implanted with tech I'm convinced was streaming holo back to the Source. If we're lucky, putting him down like that bought us some more damned time."

And what was going on out in the streets was pissing it away. Motherf—

"Tech?" Riggs asked.

"I'm sure Crandall can confirm." Shithead had to be good for something.

"There is evidence of plaz contamination, though given the condition of the corpse, we're unable to ascertain its purpose."

The room didn't chew on that for nearly long enough.

"And your use of talent, Lord Scot?" Riggs pressed.

"I told you, I contained the blast and severed his channel."

"I'd say you did a bit more than that," someone snorted.

Riggs kept looking at Flynn. He rocked back in his seat, trying to pull up that blanket of calm... The noise from outside crested again, more projectiles striking the windows.

The Assembly waited.

Fuck them. He dropped the legs of his chair, disgusted. Kara leaned against him and he put his arm around her. She needed to go home. He tamped down his rage, done with all of their bullshit. They wanted to indict him, have fucking at it, and send him a memo when they'd figured it out.

Riggs adjusted his glasses, looking around the chamber. "Well, then, anything else?"

Crandall smirked and Flynn wanted to pummel the fucker.

"Yeah," he spat, standing. "Instead of raking us over the coals, you should be asking how that Breaker was released from the constabulary's drunk tank three days ago, despite his description being posted throughout the city. If Crandall had been doing his job, none of this would've happened. I won't apologize for cleaning up his mess. Any further questions can be directed to my lawyer."

Flynn picked Kara up, pulled talent, and phazed them through the mob.

The surprised indignation on the Intelligencer's face as the room turned its attention to him was almost worth being hauled in for.

Want More?
GET YOUR COPY AT: books2read.com/Split-Vol3

ACKNOWLEDGMENTS

Once again, my thanks goes to my editor, Jonathan Oliver, for his unwavering faith in my work and mind-boggling patience in dealing with my grammatical errors. (And guys, there's *a lot*.) He is truly a prince among editors.

I also need to thank JJ Graham for reading (and re-reading…and probably reading again) whatever I happen to throw at him. He's become an invaluable part of my process, and I don't know what I would do without him. Okay, yes I do. I would cry. A lot. Because he's amazing. OMG dude, never leave me.

He also introduced me to Stacy, and lady, I can not thank you enough for your support! It means the world to me to have someone as excited about my worlds as I am. I live for your feedback, and have to admit I've imagined your reaction when writing more than one scene.

And finally, to my family. Thank you so much for dealing with me when I'm in my head, oblivious that the house is burning down around me. D, you are my rock, and T, I am so impressed with how you step up and get shit done. As far as the littles are concerned, thank you for being cool and remembering to feed the cat. Pretty sure he thanks you for that, too. Well, with his teeth.

My mom? She got another dedication. I mean, I'd thank her again, but she'd totally let it go to her head and nuts to that. She's already impossible to live with. So instead, I'll sign off by heading on over to the next installment.

Hope to see you all over there.

BOOKS BY AK NEVERMORE

THE DAE DIARIES - URBAN FANTASY WITH SPICE

- *One Night in Bliss* — FREE TO READ
- *Flame & Shadow*
- *Air & Darkness*
- *Playing with Fire* — FREE TO READ (October 2024)

THE PRICE OF TALENT - SPICY DYSTOPIAN SCI FI ROMANCE

- *Breeder* — FREE TO READ
- *Breaker*
- *Destroyer* — FREE TO READ
- *Binder*
- *Conspirator* — FREE TO READ (October 2024)
- *Split*
- *Overlord* — (January 2024)
- Exile — (March 2025)

THE MAW OF MAYHEM - PARANORMAL MC EROTICA

- *Bites of Mayhem* — FREE TO READ
- *The Maw of Mayhem* — FREE TO READ
- *Grimdarke*
- *Darker*
- *Kit-Kat*
- *Katherine*
- *Deuce* — (Forthcoming)

ABOUT THE AUTHOR

AK Nevermore writes science fiction and urban fantasy. She enjoys operating heavy machinery, freebases coffee, and gives up sarcasm for Lent every year.

A Jane-of-all-trades, she's a certified chef, restores antiques, and dabbles in beekeeping when she's not reading voraciously or running down the dream in her beat-up camo Chucks.

Unable to ignore the voices in her head, and unwilling to become medicated, she writes full time. Her books explore dark worlds, perversely irreverent and profound, and always entertaining.

Want more Nevermore?
Sign up for her newsletter and never miss a release!

aknevermore.com

Cover design by Beholden Books

Hardcover ISBN: 978-1-964466-01-9

Paperback ISBN: 979-8-9887464-9-2

Digital ISBN: 979-8-9887464-8-5